DIE AGAIN, MR. HOLMES

THE SHERLOCK HOLMES
AND LUCY JAMES MYSTERIES

The Last Moriarty
The Wilhelm Conspiracy
Remember, Remember
The Crown Jewel Mystery
The Jubilee Problem
Death at the Diogenes Club
The Return of the Ripper

The series page at Amazon:
amzn.to/2s9U2jW

For a FREE copy of
THE CROWN JEWEL MYSTERY – the prequel to the series
please visit sherlockandlucy.com

OTHER TITLES BY ANNA ELLIOTT

The Pride and Prejudice Chronicles:
Georgiana Darcy's Diary
Pemberly to Waterloo
Kitty Bennet's Diary

Sense and Sensibility Mysteries:
Margaret Dashwood's Diary

The Twilight of Avalon Series:
Dawn of Avalon
The Witch Queen's Secret
Twilight of Avalon
Dark Moon of Avalon
Sunrise of Avalon

The Susanna and the Spy Series:
Susanna and the Spy
London Calling

OTHER TITLES BY CHARLES VELEY

Novels:
Play to Live
Night Whispers
Children of the Dark

Nonfiction:
Catching Up

DIE AGAIN, MR. HOLMES

A SHERLOCK HOLMES/ LUCY JAMES MYSTERY

BY ANNA ELLIOTT AND CHARLES VELEY

Typesetting by FormattingExperts.com
Cover design by Todd A. Johnson

ISBN: 978-0-9991191-6-7

I beseech you,
Wrest once the law to your authority:
To do a great right, do a little wrong.

William Shakespeare,
The Merchant of Venice (1596-8) act 4, sc. 1.

PROLOGUE

Darkness had fallen by the time we reached Greenwich. A few harbor lights glittered over the wide expanse of black river, barely illuminating the low outline of HMS *Daring* along the dock. Secretary of War Lansdowne was waiting for us, hatless, at the entrance to the West Building, his aquiline features readily identifiable. His tall frame was stooped and hunched against the cold. He gave a momentary glance to our group, which consisted of Mycroft, Lucy and me. We had left little Becky in Baker Street, in the care of Mrs. Hudson.

To Lansdowne we were all familiar faces. All of us had been inside Lansdowne House, and with him in the adjoining Devonshire House just six months earlier when the Jubilee Ball had nearly ended in catastrophe.

On that occasion a traitor had been unmasked, and we had shared with Lansdowne a grim triumph. Now, I could not help thinking that there was no triumph. There was catastrophe.

"I am so terribly sorry for your loss," Lansdowne said. "Lieutenant Commander Bradley is inside. I will take you to him."

The commander, clean-faced and ruddy, about forty years old, stood in his blue uniform at attention outside a tall door just off the front entrance. His blue eyes looked inquiringly at our little group, then at Lansdowne as we approached.

"Commander Bradley, I shall introduce you to each of these people in turn. They are the next of kin to Mr. Sherlock Holmes."

We each shook hands with him as Lansdowne made introductions. Then he opened the door to reveal a well-lit conference room, with a large oak table surrounded by a dozen empty chairs. On the table lay a misshapen dark pile of fabric.

"His coat," said the commander. "It's all we have, I'm afraid."

I picked up the coat to inspect it, catching the scent of damp wool and river water. It was Holmes's black tweed Inverness. I put my finger through a small hole in front of the cape, through to the coat beneath, and then through the heavy wool fabric at the back. As I did so I realized that traces of reddish liquid were coming off on my hands. There was no mistaking the coppery scent of blood, diluted though it had been by the waters of the Thames.

There was also no mistaking the inevitable conclusion. A bullet passing through Holmes's cloak in this manner would inevitably have gone through his chest. From the angle between the holes, the shot might have missed the vital organs, but there was no question that significant blood loss would have ensued.

"A miracle that he survived to take this off and attempt to swim," said Commander Bradley, looking from me to Lucy and to Mycroft.

We took chairs around the table. Bradley told us what had happened. Authorized by Lansdowne, Holmes had asked for his assistance to watch the Red Dragon Inn and monitor boat traffic in and out. "Something to do with opium smuggling," the commander said. "We hove to on the south side of the river, just opposite Limehouse Basin. We had a good view of the Red Dragon. It was a gray afternoon, but the weather was clear enough."

"What time was this?" Lucy asked.

"About three o'clock," the commander said. "We saw a motor launch pass us, heading straight for the Red Dragon, close enough so that we could see the crew was Chinese. There was no name and no flag. The boat docked briefly under the pier, unloaded a few barrels of cargo, and then maneuvered away from the dock, to head downstream. At that moment Mr. Holmes appeared on the dock, running at full tilt."

"You could identify him at that distance?" Mycroft asked sharply.

"Not at that time. I had my binoculars, but no, I could not distinguish his features as he ran. I did see that he was brandishing a revolver. He jumped onto the Chinese boat just as it was pulling away from the Red Dragon dock. In a few moments, however, I could identify Holmes. He was on deck, and the Chinese boat was moving rapidly in our direction. Then there were shots fired. The man I now know to be Sherlock Holmes was clearly visible, and he was hit by one of the shots. He fell into the river."

"Could you see his face when he was in the water?"

"Yes. Plainly. It was Mr. Holmes."

"You had met him before?"

"Yes. This was the man who had asked me to keep the Red Dragon Inn under surveillance."

"And he had identified himself as Sherlock Holmes?"

"He did, and to confirm his identity he asked me to call Secretary Lansdowne in his presence."

"Holmes made the request to me on the phone," Lansdowne said, "I recognized his voice. Then he put Commander Bradley on the line, and I gave the authorization."

"What happened then?" Lucy asked.

"I knew the water was dangerously cold. As you know, freezing water can paralyze a man's limbs in no time. There were blocks of ice here and there, but none close enough for Mr. Holmes to hold onto. We lowered a dinghy to rescue him. I watched throughout. He was struggling to stay afloat. He took off his coat, which was dragging him down, and tried to swim to the dinghy. It was a valiant effort, but before we could reach him, he went under. He was gone."

PART ONE

OUTWARD BOUND

1. AN OLD ENEMY,
AND A NEW APPEAL

From the upper gallery, Holmes and I had a clear view of Thomas Newman as the jurors filed into the courtroom. His close-set, pig-like eyes glittered with determination, and on his massive jaw, a purple bruise—caused by a solid punch from Holmes two months ago—had faded. I detested Newman. I had hoped to see some anxiety on his coarse features as he waited to learn whether the jurors would set him free or send him to the hangman. But to my disappointment, the leader of the East End gang known as the Bleeders sat stolid and impassive in the prisoner's dock.

From time to time, however, Newman would glance up to the gallery opposite ours to wave—in an oddly delicate manner—to a veiled woman in the front row.

I had been told the woman was Newman's wife. She sat quietly, as stoic in her appearance as her husband, though she never waved back.

I had seen most of the trial, and the veiled woman had occupied the same front row seat each time I had attended.

The proceedings had been difficult for the prosecution. We had known Newman was guilty, of course, but proving it was another matter. Newman rarely soiled his hands with the face-battering and leg-breaking that were the usual enforcement techniques of his organization, preferring to let other thugs do the dirty work. Holmes and I had both been his intended victims two months earlier, so we had both been able to give what I thought was completely convincing testimony as to his guilt on the charge of attempted murder.

But Lestrade wanted the death penalty. He had brought in three former Bleeders, who had witnessed Newman—they said—in the act of ordering and overseeing several murders. They were now members of a rival gang on the south side of the Thames, and Newman's barrister had made much of that fact when attempting to impeach their credibility.

Had he been successful?

We would know the answer in the next few moments.

The judge emerged from his chambers, moving slowly, with an old man's careful step. His powdered wig, which no doubt had fit him properly at one time, was now too large for him and made him look older still. He spoke in a reedy tenor voice. "Will the defendant please rise."

Newman got to his feet.

The judge continued. "Gentlemen of the jury, have you reached a verdict?"

"We have, Your Honor," said the jury foreman.

"Will you please read your verdict."

"We find the defendant Thomas Newman guilty on all charges."

Newman never flinched. He might have been standing in

a theatre queue, patiently waiting for a seat. He kept his jaw clamped shut and his chin tilted upward. His fists remained firmly clenched at his sides.

The judge nodded. Turning his gaze to the dock, he continued, "Thomas Newman, you have been found guilty by a jury of your peers, of four counts of willful murder. It is my duty to sentence you. The jury has not recommended mercy, and I have been told your associates have made every effort to influence the jurors in their deliberations, first with threats and then with bribes. Your associates are not on trial here, of course, but I can take their actions into account when passing sentence."

A murmur went through the court. The judge rapped his gavel, and the crowd grew silent once more.

The judge spoke. "Have you anything to say before sentence is passed?"

Newman did not look at the judge nor at anyone else. His beady little eyes seemed to be staring at a fixed point in the air.

Then he said, "I'm not done yet."

The judge shook his head in irritation. "Do you mean that you wish to say more at this time? Or are those words intended to convey some other meaning?"

Newman said nothing.

Holmes stared intently at the gallery opposite us, at the end of the row farthest from Newman's soon-to-be widow. He seemed to be watching an attractive, blonde-haired young woman, whose feathered hat was causing some annoyance to a man on the bench behind her. The young woman was repeatedly shifting the direction of her gaze, first to look down at Newman, and then to look across at Holmes.

The judge went on, "Very well. You have had your opportunity to speak. Thomas Newman, I sentence you to be hanged from the neck until you are dead, sentence to be carried out on the morning of January the 13th, one week and two days from today."

The courtroom erupted in cheers.

* * *

A short while later we had left the Old Bailey and were walking away in the harsh January wind, looking for a cab, when a woman's voice came from behind us. "Mr. Holmes! Please wait!"

Holmes stopped and turned. I recognized the young blonde-haired woman we had seen across from us in the opposite gallery. She still wore her feathered hat. Her round, pleasant features widened in a glad smile of relief and she spoke rapidly and urgently. "Thank you for stopping, Mr. Holmes. You gave testimony at the trial several weeks ago, and I recognized you today. Please pardon me for staring at you so repeatedly back there in the courtroom. I fear I am very much in need of your help. My name is Florence Janine, and I need you to find my fiancé."

"Miss Janine, I am sorry to have to disappoint you—"

But she interrupted him, her words spilling out in an even more desperate tumble, almost breathless with her anxiety to prevent Holmes from walking away. "His name is John Swafford. He is a police detective, and he works at Limehouse Station, but none of the policemen there will speak with me. I have not seen him since Christmas. John was investigating that man Thomas Newman. I came to the trial every day last month hoping I would see him, but he wasn't there. And he wasn't there today either. Or yesterday. Unless you saw him today and I missed him?"

"Now why should you think that, Miss Janine?"

"John said Thomas Newman had an escape plan and more than enough money to bribe his jailers. He told me he was going to speak to you about it. He said you would want to know."

WATSON

2. A COOPERATIVE CLIENT

Miss Janine was shivering with cold, and passers-by were beginning to become a distraction, so we repaired to a nearby teashop and found a table. Soon we had a pot of tea and a plate of scones before us. Holmes was trying to be friendly and helpful, although I could tell he was still skeptical of Miss Janine. He waited patiently until she had consumed half a cup of hot tea and one of the scones.

Then he said, "Now, Miss Janine, would you please tell us what you can of Detective Swafford? When did you inquire about him at Limehouse Station?"

"I called on Boxing Day, but, as I said, they would not talk to me about him."

"You never saw him go into the station."

"Oh, no. I wouldn't go to Limehouse. I live in Kensington. Besides, he told me not to get too close."

"He wanted to marry you?"

"Of course he did."

Holmes looked at her bare left hand. "But he did not provide an engagement ring?"

She reddened. "John said he would need to save up for that. He hoped to have enough very soon."

"I see. Now please tell us about the last time you saw him. What happened? Please do not omit any detail, no matter how trivial it may seem."

"It was Christmas Eve. We went to a candlelight service in St. Philip's Church. Ever so moving."

"What did he wear?"

"Why, just ordinary clothes. White shirt, nicely-starched black tie, black overcoat. Perfectly respectable."

"Nothing to indicate that he was a policeman?"

"Oh, no."

"Nothing to indicate an association with Mr. Newman or his gang, the Bleeders?"

"I wouldn't recognize anything like that, I'm sure."

"What hymns did you sing?"

" 'O Come All Ye Faithful,' I remember that. And a German one, 'Silent Night.' I remember him saying it wasn't like London. Nothing silent about nights in London."

"What kind of voice did he sing in? Tenor, baritone, bass?"

"Oh, he was a tenor. Right enough. A nice clear tenor and very pleasant."

"Had you been to his home? Met his parents?"

She shook her head. "He never brought that up. I was under the impression that his parents were dead. He did say something about a brother, though. A sailor. They were from a seacoast town, I think it was. He said he liked to hear the sound of the ocean as a boy."

"Please tell me where you were when he proposed marriage."

"Why, it was at the church. Christmas Eve."

"And where did you first meet Mr. Swafford?"

"It was at a church tea."

"At St. Philip's?"

She nodded. "Just after Guy Fawkes, it was. I went with my mother. I don't do much in the way of getting out on my own. She says she's glad of the company, with my father gone."

Holmes raised an eyebrow. "Gone?"

"Of the diphtheria. He passed away when I was only a little girl."

"And how old are you now?"

"Eighteen, sir. My mother said it was time for me—"

"I understand. So she took you to the church social at St. Philip's."

"Very wholesome," I interjected.

"Please describe Mr. Swafford. Did you find him handsome?"

"Well, not in the way of the actors on stage. But he is a strong-looking fellow. Not much fat on him, but strong. Wiry, you would say."

"His features?"

"Oh, nice big dark eyes. A nice strong brown mustache. Nice dark hair. He's very energetic, too, is John. I think he will go far on the police force."

"Thank you, Miss Janine. This will all be most helpful."

"How long do you think it will take to find him?"

"It is too soon to know. But it would also be most helpful if you would please tell me everything you can about what John told you about Mr. Newman."

"Oh, I see. Yes, of course you would want to know that. But can you not get that information from the police? Surely he would have made a report."

"He may not have had time for a report. If he went missing—indeed, truly missing—then it's more likely than not his superiors at the Limehouse station do not know the latest points of his investigations."

"Will you promise not to get him into trouble?"

"I cannot promise to conceal a crime."

She gave an embarrassed half-smile. "He said Newman's gang continues to rule in Limehouse, even though Newman himself has been in prison for—well, at that time it was nearly two months."

"John thought this was unusual?"

"Yes. He thought that Newman might have some secret plan to get away. He said Newman had offered two thousand pounds to whoever could manage his escape from prison."

"Did John know where Newman was getting such a large sum?"

"John thought he knew but, of course, he didn't tell me. He said that with such a lot of money involved he was sure to get a reward out of it. That was how he would be able to get me my engagement ring."

"And why did he say he was going to speak with me?"

"He said there were some in the police force as couldn't be trusted. So he was going to tell you about it. He said you were a man of integrity."

"Where did he say he was going, after the Christmas Eve service?"

"He said he had to get back to work."

"On Christmas Eve?"

"I didn't know what he meant. I thought maybe he was going to write up a report or something." Her eyes glistened with tears. "Oh, please find him, Mr. Holmes. When I first met him at the church tea, I poured out a nice hot cup of tea for him, and he just looked up at me with his big brown eyes, ever so grateful, and I just fell in love. I know we are meant for each other. Mr. Holmes, I shall be happy to pay you—"

"That will not be necessary."

"I don't expect charity—"

"Miss Janine, I shall probably be able to settle the question of Detective Swafford's present whereabouts with a telephone call. Now, I should like to know where to report progress. How can I reach you?"

She produced a card, which displayed her address. "We have a telephone as well. The number is on the card."

Holmes glanced at it briefly and then tucked it into his pocket as she left the tea shop.

* * *

When we returned to Baker Street, Holmes telephoned Lime-house Station and spoke briefly with the sergeant on duty. He then took out Miss Janine's card from his waistcoat and gave the number to the operator. I heard him speaking.

"Miss Janine? Do you recall our meeting this afternoon? Yes, that is who I am, and I recognize your voice as well. I have spoken with a responsible party at your fiancé's workplace and am assured that he reported for work this morning. No doubt you will be hearing from him in due course. Yes, it is no trouble at all. I wish you both well in the future."

He set down the receiver.

"You were quite circumspect," I said.

"It is as well to be careful."

"You said nothing about Thomas Newman when you called the Limehouse Station."

"I shall make some inquiries on my own. And if Mr. Swafford wishes to give me information or ask for my guidance, he is welcome to do so. However, I do not think I shall hear from him. Twelve days have elapsed since he told Miss Janine of the matter, and he has neither called on me, nor written, nor sent a telegram, nor telephoned."

"Why not, do you suppose?"

"I do not suppose. I observe that he mentioned my name, and the large sums involved in his investigation, and the possibility of a reward that would enable him to provide Miss Janine with an engagement ring. I believe that my name was an embellishment. A bit of corroborative detail. He would not be the first impecunious suitor to exaggerate his own importance and financial prospects when describing them to his intended."

We would soon discover how wrong Holmes was.

3. AN UNCOOPERATIVE CLIENT

I gritted my teeth. "So you haven't yet been in touch with the local police constabulary in Lincolnshire?"

Under ordinary circumstances, I didn't have to clench my teeth when asking questions of that variety. It was an important point, but hardly the type of inquiry to arouse passionate feelings one way or the other.

In this case, though, it was the fourth time I had made that identical inquiry, and I had yet to receive anything even marginally approaching a satisfactory answer.

Lady Serena Lynley looked at me across the rim of her Spode china teacup.

We were sitting together at a table in the tearoom of the very exclusive London ladies club to which she belonged—the type of institution which catered to ladies visiting London from the country. Here they could refresh themselves after an arduous day of shopping, or even stay a night or two if their errands in the city lasted more than a day.

"I don't trust that the police will take the matter *seriously* enough," Lady Serena said.

She was a tall woman of probably forty or forty-five, with a very slim, upright bearing. Her face was long, aristocratic and narrow, and her skin was slightly sallow, almost matching her drab blonde hair. Her pale-yellow morning suit with its tight-fitted bodice, puffed sleeves, and cream-colored velvet trim was no doubt the height of fashion, but studying her, I had the uncharitable thought that she looked as though she had been put through the laundry, and all her colors had faded in the wash.

Even her eyes were a very pale blue, framed by colorless blond lashes.

She set down her teacup and fluttered her hands.

"After all, it's hardly a criminal occurrence for a young girl to leave the position for which she's been hired. Ungrateful, certainly, and a gross breach of the trust I invested in her, but not *criminal*. I don't see that there is anything for the police to investigate, and besides, people in the country do *talk* so. The amount of gossip and scandal that circulates through our part of Lincolnshire alone is simply *frightful*. The police have no discretion, no discretion at all about that sort of thing. And I heard from my dear friend Charlotte Teal before she and her daughter-in-law left for Canada how very discreet you were during that *dreadful* affair with her son, and how I could absolutely rely on your discretion—"

I stopped listening.

This was exactly the response that I had gotten the first three times I had brought up the question of contacting the police.

Lady Lynley would start waving her hands ineffectually and launch into a twittering speech in which the words *scandal* and *gossip* were each mentioned at least once, and *discreet* or *discretion* at three times minimum.

"What can you tell me about Alice Gordon?" I asked.

Lady Lynley blinked, possibly because I had just cut her off in the middle of saying *discretion* one more time.

"Tell you about her? Well, she is—was—my personal maid. I hired her about a year ago."

She stopped.

"And?" I prompted.

A slight furrow appeared between Lady Lynley's plucked blond brows. "What do you mean, 'and'?"

"What more can you tell me about her? If I'm to look for her, at the very least, I need to know her appearance. Do you happen to have a photograph of her?"

Lady Lynley's look of bemusement deepened. "Why would I have a photograph of my maid?"

"Can you tell me what she looks like, then?"

"Well." Lady Linley looked blank another moment, then frowned. "She has blonde hair. And blue eyes."

The next time I had occasion to visit the dentist, I'd be able to tell him that I knew exactly how it felt to pull teeth with metal pliers.

"How old is she?"

Lady Lynley blinked again. "I don't know. I never asked her age. Somewhere between … oh, I don't know. Eighteen and thirty, I suppose."

"Blond hair, blue eyes, age between eighteen and thirty."

"That's right." Lady Lynley nodded.

"And she went missing two days ago?"

Lady Lynley nodded again. "Yes, on the 4th of January. It was very inconvenient, because we were hosting a dinner party that night, and Alice didn't turn up to help me dress and arrange my hair. I had to call on the under-parlormaid to assist me, and the results were *most* unsatisfactory. Alice always had a particular skill with hairdressing." Lady Lynley sighed.

"And can you tell me anything else about her? Where her family is from, for example? Anything about her interests or ambitions?"

Lady Lynley drew herself up, an affronted look crossing her narrow features. "Certainly not! I am not in the habit of asking my staff for details about their personal lives."

I nodded, bending over the small notepad I had brought with me and pretending to jot down a note—which had the obvious benefit of helping me to *not* upend the teapot over Lady Lynley's silly aristocratic head. And the not-so-obvious benefit of allowing me a moment to study her from under my lashes without her being aware that I was doing so.

"So why is it that you want to find Alice?" I asked. "You must have some reason for being concerned about her."

I continued to scribble meaninglessly in the notepad, but I watched Lady Lynley's face as I asked the question.

A shadow of something hard crossed her features—annoyance or vexation, although whether it was because of me or the missing maid, Alice Gordon, I couldn't be sure.

"Well, I hired her as my maid. I feel a certain degree of responsibility to make sure that she has not gotten herself into some kind of trouble," she finally said.

I made another note. "Mmmm." I had found that sometimes a vague murmur of agreement followed by silence would prompt people to fill that silence with more talk.

In this case, Lady Lynley simply sat, fiddling with the edge of the lace tablecloth.

On the surface, everything about her, from the plume of ostrich feathers on her hat to the onyx buttons on her boots, proclaimed her a typical member of the aristocracy—the class of landed gentry born into the lap of pampered luxury, who never did anything so vulgar as a day's work in their lives.

But that wasn't the full picture.

Her accent was quite good. Almost as good an impression of an upper-class English accent as I could do, and I'd not only spent years training as a vocalist and actress, I'd had the private tutelage of Sherlock Holmes, who could sound like a native in any language, from Bahasa Indonesian to Hindustani.

But she still—just ever-so-slightly—over-emphasized her h's. *Habit* had been more like, *hhabit*—a mark of someone who'd grown up dropping her h's in the manner of a working-class Londoner and had trained herself out of it.

The club tearoom had a pianist playing soft music in one corner, and I'd noticed the way that Lady Lynley's head unconsciously tilted in that direction, her body starting to sway just a little in time to the melody until she stilled the motion.

I caught myself doing the same thing, after nearly three years of almost nightly musical performances at the Savoy Theater.

If Serena Lynley hadn't been an actress or dancer of some variety before her marriage to Lord Lynley, then I deserved to have Holmes disown me as both his investigative partner and his daughter.

A ballet dancer in a second-rate company would be my guess. Her high-button boots were very fashionable—and no doubt incredibly expensive—with slender heels and narrow toes. But I'd seen the way she winced just slightly with every step when she came in to meet me, her feet clearly protesting in the way they would if she'd spent her youth dancing *en pointe*, stressing the tendons and bones.

I set my pencil in the crease of my notebook, and folded the book shut to hold it in place.

"What exactly is it that you'd like me to do?"

"Well—" Lady Lynley made vague fluttering motions with her hands. "I thought that perhaps you could ask about—investigate—whether there is any sign that Alice has indeed come to London? Just quietly—discreetly, mind you. There must be places where you could look—places where girls of Alice's type might be found?"

I rubbed my forehead. "You missed another two 'discreets.' " That had only been one.

Lady Lynley looked startled. "I beg your pardon?"

"Never mind."

There was no reason that this case—not even a case, really; at most a *potential* case—should be setting off faint alarm bells inside my mind.

A maidservant deciding that she'd had enough of her employer and deciding to seek her fortune elsewhere was—as Lady Lynley herself had said—hardly a matter for criminal investigation.

And a bare twenty minutes of Lady Lynley's company had already persuaded me that if I had been in Alice Gordon's place I would have jumped with both feet at practically *any* chance of alternative employment.

And yet I couldn't shake the cold, unpleasant feeling that was currently crawling along the length of my spine. I'd had the same feeling before in the course of joining my father's investigations, and it generally meant that something was very, very wrong.

Lady Lynley had expressed absolutely no affection for her former maid. The only note of genuine regret I'd heard in her voice was for the loss of Alice's skill at arranging hair.

And yet—despite the fact that she was avoiding involving the police at all costs—she had traveled all the way from Lincolnshire to London, a journey of three hours by train, just to speak with me about a maid whom she barely knew and didn't appear to particularly care about.

It didn't make sense.

"I could make a few inquiries, certainly," I said slowly. "Although I can't entirely promise no police involvement. My husband is a police sergeant with Scotland Yard. If I discover any evidence that harm has come to Alice or that she's gotten involved in any sort of criminal activity, I'll have to tell him."

Depending on circumstances, I would probably have reported the matter anyway, but I especially didn't keep secrets from Jack.

Lady Lynley raised her brows and she caught her breath—though not, it appeared, at the idea that Alice might be in danger.

"Your *husband?*" Her eyes narrowed, a look of appraisal in their depths. "You could easily have married someone of a *much* higher social standing, too; you're quite pretty, and many of the aristocracy don't mind American wives. And yet you married a policeman? How very ... broad-minded of you."

Once upon a time, I might have been tempted to answer that I miraculously went whole days without caring about Lady Lynley's opinion on my personal life.

But now I didn't even care enough to bother with the reply—although I did take note of her mannerisms so that I could mimic her to Jack when I went home tonight. He would think her statement about aristocrats being willing to tolerate American accents very entertaining. Becky would, too.

Lady Lynley's shoulders twitched, and she said in a slightly brisker tone, "Well, it can't be helped, I suppose. You will make inquiries?"

She still hadn't reacted to the suggestion that Alice might have come to some harm. And yet she *was* troubled. By now I was certain of it. I could see it in the tightness of the skin around her eyes, the tension in her fingers as she gripped the handle of her teacup.

Lady Lynley was frightened about something—just not her missing maid.

Of course, that didn't mean that I was obligated to investigate on her behalf. Before today, we had never even met, and I didn't have any concrete reason to think that Alice was in danger.

But Mrs. Charlotte Teal—whom Lady Lynley had also dragged into the conversation at every available opportunity—apparently was a friend of hers.

That still didn't mean that I owed Lady Lynley any favors … and yet, I couldn't shake the feeling that it actually *did*.

I sighed. I occasionally wished in the course of investigations that I could be more like my father. Sherlock Holmes wouldn't feel morally obliged to take the case of a vain, silly, snobbish woman just because he had been instrumental in getting the son of the woman's friend arrested for murder.

Or maybe he would. If I had learned one thing about my father, it was that he was more human than he cared to admit.

"I'll make inquiries," I said out loud. "And report back to you if I find anything at all about whether Alice has turned up in London."

4. A MURDER VICTIM

Holmes and I were attending an evening concert when we had the news from Lestrade that a police inspector had been murdered. While dying, the man had asked for Sherlock Holmes. His body was at St. Thomas Hospital. Would we come?

I had an uneasy feeling in the pit of my stomach as we arrived. I feared that the dead man was Miss Janine's missing fiancé.

My fears were confirmed when we entered the hospital mortuary and saw Lestrade standing beside a body on the marble slab at the center of the room.

"This is Inspector John Swafford. Or was," said Lestrade. "He died asking for you."

"I blame myself," said Holmes. His eyes gleamed with a bitter intensity, and his voice was dry and tight.

"Why would you say that?" Lestrade asked.

Holmes was already bending over the body. "After Newman's trial this past Tuesday, a woman calling herself Miss Janine approached me outside the Old Bailey. She named Inspector John Swafford as her fiancé, said he had gone missing, and that he was investigating Thomas Newman." He told Lestrade what had happened since, and continued, "Now it is painfully clear to me that I ought to have done a great deal more."

I was at Holmes's side. I heard the resignation in his tone as he continued: "This man's appearance perfectly matches the description given by Miss Janine."

Indeed, the body of Inspector Swafford was that of a middle-aged male, Caucasian, thin, wiry, still fully-clad, though in shabby attire. He had the look of a laboring man: coarse and careworn, his features gaunt and raw-boned, framed by a thatch of thick black hair and a full black mustache, cut in the tooth-brush fashion. His bloodstained overcoat lay in an untidy heap on a table beside the slab, beneath a metal bowl containing spectacles, a wallet, and a few coins.

I recalled Miss Janine's adoring description. Nice dark hair. Nice dark mustache. Nice dark eyes.

In an act of mercy, someone had closed both the inspector's eyelids. I lifted one, and saw the sightless, lifeless brown iris.

The upper front of his shirt was deeply discolored by dark brown bloodstains.

The cold electric light of the mortuary illuminated the source of the bloodstains. The man's throat had been ripped open from his chin down to his thorax. Both the jugular vein and the carotid artery had been severed. Blood loss was clearly the cause of death.

"He was still alive when they found him outside the Red Dragon Inn, in the Limehouse area of the Docklands," Lestrade said. "His last words were, 'For the love of God, get Sherlock Holmes.' "

Holmes grimaced. "I ought to have spoken with him directly."

"You cannot blame yourself, Holmes," I said.

"You did all that the law and your profession required of you," said Lestrade.

Holmes gave each of us a long, searching look. "That is never enough," he said.

He bent down over the body once again. "The wound appears to have been made with a docker's hook."

"Swafford was working undercover, following up on that diamond smuggling case we concluded last November," Lestrade said. "Yesterday, he reported that he had made a breakthrough. He had an important meeting at the Red Dragon this afternoon. We thought that odd."

"The Red Dragon is nowhere near the diamond district," Holmes said.

"Nevertheless, we approved the meeting. We had two officers outside."

"What happened?"

"There was a diversion. Deliberately set, it now appears. By the time the two officers returned, Swafford was wounded as you see him now, having been dragged to the edge of the pier, about to be thrown into the water. Our men returned in time to prevent that. The man dragging Swafford dropped him and fled. Our two men chose to provide aid rather than pursuing."

Holmes picked up Swafford's overcoat and sniffed at the pockets. His brow furrowed for a long moment, as though the scent was unpleasant. But he said only, "So Swafford was on the diamond case. And he told his fiancée he was investigating Thomas Newman."

"Then Newman's gang may still be involved in the diamond smuggling affair. We shall pursue that line of inquiry."

"As shall I," Holmes replied. "And I should like to visit Swafford's residence immediately."

"Of course." Lestrade gazed at the body for a long moment. Then he shook his head. "We would have taken him off this case if we had known he had gone and gotten himself engaged. The department does not allow family men to do undercover work. Too dangerous, and the hours are unpredictable. The wives—"

Holmes interrupted. "Where is the telephone?"

Moments later he had called our Baker Street number and was speaking with Mrs. Hudson, our landlady. He wrote on a notepad, thanked her, and rang off. A moment later he was reading a telephone number to the operator.

We waited.

"Ring again," he said, and repeated the number.

We waited again.

Holmes set down the receiver and handed the notepaper to Lestrade. "Would you please have a constable sent to this address? It is the home of Swafford's fiancée. She lives with her mother. She should be notified of Mr. Swafford's death, and warned that she herself may be in danger."

WATSON

5. A TRIP TO KENSINGTON

We found Swafford's lodgings situated within a modest row of brick buildings in Kensington, on Stratford Road. The two constables who had come with us in Lestrade's police van waited outside as Holmes knocked. Soon Swafford's landlady appeared. She had been asleep, as was plain from the rumpled condition of her hair and dingy calico dressing gown. After a brief introduction and a long look at Lestrade's badge, she led us up a gloomy flight of stairs to Swafford's room. She lighted a cigarette and waited inside the doorway.

A solitary bed occupied the centre of the room, its sheets and blankets crumpled and tangled. At the side of the room was a shabby bureau, and an uncomfortable-looking canvas cot topped with a gray wool blanket and pillow.

"Madam, if you please," Holmes said. "Could you describe Mr. Swafford's most recent visitor for us?"

"The sailor fella?"

"His appearance, if you please, and can you give us an idea of what they talked about. If you know, of course."

"Why, he were wearin' a sailor's cap and navy jacket. Mr. Swafford said he was his brother."

"Older, or younger?"

"Younger, I'm sure. And they looked quite alike, though the younger was all sunburned from the sea voyages he'd been on, I suppose. And had a seaman's roll to his step. He were clean shaven, not like Mr. Swafford. And a good deal more spry. I didn't hear their conversations. I'm not that kind of landlady. But the brother did surprise me."

"In what way?"

"I thought he would be staying. But the two of 'em left together about a week ago, and only Mr. Swafford came back."

"The exact date that he left, please, if you can recall it."

"Why, Christmas Day. He said they were goin' home for the holiday."

"And his return?"

"Tuesday."

"No visitors since?"

"None at all. I would know. I can hear—"

"What made you think the younger brother would be staying here?"

She gestured towards the corner, where a dirty and battered seaman's trunk reposed, its wooden surface tarnished by pitch. "It took two of 'em to haul it up these two flights of stairs."

Holmes nodded. "Thank you, madam. You have been very helpful. You can leave us to it now. We shall see ourselves out."

He waited for the door to close behind her. Then, taking a folding knife from his pocket, he bent over the seaman's chest and pried open the flimsy brass lock. Then he lifted the lid.

Inside were what appeared to be twelve heavily rusted cannon balls, arranged in rows and placed into individual compartments. The balls were dark brown in colour, and with an irregular surface that appeared to be flaking away, like badly-weathered paint. One of the balls was missing. From the chest emanated a pungent scent reminiscent of charred wood, decay, and heavy perfume.

"What are those? They look like cannon balls," said Lestrade.

Holmes was kneeling above the chest. Then he grasped the frame of the empty compartment and lifted it, briefly and only for a few inches. "There is another tray below the top one," he said. "Both trays contain balls of raw Indian opium. The characteristic colour and scent are unmistakable."

"I thought opium was a white powder," Lestrade said.

"This is the most common and reliable form for transport of the raw product," Holmes said. "The cooked sap from the poppy bulbs is formed into a ball, and petals from the poppy flower are pressed onto the surface, which is clay-like and sticky. The petals act as a protective wrapping, preventing the opium from sticking to the fingers of those who handle it. When dry, the petals create the surface irregularity which we observe here."

Holmes had taken out several of the balls and set them down carefully on the shabby carpet. "Each one of these balls weighs nearly three pounds," he said.

"How much would it cost?" asked Lestrade.

"This chest is worth approximately two hundred pounds sterling at auction in Hong Kong."

"More than I earn in ten years," said Lestrade. Then he shook his head, and added, his tone now bitter, "So Swafford was bent. That's all we need, that getting into the papers. Worse than him being dead."

"There may be another explanation," Holmes said.

"You think he was innocent because he asked for you?"

Holmes merely motioned for me to help him remove the upper tray. Kneeling, I grasped the thin, rough wood of one empty compartment, taking the end opposite Holmes. Together we lifted out the tray. Holmes carefully removed the remaining balls—each about the size of a melon—and tilted the tray forward and over.

Branded into the bottom of the tray was the stamp of the British East India Company, alongside an inscription scratched into the wood: #202 Bengal. 08 March 1894.

"Lestrade, would you please make a note of the inscription?" Holmes said.

Holmes and I wrestled the massive chest down the stairs, step by laborious step, and outside to the pavement where the police van waited. The darkness on the street outside was broken only intermittently by a flickering gaslight. We made our way to the police van and set the chest down a few feet from the closed rear doors.

"Where's the constable?" Lestrade called to the driver, a shadowy figure, hunched over the reins in his police greatcoat and helmet. "Give us a hand with this chest. We haven't got all day!"

"In the back," the driver said.

Lestrade opened one of the rear doors.

Two strange men stood at the back of the van. They were coarse-featured and grimy, though incongruously clad in clean police overcoats and helmets. They were not our constables. Each man held a revolver pointed in our direction.

Behind the two men were two recumbent figures in just their shirts, trussed up like cattle. I realized that our two constables had been overpowered and their overcoats and helmets taken.

One of the two gunmen pointed at the chest. "Bring it here and lift it into the van," he said. "Easy, like."

Holmes nodded, silent. He held up one hand in a gesture of peace as he crouched down to the chest. Then he opened the lid.

"No, you don't," said the gunman, and leaped from the van, taking a quick few steps at a run. Before Holmes could respond, he was beside Lestrade, with his revolver held against Lestrade's temple.

"Just do as he says," said the other gunman, now standing beside me, his own revolver at the ready.

Holmes took hold of one end of the chest, and Lestrade, crouching down, the gun still at his temple, took the other. I supported the middle. Under the watchful eyes of the two gunmen, we soon placed the chest into the van. I then saw that a third gunman had been behind the others and that he now was pushing the two tied constables out of the back of the van, both gagged and wriggling in their ropes, straining to position their bodies to avoid falling onto their heads. As it was, each hit the ground awkwardly and toppled over, landing heavily.

Moments later, the two gunmen clambered back up into the van, grabbing the bars of the windows and banging the doors shut behind them. I heard two sharp raps from the interior, plainly the signal to the driver to whip up the horse.

As the van lurched forward, Holmes ran to the rear doors. He grabbed hold of the handles and hauled himself up, bracing his feet against the bottom while keeping his head away from the windows.

Holmes clung like a shadowy limpet to the back of the van as it gathered speed and drove away.

I bent to untie the two constables, my fatigue washing over me like a wave of ice water. I heard the chimes of a church clock strike the hour of one.

6. A CALL TO BAKER STREET

It was nearly dawn when I arrived home at 221B Baker Street. As I came into our entry hall, Mrs. Hudson opened her door, looking tired and a bit indignant in her dressing gown and night bonnet. But she gave me a relieved nod. "Someone's been ringing your telephone for the last hour," she said. "Every ten minutes. Like clockwork. I do hope you'll answer it." She shut the door firmly.

I climbed our stairs and entered our rooms.

Our telephone rang.

A terse voice said, "This is Detective Inspector Paul Plank of the Limehouse Street station. Is this Mr. Sherlock Holmes?"

"He is not here at present."

"That is what I had hoped you would say. He is with me. I have been attempting to verify his identity. We found him driving a stolen police van."

"Mr. Holmes did not steal the van," I said. "I am Dr. Watson, and I was with him and Inspector Lestrade—"

"Yes, yes. He said as much. And now that you have confirmed his story, I shall release him."

The line went dead.

I hung up my cape and put away my hat. I sat down heavily on my desk chair and looked down at Baker Street from our bow window. Soon, I hoped, a cab or a police coach would stop in front of our home and Holmes would step out. In the meantime, there was nothing to be done but wait. I was too overwrought for sleep in any event. At least Holmes was safe. Over the past decade we had been bombed, set ablaze, our rear door broken, and Lucy kidnapped—and the decade was not yet done with us—yet we had endured. We had done some good in a world that seemed always to be swirling with new evil.

But what was the new evil this time? As I waited, I tried to sort out the elements in the case. A police detective is working under cover, possibly for his own profit, but possibly not, since he had wanted to meet with Holmes. That detective is murdered, perhaps for a ball of raw opium. A chest of opium, worth ten years' salary to a policeman, is stolen. A carriage, with Holmes clinging to the outer surface, vanishes into the January fog.

In my imagination, I could see the fog swirling around me. *Most appropriate for my state of mind*, I thought.

LUCY

7. A WARNING SHOT

"So you want me to ask around? See if I can turn anything up about this Alice?" Jack asked.

I looked at him and smiled.

Ordinarily, Jack's whole body radiated a kind of tightly-controlled energy, his expression guarded and alert, his dark eyes watchfully intent with an expression that could turn hard-edged in a blink. The criminals and drunks he encountered as a police sergeant usually took one look at him and decided to either run or cooperate.

His recent promotion to Scotland Yard, though, meant that he was no longer called in to work night shifts as often, and right now he was sitting next to me on the living room sofa with his posture relaxed and the firelight painting shadows on his lean, handsome face.

"Do you mind? I know it's worse than a needle-in-a-haystack operation. At least there, you have some guarantee that you'll actually *find* a needle if you sort through enough hay."

Icy January sleet was hissing against the windows. The curtains were all drawn against the dark outside, and Becky was—theoretically, at least—asleep upstairs.

In practice, it had been roughly thirty minutes since Jack and I had told her good night, which meant that we were probably due for an appearance in which she announced that she wasn't tired in the slightest and couldn't possibly be expected to stay in bed.

London was never entirely quiet, even on an icy winter night, and carriages rattled past in the street outside, punctuated by the occasional shout of a newspaper boy or a spirited argument between flower or orange vendors. I actually loved that about the great city—or cesspool, as Watson had famously called it—that it was constantly beating with fierce, irrepressible life.

But I also loved that inside, our lamps were lighted and a fire was crackling in the grate in front of us. The small room was quiet, cosy, and ... *homelike.*

Even after nearly three months, it still struck me with a small, half happy, half almost painful jolt every time I thought the word *home* about the small row house that had been assigned to us as housing by the police force.

I'd waited my entire life to be able to say that I had a home and a family of my own. Now, a tiny part of me was afraid every time I turned onto our street that I would arrive to find that the house had burned down or been simply winked out of existence like the Scottish village in the old fairy tales.

"I don't mind," Jack said. "Although it would help if you could give me more of a description of Alice."

"Which is exactly what I can't do. According to Lady Lynley, she has blonde hair and blue eyes—which narrows it all the way down to roughly half the female population. Slightly less, of course, when you factor in that she's somewhere between eighteen and thirty years old. Lady Linley doesn't have a photograph of her, and doesn't know anything about her interests or family background, because she's 'not in the habit of asking her staff about their personal lives.' That's a direct quote."

"And she couldn't give you any idea where in London Alice might have gone?"

The most recent census reports estimated the London population at over three million people, spread out across twelve metropolitan boroughs, which meant that the odds of finding a single female were small to none.

"Not just that. She couldn't really give me any actual reason for thinking that Alice would have turned up in London at all. All she would say was that 'girls of Alice's class are always thinking that they'll improve their lot in life in a big city.' Another direct quote."

Jack's dark brows edged together. "So she wants you to look for she-doesn't-know-who, who may be she-doesn't-know-where, doing she-doesn't-know-what."

"More or less. And that's just it." The same nameless, formless uneasiness I'd felt during my meeting with Lady Lynley danced across my skin. "She doesn't appear to have known Alice well—not well enough to care about her personally. She wants at all costs to avoid going to the police, because she's afraid of causing a scandal in her neighborhood. If I had a shilling for every time she said the word 'discretion' during our conversation, I'd be ... well, not rich, because that would take a lot of shillings, but I'd have enough to buy Becky penny candy for an entire month. I didn't get the impression Lady Lynley was afraid *for* Alice exactly—and yet I did have the sense that she was afraid or at least worried about *something*."

I frowned, then shook my head to clear it. With my performance schedule at the Savoy, it was too nice—and too infrequent—an occurrence that Jack and I got to be together at home in the evenings. I didn't want to spoil it with talking about Lady Lynley the entire time.

"Never mind. If she doesn't want to fully confide in me, I can't make her. And short of traveling to Lincolnshire, I don't have any good way of finding out more about Alice herself. Could you ask whether any girls matching Alice's description have turned up, either in hospitals or in the morgue? And I can ask at some of the boarding houses where country girls looking for work in the city often stay. I can take Becky with me tomorrow, she'll love that. Then I can tell Lady Lynley that I've done my best, and that will be the end of it."

Jack nodded. "I can—"

A patter of feet descended the stairs and the sitting-room door opened, revealing Becky in her white cotton nightdress, her blonde braids askew.

At ten years old, Jack's younger sister was still small for her age, with blue eyes, a heart-shaped face sprinkled with freckles across her cheeks and nose—and enough energy to make a seasoned army major general beg for mercy.

"I've tried shutting my eyes and counting sheep, but I'm not tired at all, and—"

"Sleep!" Jack and I spoke at the same moment, both of us pointing to the stairs.

"*Fine.*" Becky sighed dramatically and retreated, shutting the door again. A few seconds later, I heard the creak of springs overhead as she flopped back onto the bed in her room.

I glanced at the clock above the mantle. "At least she's right on schedule, you have to give her that."

Jack's mouth twitched, and then we both started to laugh.

My heart turned over. In the eighteen months or so that I had known him, I had seen Jack look determined, competent, grim, thoughtful, and occasionally dangerous. But it wasn't often that I had seen him look purely, unguardedly *happy*.

I caught hold of his shirt and pulled him towards me so that I could kiss him.

His breath caught in a soft murmur of surprise. "What's that for?"

I drew back enough so he could see me roll my eyes. "Not even two months of marriage, and already it's, 'What? My wife wants to kiss me *again*?'"

I broke off, laughing, as Jack pulled me onto his lap.

"Not what I meant."

A knock sounded on the front door.

Jack pulled back, frowning, and I sat up. "A visitor? At this time of night?"

"It might be my father or Dr. Watson, but they would be more likely to telephone first than come in person."

Jack got up and went to the door. I heard a young, deeply adenoidal voice say, "Special delivery message for you, sir."

Then the door closed again.

When I came into the hall, Jack was still standing in front of the door, staring at a sheet of paper he'd obviously just unfolded from the envelope in his hand.

"What—" I stopped as I caught sight of his face, cold stabbing through me even before I crossed to read over his shoulder.

The letter was on expensive-looking cream-colored stationery, with a gold letterhead printed at the top.

Office of Abelard S. Shirley, Esq., attorney at law.

I noticed those details mechanically, my eyes moving down to the words on the page.

Dear Sir,

I represent my client, Mr. Benjamin Davies. Having served his appointed prison sentence and paid for the mistakes of his past, he is naturally most anxious to be reunited with his daughter Rebecca Davies—

My breath caught. I looked up at Jack. "Becky's father is out of prison?"

Jack's expression was hard, grimmer than I had ever seen it before.

"Not just that. He wants to take custody of her."

8. RETURN FIRE

"He can't do that!"

"Yeah, he can, actually." Jack's voice was flat, his expression so stony it could have been carved in granite. "He's her father. That gives him every right to take custody of her in the eyes of the law."

"But you're the one who's been taking care of her."

When he was younger than Becky was now, Jack's mother had abandoned him, leaving him to grow up alone on the London streets so that she could take up with Benjamin Davies, the man who would become Becky's father.

Then, three years ago, Jack's mother had turned up on his doorstep with seven-year-old Becky in tow. His mother had been dying of tuberculosis, her husband had been imprisoned for smuggling, and she had begged Jack to look after Becky when she was gone.

Jack hadn't even been twenty-one at the time, but he'd taken care of Becky ever since. Until I met them, they'd been their own small family: the two of them against the world.

"Doesn't matter," Jack said. "It's not like I ever adopted her legally. I'm not even her full brother, only half. Any court in London would rule in Benjamin Davies's favor."

He set the letter with an almost chillingly careful precision on the hall table. Then he turned to the door.

"Where are you going?"

He didn't answer. I wasn't even sure whether he heard me.

Jack didn't lose his temper often, and when he did, he got deadly quiet instead of loud. Right now, he was monumentally angry.

He reached for the doorknob, and I caught hold of his arm, trying to hold him back—which was like trying to wrestle a stone statue.

"Wait! What are you going to do?"

Finally, Jack turned his head to look at me, though his dark brown gaze was almost flat, his eyes dull as though brushed with coal from the fireplace.

"There's an address on the letter. I'm going to go and ask this Abelard S. Shirley where I can find Benjamin Davies."

Judging by Jack's expression, it wouldn't end well for either Benjamin Davies or his attorney.

"You can't do that!"

Jack didn't try to pull away; he just opened the front door and set me gently to one side. "Yeah, I can."

"No you can't! If you murder Becky's father, I'll have to break you out of prison, and then we'll have to emigrate to America and live as outlaws in the Wild West—which Becky would probably love, but it could get inconvenient after a while."

Jack stood a moment in the doorway, his shoulders taut, braced. I held my breath. Then, after a seemingly endless wait, his muscles relaxed and he turned back to me, one eyebrow raised.

"You'd break me out of prison, would you?"

"Obviously." I looked up at him, scrutinizing his face. "Are you all right now? You're not going to do anything crazy?"

"Define crazy."

"Going to see Abelard Shirley and giving him the choice whether to die quick or die bloody unless he gives up Benjamin Davies's address ..."

Finally, one corner of Jack's mouth tipped up. "I think you're safe there."

I exhaled. "Good. Then can we please go back to me being the impulsive one and you being the sensible, level-headed one? Because I'm really not good at it."

Jack at least let me lead him back into the sitting room. He dropped silently onto the couch, and I curled up beside him.

A leaden weight was pressing on my chest.

Jack was unfortunately all too right about the courts being likely to rule in favor of Becky's father.

From Norman times coming right down through history to today, the law had a grand old English tradition of being almost obscenely biased in favor of the male patriarchy.

A man could be an abusive, drunken monster who beat his wife and children daily, and yet if his wife sought a divorce on grounds of cruelty, she would nearly always forfeit the right to even *visit* her own children because he husband would have sole, exclusive custody.

Jack finally spoke, his gaze fixed on the dying embers of the fire. "I remember the first week I had Becky with me. Her mother had just died, and we were living in a hole in the wall boarding house room in Whitechapel, because that was all I could afford. I was going through police training so that I could have a job that would keep a roof over our heads. My first day, I was out on the London Streets for ten, twelve hours, breaking up street brawls, chasing down thieves ... then I got back to our room and Becky told me I had to braid her hair and tell her a story before she'd go to sleep." He exhaled a half-laugh. "And I realized the police training had actually been the *easy* part of my day."

I took Jack's hand, lacing our fingers together. Something sharp and painful gripped inside my chest. I couldn't let Becky's father take her away from Jack, I just couldn't.

I couldn't give Becky up, either. Even before Jack and I had been married, she'd been like the younger sister I'd always wanted but never had.

The fire crackled in the hearth, sending out a shower of sparks. I took a breath. Panicking never solved anything.

"How likely do you think it is that Benjamin Davies's offer is sincere? That he really has paid his debt to society and wants to turn over a new leaf?"

Jack raised one shoulder. "I haven't seen him since I was a kid. Besides, I'm not exactly unbiased."

Neither of us was. Becky didn't speak of her father very often, but from what she had said, Davies had been an indifferent father at best, harsh and uncaring at worst. And—though she'd never directly said it—I suspected him of outright cruelty to Becky's mother.

"That doesn't matter. You're a police officer. You know his type. If this were someone else who'd served time for smuggling—some other criminal you'd never met—how likely would you say it was that he'd stay on the straight and narrow?"

"Ten percent?"

Police officers tended to have a cynical view of human nature, but the truth was that they were all too often proven right.

And compared to my father's view of humanity, Jack was practically an incurable optimist.

"So it's roughly ninety percent likely that Benjamin Davies is still involved in his old criminal ways?"

"Actually, it's more likely even than that," Jack said slowly. "He's just out of serving a four-year prison sentence, but he's somehow got the money not just to buy a house but to hire expensive lawyers as well?"

"You're right." That was why I'd fallen in love with Jack. He wasn't just handsome and brave and honorable; he was also one of the most intelligent people I'd ever met. "Unless he's got a rich uncle who died and left him a fortune, he obviously has a ready source of income. Which, as you say, isn't likely for someone just out of jail."

That was *why* there was only a ten percent chance of criminals going straight; after a month or two of digging ditches or hauling cargo down at the docks, they usually decided that it was far easier to make a living by breaking the law than by keeping within its narrow confines.

"And Abelard Shirley's address is here in London." I had picked up the letter from the hall on our way back to the sitting room, and now unfolded it again, looking at the letterhead. "Number 85 Chancery Lane. So it stands to reason that Davies is somewhere in London, as well, otherwise why hire a lawyer here?"

Jack glanced at me, a slight frown etching his brows. "What are you thinking?"

"I'm thinking that I feel a sudden urge to investigate Alice Gordon's disappearance in person."

Jack's expression cleared; he saw where this was leading. "Which I'm guessing means you'd need to go to Lincolnshire?"

"Taking Becky with me," I agreed. "If we're out of the city, short of sending the police after us—which I would lay odds on the fact that, as an ex-convict and probable still-criminal, Benjamin Davies *doesn't* want to do—there's very little he can do to take Becky away. Besides, except for you, my father, and Uncle John, no one will know where we've gone."

"What about your performance schedule at the Savoy?"

"I don't care. I'll tell Mr. Harris that he'll have to give my part to someone else."

Jack's frown deepened. "You shouldn't have to—"

I stopped him, putting my hand over his mouth. "Yes, I should. I'm *going* to. Becky's my family, too. I'm not letting you cope with this on your own or letting her go without a fight. I'll take her out of London. Meanwhile—"

Jack gave up arguing. "Meanwhile I'll start looking into Benjamin Davies's affairs and see what I can turn up." The expression in his eyes turned calculating, hard. "If he's involved in anything criminal, I'll find out about it, and see he's arrested again."

I didn't doubt that he would.

Davies wouldn't be able to take custody of Becky from inside a prison cell.

Cold bloomed inside me. "Just be careful," I said.

In the course of the last year, I'd found out that every person you cared about was someone you were afraid to lose.

"You, too."

"I'm investigating a maid who more than likely got sick of catering to her employer's whims and left. You'll be looking into the criminal underworld. I don't think I'm as likely to run into trouble as you are."

"Yeah, I don't know about that." Jack turned to look at me, his expression serious. "There's something about this case—I don't know what it is, but there's something about the whole setup I don't like."

That so exactly echoed my own feeling that fresh worry inched through me, one drop at a time. But I tried to speak lightly. "Are policemen allowed to have premonitions? I thought it was against regulations."

"Very funny." Jack pulled me close to him, resting his chin on top of my hair. "Just don't take any crazier risks than usual, all right?"

"No crazy risks." I tilted my head to look up at him. "You're not alone in this, all right?" From childhood, Jack had spent the better part of his life on his own, not accepting or relying on help from anyone. "Talk to my father. I know he'll want to do anything he can. And Mycroft, too. He's bound to know lawyers who might be able to help. If anyone can bury Benjamin Davies under an avalanche of legal counter-claims, Mycroft can."

Jack nodded, though the tension didn't entirely leave his expression.

I laced my fingers together with his. "We can do this. Six months from now, Benjamin Davies will just be one more criminal we can look back and say, 'There. We beat him, too.' "

9. A NEW ALLIANCE

"Psssst! Psssst!"

Becky sat up in bed, which made Prince sit up, too, and start to bark.

"Shhhh!" She clamped both her hands around Prince's jaws. "Don't make noise, it's only Flynn."

Normal people knocked on front doors when they wanted to talk to you. Flynn only ever climbed up the drainpipe next to her window and tapped. He also never cared whether it was the middle of the night for most people. But then again, Becky didn't care, either, right now.

She got up, opened the curtains, and pushed up the sash of the window. A blast of cold air rushed in, but Flynn stayed where he was, half perched on the window ledge with his arms and legs wrapped around the drainpipe for balance.

Maybe it was because he was used to living on the streets, but Flynn didn't like being inside. He hadn't ever admitted it to her, but Becky could tell that any time he was under a roof with four walls around him—at Baker Street or anywhere else—it made him jittery.

He was the same age as Becky—ten—and skinny, with blond hair that hung down into his eyes. His face was always streaked with grime and soot, and his clothes were always so dirty you practically couldn't tell what color they had been to start with.

"What's happened?" Becky asked. "Did you find anything out?"

She kept her voice down to a whisper, just in case Lucy and Jack were still awake. They wouldn't mind Flynn coming here; Flynn was one of Mr. Holmes's Irregulars. They might not even object to the secret line of investigation she and Flynn had been carrying out for the past weeks. But they probably would say it could be dangerous, and what they didn't know, they couldn't worry about.

"You got anything to eat?" Flynn whispered back.

Flynn was always hungry. Becky reached for the tin of biscuits she kept in the top drawer of her dresser and handed him one.

Flynn took it one-handed, somehow managing to still cling onto the drain pipe. "There's nothing much to report," he said around a mouthful of the biscuit. "I've been askin' around, but no one's 'eard anything about a new gang dealing in sparks."

Sparks meant diamonds, which was what the people who had kidnapped Lucy and tried to kill Mr. Holmes had been smuggling.

"You've been watching Mr. Holmes, though?" Becky asked.

Anyone who'd wanted to kill Mr. Holmes badly enough to shoot him was bound to try again. So that was part of their plan: to make sure they were watching in case someone did make a move.

Flynn reached for another biscuit. "Yeah, but 'e's been quiet, too. Only time 'e went out this week without Dr. Watson was to see an estate agent."

Becky tilted her head. "An estate agent? Why would he do that?"

Flynn shrugged. "What do I know? Maybe 'e's thinking about buying a new 'ouse."

That wasn't very likely. Mr. Holmes wasn't the sort of person to care about buying new houses, and Becky couldn't imagine him living anywhere but Baker Street.

She couldn't see that an estate agent had anything to do with smuggled diamonds, either. Well, that wasn't true. On an ordinary night, she could probably think up a dozen possible ways that an estate agent could be a secret villain, and some of them might even be plausible, as Mr. Holmes would say.

But right now she couldn't seem to make herself take an interest in coming up with theories.

She realized she'd just missed something Flynn had said, too. "What's that?"

"I just said I should be getting back." Flynn frowned at her. "Something wrong?"

"No. Yes. Maybe." Becky hadn't made up her mind whether she wanted to talk about it yet.

"Well, that narrows it down." Flynn took another bite of the biscuit. "Come on, spill. What's 'appened?"

Becky sighed. "Fine. But you have to come in, I'm not telling you through an open window." One of the neighbors would see them if Flynn stayed here long enough, and besides, her feet were turning into frozen blocks of ice.

* * *

"So, your father's out of the clink," Flynn said. He was sitting cross-legged on the floor, and there were biscuit crumbs scattered all around him.

Prince snuffled, trying to lick some of them up, and Flynn almost jumped out of his skin.

Flynn wasn't afraid of much, but Becky suspected that dogs were on the list. Not that he would ever admit it to her.

Becky nodded. "Lucy and Jack are going to talk to me about it in the morning."

That was one of the many good things about them, they didn't keep secrets. She really hadn't meant to eavesdrop. Except for when she wanted to stop them from worrying about her, she didn't keep secrets from Jack and Lucy, either. But then she'd heard Jack say her father's name, and she hadn't been able to move or keep from listening to the rest.

She felt a little less guilty about having listened, since they were going to let her know anyway.

"What's 'e like?" Flynn asked. "Do you remember 'im?"

Lucy, who'd been brought up in fancy finishing schools, would say that it wasn't good manners to ask prying questions like that—unless, of course, you were doing it for an investigation, in which case being polite didn't count. But Flynn wouldn't know good manners if some of them walked up, curtsied, and invited him to waltz. And to be fair, Becky was the one who'd started this conversation.

"Some."

"Well then?" Flynn prompted.

"I don't know." She picked at a loose thread on her dressing gown. The cold, sick feeling she'd had ever since she'd heard Jack and Lucy talking was getting worse.

Lucy also sometimes said that the best defense was a good offense. Which was really just a fancy way of saying that when in doubt, you should try to turn the tables on whoever was giving you trouble.

"What about your father? What's he like?"

"Dead."

"I'm sorry."

Flynn himself didn't sound particularly sorry about it, but Becky still felt as though she ought to apologize.

"Died before I was born," Flynn said. "And my mum died when I was a baby. Never knew either of 'em."

"So who looked after you, then?"

"Nobody."

That couldn't be the real answer, but from the way Flynn's mouth had gone all pinched around the edges, Becky knew it was the only one she was going to get. She'd known Flynn for months now, and she knew he didn't like to talk about his past any more than she wanted to talk about her father.

Flynn shot a glance at the window, the way he always did when he was stuck indoors, checking to see whether he had an easy way to escape. Becky had left it cracked open a little bit, just for that reason.

"Tell me 'is name and I could ask around a bit for you. See whether anyone around town knows anything about 'im."

"What good would that do?"

Flynn shrugged. "You never know."

That was true, and the more you knew, the better. Becky scratched Prince behind the ears and tried to think things through.

Jack and Lucy were going to fight to keep her father from taking her. But they were also smart, both of them, and sooner or later they would realize the same things she had, as soon as she'd heard her father's name tonight.

She nodded at Flynn, even though the cold feeling inside her now felt like it was crawling through her veins. "All right. His name is Benjamin Davies. Go ahead and see what you can find."

10. A VISIT FROM LUCY

I felt a hand on my shoulder and realized that I had fallen asleep in my chair. I heard Holmes's voice.

"Breakfast is on the table," he said. "Mycroft telephoned. We are wanted at the Royal Exchange at eleven this morning."

Still fogged with my lack of sleep, I poured coffee. "Why?"

"Lestrade's report included the inscription on the opium chest that was stolen from us last night. Mycroft says the inscription is of particular interest, and that the chest may be part of a larger supply. We shall learn more when we meet him and Chancellor Hicks Beach."

I struggled to sort out this news. Sir Michael Hicks Beach was Chancellor of the Exchequer, and we had worked with him on numerous occasions, each involving substantial sums and significant consequences to the British Treasury. The larger supply Holmes had just mentioned must be large indeed.

"But you got home safely last night," I said.

"The thieves stopped about a mile away, where they had a carriage waiting. While they transferred the opium chest to the carriage, I hid in an alleyway. When they had driven off, I drove the police van and followed them to Limehouse."

"Near where Swafford was murdered?"

Holmes nodded. "A police patrol stopped me just before we reached the Red Dragon, and the carriage with our assailants got away. I believe you can deduce the rest, since you took the telephone call last night from Detective Inspector Plank."

"Frustrating to lose them after your pursuit."

Holmes shrugged. "I believe Plank was equally frustrated. He said that Swafford was a friend of his."

"He sounded like a hidebound stickler when he called last night."

"I agree. But Plank was cooperative enough to provide the file on Detective Swafford. You can examine it." He held up a dun-coloured pasteboard binder.

But before I could inspect the file, we heard Mrs. Hudson's voice from below. "Why, Lucy! How good to see you!"

* * *

To see Lucy James is for me always a complex emotional experience, and in this instance, it was even more so. She has saved Holmes's life—and mine—on several occasions. She may be the only person who has had more success than me in getting Holmes to have a care for his own health when he is preoccupied with a case. I feel both fondness and responsibility for her. Yet she has inherited the Holmes trait of bravery to the point of recklessness, particularly when confronting evil. So each time I meet her my feelings of happiness are tinged with worry, for I never know what trouble or danger she may be in at any given time.

My feelings for Lucy were further complicated by an event that had taken place in our rooms barely two months earlier—

her marriage to Detective Constable Jack Kelly, with whom Lucy, Holmes and I have had numerous adventures. Given the recent marriage, I had a shadow of concern that Lucy's attentions would naturally and properly have drifted to the care of her husband, rather than Holmes. I had no worries that Holmes would feel hurt by Lucy's shift in attention—if I may call it that— but I wanted her help with my efforts to keep Holmes safe and healthy.

I was especially concerned now that I knew the current case involved opium. I knew that this drug was far different from cocaine, acting mainly as a depressant rather than a stimulant upon the human brain. But I also feared the adverse effects any drug would have on Holmes's fine mind, and I knew that opium and its derivatives were powerful substances, not to be trifled with.

Holmes and I had seen Lucy since her marriage, of course, and we knew she and Jack were prospering. But this was the first time since the wedding that Lucy had come on her own to visit us.

She entered, dressed in her usual plain black wool winter coat and plain black wool scarf. Her striking, piercing eyes met mine for only a fraction of a second, in the look that I knew meant, "Is Holmes all right?"

I nodded, and my heart lifted, all at the same moment.

Now, Lucy's eyes turned to Holmes.

She gave him a formal nod of greeting. "I do not wish to trouble you unnecessarily," she said, "but I have a case. Lady Lynley is the name of the client. She has a maid that has gone missing. In Lincolnshire. Mrs. Charlotte Teal recommended me to her."

"The Diogenes Club murder," Holmes said.

"Just so. Now, a missing maid seems a trivial matter given the scope of affairs normally attended to by this office. But there may be something of interest."

"Indeed?"

"I met Lady Lynley yesterday afternoon at her club here in London. She was not telling me the entire story. So I would like to gather some information on the Lynley family. I plan to go to Lincolnshire to investigate. I am taking Becky with me. My train leaves this morning."

Without being bidden, I stood and took down our volume of *Burke's Peerage* from the shelf. I handed it over to Holmes. Then I opened our file drawer and consulted the entries at the end of the "L" section.

"No Lynley in our files," I said.

Holmes put down *Burke's* and was looking up from his almanac. "The Lynley estate is indeed in Lincolnshire. The nearest town is the seaside village of Shellingford, which has recently become a popular summer holiday resort. That is concerning."

"Concerning?" said Lucy.

Holmes tapped a finger on the dun-colored binder he had offered me only five minutes earlier. "Shellingford is also the former home of one Detective Swafford, and presumably of his brother, a seaman."

"Something bad has happened to them. That's why you have the folder."

"The detective was found murdered last night. The brother is missing. They left behind a most valuable chest of opium, which has since been stolen. The opium may be part of a larger supply. Worth killing a detective and making a sailor disappear for."

Lucy's eyes flashed. "And certainly a maid."

"And possibly anyone who tries to investigate." Holmes's tone was more serious than Lucy's. He was always this way when she became involved in a new case. He went on, "I might add that I telephoned the detective's fiancée last night but got no answer, and I have not yet heard from Lestrade, who sent two constables to the fiancée's home."

Lucy gave Holmes the same flickering, tight smile that I had seen him employ in similar situations.

"Then Becky and I will have to be careful."

LUCY

11. A PROMISE

The train whistle blew a sharp, piercing blast that announced there were only five minutes until departure time. Already I could feel the rumble of the steam engine jolting through our carriage.

Outside the train's window, King's Cross railway station was busy with the morning bustle: porters carrying suitcases or pushing whole carts of luggage, vendors selling chocolates and newspapers, mothers herding and hurrying children towards the trains, men in business suits and bowler hats arriving from one of the London suburbs for their day's work in the city.

However, our train platform was comparatively quiet. Shellingford was a seaside town on the Lincolnshire coast of the North Sea, roughly one hundred and fifty miles north of London.

In the summer, it would be a popular vacation spot for those looking for fresh sea air and a respite from the city's heat. But very few people traveled north to the seaside at the beginning of January.

The train was so empty that Becky and I even had an entire carriage all to ourselves.

A vendor selling hot roasted peanuts approached our train window, calling and motioning for me to open the transom window so that I could buy a packet.

I glanced at Becky. "Would you like some?"

Becky shook her head. "No thank you."

Late last night, I had sent word to Lady Lynley's club that I thought the best way to move forward with the investigation was for me to travel to Shellingford and begin the search for Alice there.

Lady Lynley had mentioned that she would be staying in London for another few days, so she wouldn't be in Shellingford. But her husband would, and I had asked in my message that she telegraph ahead to let him know to expect our arrival.

Jack had accompanied us to the station. He'd had to report for duty at Scotland Yard, though, so he hadn't been able to wait with us until the train departed. Becky hadn't cried at saying goodbye to him, but she'd hugged him so tightly she looked as though she never wanted to let go.

Now she was sitting quietly on the seat beside me, her hands folded in her lap, looking as though she were modeling for an illustration of a book on good behavior.

The skirt of her dark blue sailor dress was smoothed over her knees, her gloves were spotless, her black patent leather boots were crossed at the ankles, and her blonde braids hung in perfect order over the shoulders of her blue wool winter coat.

Watching her, I wished that Benjamin Davies would appear in our train compartment so that I could punch him in the face.

Becky was *never* quiet or well-ordered. It was part of her charm, that she approached life with the tenacious ferocity of a whirlwind. This was her first real train trip too—and, apart from coming to London from Liverpool with her mother three years ago, her first time journeying anywhere outside of the city.

Ordinarily, she would have been bouncing on the seat, barely able to sit still or contain her excitement.

Now she turned to me. "Shouldn't the train be leaving soon?" Her small face looked pale and tense.

"Any moment now. You heard the whistle. They're just waiting for any last-minute-comer, and then we'll be off."

Becky nodded, though the set of her shoulders didn't relax. *I watched her, debating. Should I bring up her father or not?*

Jack and I had told Becky the full truth about the letter from Benjamin Davies's attorney. I would have easily given up ten starring roles at the Savoy to avoid doing it, but there was no point in trying to keep it secret.

Jack and Becky might look absolutely nothing alike, but Becky had every bit of Jack's quick, logical mind and determination when it came to solving a mystery. She would find out the truth sooner or later, whether we wanted her to or not.

She'd said very little since then, and I didn't know whether it would be better for her to talk about it now, or wait until she was the one to raise the subject.

I reached for the manila file on the seat beside me. "We could look over the materials on Inspector Swafford."

"Who?"

"The victim in a case Holmes is working on. He is from the same area as we're going to. Holmes gave me this file early this morning, just in case we might spot something that he missed."

I didn't—of course—have the autopsy photos to show Becky, but I had Inspector Swafford's notes on his recent investigations, and a file on his history of service with the London police force.

The file fell open to a photograph of the inspector taken in the earliest days of his enrolment on the force, before he had risen in the ranks: a gaunt face, scowling out at the camera from under the brim of a beat constable's helmet.

Usually, giving Becky even the slightest hint of a mystery was like offering a kitten a pile of yarn. But now she only glanced at the photograph, then shook her head.

"We're not *really* going to find anything that Mr. Holmes missed. You're only saying that to try to cheer me up."

With a lurch and a fresh blast of the whistle, the train began to chug out of the station, gathering speed as it rolled down the tracks.

Becky lifted her head, watching out the window as the gray, smoke-stained bricks of London buildings rolled past.

"This doesn't seem very hard." Her voice was so low that I could barely hear it above the noise of the train's engines. "Buying a ticket and traveling by train out of London. My father could do it, too, couldn't he?"

"He could," I said. "But it's not very likely that he will. He wouldn't know where to find us, for one thing." I gestured to the busy, noisy station outside. "You can see for yourself. Hundreds of trains depart from here every day. And that's just from King's Cross. There's also Victoria Station and Charing Cross ..."

I stopped, studying Becky's expression. "Unless ... do you *want* to see him?"

It occurred to me that Jack and I hadn't asked Becky that yet.

"Jack would understand if you did want to," I told Becky gently. "He is your father, after all—"

"*No!*" The word burst out of Becky almost violently, and she shook her head. "I was only five when he was sent to prison.

My mum held on for another two years in our house, hoping he'd get out again—until she got sick and then the money ran out." Becky clasped her hands tightly together, her head bent, and her face shadowed by the brim of her blue velvet hat. "But I remember how he was angry all the time—always growling at me to keep quiet and not pester him or get in his way. And he shouted at me once for going into his private office when he wasn't there. I remember how he and my mum would fight. I'd hear them screaming at each other, after they thought I was asleep in bed. And then I'd hear my mum crying afterwards."

Becky stopped, her blue eyes flooding with tears. "Could he really take me away from you and Jack, and make me live with him?"

Her voice caught.

I had promised myself that I wouldn't lie to her. Much as I would have liked to. "Legally speaking, he *could*. But he's not going to," I said. "Because Jack won't let that happen. *I* won't let that happen. Holmes and Uncle John and Mycroft won't let that happen."

Becky looked up at me. Usually she was so bright and ir-repressible that it was easy to forget how much ugliness she'd already seen in her young life.

Right now, though, her gaze was shadowed by an almost adult look of world-weary sadness.

"You can't promise that, Lucy."

I could remember myself at Becky's age. Watching all the other girls at school going home for Christmas and summer holidays, and knowing that I had no family or home of my own. I couldn't change that past, but I could make sure that Becky wasn't ripped away from us. Not as long as I breathed.

I put an arm around Becky anyway and hugged her tightly. "Too bad. Because I just *did* promise. You're part of our family and no one is going to take you away."

12. Three Missing Ships

The January wind tore at my hat and scarf as we climbed the granite steps of the Royal Exchange. As we passed through the entrance to the Society of Lloyd's, Mycroft Holmes was there to meet us, standing well inside, out of the cold. Beyond the hallway we could see a huge room with a high ceiling, and a vast expanse of desks, mainly unoccupied.

"We meet in the underwriting room," said Mycroft. "Where Lloyd's conducts business." He gave a nod to a uniformed attendant.

The uniformed man retreated and a moment later a small, dapper fellow hurried up to us, a broad smile on his quite handsome features. He had a boyishly thick shock of blond hair, which had gone slightly gray at the temples, where it spilled wispily over the tips of his ears.

"Gentlemen! I am Avery Jacoby," he said. "And I cannot tell you how delighted the Society is to see you. It is not every day that we have visitors who bring promise of repayment of a million pounds. Please let me show you to a table where we can have a bit of privacy."

"Where is the chancellor?" asked Holmes.

"We will join him in another room, after we discuss a few mundane matters."

We walked within the cavernous space of the underwriting room. The lofty structure called to my mind the impressive size of the Crystal Palace or the Royal Albert Hall, but across the wide hardwood floor here I saw polished wooden desks, small tables, and upright chairs clustered, in little groups. The focal point of the room was an elevated rotunda, with carved dark wood columns that soared thirty feet high and reminded me of the altar area in a cathedral. Enshrined within the stately columns hung a shining brass bell.

"That's from HMS *Lutine*," Jacoby said, pointing up at the bell. "A treasure ship—our most famous loss ever, but we paid the claim in a week. It's become a symbol of honor for us— a reminder that we live up to our promises. Now it has a practical use as well: we ring it when big news comes in, so that everyone hears at the same time. One ring means bad news, and two is good."

Moving on, Jacoby then stopped before a table that had a green cloth spread across it. "Maybe you'll give us some good news someday, Mr. Holmes. Maybe you'll help us salvage something big."

Holmes said nothing.

Atop the table awaiting us I saw a silver tea service, with a large plate of scones, clotted cream, sugar, and jam. There were four chairs; we each took one. I settled gratefully into mine while Jacoby served us. The tea was hot and with cream and sugar, precisely what I required to thaw my frozen faculties back to life.

"Please tell us about the discovery you have made, Mr. Holmes." Jacoby said.

"If you mean the opium chest we discovered last night," Holmes replied, "it was stolen shortly after we found it."

"So I heard." Jacoby bent to his briefcase, hefted it onto the table and produced a file, from which he extracted a photograph. He handed the photograph to Holmes.

"Did the chest look like this?"

Holmes returned the photograph after a momentary glance. "The construction was identical, as was the inscription—except for the number of the chest and the date."

"Tantalizing." Jacoby rummaged in his briefcase once again and extracted another photograph, this time of a ship at harbor, taken from possibly a hundred feet away so that the full length of the vessel was visible.

"This is the *Chichester*, a cargo vessel that sailed from Calcutta with its two sister ships, the *Scallion* and the *Bottlenose*. Each of them held two thousand chests of opium. All three vessels were doomed—at least that is what we have thought until now."

Jacoby gestured towards the Lutine Bell. "More than a year ago, that bell rang one single time, when we received word that all three ships had sunk in a typhoon. A very sad occasion that I shall not forget, for it meant that I and others of our subscribers would have to empty our pockets to the tune of one million pounds. It would have been more, had we insured all three ships for their full value." Jacoby paused, taking a small sip of tea. "What I wish you to consider, Mr. Holmes, is that the chests were loaded into the hold of the vessel you see here, under inspection of company officials from both our company and our client, the Red Dragon Company. The hatchway was sealed immediately, to be opened only upon arrival in Hong Kong port."

"I follow you," Holmes said.

"So how could the chest that you saw have been spirited from—what to all reason and logic—would have been a watery grave, and be found in a seaman's rented room in Kensington?"

"I can enumerate several possibilities," Holmes said. "But first, may I know the source of the reliable information that you received that indicated the ships had gone down in a typhoon?"

"A Red Dragon vessel, the *Tsing Po*, was inbound for Calcutta at the same time that the three ships whose cargo we insured were outbound for Hong Kong. The *Tsing Po* became caught in the same storm. However, it was sailing with a nearly empty hold, and hence was far more buoyant and maneuverable than the three vessels headed south-east and east. It saw them from a distance as they were swept up in the storm. Later when the skies cleared, the *Tsing Po* searched the area. There was nothing. Only a few bits of flotsam that indicated they had come from the *Chichester*. That was the report that the *Tsing Po* captain gave to its company office in Calcutta harbor."

"And you believed the report," Holmes said.

"I see what you are getting at. The captain could have given a false report. But why?"

"The Red Dragon Company may have sailed the three ships to another port, and subsequently renamed them. They may have then unloaded the opium and sold it elsewhere."

"We thought of that possibility. We obtained the names and addresses of the crewmen of the three vessels. We checked with the relatives of each crewman. All were grieving the loss of their family breadwinner. There were no exceptions."

"The men could have been relocated and taken new names, waiting for time to pass before reuniting with their families."

"We thought of that possibility as well. We had our agents watch the families for six months before we paid the claim. With approximately one hundred and fifty men and their families, we would have expected the secret to come out somewhere. Yet no one talked, as much as we could determine."

"There are two alternatives. Each is more sinister," Holmes said. "The crewmen may have been lost, but not lost at sea. They may have been party to the theft. Then, upon the delivery of the ships to whatever the alternative destination, they may have been killed. The effect on the grieving families would be the same."

Jacoby paled, and he brushed his hair back from where it had fallen over his forehead. "Murder of one hundred and fifty men. Difficult to contemplate. What is the other possibility?"

"That the opium chests were never loaded onto the three ships."

"Our agent saw them go into the holds—"

"You mistake my meaning," Holmes said, interrupting. "What went into the holds may not have been opium. Balls of wood or some other material may have been coated with opium paste and poppy petals, and then loaded into duplicate chests."

"To guard against that possibility, before each chest is sealed at the East India Company factory, one of the opium balls is cut into, and a small wedge is removed."

"I see," said Holmes. "And then?"

"The sealed chests are loaded onto a caravan of carts and driven under army protection to Calcutta Harbor. At the harbor, they are taken off the carts and loaded into the East India Company warehouse where the auction is held. The winning bidder—in this case, the Red Dragon Company—then takes possession at the auction warehouse and is responsible for the cargo from that point on."

"Does the winning bidder also perform the test on the opium—cutting into the ball of one of the chests?"

"They may if they choose to do so. I will have to check to see if they did."

"The Society does not supervise?"

"We insure delivery, Mr. Holmes. Not quality."

"So the Red Dragon Company might easily have falsified the test. Moreover, the false cargo may have caused the ships to vanish. Some of the balls may have contained enough explosives to demolish the hull of each vessel. With a timing device on each, all three could have gone down at the same time. The scheme then needs only the captain of the *Tsing Po* to report a typhoon instead of three explosions."

"What you have described is piracy," Jacoby said. "Combined with fraud on a gigantic scale, against Her Majesty's Government. But I do believe it could be accomplished as you have described."

He got to his feet. "Let us go to our director's room."

WATSON

13. A REJECTION

I had met the Chancellor of the Exchequer, Sir Michael Hicks Beach, on several occasions, and he was not in the director's room. The two gentlemen at the table were both strangers to me.

Mycroft indicated the man nearest us, a dour-looking fellow, with long, luxuriant gray whiskers, which oddly split into two long flowing parts, the pointed tips of which nearly touched his shoulders. His light blue eyes had a subdued, dream-like quality, almost sorrowful. His expression had a worried cast.

I found myself staring.

But Mycroft introduced him. "This is Sir Halliday Macartney, English Secretary in the Chinese Legation."

Macartney nodded coolly at Holmes and me. I took an instant dislike to the fellow. Contrary to his sorrow-laden gaze, there was something haughty and dismissive in his demeanor. There was also something about his name that nagged at my memory.

"And this is Lord Ernshaw," Mycroft continued, indicating a tall, middle-aged gentleman so extremely thin that his neck jutting up from his collar put me in mind of a stalk from the circular rim of a flower pot. He wore his dark hair shoulder length.

His pallid, yellowed complexion reminded me of a consumptive patient, yet his dark eyes seemed alert, and even forceful, as they surveyed us. He rose slightly, supporting himself with his hands on the armrests of his chair.

"The chancellor could not attend this morning," Ernshaw said. "However, he does not wish you in any way to underestimate the importance of the task which we will present to you, Mr. Holmes."

"What task would that be?" Holmes replied.

Macartney cut in before Ernshaw could reply. "I am here to represent the government of China," he said, the words coming in a broad Scottish brogue that seemed preposterous to me, given the association with an Asian country. "My principals in the matter, including His Serene Highness the Emperor, also have a view on the task; however, ours is not perfectly aligned with that of Lord Ernshaw here."

"Your views do not concern me," Holmes said. "What is the task?"

Both men looked astonished. "Why, we want you to recover the opium, of course," said Ernshaw. "Since Jacoby here has determined that there is a possibility that the missing cargo still exists. Is that not so, Mr. Jacoby?"

Jacoby nodded.

"Whatever opium there is," said Macartney.

"We want it," said Ernshaw.

Holmes raised an eyebrow. "Who, might I ask, is 'We'?"

"Lloyds will no doubt assert title" Jacoby said. "Also, the Red Dragon Company may assert a claim."

"And you represent the Red Dragon, Mr. Macartney?" Holmes asked.

"They are not my primary client. Of course, the Red Dragon will wish to acquire the opium and bring it into China for sale at a very considerable profit, which was what they would have done if the cargo had not been lost. But it is His Serene Highness the Emperor's official wish that the opium does not enter China. His Majesty has been very vocal on that point. He deplores the disastrous effect of the drug upon his subjects."

"Then His Majesty would want the opium destroyed," Holmes said.

To my surprise, Macartney shook his head, the two tips of his beard moving sidewise like a gray broom in front of his chest. "The matter is a complex one. Under certain circumstances recovering the opium would be acceptable to His Majesty."

"What circumstances?"

"As you may know, His Majesty's government is currently negotiating a new treaty regarding the territories north of Hong Kong and Kowloon. It would be helpful if those negotiations were to include a provision for payment for the sale of opium," Macartney said. "In any event, some monetary compensation is only fair. The opium, if recovered, will cause trouble in His Majesty's kingdom. His Majesty should be compensated for that trouble."

We all waited for Holmes to respond. He sat silent, his lips compressed and twisted in a grimace of distaste.

Finally, Holmes spoke. "I decline."

"Decline?" asked Ernshaw, with an astonished look.

"On what grounds?" asked Macartney.

"I am free to select my own clients," Holmes replied.

"If it is a question of your fee—"

"It is a question of my integrity. I decline to perform a task that will ultimately deepen the degradation of thousands of opium addicts and impoverish and enslave thousands of new ones."

"We can pay you a hundred thousand pounds," said Ernshaw.

Holmes shrugged. "I have no interest." He rose from his chair.

"Five hundred thousand, then," said Macartney. "Upon recovery of the opium."

"I shall not recover the opium," Holmes said. He was standing now.

"Your authority would be virtually unlimited," said Ernshaw. His eyes were wide with excitement, but then I thought I saw them narrow as he went on. "Anyone who interfered with your investigation or, in particular, with the opium, would be stealing government property, which, on a scale of the amounts we are discussing here is—" he paused for effect, and delivered the next word slowly, in a stentorian tone, rolling each of the four syllables off his lips "—*trea-son-a-ble*. And *that* is a hanging offense, Mr. Holmes."

Holmes appeared to have heard nothing of this. He was opening the door.

Standing just outside the doorway with one hand upraised to knock was the uniformed attendant whom we had seen at the entrance to the Society offices. "My apologies, gentlemen," the attendant said. "I have a telegraph message here for Mr. Holmes from Inspector Lestrade of Scotland Yard. It is marked 'Most Urgent.'"

Holmes opened the yellow envelope, glanced at the contents, and then turned to the men at the table. He said, "Dr. Watson and I will be leaving you now."

He handed the message to me. It read:

COME AT ONCE ST. PHILIP'S CHURCH.
MISS JANINE AND HER MOTHER FOUND MURDERED.
LESTRADE.

14. A DEADLY DELIVERY

My first thought on meeting Lady Lynley's husband was that he could have stepped straight off the stage. Not because he was unusually handsome or had a commanding presence, but because any theatrical producer would take one look at him and instantly cast him in the role of "*Country Squire.*"

Lynley House was a large, handsome manor house built in the Palladian style, and we were seated in Lord Lynley's private study.

A gas fire in the grate showed walls covered in dark burgundy hangings. Heavy velvet curtains framed the windows. A tall bookshelf filled with ancient-looking leather-bound volumes stood to one side of Lord Lynley's desk. On the wall, the portrait of a gentleman in the white neck ruff and doublet of the late 17th century scowled down from the back of a rearing black stallion. The scowling man bore a striking resemblance to the current Lord Lynley.

Lord Lynley himself looked to be somewhere around fifty, with graying hair just beginning to thin on the crown. His face was heavy in the brow and jaw, with deeply-set brown eyes and a ruddy, weathered look to his skin.

He was wearing an impeccable suit of country tweed, but it wasn't hard to picture him sitting astride a horse and wearing a hunting jacket, shouting *yoiks!* and *tally-ho!* as he galloped after an unfortunate fox.

"I really don't know what more I can tell you," Lord Lynley said.

Becky spoke up beside me. "But you haven't actually—"

I interrupted her before she could finish saying what I was certain she was going to, which was that in order for Lord Lynley to tell us anything *more*, he would have to have already told us something in the first place.

I smiled politely. "You haven't yet told us where you think Alice might have gone. Do you think your wife's theory is correct, that she may have traveled to London?"

Lord Lynley moved his shoulders. "No idea." He had a gruff, hearty baritone voice that matched his appearance so perfectly that it was almost uncanny. "Who knows what odd notions these girls get into their heads, eh?" He laughed, then leaned forward towards me across his desk, spreading his hands out, palms open. "Look here, Mrs. Kelly, I'll be honest with you …"

I kept my polite smile firmly in place, but inside my head, my father's voice came to mind, commenting sardonically with one of his favorite sayings:

Any time a witness volunteers to speak honestly, you can be reasonably assured that the statement to follow is a lie.

"My wife sent a telegram this morning, letting me know you were coming, but until that moment, the truth is, I had no idea that my wife was planning to consult you. I'm da—" he glanced at Becky and checked himself. "—dashed sorry that you were dragged into our mundane little domestic trouble. I don't know where Alice Gordon is, but I'm sure there's no mystery about it. She was unsatisfied in her work and wanted a change of scenery."

He glanced out the study window, where beyond the house grounds flat, marshy land stretched out like dull brown carpet beneath the iron-gray sky.

I had never been to this part of England before. The Fens, also sometimes called the Fenlands, were a vast coastal plain covering five counties and roughly 1,500 square miles. The land here alternated between marshes, and places where the marsh had been drained and turned into flat agricultural lands threaded by drainage channels and dikes.

Maybe it was the chill weather outside. Maybe I had simply lived amidst the constant noise and bustle and fierce, rushing life of the London streets for too long.

But everything about the landscape outside felt bleak, almost eerie.

Lord Lynley went on. "It's a common problem we've had, I'm afraid, with keeping staff out here. I have hopes to oversee the drainage of more of the lands on the estate, which would encourage more neighbors to settle nearby. But for right now, we are rather isolated."

I'd already seen the books on agriculture on the edge of His Lordship's desk.

"Drainage?" I repeated.

"That's right." For the first time since the beginning of the conversation, a spark of what sounded like genuine enthusiasm warmed Lord Lynley's voice. He brought his fist down on the edge of the desk. "There's good land out there—good, farmable land. But it's under feet of water. The idea is to divert the water, channel it into dikes and canals so that the land can be drained and cleared for farming. We've made a start, up to the north of the estate, but we've run short of—" he stopped, clearing his throat. "That is, it takes time. Time and the most modern advances in agricultural engineering. In the meantime, girls like Alice believe they'll find more life and company of their own age in a town, rather than stuck out in the country."

"Your wife seemed worried that something might have happened to Alice."

For a split-second, a shadow of something hard, almost angry, seemed to pass across Lord Lynley's expression. Then it vanished, and he gave me a tolerantly-amused smile. "My wife was very fond of Alice. Naturally, the girl's departure wounded her feelings deeply. Serena is of a highly sensitive, nervous temperament, and her health is … not what it should be, a good deal of the time. She gets these strange fancies that something sinister has occurred, and nothing will dissuade her from that theory." He chuckled. "Bless you ladies, but you do get the oddest notions into your heads and then nothing and no one will get them out again. But there's nothing to them. Just nervous fancy."

I took a sip of tea from the cup that a uniformed parlormaid had brought. A part of me was tempted to ask whether he wouldn't like to simply pat my head and offer me a sweet if I behaved like a good little girl and let the matter drop.

But I studied Lord Lynley instead.

As unsuited for one another as they seemed on the surface, Lord Lynley and his wife had one thing in common: like Lady Lynley's upper-crust accent, everything about Lord Lynley—and his study—was trying just a little too hard.

Of course, I was slightly cheating. Thanks to Holmes's files, I knew already that Lord Lynley's father was the first of the family to have gained the title, after making his fortune as a merchant in the China trade.

But even without that information ...

The books on the bookshelf might be expensive and leather-bound, but they weren't actually old. I had glanced over the gold-embossed titles, and the oldest book on the shelf was a copy of Dickens's *Pickwick Papers*. None of them looked to have been so much as cracked open, either. The only books that looked to have been read were the ones on agriculture and drainage.

The portrait, too, of the 16th-century man who so strongly resembled Lord Lynley, used colors that no actual 16th-century painter would have possessed. It was a modern work, probably made with Lord Lynley himself as the model, designed to lend a baronial air to the room.

"Did you ever hear Alice express a desire to go to London?" I asked.

"I'm afraid I hardly had any dealings with the girl," Lord Lynley said. "She was my wife's servant, not mine, you understand. Although now that I come to think of it—yes, I did hear her say that she wished she could find work there. And, of course, if she had a day off, that was how she spent it—traveling to town so that she could see a theater revue. And she—"

He cut off.

Becky fidgeted in her chair. I waited a count of three. Long enough to still appear polite—not quite long enough to allow time to come up with a really convincing untruth if that was what His Lordship was trying to accomplish in the silence.

"She did what?" I asked.

Lord Lynley's already ruddy cheeks turned a shade darker. "She applied for work in Shellingford. At—at the bakery, I believe."

My eyebrows lifted. "The *bakery*?" It was an odd choice of employment for a former lady's maid. Most girls with Alice's background would apply to a millinery shop or dressmaker's. "Had Alice experience in cookery?"

"Yes, her mother was a cook in a London patisserie shop, as I understand it." Lord Lynley cleared his throat, shuffling a few of the stray papers on his desk. "Perhaps that might be a fruitful avenue of inquiry in London. Checking bakeries and pastry shops."

"Possibly," I agreed.

I *could* have said that anyone who couldn't tell lies better than Lord Lynley ought to give up entirely on even making the attempt. I had met two-year-olds who were significantly more adept at prevarication.

But that would accomplish nothing except to get me thrown out of His Lordship's study—and I couldn't afford that yet.

"The first step, though, is to see whether she left behind any clues here as to where she might have gone. Has someone looked through her things?"

Lord Lynley tilted his head inquiringly, a frown knitting his brows. "Things? How do you mean?"

"Her possessions." It actually wasn't hard to speak patiently. I still had no idea what had happened to Alice or what His Lordship's not-very-skillful lies were covering up. But I didn't like anything about the feeling that this conversation was giving me.

Uneasiness—the same uneasiness I'd felt during the interview with Lady Lynley—was raising all the tiny hairs on my neck and arms. It made it comparatively easy to smile blandly at His Lordship's overdone look of incomprehension. "Surely someone must have looked through Alice's room?"

"Oh." Lord Lynley's face cleared. "Ah, yes. We tried, but she'd taken all her things with her. The room she shared with one of our other maidservants was entirely cleared of her possessions. She didn't leave so much as a stitch of clothing or a pencil stub behind."

The study door opened to reveal the same stately, gray-haired butler who had shown Becky and me in.

Lord Lynley glowered at him. "Yes, Rothwell? What is it?"

"A parcel for you, sir." Rothwell carried a paper-wrapped bundle on a silver tray. "The boy who delivered it said that it was quite urgent."

"Parcel?" The line between Lord Lynley's brows deepened. "I don't remember ordering a delivery of any kind. Must be some tom-fool notion of Serena's—"

He reached for the silver letter opener that lay on his desk, making to cut the strings that tied the package shut.

"Don't!" I sprang up out of my chair.

Lord Lynley jumped, nearly slicing his finger with the edge of the letter opener, and ground out a muttered curse. "What on earth—" He transferred the glower to me.

"I don't believe that you should open that. At least not without proper protection. Look." I pointed to two small holes that had been punched into the brown paper covering and through the pasteboard box underneath. "Those look to me like breathing holes."

"*Breathing* holes?" Incredulity stamped Lord Lynley's face, then he gave a dismissive snort. "Nonsense. The parcel probably just got damaged in the mail." With a quick twist, he severed the string and tore open the parcel's wrappings, then tipped open the lid of the box.

A wriggling, slithering mass of dark brown bodies squirmed out onto Lord Lynley's desk.

His Lordship sprang back with a sharp cry, and I caught hold of Becky, dragging her back towards the door. Strictly speaking, maybe I ought to try and help Lord Lynley, but I'd already recognized the diamond pattern of the snakes' scales— and given the choice between protecting Lord Lynley's life or Becky's, there was no contest.

The writhing knot fell apart into three snakes that slithered towards the edge of Lord Lynley's desk. His Lordship was still holding the letter opener. In a single, swift movement, he brought the blade down onto the head of the first snake, wrenched open the drawer of the desk and knocked the other two snakes inside.

He turned the key in the drawer's lock, then looked up at the butler, breathing hard. "Rothwell. Get Faraday to come up here from the stables to deal with the bloody creatures."

The butler was standing frozen in the center of the room, momentarily shaken out of his polished, stately calm. "But sir, Faraday has no experience with snakes that I know of—"

"I don't care!" Lord Lynley's voice cracked. "Tell him to bring in some rat poison or something and just get rid of the things!"

"Yes, sir." Rothwell bowed and departed, quickening his pace to almost a run as he left the room.

Lord Lynley mopped his forehead with a handkerchief and sank back into his chair—though he kept it pushed well back from the desk. He kept eyeing the drawer. He was probably wondering—as I was—whether the snakes would be able to wriggle their way out.

"I beg your pardon, Mrs. Kelly, that you were forced to witness that … unpleasantness."

The dead body of the snake that he had stabbed still lay limp across the blotting pad on his desk. I had seen uglier sights, and bloodier ones, too. But I still fought a shiver.

"Unpleasantness is certainly one word for it. Those are swamp adders. Their venom won't necessarily kill you, but it will certainly cause pain and possibly serious illness. I hope you'll forgive me for pointing it out, Lord Lynley, but it would appear that someone dislikes you a good deal. Sending poisonous snakes through the mail isn't exactly a subtle message."

Lord Lynley's face was blotchy: splotches of red patterned across his pale, almost grayish skin. But he straightened, appearing to pull himself together. "Nonsense. Just some foolish practical joke." He rose, extending a hand to me. "Thank you for coming. I'm confident that Alice is quite safe, wherever she may be."

It was a clear dismissal.

I nodded. "We won't take up any more of your time, then. Come, Becky."

We started for the door, but after a few steps I turned back. "There's just one other thing you might be able to help with."

Lord Lynley's brows creased in a slight frown. "Yes?"

"I was hoping—" I stopped. Under ordinary circumstances, I didn't put any stock in premonitions. But right now, I felt as though someone had taken a cube of ice and dragged it down the length of my spine.

"We'll need somewhere to stay for tonight," I finished. "Preferably somewhere near the train station. That's where we left our bags."

Upon our arrival in Shellingford, we had hired a carriage and come straight here.

"Ah, I see." Lynley's expression cleared. "Well, there is the Grand Hotel in town, of course, but I can't recommend it— their service is poor at best and the rooms are very overpriced, especially for only a visit of a single night. You might try Susan Anderson, who lives on Applegate Street. She runs a small inn and rents out rooms at very reasonable rates."

"Thank you so much. And please tell Lady Lynley when you speak to her that I hope her health improves."

"I'm sure it will." His tone hadn't changed, but there was another blink-and-you'd-miss-it tightening of his lips as he spoke. "It's largely a matter of willpower, of course. When our minds conceive health, our bodies obey."

15. A MESSAGE

I still shudder inwardly at the recollection of what we found at St. Philip's Church. We arrived after an hour-long cab ride, passing only a short distance from John Swafford's rooms. An ambulance waited on the street outside the church steps. We entered.

"A bad business, this," Lestrade said, and led us down the center aisle of the church. Two constables with stretchers waited in the outer aisle.

The bodies of Miss Janine and an older woman both lay crumpled on the floor between the back of the second row of pews and the seat of the pew behind it. Both bodies were twisted at an awkward angle. Miss Janine's feathered hat lay on its side on the floor. Her blonde hair was streaked with crimson.

Each woman had been shot in the back of the head.

"Mother and daughter," said Lestrade.

"Powder burns on both wounds," Holmes said, bending over the two bodies. "Shot at close range. The kneeling bench is down. They were both praying when they were shot. Perhaps that is a mercy."

"We don't know when," Lestrade said. "The church sexton found them when he opened the church at eight o'clock this morning."

"When did he close?"

"Six o'clock at night, but the death could have been before that. The sexton wouldn't have seen them. He wouldn't walk all this way down to the front."

"I agree. On the floor, they would have been below his line of vision," Holmes said.

"They were praying for John Swafford's soul," I said.

"Who told them Swafford was dead?" asked Holmes.

A uniformed constable stepped forward. "This is my beat. I had to break the news."

"What time was that?"

"Yesterday afternoon. Around five."

"So they went into the church, possibly immediately afterward."

"They were upset enough to need some sort of consolation, I can tell you that," the constable said. He went on, "I don't think the bodies have been touched—after they were shot, I mean. Nothing to indicate a robbery. Both purses are unopened."

"Were you followed, constable?" asked Holmes.

The man seemed surprised. "Why would anyone want to follow me?"

"Someone waited for these two ladies. Someone wanted to kill them as quickly as possible after they heard the news. Someone who would have known your errand, constable."

"Why would someone want to kill them?"

"They were likely killed because they knew John Swafford," Holmes said.

"You mean they might have known something that he knew," said Lestrade.

"They had to be killed before they could tell others." Holmes glanced at the constable. "Did they reveal anything to you?"

The constable shook his head. "Miss Janine was crying too much to talk. I told them to keep away from the streets and said I'd come back later." His gaze was downcast. "I should have stayed with them."

"Not your fault," Lestrade said. He nodded to the two attendants who were waiting to take away the bodies.

"It's not right," the constable said. "They came here for understanding and comfort. Somebody came into the pew behind them when they were praying and killed them. Somebody's got to answer."

"Somebody will," said Holmes.

"We'll take it from here," said Lestrade.

"Will there be a funeral?" Holmes asked.

The constable shook his head. "No family to make the arrangements. All they had was each other."

"A shame," I said, and immediately felt the inadequacy of my remark.

"They both worked at a clothing factory," the constable said. "Maybe the manager will do something."

"If there is a funeral, let me know," said Lestrade. "I want to keep an eye on whoever attends."

We waited in an awkward silence as the two attendants shuffled into the pew and bent over Miss Janine. They lifted her.

"Wait," Holmes said.

He sprang forward, picked up a scrap of white paper, and held it out so we could read it.

In clumsy block capitals of black ink were printed three words.

NOT DONE YET

16. FOLLOWED

"What do you think?" I asked Becky.

Despite the cold and the gray weather, she had decided that she would rather walk the two miles back into town, so I had paid off our carriage driver and let him go. Now Becky and I were making our way down Lynley House's long carriage drive.

Becky bit her lip. "He's a very bad liar."

"You're right about that."

"He said that he'd barely ever talked to Alice," Becky went on. "But he knew that her mother was a baker and that she wanted to go to London?"

It was also odd that—from the sound of things—he had personally inspected the missing girl's room. That was the kind of task the master of the house definitely didn't do himself. Ninety-nine percent of men in Lord Lynley's position would delegate the task to their housekeepers, or at the very least, their wives.

"Anything else?" I asked.

"He doesn't like to talk about his wife being sick."

I nodded. It wasn't terribly unusual for a man to dismiss his wife's nervous tendencies as mere female hysterics. But there had been an odd note to Lord Lynley's voice when he'd spoken of his wife's health. Impatience mixed with something almost like guilt was the nearest that I could come.

Becky took a little skipping step beside me. "He's hiding something. What do you think it is? Do you think he's secretly done away with Alice and buried her body on the grounds? Or maybe he threw her body into one of the irrigation dikes!"

I wasn't sure whether I should be disturbed or thankful that the prospect of a potential murder to investigate had brought life and color back into Becky's expression.

Thankful, probably, that she still had enough ten-year-old child in her to see a murder investigation as more in the light of one of Watson's stories come to life than a human tragedy.

"If he'd done that, it probably would have been found by now. Besides, that doesn't account for whoever sent the snakes."

"True." Becky shivered a little, her smile fading as she glanced over her shoulder at the house behind us. Lynley House was still visible through the bare, skeletal branches of the trees that lined the drive. It stood, its white marble columns and domed roof bleak and solitary, set off from the gray and brown landscape like a half-buried skull in a muddy field.

"There's something badly wrong in that place," Becky said. Her voice was smaller now. "Is that why you didn't ask to question any of the other servants?"

"Yes. I wasn't sure whether Lord Lynley would agree to let me for one thing. But I also wanted to let him think we believed that Alice had just gone off of her own accord, too."

It was also the reason I'd changed my mind about my final question for him. I'd come to Lynley House ready to see whether I could talk my way into being allowed to spend the night as a guest there.

It wouldn't have been an unreasonable request. I'd come in response to his wife's plea for help, and I'd counted twenty bedroom windows on the second and third floors. They weren't exactly hurting for spare rooms.

Becky slipped her hand into mine. "You think something has happened to Alice? Something bad?"

"I'm afraid I do."

I still had no idea why Alice had left her post—whether she'd chosen to go or been dragged off. I didn't know whether she was alive or dead. But I was sure, with a cold, deep-rooted certainty, that whatever unseen forces were at play behind all of this were dangerous.

I hated that feeling. I'd followed my father into his chosen profession because a part of me couldn't be happy without a problem to solve or an injustice to put right. But I hated standing on the outer edge of a problem or danger and not knowing what I was dealing with.

Becky turned to look up at me from under the brim of her winter hat. "You're worrying that you shouldn't have brought me here."

"What?"

"Your face got all frowny," Becky said. "The way it does when you're worried that something is going to be dangerous. But I can help you!" She spoke with fierce determination. "I know I can!"

I sighed. My father had a book on eastern philosophy that he'd picked up during his travels to the Dalai Lama in Tibet. It was probably karma that I'd spent most of my own childhood jumping to take every possible risk I could find—and now I had charge of Becky, who insisted on doing exactly the same.

"I know you can help," I said.

I was telling the simple truth. Becky had been invaluable during our past investigations. She was bold, quick-witted, and she had one surpassing advantage: that no enemy would ever perceive her as a potential threat.

I'd learned a long time ago that one of my own best weapons was that men tended to underestimate anyone who was both young and female—and there were few people easier to underestimate than a small ten-year-old girl.

"Do you want to keep investigating Alice Gordon's disappearance?" I asked.

Becky nodded instantly. "Yes." She was still looking up at me, her blue eyes clear in the gray winter light, her cheeks rosy with the cold. "Not just because it's exciting." She bit her lip, seeming to search for the right words. "No one really minds that she's gone," she finally said. "You said before that Lady Lynley didn't care about her. And Lord Lynley just wants to believe that she's gone off and not have to think about her anymore. Someone needs to care that she's missing."

I suppressed another sigh. I might still wince at the thought of leading Becky into another investigation—without Jack, without even the benefit of Holmes's presence, this time. But she wasn't wrong.

"All right." I squeezed her hand. "We'll keep asking questions. But we have to promise each other that we're both going to be very, very careful about this. No going off alone. No doing anything dangerous."

Becky nodded solemnly. "I promise—"

Something rustled in the bushes behind us, off past the right side of the drive. I stopped Becky with a quick hand on her arm, and she fell instantly silent, her eyes widening.

I tipped my head just fractionally in the direction the noise had come from.

It could be a rabbit or a bird or even a deer.

Keep talking. I mouthed the words silently at Becky, taking her hand at the same time and drawing her further up the path.

Her eyes were still big and round, but she nodded, taking a breath.

"It's frightfully cold, don't you think, Lucy? Do you think we'll see any snow while we're here? Those trees would look so pretty all covered in snow, and then maybe we could find somewhere to go tobogganing ..."

Becky could, when asked, fill a silence with an almost endless supply of cheerful, innocent prattle.

I listened hard, straining above the creak of wind in the trees to catch any more sounds from behind us. For a moment, everything seemed quiet. Maybe it really had been just a bird or a rabbit, combined with my own overly-suspicious—

A twig snapped behind us with a sharp crack.

And there went all thoughts of there being a non-human explanation to the sounds of our being followed. Birds and rabbits didn't snap branches as big as that when they walked.

My heart sped up as I took quick stock of our surroundings. There was a huge, solid oak tree standing maybe ten feet up ahead of us, and perhaps five feet from the edge of the gravel drive. The trunk had to be nearly five feet in diameter. Easily big enough for our purposes.

I touched Becky's arm, motioning to the tree silently. She swallowed, nodding again, and I held out one hand in front of me, silently counting down on my fingers.

3 … 2 …

On one, Becky stopped speaking and we both broke into a run, sprinting as fast and as quietly as we could towards the big oak tree.

We reached it, and I pulled Becky behind the enormous trunk. We flattened ourselves against the rough bark.

"What—" Becky started to whisper, but I shook my head, putting a hand to my lips. This was the part of any attack that made my skin crawl, far more than any actual fight—having to just keep still and wait for it to begin.

Every second that passed felt like rough burlap being dragged over my nerves, and I had to fight the urge to step out of our makeshift hiding place and demand that whoever was following us just step into the open and get it over with.

But I was currently unarmed, and I had Becky's safety to consider. I couldn't give up the element of surprise; it was one of the few advantages I had.

Twigs snapped again, as though someone was pushing through the bushes with less consideration for stealth than before.

Gravel crunched under booted feet.

I breathed slowly, running through quick calculations as the footsteps came nearer. The person paused as though scanning the scenery, looking for us, then started towards us again.

Male. Over six feet tall and heavyset, judging by the amount of noise he was making and what I estimated to be the length of his stride.

The crunch of gravel stopped again.

Our follower had just stepped off the drive and was coming towards us across the grass, approaching our tree.

Closer … closer.

I held myself tight in check, waiting for him to come near enough for this to work.

Becky's eyes sought mine, questioning, and my pulse sped up another notch. What were the odds that if I told her to stay safely behind the tree she would actually obey?

Probably zero to none.

Stay low, I finally mouthed.

She nodded.

The footsteps were very close, now, starting to circle round the massive tree trunk.

"Now!" I whispered.

Becky dove out of our hiding place, so fast she was practically a blur of motion, and struck our attacker full in the legs, knocking him off balance.

Before he could regain his footing, I was already beside him, stepping out to twist his arm up behind his back in the way Jack had once shown me.

"Unless you woke up this morning hoping for a dislocated elbow joint, I suggest you don't move."

The man was big, and broadly built. He wore the clothes of a farm worker or stable hand, and beneath the threadbare wool of his coat, his arm muscles felt like bands of iron under my grip.

Despite what I'd just said, if he fought back, I wasn't sure that I could hold him.

But his breath caught in a wheezing gasp of surprise, and he flung up his free arm. "Sorry, miss! I didn't mean any harm!"

I exhaled slowly. "Explain yourself. Why were you following us?"

The young man gulped and turned his head back over his shoulder to look at me. "My name's Connor Faraday. I need to talk to you about Alice Gordon."

LUCY

17. AN UNREQUITED ADMIRATION

"I ma-manage His Lordship's stables," Connor Faraday said. Seen up close, he looked to be somewhere in his late twenties, with wheat-blond hair, and a square-cut, rugged face. He also had big, work-roughened hands, broad shoulders and arms slabbed with muscle.

"I help t-train his horses," he went on.

We were standing in the partial shelter of the big oak tree. The branches overhead might be bare, but at least we were somewhat shielded from the biting wind.

"Is Lord Lynley fond of horses and riding?" I asked. My heart was finally settling back into its normal rhythm.

Connor nodded.

Despite his size, there was something hesitant, almost diffident about the way he spoke. His eyes rested on the ground far more often than they met mine, and he brought each word out slowly, with a perceptible effort.

"Rides every d-day," he said. "Lady Lynley, too. Or she used to. Hasn't been riding so much anymore lately."

He stopped, looking down at the ground again and twisting his cloth cap back and forth in his hands. I could see a pattern of a raised scar on his right forearm, disappearing beneath the cuff of his shirt.

Another scar ran up his temple and into his hairline.

"Did you manage to get the snakes out of His Lordship's desk?" Becky asked.

Connor's gaze flashed to her in quick surprise. Becky gave him a patient look. "Lord Lynley told his butler to get Faraday from the stables. That's you, isn't it? So were you able to get the snakes out? They didn't bite you, did they?"

The young man's face softened slightly as he looked at her. "No, miss. I didn't get bitten. I—" He stopped. "Well, let's just say the snakes won't be troubling anyone else again."

He stopped, still twisting his cap in his hands.

"You wanted to speak to us about Alice?" I asked when the silence had gone on for a beat or two.

Connor's blue eyes flashed up to my face. "When I was up at the house dealing with the snakes in His Lordship's office, I heard from Nell—she's the house parlormaid—that you were talking to His Lordship about Alice. Do you know her? Do you know where she's gone?"

There was urgency in his voice, and in his gaze as he looked at me.

Becky had said just a moment ago that no one seemed to care that Alice was missing, but this young man obviously did. All the anxious worry that had been missing from Lord and Lady Lynley was visible in Connor Faraday's tight expression.

Although, as an aside, it was worth noting that apparently Lord Lynley's parlormaid listened at doors. I remembered a pert-looking dark haired girl who had served us our tea, but I had been very careful to make no mention of Alice Gordon while she was in the room.

It meant that I had to be equally careful in approaching this conversation now.

"I'm sorry, I don't know where Alice is." I watched Faraday's expression as I spoke. "I'm a distant cousin of hers, on her mother's side. Our families have been out of touch for years, but I'm visiting England for a month this winter, and I thought how lovely it would be to look her up. But apparently she's left her post here. No one can tell me where she's gone."

Connor's shoulders slumped with disappointment. But he didn't question my assertion that I was Alice Gordon's cousin. Which meant that either the parlormaid hadn't heard the details of my conversation with Lord Lynley, or else she hadn't communicated them to Connor.

"Sorry," he said. "When Nell told me you were talking to his lordship about Alice, I thought maybe—" He shook his head. "I'm s-sorry to have troubled you."

"Can you help us at all?" I asked. "If you and Alice were friends maybe you have an idea of why she decided to leave?"

"Me?" Connor's eyes widened, then he shook his head. "No, I can't help, m-miss. I don't know anything about where Alice might have gone off to. She never said a word to m-me."

I studied him for a second. He was still twisting his cap so hard it was as though he were trying to wrench the fabric apart, and his big body fairly quivered with agitation.

"Were you with the army?" I asked him.

Connor looked startled. "How'd you know that?"

Becky had been quiet, but now she spoke up, gesturing. "Those scars on your arm and your cheek. They're from saber cuts, aren't they? Were you in India?"

Connor tipped his head in a nod. "I was, miss." Almost unconsciously, his fingers went to touch the raised mark on his temple. "Four years ago. That's where I got this. I was struck in the head with a horse's hoof t-too. I stayed unconscious for almost three weeks, after. My eyesight wasn't qu-quite right after that. Get headaches, too."

That probably also explained the difficulty he had with speaking—as well as the look that occasionally flashed in his eyes, as though he were looking at us and through us at the same time, bracing himself for any sign of threat to appear.

Uncle John's eyes sometimes held that same look, and he'd been out of army combat a good deal longer than four years.

Becky was eying Connor, as well, then she tugged lightly on my hand. "Lucy? May I go and climb that tree over there?"

She gestured to one of the maples a short way off, which had an inviting spread of branches low to the ground.

Knowing Becky, I was certain she really did want to climb it. But she'd also clearly decided that Connor would be more likely to speak freely to me, an adult, than he would in front of a child.

"You may. Just don't go too high, all right?" I told her. "And if you could avoid falling and breaking any bones, too, that would be ideal."

Becky giggled and skipped off. The look she threw me over her shoulder was an unspoken request—or probably closer to a demand—that I fill her in on whatever she missed of the conversation once we were alone.

"So, you and Alice are friends, then?" I asked Connor.

"Friends?" Connor sounded shocked. "Oh, no, miss. I never even t-talked to her, not really. She'd come and visit the stables, sometimes, when Her Ladyship was gone out visiting or taking one of her rest cures, and Alice had some time off. She liked to s-see the horses, and she'd say a w-word or two to me, sometimes. She was so lively—always full of jokes and good spirits. Happy. Like she was just lit up from the inside. But I never knew what to say back to her. The words, they'd get tangled up and stuck and I'd just keep quiet. She used to laugh and say she was going to get me to talk to her one of these days, if it was the last thing she ever did."

Connor stopped, an expression of pain flashing across his face.

"Did Alice have any particular friends among the rest of the household staff, or in the neighborhood? Do you think they might know where she is now?"

"Not to speak of." Connor frowned. "She was friendly enough with the other house servants, I suppose. But then she got mixed up with that foreigner."

"Foreigner?" I'd been in England long enough to know that in country terms that could mean anything from Welsh to Italian to a visitor from two villages over.

Connor grunted. "Chinese fellow. Chang Kai-chen, his name is. He works for Lord Lynley's partner in His Lordship's import business. And he runs errands for Lord Lynley sometimes, too. Used to bring Her Ladyship's medicine to her. That's how he and Alice g-got to know one another."

I glanced over towards Becky. Her hat had already been knocked off and lay on the muddy ground underneath the tree, but she was otherwise fine, clambering skillfully onto a branch maybe ten feet from the ground. It was probably a good thing she'd taken herself out of this conversation.

I widened my eyes in an expression of surprise that was only partly feigned. Romances between an English lady's maid and a Chinese servant didn't happen often. "And you think Alice and Kai-chen were ... involved?"

Connor's broad shoulders twitched, and he gave a short, miserable nod. "I know they were. I was awake one night, sitting up with one of His Lordship's horses that had the colic. I saw them walk past the stables. Alice and Chang, together. She must have snuck out of the house to ... meet up with him."

His big hands curled, balling up into fists.

"Do you think she could have gone off with this Chang?" I asked.

Connor shook his head. "He was up at the house just this morning, bringing a message for His Lordship." He stopped, his work-roughened hands flexing once more. "It's not that I've got anything against the Chinese. I saw some of them when I was out in India, and they were decent people. I just ... he didn't seem right for Alice." He looked at me, his eyes miserable, almost pleading. "She hadn't been coming out to the stables lately, either. But the couple of times I saw her these last few weeks, it was like—" he stopped "—like all the happiness and brightness had gone out of her, somehow."

18. NEWMAN AT NEWGATE

It took us an hour to travel from St. Philip's to the Old Bailey by cab, and the late afternoon was turning to twilight by the time we entered the formidable building.

Thomas Newman had a cell to himself, due to a Newgate policy intended to keep other prisoners out of reach of the men under sentence of death. The fat gang leader lounged on a pallet bed, which hung suspended from the stone wall by iron chains. The chains creaked as he twisted his walrus-like frame to look up at us.

"Come to gloat, have you?"

"I have come for information," said Holmes.

He showed Newman the scrap of paper which had been found beneath the body of the murdered Miss Janine.

Newman glanced at it briefly. "What of it?"

"You can read, Mr. Newman?"

"It says, 'Not done yet.' What I said at my trial upstairs two days ago. Been in the papers since, I hear."

"Correct."

"So what are you doing showing me the words I said upstairs on Monday? More for the newspapers?"

"The paper was found in St. Philip's Church in Kensington."

"So?"

"It was found under the body of a young woman. In a church. She was in a pew, kneeling, praying alongside her mother, when they both were shot. From behind."

Newman made a face. His disgust seemed real. "Bleeders don't work in Kensington. This is some other bloke, trying to make it look like my boys did it. Anybody could 'a seen those words in the paper. None of my boys would be that stupid."

"Are you sure about that?"

"We've got no quarrel with two women in Kensington, at a church—"

"Some other gang?" Holmes held the paper out again. "Think about who it could be. Who else would do this and implicate you? Who do you suspect?"

"Could be anyone. Like I said, it was in the papers."

"What do you know of John Swafford?"

"The dead copper at the Red Dragon? That wasn't us neither."

"Did you know he had a ball of opium with him when he was killed?"

"Couldn't care less."

"The police will ask you about the note and the women. They may not be as polite as I am."

"Is that a threat, Mr. Holmes?"

"I understand you have a wife and son."

The burly criminal boss turned his face to the wall.

"You can turn away from me," said Holmes, "but you cannot escape your position. Or do you think you have sufficient funds to bribe the prison guards, and find a way out of here, and then pay someone else to spirit you and your wife and son away from

England?"

Newman said nothing.

"Perhaps someone promised you that rosy future. But why should you believe in it? You are a practical man. You have heard many false and fanciful promises in your time. Has someone told you about the great hoard of opium that will somehow provide funds to enable your personal freedom?"

"What of it?" Newman said.

"I wonder what you could do for that someone in return for such a huge change in your fortune. After all, you are in prison, and your associates have no reason to be loyal. They will be thinking only of themselves."

"Maybe I know things, Mr. Holmes," the big man said. He shifted his bulk, so that he was lying on his back, staring up at the ceiling. "Maybe I can name some high and mighty blokes who would just as soon I kept mum. Maybe I've written some names down somewhere."

"And those people have the opium?"

"I'm not sayin' what they have or don't have. Except they do have money, and they want my silence."

"They can rely on the hangman to keep you quiet," said Holmes. "But if you divulge the names now, your wife and your son may have a better future."

Newman turned his face to the wall once again.

"Think about it," Holmes said.

* * *

A few minutes later we stood on the snow-covered pavement outside the prison, looking for a cab and bracing ourselves against the cold wind.

Holmes was shaking his head, with an expression on his aquiline features that was more chagrined than I could ever recall seeing.

"These are dark waters, Watson," he said.

"Newman gave us no help," I said.

"We have no obvious direction. Our client has been murdered. Her fiancé has been murdered. We have no client, and we cannot accept the offer of those who would retain us."

"Because they want to recover the opium and sell it," I said.

Holmes went on, as though he were talking to himself. "Yet we cannot allow the lives of Miss Janine, and her mother, and Inspector Swafford simply to vanish into oblivion. We cannot allow their murderers to go unpunished. And we cannot allow those who have ordered the murders—" He broke off and looked at me, as though he had just become aware of my presence. "What did you say, Watson?"

"I was talking about Ernshaw and Jacoby, who want to recover the opium and sell it."

His piercing gaze held mine for a long moment. "Good old Watson," he finally said. "I can always rely on you for illumination. Now you have shown me the path forward."

"I don't see—"

"It is a difficult path," he went on, "but it is the only way. And we must take it."

Whereupon he gave me one of his tight little smiles and turned towards the oncoming traffic, vigorously waving down a four-wheeler cab.

The cab stopped before us. "Where to, gents?" the driver asked.

"To Limehouse, cabbie," Holmes said. "To the Red Dragon Inn."

PART TWO

HEADWINDS

19. TO THE GRAND HOTEL

"What now, Lucy?" Becky hopped from one foot to the other. "Are we going to go and talk to this … do you think he calls himself Mr. Chang?"

I eyed the sun, which was sinking lower on the horizon. Eventually we would have to talk to Alice's sweetheart, insofar that he was almost the only tangible lead we had.

"I'm not sure," I said. "Chinese people do put their last names first when they're speaking or writing. That way, you know right away who someone is, where they come from and which family they belong to. According to Chinese custom, I'd be Kelly Lucy, and you'd be—"

I cut myself short, silently kicking myself as I realized what I'd been about to say. But it was too late.

All the liveliness and color went out of Becky's expression like someone had just snuffed a candle. "Davies Becky," she said quietly.

She was right. Becky had gone by Becky Kelly, for as long as I'd known her. I'd always thought of her that way. But, of course, her actual legal name would be the same as her father's.

I took her hand. "Come," I said. "We can save speaking to Chang until tomorrow. For right now, we still have a two-mile walk back to town, and it's going to be dark within the next hour or so. I think we'd be better off finding somewhere to spend the night."

Becky nodded, scuffing the toe of her boot in the dirt. "Where are we going to stay?"

"I don't know. Why don't you tell me?"

Becky glanced up at me, a furrow creasing her brows. "What do you—oh!" A faint spark of interest came back into her gaze. "You're thinking about Lord Lynley telling us he couldn't recommend staying at the Grand Hotel."

If nothing else, I could at least distract Becky. I nodded. "Exactly. Maybe it really is an inferior establishment with poor service, and His Lordship's warning was purely benevolent. But I think it's worth finding out for ourselves just what kind of a place the Grand Hotel really is, don't you?"

* * *

"Let me see." Mr. Torrance, manager of the Grand Hotel, consulted his leather-bound ledger, then looked back at me and beamed. His smile displayed a row of teeth so even and blindingly white that they almost had to be dentures. "Why yes, Miss James. It just so happens that we do have an unoccupied room to offer you for tonight."

Mr. Torrance was a short, dapper man in his early forties, with slicked-down black hair and a rotund face. His tone made it sound as though it were nothing short of a minor miracle that he had a room for us, but my guess would be that he, in fact, had several.

The Grand Hotel actually lived up to its name. It was a big, elegant building, set on the edge of town nearest to the seaside. Built of yellow brick on the outside, it had four floors, the uppermost crowned by turrets at the corners.

As we approached, Becky had said that it looked like a castle.

Inside, the hotel lobby was every bit as grand, and expensively furnished. The floors were made of polished marble, the walls hung with ornately gilded mirrors, and the furnishings were fashioned in gilt and gold brocades. Everything was impeccably clean too: the potted palms that dotted the lobby were all watered and well-cared-for; the floors, tables, and mirrors all spotless.

Clearly, Mr. Torrance could afford to keep a large and competent staff of employees. And yet the hotel seemed empty. When I'd signed the registry, the last entry to mark a guest's arrival had been made three days before. And the only other guest I saw in the lobby was an elderly man, dozing in one of the armchairs in a corner.

"Thank you so much," I said. "I was wondering whether you might be able to tell me something else."

"Yes?"

"A cousin of mine named Alice Gordon was employed not far from here, out at Lynley House."

I'd already made up the fiction of being Alice Gordon's American cousin when we'd spoken to Connor Faraday. To that end, I'd signed the hotel register Lucy James and introduced Becky as my niece.

"You want me to pretend to be American, too?" Becky had asked on our walk to town.

"I think so. We can both be distant cousins of Alice Gordon, come to visit from across the Atlantic. You can do a quite good American impression by now." I'd been coaching her. "And besides, being American has an advantage, sometimes, in an investigation when it comes to asking questions."

Becky's forehead crinkled as she frowned. "How?"

"A lot of English people just expect Americans to be rude, brash, and overly-inquisitive about personal matters. And that means they don't blink an eye if you live up to at least one expectation out of three."

Becky had still looked—for her—much too serious. But a small smile had crept onto her lips at that.

"Also, it's fun, pretending to be someone you're not."

I'd smiled back, because I knew even Holmes would agree with her. Investigating was exhausting, messy, brutal, and often dangerous. It could warp your whole view of humanity and the world.

But, call it a quirk, a character defect—or a slight madness— as Uncle John frequently had—a part of me did still love the exhilaration.

"Well, yes. Also that."

Now in the hotel lobby, Mr. Torrance's expression was polite, but not particularly interested. "Yes?"

"Our families have been out of touch, but I'd heard my cousin was in the area and I was hoping to reconnect with her again. But when I called at Lynley House, I found that she'd left her employment there. I don't suppose she's applied for work here, has she?"

"Alice Gordon?" Mr. Torrance frowned. "No, I don't believe so. We do employ some local girls, but we haven't hired on any new maids in the past six months. Although you could ask my wife, of course, to be absolutely sure that she hasn't come to ask about a job," he said. "She takes care of all the hiring and managing the staff."

He turned and spoke into a brass-plated speaking tube mounted on the wall behind the front desk.

Another sign of affluence: they could afford modern devices to allow instant communication between different floors and different areas of the building.

"Louise? Would you come out to the front for a moment, please?"

He waited a moment, but there was no answer. "Louise?"

Another wait, but the speaking tube remained silent until finally Mr. Torrance turned back to us with a slightly awkward smile. "She must be in another area of the hotel. Although I would have sworn I saw her—"

He turned, pushing open the swinging green baize door that stood in the center of the wall behind the desk.

Through the open doorway, I caught sight of a small room that I assumed must be the hotel's private office.

Where the outer part of the hotel was all ornate luxury and elegance, this room was small and furnished in a simple country style, with a pair of yellow pine desks against one wall, and a bookcase, and a couple of over-stuffed armchairs upholstered in sprigged flowery chintz against the other.

A plump, dark-haired woman was slumped in front of a chair by the fire, asleep with her head sunk on her chest.

"Louise!" Mr. Torrance barked.

The woman startled at the address, her head lifting. Her face was round and full-cheeked, with a small mouth. She blinked at us dazedly. "Oh. Was I asleep?"

"You were." Mr. Torrance's jaw clenched, the muscles standing out in his cheeks, but he turned to us with an apologetic smile. "My dear wife works so hard. She runs herself ragged seeing to the comfort of our guests, don't you, my love?"

Mrs. Torrance struggled upright from her chair, making ineffectual efforts to tuck untidy wisps of hair back from her face as she came out of the office to stand behind the desk with her husband. "I'm so sorry." She shot Mr. Torrance a quick, nervous glance before settling her gaze on Becky and me. "Did you want me for something?"

"Louise, these two ladies are inquiring about a local girl named Alice Gordon." Mr. Torrance put a hand on his wife's shoulder. She flinched visibly at the touch, but he kept the hand in place. "You haven't hired anyone of that name, have you?"

Mrs. Torrance blinked again, then shook her head. "No, I don't think … no, I'm certain we haven't."

"I thought not." Mr. Torrance nodded, squeezed his wife's shoulder and turned back to us. "Now, ladies. Is there anything else that I may help you with?"

I studied Mrs. Torrance's flushed cheeks and vague, glassy-looking eyes—mentally setting them beside Lady Lynley's quick, nervous manner.

In the same moment, an echo from Connor Faraday's statement slipped smoothly into my mind.

"Is there a local chemist's shop you could recommend?" I asked.

"A chemist?" It might have been my imagination, but I thought the skin around Mr. Torrance's eyes tightened briefly, even though his politely attentive expression remained firmly fixed in place.

"Yes." I smiled at him again. "Would you believe it, we managed to leave our tooth powder at the hotel in London! But I was sure we would be able to purchase another tin somewhere in town."

"Ah." I thought there was a very faint relaxing of Mr. Torrance's tense posture before he nodded. "In that case, you ought to go to Seewald's, in the high street. Mr. Seewald is our local pharmacist; he can see that you get whatever it is you need. Isn't that right, Louise?"

"What?" Mrs. Torrance startled again, looking as though her husband's voice had just roused her out of a happy dream. "Oh. Oh, yes. Mr. Seewald will take care of everything for you."

"Excellent. If there's nothing else, here is your key." He handed a key over, then pressed a bell on the desk. A moment later a red-haired boy of around eleven appeared dressed in a bellboy's uniform. "This is Bill. He will carry your bags up to your room."

20. NEWS FROM A BELLBOY

Becky's muffled voice pulled me out of sleep. "You're—how old? Ten?"

My eyes snapped open, and I sat up with a jolt. Morning light streamed in through the chinks around the hotel room curtains. I was alone in the room; the small twin bed Becky had occupied the night before was empty.

Her voice was coming from the hall just outside the door.

"Or maybe even eleven?"

"Eleven and a half." The voice that answered her was young, male, and more than slightly sulky-sounding.

Bill, I realized. The same bellboy who had carried our bags the night before.

"So what's your point?" I obviously couldn't see Bill, but he sounded as though he was probably scowling and folding his arms across his chest.

"My *point*—" Becky's voice filtered through the doorway in near-perfect American tones "—is that you must have lost some of your baby teeth by now, and had the adult ones come in. Which means that if I knock out any of them, they're not going to grow back."

I jumped up out of bed, reaching for the dressing gown I'd left across the back of a chair and slipped it on as I went to the door.

I shouldn't really have worried. When I opened the door, Bill was standing with his palms up in a gesture of surrender, his freckled, snub-nosed face looking more than slightly scared.

Somewhat comically, since he was a good six inches taller than Becky and probably outweighed her by twenty pounds. But to judge by the rumpled state of his gold braid-trimmed uniform, she'd already given him a demonstration of her skill in putting a much larger opponent on the ground.

I'd been giving her training in that area, too, in addition to speaking as though she'd been born across the Atlantic.

"All right, all right. Can't blame a fellow for trying, can you?" Bill said.

I cleared my throat. "What's going on?"

"Oh. There you are, Lucy." Becky gave me a bright smile before gesturing to Bill. "This boy has something that he'd like to tell us about Cousin Alice. At first he thought that maybe he would try to charge us money for the information. But he's thought better of that, now. Isn't that right?"

Bill's face blanched again. "Right. I mean, yes, miss." He looked at me and swallowed, his tone an odd blend of nervousness and sullen defiance. "I don't see what the fuss is all about, anyway. All I really know is that she was here."

I tied the belt of my dressing gown, looking up and down the hall, which was as deserted as the hotel lobby had been the night before.

"Who was here? Alice?"

"Yeah, that's right." Bill nodded his head. "Came here to

look for a job, didn't she?"

"When was that?"

Bill shrugged. "A month ago? Maybe three weeks?"

"And who did she speak to? Was it Mr. or Mrs. Torrance?"

"I dunno." Bill shrugged again. "Never heard her say which of them she talked to. I just overheard her talking to Jane—she's one of the housemaids—saying that she was hoping for a job, and wouldn't it be a barrel of laughs if they were both working here." His face wrinkled with scorn. "She was wrong about that, I can tell you. It's dead boring here most of the time. Except when it's a spa weekend, and then it's 'get this, fetch that, carry those bags there.' Hop, hop, hop all day long and you don't hardly get time to even eat or sleep."

I breathed out, slowly. Bill struck me as the kind of witness who would clam up the moment he suspected that what he had to say was actually of any value.

Besides, Becky and I were supposed to be cousins of Alice Gordon's, nothing more. We didn't care about the running of the hotel.

"Spa weekends?" I made my voice sound casual. "That sounds exciting."

Bill's shoulders jerked in yet another shrug. "Only if you like fetching and carrying and getting yelled at by a lot of rich foreigners—"

Bill cut off speaking so abruptly it was as though the word had been snipped with a pair of scissors. His eyes went wide, focusing on something behind me.

"Sorry, Mr. Torrance." He touched the edge of his bellboy's cap. "Were you wanting me?"

Mr. Torrance was stumping down the hallway, his lips

pinched at the edges, his brows drawn. "You're supposed to be downstairs in the lobby, Bill."

His voice wasn't quite a growl, but Bill still swallowed visibly, his throat bobbing.

"Yes, sir. Sorry, sir."

He took off towards the elevator at the end of the hallway, almost at a run.

Mr. Torrance watched him a moment before turning to us, his face wreathed in a smile. "I do hope Bill wasn't annoying you ladies?"

"Oh no, not at all." My own smile was—I hoped—more convincing than Mr. Torrance's, otherwise I deserved to be thrown off the London stage. "I just wanted to ask where the nearest telegraph office might be located."

Actually I knew that already, since before coming to the hotel yesterday evening, I'd already found the local office and sent two telegrams: one to Jack and one to Holmes, telling them that Becky and I had arrived safely and where we could be found. I would have given almost anything to be able to actually speak to Jack, but Shellingford didn't yet have long-distance telephone service that could reach all the way to London.

Mr. Torrance's eyes narrowed just fractionally as he looked at me; then he nodded, his white-toothed smile flashing out again. "There is a telegraph office on the high street. Or if you prefer, you could hand whatever messages you wish to send in to me, and I will see that they are delivered."

LUCY

21. A DECISION

"Mr. Torrance pretends to be nice," Becky said. "But I don't think he is. Not really."

We were outside the hotel now, and walking along the town's main street. A few crumbs of the raisin scones we'd purchased for breakfast at the local bakery still clung to Becky's mittens.

Despite it being market hour, the street wasn't busy. A few women with shopping baskets over their arms and shawls over their heads hurried past us, and the odd horse and cart clip-clopped down the cobblestones.

Shellingford wasn't a large town by any means, and Becky and I had nearly traversed the whole of it in the half hour or so since we'd left The Grand. Apart from the hotel, there was a stationer's shop, a butcher's, a grocer's, a tea room, and a few other assorted businesses.

"I'm inclined to agree with you," I told her.

Mr. Torrance's disingenuous offer to take down any telegrams we wished to send might have been the same one he made to all hotel guests, but inasmuch as it would also allow him to *read* any telegrams I sent, it was an offer I would never accept.

"It's not just Bill who's scared of him, either," Becky went on. "His wife acts as though she's afraid of him, too."

I nodded, remembering the way Mrs. Torrance had flinched at her husband's touch.

Becky fell quiet for a moment, then glanced up at me. "You're worrying about Jack, aren't you?"

I sighed. This was the disadvantage of traveling with anyone as bright and observant as Becky; the idea of trying to keep anything from her deserved to go into the dictionary under the heading *exercise in futility*.

"Yes," I said honestly. "A bit."

In addition to the bakery, we'd already stopped at the telegraph office and been informed that there had been only one reply to my messages sent the day before.

Holmes, with characteristic effusion, had sent back two words: *message received*. Jack hadn't answered yet.

"But just because he hasn't sent us a telegram doesn't mean that anything is wrong," I said.

To keep down the number of people who knew where Becky and I had gone—and thus who could tell Benjamin Davies or his lawyers—I'd sent the telegram to our house only, not to Scotland Yard. "It's probably that Jack got called off to work on a case and just hasn't had a chance to go home yet."

Becky nodded, but the corners of her mouth drooped down. I was beginning to have an idea of what could be at the root of Alice Gordon's disappearance. And the more I learned, the more I strongly disliked the direction all of this was leading.

I debated. Becky could use a distraction right now, and provided that we were careful, I couldn't see any danger in the next logical step of the investigation.

"Come along," I said. "Let's go and visit the chemist's shop."

22. A DOMESTIC ALTERCATION

Mr. Torrance was right: Seewald's pharmacy was impossible to miss. A brick-built shop set on the far end of the high street from the hotel, it stood out as easily the largest and most modern of the shops in town. Even on this misty day, the plate glass windows were sparkling clean and filled with assorted goods: bottles of patent medicines, brightly-labeled jars of beauty creams and cosmetics, kid gloves and ribbons, ivory-handled shaving razors, hair nets and modern electric curling tongs.

Mr. Seewald, whoever he might be, was clearly doing a brisk trade.

Inside, Becky tripped off to look at the shelf that held big glass jars of candy, while I got into line in front of the counter.

Only one other customer was in the shop before us: a slender woman dressed in heavy black mourning clothes, her dark hair topped by a black velvet hat with a black lace demi-veil.

"... sorry to hear the headaches haven't improved," I heard the man behind the counter say.

There was a perceptible pause before the woman answered. "Headaches. Yes. Of course." Her voice was low and husky, and her fingers clenched and unclenched on a black-edged handkerchief as she spoke. "Just give me the usual bottle of tonic quickly, Mr. Seewald. Please," she added, clearly as an afterthought.

"Certainly, certainly." Mr. Seewald looked less like a chemist and more like a lump of undercooked dough wearing clothes: big, pallid, and obese, his scant few strands of dark hair were combed, with rather pathetic optimism, over a mostly bald, domed head. His features were lost in rolls of fat, and the white apron he wore barely stretched over his girth.

He beamed at the female customer, his eyes nearly disappearing into heavy pouches of flesh.

"I have it right here."

"Fine." The woman's hands clenched again, and she threw a quick, nervous glance over her shoulder at the main entrance. I caught sight of a thin, careworn face. "Just *hurry*."

He turned to a shelf behind the counter, selected a brown bottle with a pink, flowered label, and handed it across to the woman, who almost snatched it out of his hands.

"Thank you." She clutched the bottle in one hand and started to root through her handbag. "I know I have it. I know I have the money here—" She muttered the words under her breath.

The bell over the shop's door chimed, and the woman jumped, letting out an audible gasp as she whirled to see who it was.

A young Chinese man stepped into the shop, glanced towards the counter, then moved to a display of shaving creams and brushes.

"Here." The dark-haired woman flung a handful of coins onto the counter. "You can keep any extra change."

Mr. Seewald didn't seem at all discomposed by her hurry. His face creased in another smile and he started to pick up the coins the woman had dropped.

"Thank you, Mrs. Slade."

The door to the shop opened again, and a broad-shouldered man wearing a police uniform strode through.

Mrs. Slade froze in the act of turning away from the counter.

For a moment, I thought she would bolt back behind the counter with Mr. Seewald. But then her chin lifted.

"What are you doing here, William?"

The uniformed officer was a heavyset man, more than six feet tall, with dark brown hair just beginning to turn gray at the temples and thin over his crown. He had a firm jaw, and his face was strong and weathered, with a ruddy complexion.

He looked hale, hearty, and as though he ought to be jolly, in a fatherly sort of way—except for his eyes. His eyes were dark brown, and held a kind of weighted sadness, even when he smiled. They were the eyes of a man who had been gutted by life and was struggling on, but was continuing to bleed on the inside.

His gaze darkened as he looked at Mrs. Slade. "I was looking for you. I heard—that is, I went to the house and you weren't—"

Mrs. Slade interrupted, drawing herself straighter and folding her arms tightly across her chest. "I can't even do some shopping without you spying on me, now? How did you even—" She stopped, the pitch of her voice rising with disbelief. "Have you sent Constable Meadows to—to *watch* me?"

She scrutinized the man—who had to be her husband—as she said it, and whatever she read in his expression seemed to give her an answer. "You *have*! William, how could you?"

Her husband glanced around at the rest of the shop, his expression creasing in discomfort. "Emily, this is hardly the time or the place—"

Bright spots of color had appeared in Mrs. Slade's cheeks below the edge of her black net demi-veil. "Oh, and when *is* the right time or place, exactly, to discuss the fact that you've been spying on your wife as though I'm a common criminal?"

Pain tightened his expression. "You know it's not like that. I'm worried for you, Emily." His gaze focused on the dark brown glass bottle in her hands, and the line of his mouth flattened into a grim line. "With good reason, I see."

"No!" Mrs. Slade stepped back, clutching the medicine bottle more tightly. "I *need* it, don't you understand? It's the only thing that helps. The only thing since—"

Her voice cracked. A moment ago, her whole body had been stiff with pent-up fury, but now she seemed to crumple, folding inwards. She covered her face and started to cry with deep, wrenching sobs.

"I know." The same terrible, bone-deep pain and weariness I'd seen before were still visible in her husband's expression. But he moved forward, putting a gentle arm around his wife and murmuring the words as one would to a child. "I know, Emily, I know. Come along, now. Come along home."

Mrs. Slade didn't resist as her husband drew her towards the door of the shop. Her shoulders still shook, but she was weeping quietly, now, as though the pain were too stark for further words.

Just as they reached the shop's exit, though, the uniformed man looked over his shoulder at Mr. Seewald. I almost startled. I wouldn't have been surprised by anger, but the look that Mrs. Slade's husband directed in the chemist's direction was filled with so much stark, naked hatred that I could almost see the intensity and violence of the emotion arcing through the air.

Mr. Seewald's lips curved in a small, private smile. Then he focused his attention on me, his pudgy hands folded across his capacious middle.

"Now, miss, what may I help you with today?"

Since I had first joined Holmes in criminal investigation, I'd had to grow somewhat accustomed to bearing witness to the worst moments of other people's lives: pain, fear, loss. And yet, after the scene between Mrs. Slade and her husband, I still felt as though I wanted to take a bath in scalding hot water just to wash away the residual pain and tension.

Mr. Seewald, on the other hand, looked perfectly ready to pretend that nothing at all out of the ordinary had occurred.

"Tooth powder, please." I glanced at Becky, who was still eyeing the penny candy. "And a bag of the peppermint sticks."

"Certainly, certainly."

I lowered my voice. I was already resolved not to take any risks while I was in this shop, but after the scene we had just witnessed, *not* asking questions would almost be odder than asking them.

"Who were those people who just left?"

Mr. Seewald turned to his shelves and selected a tin of tooth powder. "Ah, the Slades. He's the chief constable of the village and, of course, Mrs. Slade is his wife. They lost a child— a daughter—just over a year ago. A tragic case. Very sad."

Mr. Seewald shook his head, his lips pursed in an appropriately sober expression, but his small eyes were sharp as he studied me. "If you don't mind my asking, you're not from around these parts, are you, miss?"

"Just visiting family." I smiled. "I know it's hardly the time of year for a visit to the seaside, but we're only staying in England through the winter."

"Ah, American, are you?" Mr. Seewald nodded. "Whereabouts are you from?"

"Milwaukee." I'd never been to Wisconsin in my life, but it didn't matter; in my experience—beyond having heard of New York and possibly Chicago—almost no one in Europe knew specifics of American geography. Whichever city I identified would be greeted with exactly the same look of polite, blank unfamiliarity.

Mr. Seewald was no exception. "Lovely, I'm sure." He slid some peppermint sticks into a small brown paper bag. "There you are. That will be three and six."

I took a breath. "There was just one other thing. I've been suffering from headaches, lately." I touched my fingertips to my forehead. "Dreadfully painful ones, so bad that I can't sleep at night. I was wondering whether you might have anything to suggest."

"Headaches, is it?" Mr. Seewald's expression turned sympathetic. "Ah, that's bad, that is. Well, now, it just so happens that I do have something that might help. A bottle of this mixture here."

He turned, selected a brown bottle from his shelves, and passed it across to me, still smiling paternally. "It's specially formulated with the ladies in mind and will do you a world of good. Just take a dose when your head is paining you, and you'll soon be sleeping like a newborn babe in arms."

LUCY

23. A WARNING

"Excuse me. Miss!"

I turned on the doorstep to Mr. Seewald's shop to find that the Chinese gentleman had followed us out.

A light, misting rain had started to fall, but he hadn't yet bothered to put up the black umbrella he carried.

"Miss! A word, if you will please excuse the liberty."

Seen up close, he looked to be somewhere around thirty, with a face so handsome he was almost beautiful: sculpted features and deeply brown, angular eyes.

He spoke English very well, with only a trace of an accent, and his clothes were entirely Western: a knotted silk cravat and a well-tailored gray suit topped by a wool overcoat. He might be Chinese by birth, but he'd clearly been in this country for some time.

"Yes?"

He shut the door securely behind him, then nodded to the parcel I was carrying. "I would not take the medicine if I were you, miss."

I could have told him that I was more likely to send Mr. Seewald special box seats to a performance at the Savoy, but instead

I first squeezed Becky's hand, signaling her not to interrupt. Then I summoned up a puzzled frown. "Why ever not? Does it not work? Mr. Seewald promised me—"

"Oh, it will work. Only too well." The Chinese man leant forward, his voice increasing in intensity. "It will cure your headaches—or so you will think. You will take it and feel wonderful. As though you are caught up in a happy dream. So you will take it again the next night. Then the next. Then you will think to yourself, *Why should I not allow myself this happiness, these lovely dreams, during the day?* So you will take it the next morning. And then a little more. Each day, you will take a little more—and each day, you will care a little less about the rest of the world. Family, friends—all will speedily fade in importance when compared to the medicine and how it makes you—"

He cut off abruptly, drawing in a sharp breath as the door to the shop opened again. Mr. Seewald's paunchy face scowled out at us.

"Is there a problem?"

"No, no, no. No problem." The Chinese man shook his head and I almost blinked at the transformation. His face split in a wide, slightly uncomprehending smile and he put his hands together, sketching a shallow bow. "Velly solly, honored sir. Velly solly." In addition to his mannerisms, his accent had gone from being slight to so thick it was almost incomprehensible. "I only ask these ladies whether they enjoying their stay here."

Mr. Seewald didn't speak, but his eyes narrowed a fraction.

"Good day." With another bow, the Chinese man turned and hurried down the street—finally putting up his umbrella against the quickening rain.

Mr. Seewald growled something under his breath. He glared

at the man's retreating back for what seemed an eternity—then transferred his scowling gaze to his storefront step, apparently checking to make sure that it had been swept well enough.

I curled my fingers towards my palms as the seconds ticked past, resisting the urge to shove Mr. Seewald bodily back through the door.

Finally, he shook his head, turned, and lumbered back inside the shop—just as the Chinese man's umbrella vanished around the nearest corner.

I suppressed a word that I wouldn't want Becky repeating and took her hand. "This way! Hurry!"

Becky was small but fast and kept pace with me easily as we raced down the street and turned the corner.

The Chinese man was nowhere in sight.

I stopped running and turned to scan the road, looking for any sign of him—or a clue as to where he might have gone.

But this was a residential street rather than a market one, lined with narrow row houses. Nothing to suggest he would have gone into one over another, and I could hardly go up and down the road knocking on doors, demanding to know whether anyone matching our man's description had just come in.

"His umbrella had a small tear in it," Becky said. "If that helps at all."

"Well spotted. You're right, it did. And a red handle. But I still don't see him anywhere here."

A few pedestrians were hurrying along the pavement in front of us, many carrying black umbrellas—but none of them matched the Chinese man's.

Becky looked up at me, wiping rain out of her eyes. "I don't understand, Lucy. Why are we following him? And what's in that bottle of medicine that he didn't want you taking?"

I scanned the street one last time, then gave up. "The medicine has laudanum in it—opium, in other words—and he warned me not to take it because it can be very addicting. Legal, but often lethally habit-forming. As to why we're following him, I can't be entirely sure, but unless I'm very much mistaken, that man was Chang—the man Connor Faraday said knew Alice Gordon."

LUCY

24. AN INCONCLUSIVE INTERVIEW

"I don't know." Mrs. Torrance looked dreamily at the lace she'd just spread out on the back of the big, cushioned armchair. "I had thought that white lace antimacassars would look nicest with the flower pattern. But maybe I should have bought the ecru ones instead." Her brow furrowed, her expression deeply pondering. Then, with a slight start, she raised her head and looked at me, her hazel eyes dazed and blinking. "I'm so sorry. Did you ask me something?"

"I asked you about Mr. Seewald."

"Mr. Seewald?" Mrs. Torrance looked blank.

"Yes, the man who runs the chemist's shop."

"Oh! Oh, yes, a lovely man. So sympathetic ..." Mrs. Torrance's voice trailed off as her gaze wandered to the white antimacassar again. She reached to stroke the lace gently, the way you would a cat or a puppy.

Becky shot me a look that plainly asked what on earth we were doing here and why we had waited half the afternoon for this.

I wasn't entirely sure, either—beyond the obvious answer of

wasting our time. But I needed answers, and my options at the moment were limited as to where I could go to get them.

After returning to the hotel, Becky and I had eaten lunch and checked to see whether any letters or telegrams were waiting for us. There still were none.

If nothing else, talking to Mrs. Torrance was—somewhat—distracting me from thinking about what that might mean.

Becky and I had waited in the hotel lobby, pretending to read, and watching the door to Mr. Torrance's inner office. Now it was around 4:30 in the afternoon, and our patience had finally been rewarded by Mr. Torrance putting on his hat and striding out of the hotel's main entrance—alone.

We'd given him five minutes to be certain he wasn't just stepping out to buy a newspaper, then knocked on the office door.

I drew in a breath and tried again. "Mr. Seewald's shop is amazingly well stocked—really, he has as fine a selection as any shop in London. Do you know where he gets his supplies?"

"Supplies?" Mrs. Torrance peered at me as though she had never heard the word before.

Becky was right. This was probably pointless.

If the man who'd spoken to us outside of Mr. Seewald's shop really was Chang Kai-chen, it should be possible to find him. He served Lord Lynley's partner in the imports business, which meant that we could simply go back to Lynley House and ask His Lordship for the address.

But if what I suspected about the Lynleys was true, going to Lord Lynley for answers could prove dangerous. Even asking questions about Kai-chen around town carried its own set of risks.

Starting with speaking to Mrs. Torrance had seemed the

safest, most sensible option—though the universe didn't appear to be rewarding my good sense with any helpful answers.

Mrs. Torrance had gone back to staring at her antimacassar. "Maybe I should go back to the shop and buy just *one* in ecru, just to see how it looks—"

I interrupted, trying—though probably failing—not to sound impatient.

"Do you happen to have a map of Shellingford?"

I was halfway expecting her to give me the same blank look, but instead she rose unsteadily to her feet and tottered over to the small writing desk.

"Oh, yes indeed. Here you are." She took out a tri-folded sheet of paper with the hotel's name printed in red and gold lettering. "My husband had them printed specially last year. We hand them out to any of our guests who want them. There are several picturesque spots around town—ocean views, and such—that you will find marked out."

"Thank you so much."

There seemed more awareness in Mrs. Torrance's gaze as she peered at me more closely, a troubled frown crossing her brow. "You're surely not going for a walk now, are you?" She glanced at the window, where sunset was just giving way to the deepening purple shadows of twilight. "It will be dark soon, and it's dreadfully cold outside."

"No, of course not." I smiled at her. "We just want to be prepared in the morning."

25. AN ATTACK IN LIMEHOUSE

Night had fallen by the time we reached The Red Dragon. The January wind buffeted us, coming from the north bank of the Thames with a force that caused the cab to rock and lurch sideways. Newly-frozen slush on the roadway combined with ruts and holes in the pavement jolted us as we moved. Holmes barely spoke, and when we reached Limehouse Basin we dismounted from the cab, finding ourselves in a row of seedy retail shops and alehouses along Narrow Street, only a few yards from the mud bank near the Regents Pond.

Holmes told the driver to remain.

I tried to take in our surroundings. The cold stung my nostrils and caused my eyes to water. I could make out the outlines of The Red Dragon, a nondescript tumbledown affair. In the night shadows cast by a solitary gas lamp, I could see clumps of sleet-laden snow sagging off the edge of the roof. The building itself sagged as well, listing over the side of the riverbank, as if waiting to collapse into the black water and join the coal barges and lumber scows that clogged this part of the Thames.

A pale-yellow light came from behind a dirty curtain in a solitary window. Knowing that the building housed an opium parlor put me in mind of the Swandam Lane establishment Holmes and I had encountered nearly a decade earlier, along another part of the river, in a section of the great city even coarser and more dangerous than where we now found ourselves.

Holmes was already at the front door, looking into the window alongside it.

Then I heard the cab driver whipping up his horse.

Before I could interfere, the cab lurched forward, the horse picked up speed, and a moment later horse and cab were galloping away, into the darkness.

Holmes motioned for me to join him. "There are people inside. We are safer with them than out here."

At least we would be warmer, I thought. I followed him inside, where I was struck by a smoky haze that immediately clouded my vision. I caught the smell of tobacco, tinged with the unmistakable sweetish scent of opium.

I soon realized we were in a kind of reception area, partitioned off from the long room behind by two ragged blankets that had been draped over a thick clothesline rope.

One of the blankets moved, swept aside by a powerful arm. A lascar Indian seaman of immense girth stepped forward, wearing a black suit large enough to have made three suits for a man of my size. Wide and healthy looking, he radiated a jovial energy.

"Mr. Holmes," he said.

"You have the advantage of me," Holmes said. "This is my friend and colleague, Dr. John Watson."

"I am Rahim Hasson, owner of this humble establishment. My business is important to me. A constable of Inspector Plank told me you would be coming."

"Yes. I spoke with him this afternoon by telephone."

"You put Mr. Thomas Newman in jail, I believe."

"We were just speaking with Mr. Newman, in fact," Holmes said. "I have no need to further antagonize him or those in his organization. Unless they killed Inspector Swafford?"

"Who?"

In reply, Holmes took a photograph of the late inspector from his coat pocket and showed it to Hasson.

The lascar examined it for a moment. "A greedy fellow. He did not say his name. He wanted to sell me his opium. I told him I had my own sources of supply."

"His response?"

"He said he could sell below whatever price my current suppliers were asking. He brought product for me to try. A sample, so to speak."

"And did you?"

"I do not partake of the substance myself. However, I invited one of the customers who happened to be present to try a pipe. He did so. We waited. He pronounced the product of better quality than our standard fare."

"Why should Swafford's product be better?"

"His came from India, or so he said. Our source is China. We get the surplus from one of the plantations in the Wuhan district. Chinese product is not as effective and has a rougher feel on the throat."

"So, to summarize, Inspector Swafford offered you a better product at a lower price. And your response was still negative."

"One does not terminate a long-term relationship for the sake of a fleeting opportunity."

Holmes raised an eyebrow. "Fleeting?"

"There would have been retribution from those who supply

my establishments. I own several, located on other streets in London and in several other ports in England. Moreover, I had no proof that Swafford would or could honor his promise over a continued period of time."

"You declined the offer from Inspector Swafford. What happened next?"

"He bid me goodbye in a very cordial manner and left that evening. I never saw him again."

"Then allow me to repeat my earlier question. Would Newman's men want to kill Swafford?"

"I doubt it very much. Newman's people only want me to continue the weekly payment they extract from me. They do not care where I get my supplies."

"Would your suppliers wish to kill him?"

"If they knew of his attempt to replace them, they would certainly try to prevent that from occurring. They might indeed kill him. But they have no idea of Inspector Swafford's approach to me. I certainly did not tell them, and no one here overheard our conversation."

"But one of your customers was aware. The man who sampled the new product would have seen Swafford."

"No, for I took the sample to him myself."

"Where did Swafford say he had procured the Indian sample?"

"He did not say."

"But he said he had more."

"And very possibly could obtain more still. A great deal more."

"Nonetheless you do not think your suppliers or Newman's gang had anything to do with his murder," Holmes said.

He shrugged. "The incident of Swafford's murder caused me difficulty. It is to the advantage of my suppliers and Newman's gang that I continue to operate and prosper, so that I can continue to pay them."

"He was killed with what appears to have been a dockhand's hook. Does that suggest anything to you?"

Hasson blinked once but shook his head.

"If you were to guess his killer?"

"How would I guess?"

"Several alternatives suggest themselves. The Metropolitan Police will explore the obvious—people from his past—criminals he may have arrested or family members with a grudge. The alternative that I am considering is that Swafford did not own the sample that he provided to you. Perhaps he stole it. Perhaps the owner discovered the theft, followed him here, and took his revenge—along with the sample."

"That seems a reasonable assumption." A guarded look crossed Hasson's swarthy face. "But if there is such a source, others would also like to know it. Perhaps they attempted to learn the location from Swafford. Perhaps he would not tell them, so they killed him."

"Or perhaps he did tell them, so they killed him, having no further use for him."

Hasson nodded. "That is, regrettably, equally as likely. Inspector Swafford was playing a most dangerous game." He paused. "Now, Mr. Holmes, perhaps you will tell me the game that you are playing. Inspector Plank's constable said that you would have a business proposition for me."

"My objective is to uncover the truth about Swafford's murder. Yours is to continue to operate here, and to prosper."

"How are those two connected?"

"The location of Swafford's murder was an attempt to implicate you. There was also another attempt to accomplish the same objective."

"And that was?"

"Last night. More opium, from the same source as the opium Swafford obtained, was stolen, and last seen in this neighborhood."

"I had nothing to do with that—"

"I understand. I believe that the person who stole the opium is the person responsible for killing Swafford. Capturing that someone is what I want, and what you also should want."

The man features remained stolid. "So, let us assume we agree. What then?"

At that moment the door opened, and a rush of frigid air swept into the little room. A burly man in a bowler hat stood before us, muffled against the cold by a black wool scarf atop his black overcoat. "I am Inspector Paul Plank," he said. "You must be Dr. Watson. I have come to provide you and Mr. Holmes safe passage to Baker Street."

I felt a moment's relief. But then to my surprise, there immediately came the faint crack of rifle fire in the distance. Inspector Plank startled at the sound.

Then the burly inspector twisted, stumbled, and fell to the floor, clutching at his right shoulder.

Instinctively I knelt to help the wounded man. Holmes had already moved to the open doorway. He was about to close it when Inspector Plank, already down on one knee, called out, "Wait, my men are coming!"

Through the doorway I saw two uniformed constables running towards us. Plank waved them away with his good arm. But the two were already at the door, breathless. "The shot came from a boat, sir," one said.

"Out on the river," said the other.

"In the dark," the first constable continued. "Impossible to follow."

"From the river?" Plank said. "That seems an impossible shot."

"Why impossible?" asked Holmes.

"Because, Mr. Holmes, I am convinced that the shot was meant for you. You should stay away from Limehouse. The word on the docks is that someone wants you dead."

"I have heard similar sentiments many times over the years. And yet I live," Holmes said.

I helped Plank remove his coat and administered first aid, cleaning the wound, which fortunately was only superficial. I wrapped my clean handkerchief into a pad and pressed it against the damaged area for the inspector to hold with pressure until we could get the wound properly dressed.

Holmes made his way carefully around the back of the Red Dragon's entry area. Finally, he bent down and retrieved a small object from where it lay on the floor against the wall. "The bullet that struck the inspector," he explained, tucking it into his waistcoat pocket.

Plank was outside, having been assisted by the two constables, already on his way to the police carriage.

Hasson had retreated behind the ragged blanket curtain at the first entry of the police. Holmes called softly to him that we were leaving.

"A most unfortunate third attempt to disturb my establishment," the big man said, coming out to the entry area once again.

"And most unfair as well," Holmes replied. "After all, you are paying Newman's gang for protection."

We returned to Baker Street shortly before dawn, to find Mrs. Hudson waiting up for us in the front stairwell. "You've had a telegraph message from Lucy," she said, thrusting a yellow envelope into Holmes's hand.

Holmes tore open the envelope, scanned the message, and then reached into his pocket for a pen. Flattening the yellow paper against the wall, he wrote hurriedly for only a moment. Then he handed the paper back to Mrs. Hudson.

"Lucy merely wants us to know that she is safe. Please send back our acknowledgment."

Holmes headed for the staircase. I followed, bleary-eyed and looking forward to a few hours' sleep, if not more.

Above me, Holmes turned back. "And Mrs. Hudson. No callers are to be admitted. Dr. Watson is in need of rest, and I must grapple with a problem that will require my full attention."

LUCY

26. BREAKING AND ENTERING

"Did you see anyone?" Becky whispered.

I strained my eyes, peering through the nearly pitch darkness, then shook my head. "No one except the night watchman."

Shellingford had street lamps, but only on the main streets, and we were on a narrow side lane that ran down towards the harbor. It was only around eight o'clock at night, but the streets were completely deserted. The air was so cold that it seemed to slice right through my heavy woolen cloak, although at least the earlier rain had cleared.

A single pale sliver of a moon allowed me to make out vague shapes in the darkness.

Unlike the sprawling docks in London, the dock in Shellingford harbor was a much smaller affair. Only three ships bobbed at anchor out in the deeper waters of the harbor, with a handful of smaller tugboats closer to shore.

A single long wooden pier stretched out into the ocean, while on shore, the dark shadows of four or five long, single-story warehouse buildings clustered along the bay's southern curve.

Becky and I were standing in the partially sheltered doorway of a tea shop that had long since closed up for the evening.

Our eyes were on the entrance to the nearest warehouse—the one which, according to my map, was owned by Lord Lynley's import and export company.

A light bobbed in the darkness along the furthest side of the warehouse.

"It's not very smart of the night watchman to carry a lantern with him," Becky said. Our spying post was too dark for me to see her expression, but I could picture her critical frown. "It lets anyone who might be watching him know exactly where he is all the time."

"True. But that doesn't mean we can assume that there's no one else, just because we can't see them."

I looked out across the deserted, cobbled street again. In theory, this was a simple enough assignment: break into the warehouse, find the office, examine the shipping manifests and records.

There was, obviously, the danger of being caught and arrested. But it was nothing that I hadn't faced before. Still, as I watched the night watchman's lantern bobbing in the darkness, my heart was beating too hard and too fast in my ears.

"I'm not going back and waiting for you in the hotel room," Becky whispered.

I turned. "How can you possibly know that's what I was thinking? You can't even see to tell that I was frowning."

"No, but your voice *sounded* frowny," Becky whispered back.

"Maybe that's because I'm imagining myself explaining to your brother why I thought it was a good idea to bring you along on a burglary."

"Jack would understand. Besides, I thought it only counted as burglary if you stole something. We're not going to take anything, only look."

"Becky." I crouched down so that we were more on a level. "You have to understand that this could be dangerous—really dangerous."

"Because you think Lord Lynley is importing opium?"

"I think so. I'm certain—almost certain—that Mrs. Torrance is a laudanum addict." That was why I was hoping she could tell us about Mr. Seewald's suppliers. "I'm fairly sure that Lady Lynley takes laudanum, as well. And that the opium is being brought in on Lord Lynley's ships and manufactured here. Possibly even at the Grand Hotel."

It would explain the hardening of His Lordship's expression when he spoke of his wife's poor health.

It would also explain why he had tried—clumsily—to warn us away from staying at the Grand.

"I'm not sure who's in charge of the business, though— whether it's Lord Lynley, or his business partner. Or even Mr. Torrance is a possibility."

I sensed rather than saw Becky's tilting her head. "I don't understand, though. I thought you said that importing opium and selling it like Mr. Seewald does isn't against the law?"

"It's not." That was a part of the puzzle that was stubbornly refusing to make sense. Opium *wasn't* illegal. Even the seven percent solution of cocaine that had nearly claimed my father's life and health was fully within the bounds of the law. "But Alice was employed by Lord Lynley, whose wife is addicted to taking laudanum and who may or may not be responsible for its manufacture here. She was also involved with Chang, who serves His Lordship's business partner, and who warned me against taking Mr. Seewald's concoction. The opium connection is the only credible lead we have so far in Alice's disappearance—which makes me think we need to pull on that thread and see what's on the other end."

Or I would think that, if I didn't have my ten-year-old sister-in-law standing and shivering in the dark next to me.

"If you think Mr. Torrance is somehow involved, I could still be in danger, even if you make me go back to the hotel," Becky whispered beside me.

"Well, but—"

"What if he actually *suspects* who we really are, and he's just waiting for a chance to kidnap me?" Becky interrupted. "You won't be able to stop thinking about that, now. You'll worry about it the whole time you're gone if you do take me back to the hotel and return here alone."

In my mind, I imagined myself thumping my forehead against the nearest solid wall. "Have I ever told you that you are far too smart and too devious for your own good?"

Becky stiffened, drawing in a quick breath, and I turned back to the street. "What is it? Did you see something?"

"No." She blew on her mittened hands, trying to warm them. "Can we go now, do you think? The guard is all the way over there, away from Lord Lynley's warehouse. You can see his lantern."

I located the bobbing light in the darkness and watched it for a moment. Becky was—unfortunately—all too right about my worrying if I left her at the hotel now.

If we were keeping score like in a game of tennis, the tally would at this moment read *Becky: 1, Lucy: 0.*

"All right, we'll go," I told her. "Carefully."

27. A GRIM DISCOVERY

I fitted one of my lock picks into the lock on the warehouse door, and scraped fruitlessly around for what seemed like an eternity before I felt it press on the tumbler.

All lockpicking was done by touch, so the fact that it was nearly pitch dark shouldn't have made a difference—and yet it was somehow throwing me off. Or else it was the fact that my fingers were stiff and clumsy with cold.

I glanced over my shoulder at Becky's small, shadowed figure standing at the corner of the building nearest to me. She was keeping a lookout for the night watchman and was supposed to signal with two low whistles if she saw his light coming nearer.

While watching from the street, I'd timed the patrol he made of the warehouse buildings, and there was roughly a ten-minute gap between each of his circuits past the Lynley warehouse. Which had probably shrunk to seven or eight minutes by now.

I pushed stray hair off my forehead with the back of my wrist and inserted another pick into the lock. *Careful … careful …*

From somewhere not far off, a dog's bark cut through the whistle of wind from the harbor and the slap of the waves against the boat's hulls.

The sound ran down my spine and landed in my stomach like a clump of ice.

Becky appeared beside me, her whisper low and urgent. "Lucy, wasn't that—"

"I know."

I was silently kicking myself for not considering the possibility that the night watchman would have a guard dog to help him on his rounds.

Holmes would probably be able to tell me with exact precision what percentage more sensitive a dog's hearing and sense of smell were compared to that of a human. But even I knew it was much too high for our comfort.

The dog barked again. A deep, throaty bark. Likely a mastiff or bloodhound.

I bent towards the lock again. Once, twice, the picks slipped uselessly off the tumbler mechanism. Despite the cold, sweat prickled on my hairline.

Something clicked inside the lock, and finally turned. I exhaled, pushed the door open, and Becky and I almost tumbled inside—just as the first yellow tinges of the watchman's lantern came into view around the side of the building.

Every nerve in my body wanted to slam the door shut behind us, but I forced myself to ease it closed, slowly and as silently as possible.

No time to use the picks to re-lock it, and no one had been obliging enough to leave a key on the inside of the door, ready for me to find.

I ran my hands along the edge of the door frame, praying for the added security measure of a bolt or—

There.

It was pitch black inside the warehouse building, the darkness so complete I couldn't even see my own hands. But I felt the sharp outline of a barrel slide bolt.

I rammed it home, just as a short, sharp bark announced the presence of the dog and the night watchman on the other side of the door.

I held still. Becky pressed tightly against me but remained motionless, as well. The only sound in the room was the sound of our breathing.

The dog barked again, and then the doorknob rattled. The night watchman was trying the door.

The bolt held.

The dog whined, and I heard the sound of scrabbling, as though it was pawing at the door.

"What is it, y' daft mutt?" The night watchman's voice was gruff and low-pitched. I couldn't see him, but I pictured him as beefy and barrel-chested, with a weathered face and possibly a beard. "There's nothing here."

My heartbeat ticked off the seconds. *Eight ... nine.*

Fifteen interminable seconds later, I heard the dog whine again and the night watchman grunt irritably—then the sound of footsteps, moving away.

I squeezed Becky's hand, warning her not to move yet. I counted off two minutes inside my head, then one more for good measure before finally allowing myself to step away from the door.

"All right. We should be—"

My foot connected with something that lay sprawled across the floor. Something solid and heavy.

"Becky, don't move for another minute." I spoke in a low voice.

"All right."

I was still frustratingly blind, but I stooped down, feeling in the darkness by the floor. My fingertips connected with rough tweed fabric, then a cuff with buttons.

The sleeve of a jacket.

Then an unmistakably human hand.

"Lucy?" Becky sounded slightly frightened now.

"It's all right." I worked to keep my voice calm. The hand I'd touched felt cold, but no colder than mine. I moved my fingers, searching for a pulse.

Nothing.

I shut my eyes for a second then stood up, crossing back to Becky. "There's someone lying on the floor just in front of us. I'm not sure whether they're alive or dead." True, I hadn't felt a pulse, but I might have missed it in the dark—and if whoever was lying here was still alive, leaving right now to seek help would take time we couldn't afford. "I need to risk a light. But whatever we see, I need you not to panic and not to scream, all right?"

"All right." Becky's voice was small but steady.

I took one quick look around, scanning for any signs of a window in whatever room we were in, but I couldn't see any at all. And it didn't matter so much whether the night watchman did see a light; we were going to have to report this, one way or the other.

I'd brought a small stub of a candle from the hotel along with a box of matches.

I took them out and struck a match. Fire flared in the darkness; then the candle's wick caught. Dim light cast flickering shadows across what seemed to be a small office; there was a wooden desk in one corner piled high with what looked like accounting books. Ledgers and more stacks of papers were on a shelf nearby.

And Lord Lynley's body, sprawled on the floor in front of the desk. Unmistakably killed by a gunshot wound to the head.

28. CONFLAGRATION

Becky's breath went out in a small gasp, but otherwise she didn't make a sound. I still wished I could cover her eyes, somehow stop her from seeing the dead body on the floor. But she turned to me, pale but determinedly calm.

"It's all right, Lucy. I've seen dead bodies before. And anyway, he can't hurt us." She looked towards Lord Lynley. "Do you think he shot himself?"

"I don't know. It certainly looks that way."

Lord Lynley's body lay on its side, his legs twisted at an awkward angle. His right arm was flung outwards, and a gun lay on the floor just under his fingers, as though he'd lost his grip on it at the moment of death.

I stepped closer.

The gun was a .32 caliber Smith & Wesson revolver, and the bullet that had killed him had clearly entered through his right temple. The shot had been fired at close range. The wound was surrounded by powder burns. A trickle of blood dripped onto the floor, still liquid.

I touched Lord Lynley's neck. His hand had been cold, but the skin under his collar was still warm.

He could only have been dead a very few minutes.

I raised the candle a little higher, scanning the body and the floor around him.

Lord Lynley had been right-handed. I remembered the configuration of his desk: pen and inkwell both on the right side.

So far, everything pointed towards suicide.

I stepped carefully around the body and moved to the desk.

The papers had been neatly stacked to one side, and a single sheet of writing paper lay in the exact center of the desk's surface, next to a typewriter. A single sentence had been typed out on the paper:

I cannot bear to go on, living with the shame I have brought on my family's good name.

The signature scrawled just below was in black ink. *Lynley.*

The handwriting was definitely male, and the writer had obviously been in the grip of a powerful emotion. The ink was blotted in places and the letters were unsteady, as though the hand that had done the writing had been shaking. The pen had been dragged so heavily across the page that it had scored gouges in the paper.

The chair behind the desk was set at an angle, too, as though Lord Lynley had sat down to write this note, then shoved his chair back, stood up, and came out into the middle of the room to shoot himself.

Still, I stared at the note, feeling an odd sense of uneasiness prickle at the back of my mind.

Maybe it was just that it seemed odd to bother with typing a suicide note, when you were going to sign it with pen and ink anyway?

Or that Lord Lynley could just as easily have shot himself

while sitting at the desk as standing in the middle of the room?

Both of those things were true, but I didn't think either was what was troubling me.

I glanced around the room again. There was another door set into the wall to the left of the desk. Presumably it led through to the rest of the warehouse. No sign that anyone had gone through it recently—but no sign, either, that they *hadn't*.

I crossed over and tried the doorknob. Locked. Although, of course, I'd just proved that locks could be manipulated from the outside.

If I'd been alone, I might have tried unlocking the door just to see where it led, but as it was, I drew in a breath. "We need to leave now and report this."

"To the night watchman?"

"Only if we're careless enough to let him see us leaving."

If we went to him or if he caught us, the night watchman would, understandably, want to know exactly how we'd come to break into a locked warehouse and find the dead body of its owner on the floor.

"I'd rather go straight to Chief Constable Slade and tell him who we are and why we're here." I didn't usually like to capitalize on my connection to Sherlock Holmes, but at the moment I was perfectly willing to use my father's name and reputation if it kept me from being thrown into a jail cell.

Becky nodded. Then she frowned, sniffing the air. "Lucy? Do you smell smoke?"

"It's just the—" *candle*, I was about to say. But then I froze.

A harsh scent of burning, sharp and acrid, was filling the air. I raised the candle higher. Ribbons of smoke were pouring in from under and around the door behind the desk.

Something crashed in the distance, making the roof above us shake. A series of thuds followed, as though something was raining down from above. The floor vibrated under my feet.

"We need to get out of here." I spun around, unbolted the door, and turned the knob.

The door refused to budge.

I set my shoulder against it and tried again.

I might as well have been shoving against a brick wall.

"Lucy?" Becky asked.

I took a breath, ignoring the sting of smoke in my lungs, and tried to speak calmly. "That door won't open." If the docks were on fire, maybe debris had fallen and blocked the door. "We'll have to try the other one."

Although judging by the amount of smoke billowing in from around the edges, that way out wasn't any too promising, either.

I crossed to the second door and knelt down in front of the knob. I just had to hope that this lock would be easier to pick than the last one.

I pushed, twisted, and then the tumbler clicked. *Unlocked.* I swung the door open—and a choking cloud of thick black smoke rushed in.

"Lucy, I can't see you!" Becky's voice was on the edge of panic.

"I'm right here. Just reach out towards the sound of my voice." Coughing, I wiped my eyes with one hand, holding out the other towards Becky. Her fingers gripped mine. "It's all right." I peered through the thick cloud of smoke beyond the doorway. "At least I don't see any flames."

I didn't see any way out of here, either, but Becky didn't need to know that. "All we need to do is find another entrance."

"What's happening?" Becky was coughing, too, her eyes streaming. "Why is the building on fire?"

I might not have the full answer, but I was already certain there was an approximately zero percent chance that this fire was accidental.

"Here." I pulled out my handkerchief and handed it to Becky. It would be helpful if I had water to soak it in, but it was better than nothing. "Keep this over your nose and mouth and keep close to me, all right?"

Becky clamped the handkerchief to her face and nodded wordlessly.

I started to step out of the office and into what seemed to be a hallway, then stopped.

Someone was trying to destroy this building, presumably for a reason.

There wasn't time to make a more thorough examination of the room, but I stared through the smoke, trying to fix the details of the scene in my mind. Maybe whatever was bothering me would surface later.

I turned, snatched up Lord Lynley's suicide note, then swept up as many of the other papers as I could hold off the surface of the desk and tucked them inside my coat.

They might or might not provide answers, but at least it was something.

"Follow me," I told Becky. "And stay as close to the ground as possible. The smoke is less thick there."

I crouched down, bending almost double as I led the way out of the office, holding tightly onto Becky's hand.

I was still clutching the lighted candle, but I blew it out after the first ten steps. The smoke was so thick that it was still impossible to see even with a light, and trying to keep the flame from going out was only slowing me down.

I groped in the dark, identifying rough plaster walls on either side of us, about five feet apart. A hallway. One, so far, without windows or doors, but even so it had to lead somewhere.

I kept my hand on the wall to our right, letting my fingers trail across the surface so that I would know if there were any exits or turns. I counted off the steps, trying to calculate how far we had come.

Twenty feet. Fifty.

The air felt hotter with every crouching step forward. My eyes burned. Smoke scraped my throat and scoured my lungs.

I stopped short as the hallway under my fingertips abruptly ended and an orange glow lighted the smoky darkness up ahead. I blinked, trying to clear my eyes enough to see. We were standing on the edge of what looked to be the huge open space of the warehouse. Here and there, the shapes of big shipping crates loomed. But fire was everywhere, licking the wooden crates and barrels, racing in trails of flame across the floor, running up the walls.

Beneath the harsh smell of smoke, I caught a sharp odor that reminded me of my father's chemistry experiments. Someone had doused the room with something flammable, and then struck a match.

"Look out!" Becky screamed.

The fire had leaped up to reach the ceiling, and a chunk of wooden beams and slate roof came crashing down in a shower of sparks.

We both jumped backwards out of the way. Becky clung to my side. I could feel her trembling, coughing and struggling to breathe. "Lucy, everything's burning." She had to almost shout to be heard over the fire's crackling roar. "If we can't get out of here, we'll be burned up, too. We'll die!"

I crouched down, checking her over quickly to make sure that none of the burning sparks had set her coat or skirt on fire, then did the same for my own. "We're not going to die, and we *are* getting out of here."

"How do you know that?"

"Because I categorically refuse to let Mrs. Torrance's new antimacassars be the subject of the last conversation I ever have on earth."

As I'd hoped, Becky hiccupped an unsteady laugh and wiped her eyes.

"Good." I hugged her quickly then straightened. "Now help me look for a door that leads to the outside."

At least the fire was casting enough light for us to see, if only dimly, through clouds of choking smoke. We edged sideways, past a stack of wooden barrels that hadn't yet caught aflame— and another huge chunk of the ceiling caved in, blocking the way in front of us.

This time, Becky didn't even scream, but I still held her tightly, my mind racing. Flames had sprung up all around, blocking our way back to the office. Not that we could get out through there, either.

Shouting for help wouldn't do any good. I could barely even hear my own voice, much less hope that anyone on the outside would hear me.

A man's dark figure loomed up suddenly out of the smoky shadows to my left. Backlit by the glow of the orange flames, he looked for a split second like the demon in a medieval morality play.

Then he drew nearer, and I recognized the Chinese man from Mr. Seewald's shop.

"Come with me!" His eyes were red and streaming from the smoke, and he, too, held a length of cloth across his nose and mouth. "Quickly!"

I pushed back the shock of his appearance, but still stayed where I was, my hand on Becky's shoulders.

"Why should we trust you?"

He coughed and wiped sweat from his forehead. "You will forgive me for stating the obvious, but your options are somewhat limited at the moment." The exaggerated accent he'd used with Mr. Seewald was gone, leaving his voice short, clipped. He gestured back towards the way he had come. "There is a doorway, straight over there. Unless you are searching for a creative and extremely unpleasant way to die, you will follow me."

LUCY

29. UNEXPECTED AID

After ten feet, the smoky air cleared a fraction.

The stranger edged carefully around a pile of smoldering shipping containers, and cooler air washed across my face. I see the dark outlines of an open doorway with a slice of the night sky visible beyond. It was only about five feet up ahead, but even still, Becky and I almost certainly wouldn't have found it without help.

Our rescuer stepped through the doorway, then paused, looking to see that we made it safely out after him. I let Becky go first, squeezing her hand briefly.

The doorway seemed to emerge into a narrow space between two warehouse buildings. If the whole of the Lynley warehouse behind us caught fire, then the second one would be in grave danger as well, but for now the air here was comparatively clear.

I drew in a breath, stepped to the doorway, then caught my toe on the door frame and stumbled forward.

"Take care!" The stranger held out a hand to steady me.

I took it, stepped out onto the hard-packed frozen ground, and then used the leverage to yank him forward and down.

He staggered, stumbling towards me, and I hit him across the back of the neck with my joined fists. The blow wasn't hard enough to knock him out, but he at least collapsed onto the ground, face-down.

I set my foot between his shoulder blades and drew the Ladysmith revolver I'd brought on tonight's expedition.

"Don't move."

Most people either froze or panicked at the sight of a gun. The Chinese man, though, remained calmly motionless, and his voice was remarkably composed. "Is this always how you repay those who save your life?"

Becky was standing off to one side, her hands clenched. I didn't doubt that if our rescuer tried to fight back, she would throw herself straight into the fray.

One of the reasons I had brought the Ladysmith along.

"No, not always. But this strikes me as an extraordinarily good night for being cautious." I flicked the safety off the gun. "Who are you? What are you doing here?"

"I am Chang Kai-chen." He pronounced the name differently than I would have done. Closer to *Zhang*. But I'd been right about his identity. "You may call me Kai-chen."

His arms lay at his sides, palms flat on the ground. The firelight showed angry red marks on his right wrist, as though he'd already been struck by burning debris.

"I serve Ming Donghai, Lord Lynley's … for lack of a better word, business partner," he went on. "May I get up now?"

I didn't move, but I did raise my head, listening. The smoke, even out here in the open air, was thickening as the building behind us caught fire, and I could hear shouts and voices. The night watchman must have raised the alarm.

We couldn't stay here much longer. Another section of the roof in the building beside us crashed down. I startled involuntarily—

And Kai-chen twisted himself out from under my foot and sprang to his feet in one agile, fluid motion.

My heart lurched. But instead of coming towards me, Kai-chen whirled and raced away, vanishing into the smoke-filled night.

30. FACTS AND CONCLUSIONS

Clouds of shag tobacco smoke filled our sitting room. Holmes was sitting cross-legged on the floor on several of our sofa cushions, in front of his fireplace chair. On the grate the coals had been stoked and were glowing brightly. I felt grateful to see breakfast on the table.

"Watson, good morning. Do you recall last night's incident with Inspector Plank?"

"I do."

As I poured coffee for myself, he continued.

"Have you reached any conclusions?"

"The shot cannot have been for you. The inspector must be mistaken. If the shot came from the river, it would be impossible for someone that far away to have seen you. The inspector is a bulky man, and he was standing in the doorway."

"That much is obvious. However, I need your help."

"Of course."

"The wound the inspector received. I did not see it, but you did. You recall it well?"

"Very clearly."

"Would you please trace your finger along your own shoulder to indicate the wound?"

I did so. The bullet had caught the inspector's right deltoid muscle, so close to the surface as to penetrate the skin, and continued straight through it. I traced my finger accordingly.

"Now please set down your coffee and stand before me and perform the same tracing action as before."

I did so.

"Place your fingertip where the bullet went in, and the tip of your thumb to mark where the bullet went out."

I did so. Holmes stood up, came forward, and looked at my shoulder for a long moment, and with a level of interest that puzzled me. Finally, he nodded with apparent satisfaction.

"Now, Watson. We are getting at the truth of the matter, thanks to your demonstration."

"I am glad indeed to hear it, but I confess I have no idea what you have seen or how this has been helpful."

"You know my methods."

"Holmes," I protested. "I have had a very late night and have not yet taken breakfast!"

"Quite so. Let me make the situation plainer for you then. How far above the ground is the tip of your finger?"

"Why, about five feet."

"And the tip of your thumb?"

"Nearly the same height. About five feet above the ground."

"So, since your fingertip and the tip of your thumb represent the points of entry and exit of the bullet, it was on more or less a level trajectory when it struck the inspector and passed through his coat and the surface of his shoulder."

"It must have been."

"You are five feet ten inches tall. The inspector is a shade taller, but I confess not to have a precise image in my mind of the slope of his shoulders. Let us say that his shoulder was at the same height as yours. So, given that the trajectory of the bullet was a level one, how far above the floor of the Red Dragon must the shooter's weapon have been when it was fired?"

"About five feet."

"And where did the two constables say the shot came from?"

"From the river."

"From a boat on the river, Watson. Not from a ship, but from a boat, which would have been on the water. And the surface level of the Thames, I noted as we left the building, is some fifteen feet below the floor of the Red Lantern. What does that tell you?"

I did some elementary mental calculation. "That the two constables were mistaken. The shot would necessarily have come from a height of twenty feet above the river level. From a ship."

"That is one possibility. But where was this ship? When we arrived and when we left there were only coal barges and small launches. Nothing of that height."

"I am at a loss to explain."

"Consider also the aim of the shooter."

"Not very good, presumably. Though to give him some credit, if the shooter was out on the water, a hundred yards away or more, rocking on the waves, the wind buffeting him—"

"It is remarkable that he hit anything at all," Holmes finished for me.

I had an idea. "What if there was a second shooter, Holmes?" I asked. "With an air gun. The first fires randomly from somewhere out on the river. The second, closer at hand, at the same level, concealed from the constables in a building or shed, fires his air gun from there."

"There were no buildings of that sort."

"Then what did happen, Holmes?"

"There was a shooter on the water. He did fire his weapon. The inspector heard it and fell. At the same time, while rolling onto the floor and while our eyes were on the outside, where the shot had presumably come from, he whipped off the black wool scarf that concealed a wound previously made and, falling, flung the bullet against the wall."

"But Plank rode in the carriage with the two constables."

Holmes drew on his pipe and emitted a great cloud of tobacco smoke. "We assume that Plank shot himself at some time prior to opening the door and covered the tear in his coat with his scarf. He may have done the shooting before entering the police carriage and concealed his pain from his two subordinates. Alternatively, the constables may have been in on the deception."

I shuddered. "Why should the inspector wish to shoot himself?"

"He said he wanted to keep me away from Limehouse. He may be sincere, or he may not. He may want the exact opposite."

"The opposite?"

"He may have staged the incident, hoping I will be challenged to redouble my efforts. He also mentioned the rumor in Limehouse that I was wanted dead, which also may be taken as a challenge. We must add to this the fact that Limehouse is controlled by Newman's gang, and that the note at St. Philip's implicates Newman in the death of Miss Janine and her mother."

"So Limehouse and Newman are the key to the mystery."

"To the mystery of the three murders, very likely. To the mystery of the missing opium—"

"I thought you had declined that case."

"I declined to recover the opium, which has earned me the approbation of several men in high places. But we must take the opium into account all the same if we want to solve these murders and prevent many others."

He stood. "I am going to Scotland Yard. Will you come?"

31. A POLICEMAN'S WIFE IS NOT A HAPPY ONE

The London Police stations I had visited were big, modern buildings, all constructed with their intended purpose in mind, all housing not only holding cells, offices, and interview rooms, but dormitory housing for unmarried constables, as well.

The Shellingford police station, by contrast, looked as though it had been lifted straight out of Shakespearean times: half-timbered, with a thatch roof and diamond-paned windows.

Beside the police station itself sat a small, whitewashed cottage that I knew from making inquiries in the village was the private residence of Chief Constable Slade and his wife.

Beyond and behind both buildings, the fenlands stretched out, the tall brown grasses waving in the breeze, and pools of water glinting mirror-smooth in the early-morning sun.

"Are you sure this is a good idea, Lucy?" Becky asked.

The night before, we had managed to get away from the docks without being seen. Not that that was any great achievement of stealth. The fire had spread to two of the neighboring warehouse buildings, and in the chaos, as dock workers and villagers alike worked feverishly to put out the flames, an entire brass marching band could have passed through without being seen.

Miraculously, no one had been seriously injured and no other lives lost. But this morning the entire village was buzzing with the news of Lord Lynley's death.

Since the fire had started at the back of the warehouse and the office had been in the front, it had survived the blaze with the least amount of damage. His lordship's body had been discovered when those fighting the flames had broken in, and—according to what Bill had said back at the hotel when he'd brought up our breakfast—thus far, no one was questioning the idea that Lord Lynley had taken his own life.

"We don't have a choice. I have to report what we know to the police."

Which—also according to Bill—consisted of the chief constable and a single sergeant who assisted him in his duties.

"I need to give him the papers I took from the warehouse. They're evidence, after all." I studied Becky's face. "Are you sure you're feeling all right?"

She wasn't coughing or showing any other signs of illness from the smoke we'd breathed last night, but she still didn't seem like herself.

"I'm fine." Becky started up the narrow flagstone pathway that led to the police station. "Let's go in."

The station door was locked, though, and no one answered our knocks.

"Should we try next door?" Becky asked.

I considered. Most likely, Chief Constable Slade and his subordinate were still down at the docks, dealing with the investigation into the fire and Lord Lynley's death.

There was his wife, though. I remembered Mrs. Slade, sobbing and clutching Mr. Seewald's bottle of medicine as though it were a life preserver and she was drowning in the ocean.

I sighed. There were times when investigating crimes was exhilarating—and others when it just made you feel like a snake.

But set against the idea of questioning someone as fragile as Mrs. Slade was the look I'd seen pass between Chief Constable Slade and Mr. Seewald: the murderous fury on the chief constable's face; the smug satisfaction lacing the chemist's smile.

I could hand the evidence over to Chief Constable Slade, but that didn't mean he was in a position to see justice done.

"We can at least knock and see whether she'll speak to us," I told Becky.

I was expecting a housemaid, but instead it was Emily Slade herself who answered the door.

It was past ten in the morning, but she still wore a nightdress and dressing gown, both made of thick black cotton and edged with black ribbons. Her dark hair hung down in untidy straggles over her shoulders, and her feet were bare.

"Mrs. Slade?" I asked.

She looked from me to Becky, a slight frown puckering her brow. "I'm sorry, do I know you?" Her voice wasn't curious or surprised so much as dull. Flat. As though she had long since given up on taking any interest in whatever life brought her way.

I hadn't gotten a very good look at her face the day before beneath her veil. Seen up close, she looked younger than her husband, maybe thirty or thirty-five, with small, neat features that might at one time have been pretty. Now, though, her face was stamped with the same indelible marks of grief as her husband's. Lines of pain bracketed the corners of her mouth, and deep purple shadows showed like bruises under her eyes.

"No, we haven't met." I spoke as gently as possible. "But I was hoping that we might talk to you, just for a short while."

Mrs. Slade's eyes moved from me to Becky and then back again, her gaze as dully uninterested as her voice had been. Then she shrugged, her thin shoulders slumping.

"If you like. Come in." She stepped back, allowing us entrance into the house.

The interior was dim, but instantly the odors of dust, stale air, and old grease from cooking washed over me.

"I'm sorry." Mrs. Slade led the way inside. "You'll have to find your own place to sit and put up with not having anything to eat or drink. I let our maidservant go. I couldn't bear having someone underfoot in the house all the time. But now there's no one to do any of the work and I'm alone all day long, and that's even worse."

Her voice wavered as she gestured to the cottage's front room.

There were a couch and two chairs in the sitting room, but all three were piled high with an array of what looked like bed linens and other laundry, some of it dirty, some clean. Newspapers and magazines lay in stacks on the floor. Half-drunk cups of tea and plates with uneaten slices of toast littered the tables, and the rest of the furniture was thick with dust.

"That's all right," Becky said.

I knew she wasn't oblivious to the pain in Mrs. Slade's eyes or the almost palpable cloud of misery that seemed to hang over the house any more than I was. But she still spoke cheerfully.

"We can sit on the floor, can't we, Lucy? We don't mind. It will be like having a picnic."

Mrs. Slade's gaze moved to Becky and, for the first time, her dull eyes warmed. The faintest trace of a smile curved the edges of her lips. "You're a sweet child. My Amelia had blonde hair, too, although it wasn't quite as light a shade as yours."

Her voice shook again on the last words.

"I'm so sorry."

I had already noticed the one clean, well-maintained spot on the mantle; it held a framed photograph of a little girl of five or six, holding a bouquet of flowers and staring at the camera with an expression that said she'd far rather be allowed to run out and play.

"Thank you." Mrs. Slade raised one hand and scrubbed tiredly at her eyes. She sank onto one of the chairs, ignoring the pile of dirty linens and looked down at her own heavy black dressing gown as though she were seeing it for the first time. "It's funny." Her mouth twisted slightly. "I remember my sisters and I would laugh at an aunt of mine for wearing mourning clothes at night, as well as during the day. She was a Tartar for not leaving a task half done, and we used to say that she had to be thorough even about her mourning. But now I can see her point."

Becky moved to stand beside her and put one hand over hers. "My mother died. My brother told me it was all right to feel sad. But that she wouldn't want me to be sad all the time. He said she'd want me to be happy, too."

Mrs. Slade blinked, staring at Becky.

I turned, starting to shift one of the piles of laundry and other clutter from one side of the sofa, then froze.

On a small table next to the sofa's arm, something metallic caught my eye from among the plates of stale food and half-drunk cups of tea.

I picked it up, all the fine hair on the back of my neck prickling.

The item inside was made of metal, and heavy in my hand. A sixteen-pointed Brunswick star topped with a crown and blazoned with Queen Victoria's initials in the center.

I was holding the helmet plate from a London Metropolitan Police constable's uniform.

Before I could move, the cottage's front door flew open, hard enough to bang against the wall.

Chief Constable Slade stood in the doorway, glaring, his face so dark with fury I had to check the instinct to take a step back.

"What do you think you're doing here?"

Mrs. Slade sprang to her feet.

"William!" Where her voice had been dully choked with grief just a few moments ago, she now spoke with a sharp edge. "Not in front of the little girl! What are you thinking? You'll frighten her!"

The chief constable gaped at his wife in astonishment.

"It's all right." I was still holding the brass helmet plate, but I palmed it, keeping it unseen as I stepped forward. "It was really you I wished to speak to, Chief Constable. Maybe we could talk outside? Or in the station next door?"

Mrs. Slade frowned, her mouth turning downwards in a stubborn line. "Let the child stay, at least." She turned to Becky. "If you'd like to?"

Becky gave me a questioning glance, and I nodded.

"Yes, thank you," Becky said.

"Good." Mrs. Slade turned to a messy writing table that stood against one wall and started to shift some of the piles of papers. "I know I have a book of paper dolls here somewhere."

Chief Constable Slade closed his mouth with a click. Muscles played in his jaw as he turned back to me. "Outside." His voice was a rough growl. "*Now.*"

LUCY

32. A LINK TO LONDON

Chief Constable Slade's brows formed an almost perfectly horizontal slash across his forehead.

"I should lock you up for obstruction of justice and tampering with evidence."

We were next door to the Slades' cottage, seated in the low-ceilinged main room that served as the police station's central office.

Chief Constable Slade sat at his desk, glowering down at the sheaf of papers I had given him. "No matter *whose* daughter you are."

I had come to Shellingford prepared to encounter something along these lines. In addition to the suicide note from Lord Lynley, the chief constable was glaring down at a notarized document from Inspector Lestrade of Scotland Yard, as well as a letter from Holmes himself, identifying me and issuing a request—or knowing Holmes, closer to an order—that I be given every assistance in my investigation into Alice Gordon's disappearance.

"You could certainly do that," I said. "But then I would immediately send a telegraph message to Scotland Yard, and you would have to explain to them, and not just to me, why and how you're being blackmailed into turning a blind eye to the opium smuggling that's been going on at this port."

Chief Constable Slade's head snapped up, his mouth opening and closing before he managed to force words out. "What—how—"

"I assume the opium is being smuggled in to avoid the cost of import taxes," I said. "Otherwise, the business would be legal. Dirty and morally reprehensible, but completely within the bounds of the law. Which would mean there would be no need to bother with blackmailing the local law enforcement officer."

Slade continued to stare at me, his eyes bulging.

I held up the London Police helmet plate that I'd found in his living room. "You would also have to explain how and why you came to be in possession of part of a dead policeman's uniform."

The color drained from his face, leaving it ashen, with unhealthy blotches in his cheeks. He hardened his jaw. "That doesn't prove anything—"

"My own husband is a police officer with Scotland Yard." Despite his bluster, I could see the underlying fear in the chief constable's manner. I tried to speak gently. "I know what the uniform looks like. I also know that this number—" I rubbed my thumb across the row of numbers at the bottom of the plate "—is the particular identification number of Inspector John Swafford, who was found murdered down at the Docklands in London less than a week ago. He was promoted through the ranks and no longer wore the constable's uniform. But I have a photograph of him soon after he joined the force, wearing a helmet with this exact number on it."

Chief Constable Slade took several shallow rapid breaths, but he didn't speak.

I kept going, shifting my hand just slightly so that it was within easy reach of the Ladysmith I had in my bag.

I might feel horribly sorry for Slade and his wife. But I'd also known men to commit murder with far less motive than the chief constable had, and I didn't want the engraving on my tombstone to read, *Here lies Lucy Kelly. She was sympathetic but stupid.*

"Was Inspector Swafford here? Did he find out about the smuggling?"

"No!" His voice burst out, hoarse and desperate. "What you're really asking is whether or not I killed him." He pinched the bridge of his nose, shutting his eyes. "I didn't. As God's my witness, I didn't kill him. Inspector Swafford was never here. I never even laid eyes on him. But I'm afraid—" He took a shuddering breath. "I'm afraid I may have sent his brother to his death."

LUCY

33. A THREAT

I faced the chief constable across the desk between us. "Why don't you tell me exactly what happened?"

Slade swallowed, mopping his forehead with a handkerchief. When he spoke, his voice was low and uneven, but he seemed to have made up his mind to speak freely.

"A man came to see me last week. He said his name was Tom Swafford, and he'd been a seaman on some of the ships that had put into harbor here."

"Some of the ships that imported smuggled opium?"

Slade's head dipped in a short, jerky nod. "That's it. He'd started off as a seaman, then gotten sucked into the business of selling the dirty stuff—bringing it down to London to distribute."

I thought of the three opium ships from India that had been—supposedly—lost at sea. "But then he thought to cut himself in on a bigger share of the profits?"

The chief constable nodded again. "He managed to get his hands on some extra cargo. He didn't give me all the details. But he'd planned on selling it. Only his employers—the ones running the trade up here—got wind of it and didn't take kindly to being robbed. Tried to have him killed—knifed—down on the London Streets. He showed me the marks on his back. He barely got away with his life. That's what sent him to his brother."

"Inspector John Swafford, of Scotland Yard?"

Slade's throat bobbed as he swallowed again. "Yes. His brother—Inspector John Swafford—wanted to protect Tom from going to prison. He said he couldn't be seen to help him, not without losing his own place on the police force. He came up here with Tom just after Christmas, though he wouldn't show himself—had Tom give me a letter and the badge off of his helmet as proof Tom was telling the truth. John said he was going back to London, but he wanted to break up the smuggling ring at both ends—here and in London. And I thought—" His voice cracked. "I thought that maybe this was my chance to break free. If the London police wanted to get involved, maybe there was a way to cut the smuggling ring off at the root without any of the blame falling on me. Without any harm coming to Emily."

The chief constable's voice had turned almost pleading, but then he shook his head, a quick spasm twisting the corners of his mouth. "I told Tom he could sleep in the cells back there at night for safety." The chief constable nodded towards a door at the back of the room. "Then in the morning he could go down to the harbor and put out the word that he had some opium for sale. I told him I'd protect him. I said that either I or Constable Meadows would be watching at all times. He said he'd take me up on it, that he'd be back to spend the night in a cell. He just wanted to go out for a bit. But he didn't come back. He just disappeared." Slade's face worked. "I never saw him again."

I took a breath. I could have filled an entire telephone directory with the questions I had. But one took priority.

"Did you somehow suggest to Lady Lynley that she consult me about Alice Gordon's disappearance?"

Slade's head snapped up and he stared at me all over again. "But what—how did you—"

"It's too much of a coincidence otherwise. That I should happen to be called into a case in the exact location of the spot where Tom Swafford—the brother of a man whose murder my father is investigating—disappeared."

The chief constable ran both hands across his face, his breath going out in a shaky rush.

"I heard that Alice Gordon had gone missing."

I frowned. "Lady Lynley said that she hadn't reported the matter to the police."

Chief Constable Slade snorted, sounding momentarily less desperate and more like he must have done before this nightmare had come into his life. "Lady Lynley doesn't remember that the sky is blue half the time."

"She's in the habit of taking laudanum as well?" I was fairly certain I already knew the answer.

"That's how she and my wife got acquainted. Of course, Lady Lynley's too grand a lady to do her own shopping at Seewald's, but I heard His Lordship was determined to get her to give up the habit, too. Cut off her spending money and ordered the servants not to buy it for her. So she got desperate. Used to get my Emily to buy her an extra bottle, then come around here to collect it." He took a breath. "I heard her, a couple of months back, sitting right there in my front room and prattling on about a friend of hers who'd had the good luck to meet the daughter of Sherlock Holmes. Then last week, when Tom Swafford came to see me, he was talking about his brother, who was such an important man at Scotland Yard that he was looking into a case for the great Sherlock Holmes himself—involving diamond smuggling, no less. And when Alice Gordon went missing—"

"So you had your wife remind Lady Lynley that she knew someone with a connection to Holmes," I finished for him.

Slade looked at me, his eyes bleak. "I thought … I don't know what I thought." He scrubbed his hands down his face. "I knew it was a long chance at best, but I hoped maybe Mr. Holmes himself would be interested enough to come up here. But now I've dragged you into this. You and the little girl—"

"You, yourself, don't know who is behind the opium smuggling?"

He shook his head. "I know the filthy stuff's coming in through our port here. But my hands are tied."

"Because of your wife?" I asked.

The chief constable's gaze went involuntarily to the station house window. Through a side window into the cottage next door, I could see Becky sitting with Mrs. Slade and cutting paper doll clothes from a book.

A spasm of pain twisted Chief Constable Slade's rugged face. "Yes. I suppose you heard our daughter died a year ago last fall. Emily's … she's not been right, ever since. But when it first happened, she was half out of her head with grief. Wouldn't eat. Couldn't sleep. The doctor gave her something to help her rest at night."

"Laudanum."

The chief constable tipped his chin. "Yes. It seemed to help—at first. But now—" He shook his head, swallowing. "About the same time that our Amelia died, I got wind of the smuggling that was going on. Ships that were being loaded or unloaded in the dead of night, and workers bribed to keep quiet about what they carried. Harbor officials taking pay not to ask too closely what was in certain crates or barrels. I started to look into it." He stopped, rubbing a hand across his neck. "It's not just the ladies who get into the habit of taking the stuff. There's even more with the laudanum habit down at the docks, among the porters. They carry those heavy loads all day, get hurt sometimes—or just strain their backs and arms. They want to take something for the aches and pains, and the laudanum's ready at hand, cheaper even than turning to drink. Seewald sees to that. He gives them their first few bottles for mere pennies—then, once they've got the habit formed and can't stop, he starts cranking up the price."

"And you received word that if you continued to investigate, your wife's laudanum addiction would prove fatal." I didn't even make it a question.

Chief Constable Slade's shoulders slumped. "That's exactly what happened. I got a note—no name, no address—saying that if I didn't stop looking too closely into what didn't concern me, my wife's medicine would get a new ingredient added to it, one that would put her to sleep permanently." His voice turned ragged. "I've tried everything. Talking to Emily. Begging her to give it up. I thought of sending her to Ming's, but she wouldn't go."

I frowned. "Ming's?"

"Lord Lynley's business partner. A Chinese fellow who specializes in Oriental medicine. He runs a clinic out at his place, a mile or two outside the village. Helps people to get over their addictions, weans them off the habit."

That tallied with Kai-chen having warned me away from Mr. Seewald's bottle of tonic.

Slade dragged a hand across his face. "I thought maybe he could help Emily, but she refused flat-out to even consider the idea." He shook his head. "I've gotten to the point of spying on my own wife—setting my own constable to keep a watch on her, stopping her from going to Seewald's." His mouth twisted. "You saw how well that went. I know you were there, in Seewald's shop yesterday. I remember seeing you. That's why I was so angry seeing you next door with Emily. Thought you were someone Seewald had sent to sell her more of the stuff."

The raw misery in his eyes made anger burn its way through me. Whoever was behind this wasn't just selling drugs, they were feeding, parasite-like, off of other people's grief and pain.

"Do you think Mr. Seewald is the one behind it all?" I asked.

"I don't know." He seemed to debate for a moment, glancing down again at the letters on his desk from both Lestrade and Holmes. Then he looked back at me. "I suppose you may as well know, I found this on my desk this morning."

He reached into his pocket and drew out a single sheet of paper. I mentally ticked off the characteristics: medium grade paper and a, cheap watermark, the kind that could be purchased at any stationer's shop in England.

The words on it had been formed in straight block capitals, the individual lines obviously made with the edge of a ruler.

Lord Lynley died of suicide. If you know what's good for you and your wife, you'll leave it at that.

I studied the letters. Unfortunately, the effort to disguise the handwriting had been effective. I leaned towards thinking that the note had been written by a man, but I was only about sixty percent sure.

"Have you contacted Lady Lynley?" I asked. "The last

I heard, she was still in London."

Chief Constable Slade shook his head. "I've sent a telegram to the club where she's supposed to be staying, got the address from the butler at Lynley House. But I haven't heard anything back yet."

He tapped his fingers against the suicide note I'd found in Lord Lynley's offices the night before, and I mentally re-read it, running over the typewritten lines.

Something about it still bothered me, but my mind was spectacularly unhelpful in identifying what that something was.

"Is that His Lordship's signature?" I asked.

Lord Lynley might not be the man in charge of the smuggling operation, but he might still have been involved. In which case, he could have first set fire to his warehouse the night before, then taken his own life out of shame, just as the note said.

"Looks like it. I'm no expert, but it looks like his." Slade shook his head. "Poor blighter was obviously in a state when he wrote it."

I nodded, eying the shaky writing on the signature, the way the pen had dug into the paper. That was a point in favor of believing that the note was genuine. Faking a signature was comparatively easy. Faking the *emotion* behind a piece of handwriting was far harder.

"I'll tell you this, though," Slade went on. "Something's changed lately."

"Changed? How so?"

"More ships coming in at the dead of night. More of those so-called spa weekends at the Grand Hotel, with people of all sorts coming and staying."

"You think that may be how the opium is being distributed

to other parts of the country?"

Chief Constable Slade nodded heavily. "I'm almost sure it is. Though whether or not that means that Mr. Torrance is the man on top—" He stopped and shook his head.

For all his false smiles, I wasn't sure that I could see Mr. Torrance as a master criminal. I could, though, imagine him shooting another man in the head with very little difficulty.

I debated, then made up my mind. "Where is Mr. Ming?"

"Ming." The chief constable exhaled hard, a sharp burst of air. "I know. I should be the one speaking to him. He might know more about whether His Lordship really was mixed up in the opium trade. But I'm afraid if I start asking questions—"

His jaw tightened.

He didn't need to finish. If he gave even a sign that he was looking into the murky details surrounding Lord Lynley's death, his wife could die. *Would* die. The forces behind this had already proven themselves more than willing to commit murder.

"I'll go."

Chief Constable Slade made a brief, jerky movement. "You shouldn't do that. It's not safe—"

"Nothing about this affair is safe. Which is why I plan on being extremely careful."

The chief constable was right, actually. Much as I usually disagreed on principle with anyone who warned me away from danger.

We had passed the point where I could safely keep on investigating this affair alone—at least, so long as I was on my own here with Becky. Sometime today I would have to decide whether we should even remain here in Shellingford.

But the fact that Inspector Swafford's brother had been here a week ago meant that I had to report everything I could learn about this matter to Holmes—and he would need as much of a complete picture as I could give.

Chief Constable Slade gave way. "Fine. I can give you the address easy enough, but I wish you good luck. I've never gotten Ming to speak to me. Never so much as seen his face. He won't see anyone directly—it's all through his right-hand man, Kai-chen."

"I've met Kai-chen." I glanced at the cottage next door. "If it's all right with Becky, would you mind my leaving her here while I go and speak to them?"

I hadn't yet mentioned it to the chief constable, but if Mr. Ming was on a crusade to stamp out opium addiction, and if he'd recently discovered that his own business partner was bringing it into the country …

Then it wasn't only the mastermind behind the opium smuggling who would have had a clear and powerful motive for Lord Lynley's murder.

Chief Constable Slade followed my gaze, staring through the window at his wife, who was helping Becky to dress one of the paper dolls. There was so much love and desperation and longing in his expression that it was almost painful to see.

He cleared his throat. "Let the little girl stay as long as you like. That's the happiest I've seen Emily look in months." Then he dragged his gaze away from the window and turned back to me. "Be careful. Whoever's behind this, they're planning something—something big. I'd say Alice Gordon got in their way somehow, and now Lord Lynley, too. Just …"

His voice trailed off and he shook his head. "Just be careful, that's all."

34. A TRUSTED POLICEMAN

The cold wind from the Thames stung my face as we journeyed from our Baker Street rooms to Scotland Yard, and I was grateful to take shelter in the grandly towered brick and stone headquarters of the Metropolitan Police, recently built beside the broad and equally grand Queen's Walkway along the river. We had come to visit Jack Kelly, the former police constable who, after a series of promotions and adventures with us, was now a sergeant and Holmes's son-in-law.

Jack could be trusted. There was no possible doubt on that score.

Holmes announced our arrival to the patrolman on duty. We were admitted at once—such being the reputation of Holmes.

I felt a pang of sympathy for young Jack Kelly when we found him at his desk, for though he was intent on the papers spread out before him, he looked worn and preoccupied. I realized that this must be because, for the time being, he had lost the company of Lucy and Becky, and that he did not know how the litigation instituted by Becky's natural father would affect her future.

"Have you heard from Lucy?" he asked.

"A telegram. Said only that she arrived safely. You?"

"The same. But you did not come all the way to Scotland Yard to tell me that."

"I came to go over the facts in the Swafford and Janine murder cases, and to ask for your assistance."

Young Kelly stood. "It will be quieter over here," he said, leading us to a small interview room. We sat at the table and Jack closed the door.

"So, here are the facts," Holmes began. "There is a large quantity of stolen opium hidden somewhere, in a location not known to me. Swafford's brother found it and brought a small portion to London. The two brothers left London on Christmas Day. Swafford returned to London this past Monday, the day Thomas Newman was convicted. Thursday, he attempted to sell part of the opium and was killed in Limehouse. A day later, Swafford's fiancée, who had not seen him since Christmas Eve, was notified of his death. She and her mother went to a church nearby, presumably to pray, and both women were murdered. A card implicating Thomas Newman was found with their bodies. The church is located not far from where Swafford lived, and where Swafford's brother brought the opium."

"Did you speak with Newman?"

"We did. He denies any involvement."

"No surprise there."

"There is one more pertinent fact. Miss Janine was my client. She had become alarmed at Swafford's absence and she approached me on the street after Newman's trial, hoping to enlist my help in locating him. I was likely seen speaking with her. It may be that her association with me led to her murder."

"You couldn't have avoided that. Not if she approached you."

"Nevertheless, she was my client, and she was killed." Holmes shook his head. "But my feelings are irrelevant. I should like you to hear a hypothesis that fits the facts as stated. If you have other facts that corroborate or clash, I should like to hear them."

"Of course."

"I believe that the person or persons behind the murders are those who possess the stolen opium. They have it safely hidden, and it is a vast quantity—I am told six thousand is the number of chests that are missing and are now presumed stolen. Each chest is the size of a seaman's trunk."

"Hard to relocate that many."

"A daunting and difficult enterprise, particularly when secrecy must be observed. So Inspector Swafford had to be killed."

"On the assumption that he knew the location."

"Then his fiancée also had to die, on the assumption that Swafford had told her the location."

"Once she learned of his death, the natural thing would be for her to tell the authorities all she knew."

"Now she cannot."

"And you said the card at the church implicated Newman."

"He denies it."

"He would."

"He maintains that the owners of the opium hired a rival gang."

"Any gang in particular?"

"He would not say. But I think he would know. He appears to be regularly informed. I saw many entries on the visitors' docket that included his name."

"Maybe the police will get him to talk."

"Possibly," Holmes said.

"Well, for what it's worth, your hypothesis all makes sense to me."

"Thank you. Now I should like to see Mr. Newman again tomorrow. Perhaps I can induce him to say something that will help us. It would be helpful to examine the police file kept on Newman. Can you get it?"

"I can arrange for you to see the log at Newgate. Limehouse Station will have the complete file. We only have the summary here. We could ask Inspector Plank to send over the full record."

"I have particular reasons for not involving Inspector Plank," Holmes said.

Briefly, Holmes described the incident at the Red Dragon and his conclusion that Plank, for whatever reason, had falsified the attack on his person.

"I'll get our file on Newman," Jack said.

A few minutes later Holmes had examined the summary file, put it aside, and stood. "There is one thing more," Holmes said. "Swafford's brother."

Jack eyed Holmes carefully. "Are you getting at something?"

"As I mentioned, Swafford and his brother left London on Christmas Day. Both men were from Shellingford."

Jack let out a long breath. "Where Lucy is. With Becky."

"Swafford told his landlady that he and his brother were going home for the holiday."

"And only Swafford came back, so his brother may have stayed. And Lucy and Becky are nearby. And it is a small town."

Holmes stood. "This is a particularly dangerous affair, and we have very few among us who we can trust. When you hear from Lucy, I urge you to bid her to take extreme caution."

35. AN INTERVIEW WITH KAI-CHEN

Chief Constable Slade's directions led me back into the town, but away from the town's center and down a narrow side-street, little more than an alley, that ran between the butcher's shop and a dressmaker's.

I scanned the numbers above the doorways until I reached a door that, unlike all the others in the street, was painted a bright, brilliant red.

A sign emblazoned with the design of a Chinese-style golden dragon hung over the doorway, with Chinese characters above. Below, English lettering more prosaically announced, *Tea Room*.

A faint, musical chime sounded as I pushed the door open and entered.

The interior was dimly-lit, with heavy embroidered curtains at the windows. Chinese lanterns made of red paper hung from the ceiling. Low tables had been set up here and there, though there were no chairs, only silk cushions on the thickly carpeted floor.

The air was filled with an exotic, faintly dusty odor, and an air of almost reverent stillness filled the room, as though we had stepped back in time—or at least, stepped entirely out of England.

The walls were lined with shelves, some holding canisters of what must be tea leaves, others holding what looked like antiquities: a laughing Buddha made of pale cream-colored ivory; a bronze dagger with a curved blade. A wooden screen made from what looked like cinnabar stood against one wall, its surface carved with flowers and swirling vines.

I stepped closer to the nearest shelf, studying a set of figures: two tiny bronze men seated at a bronze table, with some sort of a game board between them. Miniscule bronze cups, for tea or maybe wine, sat near the figures' hands.

At the back of the room, a beaded curtain parted, and Kai-chen stepped into the room.

He drew in a sharp breath at the sight of me, although the expression of surprise instantly flattened into one of calm scrutiny. "Burial art," he said. He gestured to the bronze game players I had been studying. "From the Zhou period. Placed in the tombs of the dead to ensure the deceased would have friends in the next world, to share and enjoy all the same pleasures they experienced in life." His voice was even, but I thought there was a slight twist of bitterness to the set of his mouth as he added, "If only true friendship were as easily found as that."

"They're lovely," I said.

Kai-chen's dark eyes continued to regard me. "You are carrying a firearm. Are you expecting to have to shoot me?"

I *was* keeping my hand free to reach for the Ladysmith if need be. But it was unusual to find anyone besides Holmes or Jack who could read body language to that degree. Whatever else Kai-chen might be, he was neither stupid nor unobservant.

"I'm hoping not to. But I have a limit on one near-death experience per twenty-four-hour period, and last night's escapade in the warehouse fulfilled that quota."

A small smile might have tipped up one corner of Kai-chen's mouth, but his gaze remained impassive.

"We have carried out this exchange once before, have we not? I saved you from the fire. You and the child."

"True. But I would like to know why you sent a box full of poisonous snakes to Lord Lynley through the post."

The shock that crossed Kai-chen's expression was instantly controlled, replaced a second later by the same stony calm. But I had seen it.

"One of the adders must have bitten you. You have the bite marks there, on your wrist." I gestured to the red swelling just visible below the cuff of Kai-chen's sleeve. "I saw them last night, although at the time I thought you'd been burned in the fire."

Kai-chen eyed me. "Why have you come here?"

He made no move to come any closer, but I still stayed within a few steps of the door and kept my gaze on him, watching the way he shifted his weight.

"Unless you actually were the one to shoot Lord Lynley, I want the same thing you do: to find Alice Gordon." Holmes might eschew guesswork in detecting, but I was reasonably sure that my supposition this time was correct. "Is that why you sent the snakes to His Lordship? Because you were hoping to frighten him into telling you what he knows about Alice's disappearance?"

The impassive mask of Kai-chen's face seemed to crack, all of a sudden. "I have been at—what is your English saying?—at my wits' end! Alice is gone. But no one will speak to me. No one will tell me anything."

"Did Lord and Lady Lynley not approve of your relationship with Alice?"

"They did not. Although that is perhaps not so unusual." Bitterness sharpened Kai-chen's tone. "I do not believe you could find a single human being within the entire parish boundaries of Shellingford who would approve of a Chinese man courting an English girl." He smiled without humor. "It is ironic. Had Alice taken up with an English farmer who beat her daily, none of her neighbors would have raised an eyebrow, much less dared to interfere. Yet we must meet in secret for fear of threats and attacks, merely because my eyes are shaped differently from theirs. Alice was afraid to even let Lady Lynley suspect our relationship, for fear that she would lose her position."

"Was she happy in her job with Lady Lynley?"

Kai-chen's chin jutted forward.

When I was at boarding school, one of my classmates had been the daughter of the Chinese ambassador to the United States. I remembered from meeting her parents that the motion was the equivalent of a shrug.

"It was a job," Kai-chen said. "She did not enjoy being at the beck and call of Lady Lynley, who can be unreasonable as well as tyrannical. But she had found no other jobs available to her in this area."

I was silent, deciding how best to phrase the next question. "I'm sorry to ask this, but would she have told you if she had found another job?"

"She would." Kai-chen's answer came instantly, without hesitation. "We love each other, Alice and I. You wonder whether fear of public censure led Alice to run away—to break things off with me. But you do not know her. She would never have done such a thing. We plan to be married, as soon as we have saved enough money between us. Planned." A twist of pain darkened his face. "Something has happened to her. I know it."

I studied his face. I didn't think he was lying.

Although that didn't necessarily signify. The aphorism about love being blind had been coined for a reason, and just because he believed Alice was brave enough to defy public convention by marrying him didn't necessarily mean that she would have gone through with it.

On the other hand, the Lady Lynley's of the world couldn't and probably would never believe that I would be happy married to Jack and I'd never cared even a little.

"How did you and Alice meet?" I asked.

"Alice was concerned for her mistress. She wished to help her overcome her addiction. We began substituting tonics with a lower and lower portion of the laudanum, so that her system might be gradually purged from the drug."

"Was Lord Lynley aware of what you were doing?"

Something hard flickered briefly at the back of Kai-chen's eyes. Anger? Contempt? It was gone too quickly for me to be sure. "I do not think that Lord Lynley was aware of very much beyond the running of his estate, the drainage of his ditches—and perhaps the balance of his bank accounts. Alice was trying to help her mistress to become free of the drug. But now—" His voice cracked, and his hands clenched on the edge of the table.

"But now Alice has gone missing," I finished for him. "And

Lord Lynley is dead."

"I did not kill him!" Kai-chen burst out. "Why would I have killed him, when I still know nothing of where Alice is or what may have happened to her?"

"You think that Lord Lynley hurt her—or frightened her into running away?"

"I do not know." Kai-chen's voice trembled briefly. "I was at the warehouse last night. Since Lord Lynley would not speak to me, I had hoped to go through the papers there, searching for something—anything—that might give a hint of what had happened to Alice. But then I smelled smoke, and when I let myself in through the rear entrance, I found the place on fire. The rest you know."

I watched his face. "So you were never in the office? You didn't see Lord Lynley's body?"

"Until you spoke to me outside, I had no idea that His Lordship was inside the warehouse, much less dead." Kai-chen swallowed, frowning. "You still have not told me who you are or what you are doing in Shellingford. You surely are not with the police?"

"Not officially. But I did come here to investigate Alice's disappearance."

Kai-chen's gaze rested on me, and then his lips quirked up in a momentary twist of a smile. "You still do not trust me."

"Probably about as much as you trust me. For example, you haven't yet mentioned that you suspected Lord Lynley of smuggling opium in on his ships. Or that right now, your employer Mr. Ming is currently listening to every word of our conversation from the other side of that doorway." I gestured to the beaded curtain.

36. TEA WITH MR. MING

Kai-chen drew back, his expression shocked.

"The beads were swaying when we came in—which could have just been from you coming through. But they've clicked together twice so far while we were talking."

Kai-chen started to shake his head. "I do not—"

"Calm yourself, Kai-chen." The hanging curtain of beads parted, and a man's slender figure stepped through.

Mr. Ming was small, his back bowed, his narrow shoulders bent with age. His hair was gray and pulled into a long braid that hung down his back. Unlike Kai-chen, he wore wide-legged black silk trousers and a black brocade tunic, embroidered with what looked like gold thread.

"I am Ming Donghai." His voice was soft, cultured, with an oddly dry quality that somehow made me think of ancient parchment, so fragile that it would crumble at the slightest touch. He faced me, bowing slightly. "I apologize for not making my presence known from the beginning."

As he spoke, he stepped further into the light filtering through the windows and raised his head.

The glimpse I'd already had of his face had led me to brace myself, but I still had to swallow a sharply indrawn breath.

His face was twisted by thick, ropy scars that obscured nearly the whole of one cheek, making his left eye droop and turning the corner of his lip down. From the way he held his left arm bent, pulled protectively in to his body, I would guess that it was disfigured, possibly even crippled.

"I have discovered that in general it is more prudent to stay out of sight and allow Kai-chen to do the speaking for me." Mr. Ming's voice was level, but his black eyes were hard. "I find it preferable to women and children screaming about monsters and running away."

"Shakespeare said that one may smile, and smile and be a villain. But then he also made Richard II as monstrous in appearance as possible." I shrugged. "In my experience, that's roughly accurate. Beautiful or ugly, most people have about a fifty percent chance of turning out to be evil."

Beneath the scars, something about Mr. Ming's steady, impassive expression suggested that very little could shock or surprise him. But at that, his brows hitched up a degree.

"Remarkable," he murmured.

He turned to Kai-chen. "You have been remiss in not offering our guest any refreshment. Bring tea, please."

Kai-chen bowed, answering in a flood of rising and falling Chinese before hurrying to the back of the shop.

Mr. Ming's brocaded robes caught the light as he stepped forward. He wore rope-soled sandals, and yet his footsteps made almost no noise at all. He studied me a moment, his head tilted a little to the side.

"You are not English, I believe?"

"My father is English, my mother is Italian, and I was brought up in America. I am whatever that makes me."

"Ah, America." With an almost mercurial change of expression, Mr. Ming's scarred face brightened, the undamaged side of his mouth lifting in a sudden, beaming smile. "I have never been to that country, but I like what I have heard of it very much. A land of opportunity, where all may strive with equal chance for a better life. Is this not so? 'Give me your tired, your poor, your huddled masses yearning to breathe free.'"

"Well, theoretically." You could probably find every bit as much wretchedness, poverty, prejudice and general misery in New York City as you could in London.

Mr. Ming sighed. "Ah yes. The reality so often fails to live up to the ideal. Still, ideals are a fine thing to have. Despite everything, I hold to that belief."

He moved forward, folding his legs under him and seating himself opposite me at the low table with the flexible ease of a much younger man.

He stretched out his good hand in invitation, his face splitting in another wide smile. "Please. Be seated."

I hesitated, then took the cushion opposite his, curling my legs under me.

"You have questions you wish to ask?" Mr. Ming asked.

"I do. If you don't mind."

"Certainly, certainly!" Mr. Ming waved his good hand in an expansive gesture, still beaming. He looked like a scarred, older version of a laughing buddha statue I had once seen. "So long as you do not expect me to answer them if I do not choose to do so."

Right. I studied the man in front of me, considering my first question.

"You are in the business of curing people of their addiction to laudanum and other opiates?"

Kai-chen reappeared, carrying a bamboo tea tray which he set down on the table in front of us. The teapot and cups were porcelain, and like everything else in the shop, exquisitely made. The teapot had been painted with the design of a red and gold dragon, the handle made to look like the swirl of the dragon's tail. The dragon's eyes—inlaid gleaming enamel—peered at me from the lid of the pot.

"Ah. In order to fully answer that, one must go back many years in time," Mr. Ming said. "You are perhaps familiar with the conflicts known as … I believe you may call them the China Wars? Or possibly the Opium Wars?"

"Only slightly." I did remember them being more or less a textbook illustration of the maxim that *might makes right*.

Mr. Ming picked up the teapot and poured a thin stream of pale-amber-colored tea into my cup. "It was the Portuguese who first entered the business of bringing Opium from India into China, to sell. In 1729 so many of the populace were addicted that it became a tremendous drain, a cancer on our society. The emperor outlawed both the sale and the smoking of opium, but it did not end there."

Mr. Ming now spoke with a dry, emotionless precision that would have rivaled Holmes's capacity for sterile narration.

"You must understand that the British trade relationship with China was unequal in the extreme. Our emperors—the Quing dynasty—believed that our country provided everything that we needed; we had no need to import goods from the British. What use have we for British woolens, when we create the finest silks? And yet the English were obsessed with our tea. They could not import it fast enough or in enough quantities to satisfy the demand. So the British were importing more and more of our goods—and because they could not trade for them, they were forced to pay in silver. Then at last, someone in Britain had the ingenious idea to use opium in order to open the Chinese market and allow the balance of trade to tip in their favor. Because, of course, the opium supply comes from an English colony—that is to say, India." Mr. Ming paused to take a sip of his tea. "The English merchants and traders who came to China even went so far as to offer free samples, in an effort to create as many addicts as possible, and thus generate a demand for their filthy trade."

The full facts were even worse than I remembered.

Reading my expression, Mr. Ming gave me another of his sudden wide smiles. "Yes. It is terrible, as so much of history is. But do not grieve yourself. On the other side of suffering comes wisdom, which is the cause of true and lasting joy." He stopped to pour more tea, first into my cup then into his own. "As I was saying, we have an expression in my country. *Kǒu mì fù jiàn*, which means 'mouth of honey, heart of daggers.' That describes the British who came to our shores. My own father became an addict. He would not eat, he would not rise to see to his business or the education of his sons. He was fit for nothing but to sit in the sun and smoke his opium pipe. He died a skeleton of a man. Our family estates were lost. I was impressed into the army. We Chinese wished to stop the flow of this poisoned drug into our country. Britain's merchants wished the trade to continue. There was, as I say, a great deal of money to be made. So Britain and her allies eventually went to war—twice—to force the drug upon us, to force us to sign treaties that would allow their trade to go on. That is how I came by the burns, the scars of which you see." He gestured to the disfigured side of his face.

I watched his expression as he spoke. I would have expected anger or grief—or some sign that he was stoically expressing either outrage or pain.

But Mr. Ming was smiling as though he were describing a particularly pleasant birthday memory from childhood, involving ice cream and frosted cakes.

He tilted his head on one side. "You doubt that I can speak of it so easily?"

He was also nearly as adept as Holmes at deducing people's thoughts from their expressions.

I chose my words carefully. "I think that if I were you, it would take a very great deal of joyful wisdom to make up for a story like that."

"Ah, you *lo-fan*—you Americans." Mr. Ming made a scolding gesture with one finger, like a benevolent grandfather chastising a wayward child. "So bound by the chains of the quantifiable— weights and measures and inches. So unwilling to be ruled by anything other than your own reason and logic."

If I were actually ruled by my own reason and logic, I wouldn't be here on my own, talking to a man I suspected of murder.

I gave Mr. Ming a polite smile. "Perhaps. But I do know enough Chinese to know that *lo-fan* doesn't mean 'Americans.' It's an insult—roughly the equivalent of 'barbarians.'"

Mr. Ming tipped back his head and laughed with what sounded like genuine amusement. "We have another saying— a story, rather. A great philosopher lived alone in a small temple in the country. One day four traveling monks appeared and asked if they might make a fire in his yard to warm themselves. While they were building the fire, this teacher heard them arguing about subjectivity and objectivity. He joined them and said, 'Observe that large stone over there. Do you consider it to be inside or outside your mind?' One of the monks replied, 'Everything is an objectification of mind; therefore, the stone also is inside my mind.' 'Your head must feel very heavy,' observed the teacher, 'if you are carrying around a stone like that in your mind.' "

I studied him, considering my next question.

I had in the course of my investigations with Holmes met people of all types and from all walks of life, from street prostitutes to royalty, and almost everything in between. I couldn't, though, recall ever having so little an idea of what to make of someone as I had with Mr. Ming.

"And now that you have begun a crusade of curing opium addiction in others, you are being targeted for intimidation by those who promote its import?" I finally asked.

Mr. Ming's smile didn't falter, but his gaze registered surprise.

"At least three panes of glass in the windows in this shop have been broken and replaced in the last three months," I said. "You can tell by the glazing—it's a lighter color than the older panes."

Mr. Ming brought his hands together and gave a bow, inclining just his head. "Remarkable! Yes, truly remarkable." His good eye crinkled at the edge. "You are very observant. What you say is true. In addition to this tea house, I run a clinic not far from here, where I attempt to help those who have become addict. Without wishing to sound … what is the word? Ah, yes, grandiose. Without wishing to sound grandiose, it is my calling: to fight with my utmost devotion and dedication to see that no more lives are ruined, as so many of my countrymen's lives were taken by the drug. However, all good deeds come with a cost. As the British found, the business of opium trade is an immensely profitable one. Anyone who threatens to diminish those profits inevitably becomes a target—whether one is an entire nation or a single, poor individual."

"But you don't know who is responsible for harassing you?"

Mr. Ming lifted his teacup in his good hand, his expression serene. "We do not."

I waited, but he said nothing more.

I looked from Kai-chen to Mr. Ming. "It is possible, isn't it, that Alice Gordon might have been hurt or kidnapped as another effort at intimidation?"

I saw Kai-chen's hands clench at his sides, but he remained silent.

Mr. Ming studied me before speaking almost gently. "You are intelligent, as well as observant. It is possible. But if the girl Alice had been harmed—or even kidnapped—as a means of intimidation, then surely we would have received some message to that effect. And no message has come."

I glanced at Kai-chen, but though his hands were still balled in fists, his shoulders slumped with defeat. "Mr. Ming is right. No such message has come."

Mr. Ming studied me again. "You have another question you wish to ask, I think."

If he gave me a straight answer, it would be a first for this conversation, but I still said, "Did you know or suspect that Lord Lynley was using your shared importing business to bring opium into this country?"

Mr. Ming took a long moment before speaking. Then at last he gave me another serene smile. "When I was a boy, I learned an ancient story about a silkworm and a spider, both of whom spun silk. One day the spider said to the silkworm, 'I admit that your silk is of a superior quality to that of mine. Yet you use that same silk to spin yourself a beautiful cocoon, then live inside it, falsely believing yourself to be a king. In your little cocoon you wait until the women who weave silk put you in boiling hot water to kill you, and then unwind the threads of your silk cocoon, strand by strand. What a shame, though you have the ability to create such beauty, then die because of it. Is this not stupid?' Then the silkworm, considering what the spider had said, answered, 'We spin silk so that people can weave beautiful brocades which endure for years to come. Look at you spiders; all your efforts at weaving are to create a trap allowing you to catch and eat flies. And for their deaths, you have no regrets.' "

37. NEWGATE, REVISITED

Holmes and I returned to Newgate Prison the morning after our meeting with Jack Kelly. Holmes had spent much of the intervening time out of my company. Today he had obtained a copy of the visitor's log and was prepared, he said, for a more productive interview with Thomas Newman.

The large wall clock at the prison entrance read exactly ten o'clock when we descended the stone steps. The uniformed guard outside the corridor leading to Newman's cell recognized us immediately,

"Just 'ad his breakfast," he said.

"Any visitors today?"

"Just the clergyman." The guard knocked on the metal door. "Your visitors."

There was no answer. The guard opened the small window hatch. "Sleepin', looks like."

"Open the door," Holmes said.

The heavy cell door swung open with a metallic clang to reveal the rotund figure of Thomas Newman lying on his bunk with both hands folded across his belly. A beatific smile softened his pig-like features, as though he were having a beautiful dream.

After a moment, I realized he was not breathing.

Holmes stepped quickly inside the cell and pressed his fingertip beneath the base of Newnan's ear.

"No pulse," he said. "Dr. Watson may wish to verify."

I did so.

As I stood up, I noticed a small piece of paper in Newman's clasped hands. Making certain that Holmes and the guard were watching, I pulled at a corner of the paper. It slipped out easily.

On the paper three words were written in smudged black ink, in the same crude block capitals I had seen on the note found in St. Philip's Church.

This note read: *NOW I'M DONE.*

WATSON

38. INTERVIEW WITH A WIDOW

Two hours later we were stepping out of a police carriage with Lestrade in Clapham Common, at the house where Newman had lived in for the past five years. The dwelling was modest and cottage-like. In the freshly-fallen snow it might have been the model for a children's story illustration. Our constable driver waited with the coach as we walked up the snow-covered front footpath towards the house.

The woman I had seen at the trial opened the door. She wore the same veil I had seen, but it was now draped over her shoulders. She shivered against the cold and looked sharply at Holmes.

"You were at the trial," she said. "And you as well. All three of you testified." Her voice had a soft, fearful quality that made me wonder about her life spent with Newman, who from every outward appearance would have been a brute of a husband. "Not that it matters now."

"We have news of Mr. Newman, Madam," said Lestrade quietly. "May we come in?"

"May as well," she said.

We took off our boots in the vestibule at Holmes's insistence, so as not to track wet snow over her floor and parlor carpet.

We settled ourselves on the upholstered chairs in the small parlor. "You're going to tell me he's dead, aren't you?" she said.

At Lestrade's nod, she gestured towards the dining room, where on the table stood a vase with a huge sprawling bouquet of white lilies. She went on, "Those came just before you did."

Holmes stood and went over to the table. He read the card. " 'We are very sorry for your loss. May his soul rejoice in Heaven with the Almighty God and all His Angels.' It is not signed."

"Delivery man said it was from the church. Like those others on the sideboard that came Friday."

Holmes inspected the other bouquet. "These still look nearly fresh. Do you keep them in your basement at night?"

She shook her head. "I never go down there. I change the water in the vases."

Holmes returned to his seat.

"I am very sorry to disturb you at this difficult time—"

"Oh, you go right ahead, Inspector. I should just like to know one thing before you begin."

"Yes?"

"How did he die?"

"He was found quietly resting on his bunk, his hands clasped, and a note in his hand. The note read 'Now I'm done.' "

She nodded. "Quietly resting, you say?"

"A beatific smile on his face," I put in.

"He told me he hated to be marched about and pushed around. Said that would be the worst thing, getting frog-marched and then having everyone looking at him and he couldn't do nothing but stand there and let them put the noose around his neck. So I'm glad."

"Did he take his own life, do you think?"

"'Course he did. I saw him write the note yesterday afternoon."

"Indeed?" Lestrade's ferret-like features registered astonishment. "You surprise me, madam."

"Why should you be surprised?"

"Because the note greatly resembled another that was found outside the prison."

"A note that said, 'Not done yet'? I saw him write that out, too."

"When was that?" Holmes asked.

"Night before the jury was to do their voting. He kept the paper in his pocket. So he wouldn't forget it, he said. It gave him comfort, knowin' that if the vote went against him, he would be able to remember what to say even if he felt … flustered, like."

"And you were with him yesterday?"

She nodded. "He were all smiles. He said he'd been ready for a month now, little bits of powder, brought in little by little, and now he had plenty, more than enough. He asked for the priest to come in in the morning. He said that would put everything right 'cause he'd be forgiven and shriven and all. I didn't tell him what I thought—well, it weren't my place, were it? He would do what he would do, always would. And God may do whatever he will do, no matter what a priest does or doesn't. Don't you think that's right, Mr. Holmes?"

This was the first time she had addressed Holmes directly.

He met her gaze. "My opinion on theological matters is quite unimportant in the larger scheme of things, Mrs. Newman," he said. "But I should think that any god worthy of the name would be unconstrained by human rituals. Now, may I ask you a question?"

She nodded.

"Was your husband a good provider?"

She made a sweeping gesture at the walls and furniture and the plantings visible outside the window. "You can see it."

"The home is yours?"

"Free and clear. Paid off Monday. I had the letter from the bank. Took it to him yesterday and showed him. We owed eight hundred pounds but now it's mine, free and clear."

"Have you any idea where the funds came from?"

"Thomas said his boys had done a service for a gentleman and this was the payment. Well, part of it—the boys got some, of course."

"Is your son one of the boys?"

"Oh no, Mr. Holmes. He's in the navy, is my young Tom. 'E's a British tar sure enough, an' I'm just as proud—"

For a moment she could not go on. Then she took a small flask from the pocket of her sweater, sipped at it, and then tucked it away. "You say he died peaceful-like?"

"His expression was serene," I said.

"He told me he wanted a proper funeral. Not like he would have had if—"

"I understand," Holmes said. "A proper funeral, with flowers like those." He nodded toward the vases in the dining room.

"Like those."

Holmes stood. "Thank you, Mrs. Newman. We shall not trouble you further at this difficult time."

She saw us to the vestibule where we had left our boots.

Closing the inner door, Holmes whispered to me, "Sit on the

floor while you are putting on your boots, Watson. I need you to take two minutes." Then he quickly slipped on his own pair and went outside.

I sat on the tiled floor of the vestibule and made a show of fumbling at my task, grunting and tugging while Lestrade stared at me. When I judged that two minutes had elapsed, I stood, and said rather loudly, "Whew! Not getting any younger, Lestrade." A moment later we were on Mrs. Newman's front stoop. Holmes was at the back of our police coach, motioning for us to hurry.

We clambered inside. "Scotland Yard," Holmes called to our driver.

"What was that about?" asked Lestrade, when our carriage was moving.

"The missing opium chest is no longer missing," Holmes said. "It is in this coach, but it is empty. I shall explain when we reach Scotland Yard."

Whereupon he sat back, closed his eyes, and was silent for the remainder of our journey.

39. AN UNFORESEEN EVENT

At Scotland Yard, we had the empty opium chest brought up to the interview room. Jack Kelly joined us, at Holmes's request. Lestrade brought in his notes. After comparison with the inscription on the bottom of the chest, Lestrade pronounced the numbers to be a match.

"The same chest," he said. "How did you know it would be at the Newmans's house?"

Holmes shrugged. "It was a combination of good fortune and observation. Outside the house, I saw footprints to and from the rear entrance. Flowers had come just before we arrived. I was curious about the florist, of course, and about the identity of the sender, since we had only an hour earlier discovered that Newman was dead. So I took the opportunity to examine the flowers and to read the card. From the dining room, I had a clear view into the kitchen where I observed still-wet footprints coming from the rear entrance to the home. So the flower delivery man had not troubled to wipe his boots. I was noting that this indicated a certain disregard for Mrs. Newman, or at least carelessness, which might help identify the florist and the sender.

"Then, following the footprints to where they returned to the back entrance, I saw the chest. It was beside the back door. The lid was open, and the chest was being used as a receptacle for Mrs. Newman's boots. I saw the resemblance to the chest we had found at Swafford's. So when we departed, I took my opportunity. I quickly went around to the back of the house and purloined it." Holmes looked at his watch.

"This has been a most instructive morning," he continued. "To take what we have learned today into account I must revise my hypothesis of the case, but only slightly."

"How did the chest come to be at Mrs. Newman's?"

"Let us review once more what we know," said Holmes. "There is a great deal of opium stored somewhere. Hidden away. In thousands of chests similar to this one. The owner of the chests—we will call him 'X'—retained the Bleeders to watch for the missing one in case it made its way to London. They did so. They may have murdered Swafford at the Red Dragon. They followed Swafford's body to St. Thomas, and then followed us from St. Thomas to Swafford's house. They recovered the opium chest and brought it first to the Red Dragon, in order to throw us off the scent, and then to Newman's home, placing the chest in the basement where his wife never goes.

"Shortly thereafter the Bleeders, wanting to be paid, must have given all or most of the opium balls to their client 'X'— possibly through the florist's delivery man, the handover being supervised by one of 'the boys,' as Mrs. Newman calls them. There was a delivery of flowers on Friday, she said. The chest itself would be useless to 'X'—in fact, he would not want to be found with it in his possession. So it was left behind. Mrs. Newman saw it and used it for her boots."

"Do you believe her story that Newman committed suicide?"

"She appeared perfectly sincere. Also, she knew the inscription on the note found at St. Philip's Church."

"How did the note get to St. Philip's?"

"Newman must have given it to one of his visitors—likely the visitor representing 'X,' or possibly 'X' himself."

"Why would 'X' want a note written by Newman found at a murder scene? Clearly Newman was not present."

"It was a message for Newman. It told Newman that 'X' was behind the murder of two innocent women and would not hesitate to murder a third. Newman did care for his wife, as we learned from her today."

"But now we've got a good clue to the identity of 'X,'" said Lestrade. "His name will be on the visitors' log."

"Or the name of his emissary," Jack added.

"Assuming that all Newman's visitors gave truthful names," said Holmes. "You should investigate that line. I also recommend you should investigate the florist, the priest, and—as I mentioned earlier—the guard. Both shifts."

"Someone brought Newman a lethal narcotic," Jack said. "That someone might have a connection to 'X.' He deals in narcotics."

"You're sure it was a narcotic?" Lestrade asked.

"He was not feeling the pain of an ordinary poison as he died," I said, "or the horror caused by a vegetable alkaloid. It was likely an opiate of some sort."

Holmes glanced at his watch again. "Also investigate who paid off the mortgage loan on Newman's house. It will likely have been a cash transaction, but one should at least try."

"Someone may remember someone," said Lestrade. "But

where is the missing hoard of opium? Where are the six thousand chests?" He looked meaningfully at Holmes. "We need to find Swafford's brother. He had to have stolen that chest from somewhere."

"Where was Swafford's brother before he brought the opium to London?" Jack said.

"These are lines of inquiry that show great promise," said Holmes. He stood. "The point I wish to emphasize at the expense of all others," he went on, "is that 'X' may be connected with insurrection against England. We know that last fall the Bleeders were hired to work for Burleigh and Mrs. Scott, the diamond smugglers. As a form of anonymous currency, opium can serve as expediently as diamonds. Internationally, opium can readily be converted to cash and the cash used for the same insurrectionary purposes."

"So the Bleeders may still be working for the insurrectionists they supported in the Ripper affair?"

Holmes nodded. "Watson and I shall leave you with that thought. Now I must pursue my own lines of inquiry."

* * *

Outside Scotland Yard there were several cabs. We chose the third in the rank, following Holmes's usual practice.

"221B Baker Street," he told the driver.

"Newman was more human than I had imagined," I said when we were in the cab.

Holmes said nothing.

"Or at least his wife cared for him," I went on. "And presumably his men were loyal, since they returned all or at least most of the opium to 'X' or his representative. Otherwise, the payment of the loan against Newman's house would not have been made."

Holmes still said nothing. We had slowed in traffic. Then we started again. Then we sped up, making a sharp turn.

Looking outside, I realized we were no longer traveling along the route we had taken to reach home. Holmes had the same realization, for at the same moment, he rapped sharply on the communicating panel at the top of the cab. "Driver!"

The panel opened.

To my shock, a canister dropped from the opening and bounced on the floor of the cab. From the top of the canister a red, smoke-like cloud billowed. I caught the scent of a strange suffocating odor.

Holmes pushed open the door on his side. "Watson, get out!"

I did so, shoving open the door on my side of the cab. We were still moving, and I had difficulty leaping to the ground. I fell and hit my knee, scraping the palms of both my hands on the icy cobblestones.

The pavement wavered in my vision as I staggered upright.

Then a sharp blow struck me on the back of the head.

All went black.

40. A CALL FOR HELP

"Do you think Mr. Ming really might have killed Lord Lynley?" Becky asked.

I had collected her from the Slades' cottage, and now we were back at the hotel, climbing the stairs to our room. "I'm honestly not sure. I don't think he could have actually committed the murder—if it was murder, that is. He's old and crippled. A man of Lord Lynley's size and strength could have overpowered him easily."

I couldn't, though, overlook the possibility that Mr. Ming could have ordered Kai-chen to carry out the killing. But then, Kai-chen's anxiety for Alice and his assertion that Lord Lynley might know what had happened to her had rung true.

We stepped out of the stairwell and onto the second floor. The plushly-carpeted corridor was as deserted as before, without even Bill's uniformed figure in sight.

I glanced down at Becky. Ordinarily—even though she had agreed to have me speak to Mr. Ming on my own—she would have been full of indignation at having missed the interview, and peppered me with questions.

Now, though, her little eyebrows were knitted together, and she looked as though she was barely listening to my answers.

"Are you thinking about Mrs. Slade?" As we'd left, Mrs. Slade had begged Becky to come back and visit her again.

But Becky shook her head. "No." She twitched her shoulders, then ran the few steps ahead to the door of our room.

I sighed and followed—though I forgot to worry about Becky at the sight of the two yellow envelopes that had been pushed under the door.

"Telegrams!" Becky pounced on them, sounding much more like herself. "Maybe one of them is from Jack!" She kept hold of one and handed me the other. "Here, I'll open one and you open one!"

I started to tear open the flap on mine, but Becky was first.

"It *is* from Jack!" She scanned the words quickly. "He says everything is all right, but Prince misses me, and—"

I froze, the rest of what Becky was saying washing past me without my absorbing any of the words.

I had opened my own telegraph message, and the relief I had felt at finally hearing from Jack evaporated.

This telegram was signed, *John H. Watson*, and the message read:

Lucy. Come at once, I beg you. Holmes kidnapped.

PART THREE

CUT ADRIFT

41. COUNCILS OF WAR

More than twenty-four hours had elapsed since the attack. My numb, hollow feeling still lingered, although I was determined to discover Holmes's whereabouts and rescue him if necessary. My first thought, of course, was to enlist the aid of Mycroft, Lestrade, Jack, and Lucy, calling them to our Baker Street sitting room.

Lucy and Jack were the last to arrive. I waited as they settled themselves on our sofa.

"Bad business, this," said Lestrade.

"Whoever did this hijacked the cab," Jack said. "But how did they know you were at Scotland Yard?"

"I do not know," I said.

"So you must have been followed."

"Holmes is generally mindful of being followed, though," Lucy said. "And how did they know you were there?" Her voice showed her frustration. She was clearly the one of our number most emotionally affected by Holmes's absence—with the exception of little Becky, who had been struggling to hold back her tears—quite unsuccessfully—when I first saw her, and at the moment was downstairs in the care of Mrs. Hudson.

"Dr. Watson, please tell us exactly what happened," Mycroft said.

I did, going over the entire painful sequence of events, and ending with, "I came to my senses, face-down on the cold, wet pavement. When I looked up, several bystanders were watching me, though they seemed only idlers, acting out of curiosity. The cab was gone. Holmes was gone. When I asked the bystanders, none of them recalled anything. They saw a policeman approaching and drifted away before he could compel them to answer more fully."

"What was the red smoke?"

I had anticipated this question, and had my overcoat waiting, draped over the back of my desk chair. The reddish powder still clung to the wool fabric. I handed it over to Lucy.

"This powder is from a firework," she said. "A smoke bomb like those we use in *The Mikado* to mark the entrance of the Emperor of Japan. I can ask Mr. Ellis where he gets his supplies, but I expect it's common enough so that a particular customer would not be memorable."

"However, the use of an Asian implement is suggestive," Mycroft said. "Given what you have encountered, Lucy."

I felt a great surge of emotion as she raised her brow—the manner of her inquiry reminded me of Holmes.

Mycroft continued, "I refer to your mention of the late Lord Lynley, murdered in Shellingford. The man is, or was, known to me. His father was one of the first shippers of Indian opium from the East India Company to China. He bought the opium from the plantation and shipped it to Hong Kong. There it was sold to another intermediary, who smuggled it into the country. It is illegal in China. Yet the laws are difficult to enforce." Mycroft shook his head in frustration. He clasped his hands and rested them against his capacious waistcoat.

"We should investigate the Red Dragon," Jack said. "Holmes may be held prisoner there."

I felt a surge of revulsion and outrage at the thought of Holmes lying on one of those bunks in the back room of that foul den, insensible, forced to imbibe the foul narcotic fumes. I did not want to think how a prolonged course of that addictive drug might affect his razor-sharp mind, and what dreadful cravings the ordeal might induce, even if we were to recover him safely. Then I recalled Holmes's deductions about the shooting incident we had witnessed at the Red Dragon. "What about Plank?" I asked. "I want to confront him with our suspicions."

"I'll telephone Limehouse Station," Lestrade said. "Plank can meet us at the Red Dragon."

42. CONFRONTATION WITH PLANK

After agreeing to meet Lucy, Jack, and Mycroft at the Diogenes Club at four o'clock to report progress, Lestrade and I set out for Limehouse Basin. We took two constables with us in the police wagon. Last time Plank had brought two constables to the Red Dragon, and Lestrade thought it would be prudent to match forces. The Red Dragon had been the site of one police officer's murder and the attempted murder of a second. Lestrade said he did not want to become the third.

When we arrived, the building looked even shabbier and more downtrodden when viewed in daylight. Another police carriage was waiting on the narrow dock between the wooden structure and the dark waters of the Thames. Plank was inside. He had come with two constables once again. We could see them both on the driver's bench.

Plank got out when he saw our carriage stop. He strode briskly to the weather-beaten door where he had begun his charade the last time I had seen him here. Lestrade told our constables to wait inside the carriage.

We stepped up to face him. Plank was taller than Lestrade by half a foot and taller than me by an inch or two. He looked down to meet our gaze as if he thought his height could intimidate us. His eyes were wide and openly curious, but his stare was harder than mere curiosity. He was wearing a dark wool coat, but it was not the same as the one he had worn the other night. This one had no bullet tear in the shoulder.

"What's this about?" he asked.

"We want to know why you shot yourself," I said.

His eyes stayed fixed, not flinching, but he put on a smile of disbelief. "You're joking," he said.

"No," I said.

"Lestrade," Plank said, "what possessed you to come out here with this man and such an absurd idea?"

Lestrade was silent.

"You can take off your coat and your shirt and show Inspector Lestrade your wound," I said. "You can stand here in front of the door after you've done that. You can trace an angle from the wound on your shoulder, all the way across the river, and you'll be on the other side before you run into anything or anywhere a shooter could have shot from the night you were here with us. And the tide was out that night, which makes it even more impossible for a shot from the river to hit the top of your shoulder. Twenty feet more impossible. You shot yourself before you arrived. We want to know why."

"You're mad," said Plank.

But he did not start a fight. He just stared at me for a long moment, his hand at his chin, fingers rubbing the stubble of his black beard as though he were acting the part of an old man thinking up some words of wisdom. Then he said, "I don't have to listen to this nonsense, Lestrade. If you want to bring some sort of complaint, you know the procedure."

"You'll give us an answer," I said. I moved forward.

But then Plank sidestepped us both, moving nimbly off the entry platform and down to the dock, walking the few paces to his police carriage.

At the carriage he stopped and turned back. "I told you from the beginning: the shot was meant for Sherlock Holmes." He opened his carriage door. "He should have taken the warning. Now I have my own investigation to pursue."

Though frustrated by Plank's departure, Lestrade and I realized it did no good to pursue the man. Instead, we went inside the Red Dragon and announced ourselves to Hasson, the lascar owner. The big man watched with placid indifference as we searched his establishment from top to bottom.

But there, too, we had no success. Holmes was not to be found among the pitiful cases of stupefied individuals on the premises, and we found no evidence of hidden passageways or rooms that might have served as prison cells.

We got back into our carriage with nothing to show for our afternoon's work. We drove away in silence.

"What do you want to do about Plank?" Lestrade asked as we stopped at Scotland Yard.

"What can we do?"

"Not much," Lestrade said. "Mounting some kind of official complaint would take forever. Plank knows that. Whatever he's hiding, we won't get it from him." He hesitated. "I don't understand why he would act this way. He has a wife and two children to support. Why would he put his job at risk?"

"Unless he thinks what he's doing will earn him a promotion," I said.

"I'll see if I can talk to him privately."

Lestrade brightened. "Meanwhile, I did tell my men to find Newman's second in command and take him in. By now they may have squeezed something out of him."

"You can let me know at the Diogenes Club," I said. "Four o'clock."

43. ANOTHER DIRECTION

Returning to the Diogenes Club, I was surprised to find little Becky in the lobby, under the watchful eye of the uniformed doorman. "The child has only just arrived," said the fellow. "She mentioned the name of Mr. Mycroft Holmes, and I have sent word upstairs for him."

"I have to get away from my father," the child said, looking miserable. "He was at Baker Street. Mrs. Hudson wouldn't let him in, of course, but he said he'd be back with a constable. I knew you were coming here, so I borrowed my friend Flynn's coat and hat and went out through the kitchen."

We were soon with Lucy, Mycroft, Jack, and Lestrade in the upstairs Library. Mycroft gave a nod towards Becky, who he had last seen nearly two months ago playing the piano at Lucy's wedding. "Ah, young Miss Kelly. Please take a seat and be comfortable," he said.

Lucy pulled out the chair to the left of her own, and the two sat. Jack had taken the chair to Lucy's immediate right. Becky whispered a few words to Lucy, who in turn whispered a few words to Jack, who nodded, reaching across to pat Becky's hand.

Mycroft sat at the head of the table. His wide forehead showed furrows of worry and concentration.

"Progress?" he asked.

Lestrade spoke first. He had sweated Newman's successor for information but had obtained nothing of value.

He told of our fruitless trip to the Red Dragon, and our inconclusive confrontation with Plank.

"You may have spooked him, though," said Lucy. "Pity we couldn't have shadowed him."

Jack had done some discreet digging into Plank's affairs. "No cause for suspicion," Jack said.

Becky had just seen Flynn, but so far none of the other Irregulars had come forward with any information from the scene of the abduction.

Lucy was ticking off the leads on her fingertips. "So, Newman's successor, the Red Dragon, the Irregulars, and Plank. Four possibilities, no probabilities." She looked at Mycroft. "I hope you have something."

"What I have may or may not be of use to us," Mycroft said. "I spoke to the Chinese emperor's representative here in London, Sir Halliday Macartney, whom Dr. Watson has met. I had hoped to connect Lord Lynley and his murder with the events here. Given that Lynley's estate is in Lincolnshire, and that Swafford and his brother had a family connection in Shellingford—"

"What did Macartney say?" Lucy asked.

"Lynley had not spoken with Macartney for some time. Lynley had become somewhat of a recluse, no longer active in his business affairs with the Chinese."

"For how long?"

"Two years."

Lucy's green eyes narrowed with intensity. "Do you find that time significant, given the time that the three opium ships went missing?"

Mycroft nodded.

I felt the rush of excitement that comes of an idea, arising unbidden and claiming its due. "Macartney," I said. "He was involved in the kidnapping of the Chinese doctor Sun Yat Sen. I read it in the *Times*. It is entirely possible that the same people are holding Holmes where that unfortunate fellow was kept prisoner: the Chinese Legation at Portland Place. Lestrade, I should like you to come with me."

Lestrade looked hesitant. "We had a devil of a time getting that Chinese doctor released last year. The Foreign Office had a lot to say—"

"I shall go with you or without you."

"Unless you were invited, it would be trespass—"

My determination grew. "I repeat, I shall not be put off. There is nothing that will prevent me from finding Holmes, if there is the slightest opportunity to do so!"

"You are always the man of action, Dr. Watson," Mycroft said. "But perhaps in this instance it would be best to temper action with a strategic approach."

I clung to my position. "The Chinese Legation. They know something. And I mean to find out what."

WATSON

44. A CHINESE WALL

"Do you think me mad, Lestrade?" I asked. We were in Marylebone, having taken a cab to Portland Place, where the Chinese Legation stood with its varnished black door firmly shut against me.

Lestrade made no reply. I pounded on the door for the second time. "I know you're in there," I shouted. "Open up!"

My face felt hot with indignation and—I must admit—some embarrassment as well, for passers-by were turning to look and make remarks to one another. Still, I was determined not to be dissuaded. If there was a chance that Holmes was indeed inside, I would take it and brave the consequences.

Looking up I thought I saw movement at one of the heavily-curtained windows. There was certainly someone there. It would have been impossible for the entire building to be deserted, or that no one was curious as to the cause of the racket, which must be audible in at least this section of the building.

Sun Yat Sen, the papers had said, had been held captive in one of the upstairs rooms. There were two floors above the ground level. Possibly Holmes was in there, behind one of these windows, hearing my voice, yet unable to respond or make any answering signal. I pictured him in my mind, shackled to a bed, or—worse—sedated under the influence of some powerful narcotic. Sir Halliday had protested, of course, that the official position of the Chinese emperor was anti-opium, but in my view, this was mere hypocrisy. The emperor indeed! The fellow taxed his own people and made a profit on their use of the drug, just as Britain's government did.

I heard a coach and horses come to a stop behind me.

Turning, I saw Lestrade in conversation with a uniformed constable. Both men looked at me. Lestrade came over and tried to take my arm. I shook him off. A complaint of disturbing the peace, he said, had been telephoned to the Marylebone station house by someone within the Legation. They were responding promptly, anxious to prevent another controversial incident.

"Dr. Watson," Lestrade went on, "You have somehow got it fixed in your mind that Holmes has been kidnapped and is being held here."

"They did the same to Sun Yat Sen—"

"That is true, but it is not evidence on which I can get a warrant. We have no other evidence to get one."

"The dust from the Chinese firework, used as a distraction—"

"Is suggestive to your mind, I know. But no judge will act on mere suggestion and association. In the case of Sun Yat Sen, we had his notes begging for help, telling his friends where he was being held. The Legation has now called on the police to make you cease your disturbance, which is what any reasonable person would do under the circumstances."

"If they were innocent of kidnapping," was my prompt rejoinder.

Lestrade shook his head. "Are you to be arrested and brought to the station house and imprisoned? I don't see that this will help us to find Holmes."

My face burning, I turned on my heel and walked away from the front entrance. My thoughts were muddled. I realized that I must avoid arrest, but I still intended somehow not to abandon my efforts. I determined, then, to walk around the block. I would come back to observe whether the police coach remained. I was fairly certain that it would not, for resources would be needed elsewhere.

But then as I rounded the nearest corner, I saw two other doors to the rear portion of the building. The first, at street level and smaller than the front entrance—though equally as imposing—looked to be a side entrance for diplomatic staff. The second, at the rear corner, was smaller still, and was plainly intended for servants and service deliveries.

And just beyond this smallest door was a small shed, built within a very narrow passageway.

I knew that I was under observation by the constable and Lestrade. I could not fault them for taking the side of the law in this matter, even though I strongly disagreed. I took a few steps further. Then I turned as if I had just then remembered something. I walked back towards Lestrade, smiling inwardly to myself because, in fact, I had indeed remembered something. However, I was not about to share that memory.

On my way I took a quick glance to my left, at the narrow passageway. Then I strode up to where Lestrade and the constable were waiting.

"I've cleared my head with the short walk," I said. "You won't have any further trouble from me at this location. I see it is fruitless to ignore the strictures that govern such matters."

I had no intention of staying away, but I hoped my denial was convincing enough for me not to be followed. I looked piously upwards at the sky. A few snowflakes had begun to fall. "I shall return to Baker Street," I continued. "No need to accompany me; it is only a short walk from here."

"It is nearly a mile. And growing dark. And it is about to snow."

"Nevertheless," I said. I turned and walked away.

At Baker Street, I made my preparations, fortified myself with hot soup from Mrs. Hudson's kitchen, put on my hat, coat and scarf, and went out into what had become a snow-filled night. I was fully resolved to commit the crime of breaking and entering at the Chinese Legation.

WATSON

45. THINGS DO NOT GO AS PLANNED

At about half past eight I dismounted from my cab at the corner of Portland Place and Weymouth Street. The paved walkway was wet and slippery. The light from the corner gas lantern cast a yellow tinge onto the surface of the newly-fallen snow. Footprints from a few passers-by were visible in the slush that lay around me, ankle deep, covering the walkway pavers. From Portland Street up to the two-columned portico at the front of the Chinese Legation, however, there were more footprints, indicating the presence of many recent arrivals.

Standing on the pavement, I tried to angle my vision so as to catch a glimpse behind the curtains at the windows of the ground floor. I could see shadows moving from time to time, silhouetted vaguely against the curtains. *Good*, I thought. *People were inside.*

My plan was to walk down to the rear entrance, which would lie behind the shed at the narrow passageway that separated the rear of the Legation building from its nearest neighbor. I had brought along Holmes's set of lockpicks and I felt their weight in my coat pocket. I had practiced with them on the lock behind the outside door to our kitchen and felt sure that I would be able to fumble my way to a successful entry. Nothing ventured, nothing gained, I'd thought.

I was on the point of setting off from the street corner when I was aware of a cab coming to a stop behind me, the horse nickering and shaking its harness. I debated momentarily whether I ought to continue with my plan, or whether I ought to cross the street so as to be unobserved. The new arrival would, I felt sure, have come to visit the Chinese Legation.

Then came a Scottish brogue that I recognized. "Just wait there, cabbie. I will not be long."

It was the voice of Sir Halliday Macartney.

I shrank back for a moment, turning away, but just at that moment, Sir Halliday saw me.

"Why it's Dr. Watson," he said. "Were you the man who pounded on the door this afternoon?"

"Yes, I was here this afternoon," I said. "I wish I had thought to telephone you or visit you at your home to make my appeal, instead of coming here. I have been at my wits' end with worry over Holmes. He has gone missing, as you may or may not know."

"And you thought he was here." Halliday's forked gray beard quivered with badly-concealed amusement, as he shook his head in sympathy. "Come in with me, Doctor, and I shall endeavor to set your mind at ease on that score. Though I fear there is little I can do to assist you in learning the whereabouts of Mr. Holmes."

At the entrance he placed a hand on my chest before knocking. "You and I are Englishmen," he said, "and I have every hope that Mr. Holmes will locate the missing opium, even though he refused Ernshaw's offer to do so. I value Holmes's life and safety. Yet I must ask you to remember that in this building I am under an obligation to the emperor and must act accordingly. When we are inside, please bear in mind that others are listening at all times."

Whereupon he knocked, the door opened, and he ushered me inside, shouldering past the surprised Chinese steward, who, with a disapproving look, stood aside.

Sir Halliday explained to the steward that he had come to take me on a brief tour of the facility; he wanted to have a western medical opinion on the healthful aspects of the surroundings.

"I shall accompany you both," the man said, in perfect English.

We strode up two flights of stairs to the top floor, and down an ill-lit hallway, with doors on either side resembling those of a cheap hotel. "You are welcome to try any of these rooms," said Sir Halliday. "This is the servants' quarter."

Determined to be thorough, I went into every room. The steward had his master key on his keyring and unlocked each room in turn. All were small and simple in the manner of servants' quarters, and it was apparent that no prisoner was being held on the top floor.

"Please let me know if you see anything suspicious," Sir Halliday whispered at one unguarded moment, when we were out of earshot of the steward, "but take care that we are not overheard."

We went through the same procedure on the next floor down, with the same result.

The rooms on the ground floor were, as might be expected, larger and better furnished than those on the upper floors. We bypassed the dining room and two parlors, where there appeared to be a gathering of some sort, and stopped in front of a swinging door at the entrance to the kitchen. After a moment's wait while one of the waiters came out, we entered. There was bustling activity around a stove with bubbling pots, but this activity ceased when the chef and others caught sight of us. Then, after a few words in Chinese from the steward, the activity resumed. I took note of the cabinets, the storage shelves, and the external pantry. I saw nothing unusual.

"No prisoner here," said Macartney. "Would you like to see the basement?"

I nodded. "I shall also want to see the exit from the basement. The footprints or lack thereof will indicate whether someone has recently been hustled out of what might be a place of incarceration. I do not doubt your sincerity, Sir Halliday, but it is possible that there are those within this building that do not have your best interests at heart and may be playing their own game."

"Oh, it's hardly likely," he responded, and I had the impression that the words were just a trifle louder than they needed to be, intended for the steward's ears or for others that might at the moment be unseen.

"But before we go downstairs," he continued, "perhaps you would like to see the meeting rooms. They are in use by a number of guests. Though I cannot possibly imagine that Holmes would be held prisoner amidst a public gathering of this nature."

"I should like to see who is attending all the same," I said. I particularly wanted to see if Hasson, the lascar owner of the Red Dragon opium den, was present. I was sure I would recognize his massive figure.

Sir Halliday first showed me the dining room, where all the occupants, including the waiters, appeared to be oriental. The guests were well attired, prosperous in appearance, with an air of dignity and confidence, the surface gloss that wealth brings. All eyes were on a lovely young woman in robes and fan, who was dancing slowly and gracefully to the oddly sonorous music of a stringed instrument. "A traditional court dance," Sir Halliday said. "These guests are subscribers to a theatrical group. The dancer and her compatriots hope the guests will provide financial backing for the next production."

Until we left, all eyes remained on the dancer. I was sure no one had noticed our intrusion.

We stopped before a pair of double doors, which were shut, although I could hear voices coming from inside. "The next room is a parlor of sorts," Sir Halliday said. "It has been modified to resemble a small lecture hall. Once a month we invite enterprising Chinese citizens who may have investment opportunities for their countrymen."

He opened one of the doors and we edged inside behind the back row of onlookers, who were chattering among themselves, for the presentation had not yet begun. At the head of the room stood a man, manipulating an apparatus used for weaving.

Sir Halliday said, "This is a demonstration of a machine that can weave silk fabric more rapidly and cheaply than the old hand looms. The operator up there will soon make a demonstration of it, or rather a small replica created for demonstration purposes, and then he will distribute samples."

"You have seen this before?" I asked.

"Several times. The operator is the inventor, and his family is a friend of the emperor."

I walked to the end of the rows of chairs and looked down each. Once again, I saw no one that I recognized, and nothing out of the ordinary.

Sir Halliday showed me to the last door off the main hall. "This is the library," he said. Then, drawing me aside to where we were out of the steward's hearing, he continued, "There is another gathering here, and it is the reason why I came here tonight, for I think it may have a connection to the matter we discussed at the Diogenes Club. The principal here is Chinese, and the investment he is propounding concerns a new venture, a partnership with a German company."

The steward was drawing closer to us as Sir Halliday went on: "It offers hope for those who have succumbed to the addictive powers of opium. As a physician, you may already know of it."

My senses quickened at this, both because of the covert manner that Sir Halliday had briefly adopted, and because of the mention of opium. "My patients do not include opium sufferers," I said, taking pains to include the steward in my address, "though it might be as well to make myself aware."

Soon we were in the library, joining a cluster of hopeful-looking Chinese men who were listening to one of their countrymen: a stooped, aged fellow whose long gray pigtail braid dangled oddly above the black fabric of his evening coat. There was a marked surface deformity of the left side of his face, where skin and flesh had been scarred and pitted and misshapen, by a burn suffered in an accident of some kind. I noticed that he held his left arm close to his side, as though it, too, had been injured and failed to recover fully.

None of the men in his audience appeared to take any notice of these impairments. The faces of those listening were rapt and hopeful, with a respect and attentiveness that bordered on worshipful expectation. The man was speaking Chinese in a quiet, husky whisper, and I wondered if whatever accident he had suffered had affected his vocal cords.

He saw Macartney and switched to English immediately.

"Sir Halliday! I have something for you." He reached into his pocket and drew out an envelope, most conspicuously sealed with red wax.

Sir Halliday took the envelope and pocketed it without comment. Then he said, "My companion is Dr. John Watson. I brought him here because as a physician he may have an interest in what you are presenting here this evening."

The little man turned his black eyes on me, and I took an instant dislike to him. I had the fleeting impression of a cobra that has just awakened.

"Ah, Doctor," he said. "I am Ming Donghai, humble and obedient servant of his serene excellency the son of heaven, Emperor of China." He went on, in the same whispery tone, "Your patients suffer from opium addiction?"

"Not many," I said.

He nodded and turned immediately to the man on his right, a tall, young, robust Chinese fellow who appeared to be in excellent health. "You should observe Kai-chen, here. He was once brought low by opium, through no fault of his own, I must hasten to add. I brought him to my clinic, along the English seashore. My treatment and his exercise regimen have resulted in a complete cure, as you can see. Kai-chen, shake hands with Dr. Watson."

The young man smiled and took my hand in a powerful grip. His eyes were clear, his complexion bright and firm, his smile broad and confident. Knowing what I did of several good men who had been defeated by opium, it was difficult to believe that this man had ever been an addict.

"I have my health," said Kai-chen. "I came to it out of a loathsome weakness, but the Doctor has taught me that in weakness there can be strength."

"I am happy for you," I said.

"The addictive powers and ill effects come from the impurities inherent in the unrefined opium product," Ming said. "The treatment offering the most promise for the least effort is one that does away with the impurities. My partners in Germany made the first discovery, and they seek to spread the treatment to foreign lands. I am testing it for them here in England, trying to help those poor unfortunates who are unable to help themselves. Perhaps you would like to observe the treatment personally? Our clinic will be open for medical observers next week."

Out of politeness, and respect for Sir Halliday's obviously sensitive relationship with one so close to the Emperor of China, I declined as politely as I could. Still, something about the way he looked at me put me off-balance, and I found myself staring at his misshapen face, then hastily looked away down to his left arm, which he held stiffly at his side.

Ming saw. "You rightly observe, doctor, that my own physique is far from perfect. I suffered an injury to my arm in China. One day there may be a cure. Meanwhile, I endeavor to derive strength from my weakness, as young Kai-chen here has done from his. Strength of character, you would call it." He gave a dismissive nod, and went on briskly: "Now is there anything else I can show you before I return to my audience?"

I declined.

When Sir Halliday and I were once again in the hallway, he said, "Now we just have the basement for you to examine. And as you correctly pointed out, the entrance to the outside."

The steward led us downstairs, where two overhead electric bulbs cast sufficient light for me to see the walls of stone, the coal cellar, undisturbed, and the pathway to the door, which was clean and free from disturbance. "No one has passed inside, it seems," said Macartney.

"Yet it might have been recently swept," I said. "It would be as well to open the entry door."

I opened the door myself. Behind it, four stone steps led up to a hatchway. They were clean. There was a broom alongside.

I pushed up at the hatchway, trying to force it open. Something heavy resisted my effort. I pushed again, quicker and harder.

"What is it, Doctor?" asked Sir Halliday.

A small quantity of snow had seeped through the opening produced by my efforts to lift the hatchway. "Perhaps snow has slid down from the roof of the house and piled up on the hatchway," I said. I bent my knees and got my back and shoulder beneath the inner surface. Crouching, I then sprang upward, giving the hatchway door a powerful shove. A cascade of snow spilled over the edge of a widening gap. I tried again.

On my third attempt the hatchway flew open. From the other side, something tumbled down with more snow, landing at my feet and almost knocking me over.

Red blood stains on white snow clumps lay at my feet, clinging to the body of a man.

Behind me, Macartney and the steward were both staring, horrified expressions on their faces.

"A dead man!" the steward said, in perfect English.

I turned the body over and recognized the face, its features twisted in frozen pain, pale and stark beneath the dim light of the overhead bulb. It was the face of Inspector Plank.

46. A LINK TO A LETTER

"I should be used to this by now."

Morning sunlight filtered in through the windows as I paced from one end of the sitting room to the other. A chimney sweep was pushing his cart past in the street outside. A public disinfector's van rolled past, likely on the way to fumigate the house of someone diagnosed with smallpox or scarlet fever.

I pivoted, walking back towards the mantle. Becky was upstairs, unpacking her suitcase in the company of Prince. I could hear her opening and closing drawers, and Prince's nails clicking across the floor.

"On practically every case we've worked on together, Holmes throws himself head first into desperate danger. Or gets shot. Or abducted by the enemy. And he always gets himself out of danger again."

Logically, I shouldn't be this shaken by the news of Holmes's kidnapping. But logic was doing precisely nothing to dispel the knot of fear pulling tight under my ribcage, making it impossible for me to draw a full breath.

My hands were shaking, too, and there was a cold, shivering feeling inside me that wouldn't go away—

"Hey." Jack had been watching me from the sofa—commendably not telling me that I was going to wear a hole in the carpet if I kept pacing back and forth. But now he stood up, coming to slip an arm around me.

"You're thinking about the funeral parlor."

I shut my eyes for a second, leaning against him. He was right. I hadn't even realized it myself, but he was right. The image sat in my mind like a cold rock: Holmes, chained up in a dank and frigid basement just like the one where I'd been held captive just two short months ago.

"You got out of there." Jack's voice was steady, certain. "You'll get your father back, too."

I looked up at him. "I couldn't have gotten out of there without you."

"Nah, you were the strong one. All I did was show up and almost get electrocuted."

It wasn't true, but it made me smile just a fraction—and it loosened the knot inside me enough that I could drop down onto the sofa, pulling Jack down beside me.

"Tell me about Benjamin Davies and Abelard Shirley."

Jack looked at me. "Are you sure?"

I nodded. "There's nothing I can do for my father right now, and I need something else to think about."

"All right. Though there's not a lot to tell." Jack leaned back against the sofa. "I put out word on the streets that I was looking for Benjamin Davies, but so far nothing's turned up."

"Would it, though? Presumably he's hoping not to be found by the police."

Jack raised one shoulder. "Maybe so, but there's enough thugs for hire and petty crooks out there who'd love for the police to owe them a favor. Pretty sure I would have heard something if Davies had been seen around town or was looking to renew old acquaintances with any of the gangs."

"So he's gone to ground."

"Looks that way. Got out of Newgate Prison two months ago and hasn't been heard from since."

"Newgate?" I frowned.

"That's right. Why?"

"Nothing." Something had tugged briefly at the back of my mind, but now it was gone. "What about his solicitor?"

"Not much there, either." Jack glanced at me. "I might have gone round to his office to talk to him while you and Becky were in Shellingford."

"I see. And did this talk include the words, 'Make you see stars for a week?'"

Jack smiled briefly but shook his head. "I didn't even see him. His clerk said he's been on circuit lately in the north, but even now that he's back in London, he spends most of his days at Temple—"

Bar was what he probably said. Temple Bar in Westminster was the location of the High Court of Chancery. But Jack's voice was drowned out completely by the sudden realization that had just struck me like a dash of cold water.

"The letter!" I jumped up from the sofa. "The letter from Abelard Shirley—do you still have it?"

"Of course." Jack got up, too, and crossed to the letter rack on the mantle. "It's right here, but what—"

I almost snatched the sheet of paper out of his hand, my eyes running over the typewritten words.

I represent my client, Mr. Benjamin Davies. Having served his appointed prison sentence and paid for the—

"I *knew* it." I stopped reading and let out a breath. "It's the same typewriter!"

Jack frowned. "What's the same typewriter?"

"This one—the one that Abelard Shirley used to type this letter. Look—" I pointed to the word *prison*. "Do you see how the lower case 'r' is just a little bit crooked? It's the same."

"The same as—"

I looked up at Jack. "I'm sorry. I know I'm not making sense."

But I was right. For once in this case, I was completely certain that I was right. Whether it was good news for my father or bad news I hadn't yet had enough time to think through. But at least I now had the relief of one cold, hard fact in a sea of uncertainty to hold onto.

"In Shellingford, when I found Lord Lynley's suicide letter. Something about it kept bothering me, but I couldn't put my finger on what it was. I thought maybe it was odd that he'd type a suicide note, but it wasn't that. It was this." I gestured again to the letter in my hand. "Lord Lynley's suicide note and Abelard S. Shirley's letter to you were typed on the same machine!"

Jack wasn't easy to catch off guard, but at that his brows went up. "How sure are you?"

"Ninety-nine point nine nine percent. I noticed when Shirley's letter arrived that it had a crooked lower case 'r.' And not just that, the lower case 'm' is just slightly chipped at the top, too, see?" I pointed to *Benjamin* at the top of the page. "I had to leave it with the Chief Constable in Shellingford, but I'm absolutely certain that Lord Lynley's suicide letter had exactly those same characteristics: crooked 'r', lower case 'm' with a chip at the top."

"So Abelard Shirley at the least of it knew Lord Lynley and

had done work for him on the same machine Lynley used to write his suicide note."

"Or at most, Abelard Shirley typed Lord Lynley's suicide letter for him." I was remembering the harsh, desperate pen strokes of Lord Lynley's signature at the bottom of the page. "Lord Lynley could have been forced to sign it at gunpoint."

Jack nodded, slowly. He looked completely calm, but at the same time a hard-edged, almost dangerous look had come into his dark eyes.

"I think we'd better find Abelard Shirley so that we can ask him."

I nodded. Fear for Holmes was still sharp, scratching at my chest. But I'd learned a long time ago that you could either let fear paralyze you—or you could use it, let it sharpen you and propel you into motion. And right now, we finally had a definite direction in which to move.

LUCY

47. A PLAN EMERGES

The temperature had risen above freezing in the course of the day—although all that chiefly meant was that London was now blanketed by thick gray fog, and the streets were slick with slushy mud.

As Jack and I made our way through the crowded streets towards Westminster, smoke rose from the chimney pots and fell in flakes of soot, like grayish black snow. The carriages that rolled past us in the street were splashed nearly up to the windows with mud, and the horses that pulled them were so dirty it was almost hard to tell the color of their coats.

"How did Abelard Shirley ever come to know Lord Lynley?" Jack asked.

"You said that his clerk told you he'd been on the circuit in the north." London solicitors could travel with the Chancery judges all over the country, hearing cases that were deemed too serious for the local magistrates. "Maybe he somehow formed a connection with Lord Lynley then?"

"Or with whoever's behind Lord Lynley's death."

Up ahead of us, two flower women were vying for control of the same street corner, red-faced and screaming into each other's faces. I waited until we passed them before saying, "You don't think it really was a suicide?"

"I don't know, I wasn't there. But it's odd," Jack said. "If we're right, this means that Benjamin Davies is somehow mixed up in the business, as well."

"I know." As certain as I was about the letters, I was almost afraid to believe it. It seemed too good to be true, that we could have found both a connection to Davies, and a weapon that could be used to bring him down.

Then again, it also meant that Benjamin Davies wasn't just acting alone, he was backed by far more formidable allies than just a wealthy London solicitor.

Saying it, I was doubly glad that we had left Becky at Scotland Yard with one of Jack's constables. Ordinarily, I would have left her with Mrs. Hudson, but even Baker Street wasn't safe right now.

I only wished one of us had been there when Benjamin Davies had arrived to look for her. There was a chance that he would come back there if we waited long enough—but we didn't have the time to simply sit and hope that he would show his face again.

"This could all mean that it's just a distraction," I said. Trying to think logically helped me not to think about what might at this moment be happening to my father. "This business of wanting to take custody of Becky? It was all just a distraction—or leverage, if you want to put it that way. Someone put Benjamin Davies up to this to keep us too worried and off balance to investigate the affair of the opium."

The grimness of Jack's expression said that he'd already come to the same conclusion. But he shook his head. "Not just the opium. It started earlier than that. The letter from Abelard Shirley had to have been written days before Swafford was killed."

"And Swafford was on the track of the people behind the diamond smuggling."

We had turned onto Chancery Lane now, and although the soot and the mud and the fog were exactly the same as in the rest of the city, the whole tenor of the street had changed. The furniture shops on either side of us sold only desks and barristers' bookcases and other furniture found in solicitors' offices. The booksellers' windows were stacked with heavy legal tomes. Even the stationers' shops advertised parchment and forms for writing wills.

Despite the weather, the street was crowded. Clerks and solicitors carrying legal briefs hurried onward towards the gray, gothic style building of the Hall at Westminster. Barristers in white wigs swept past, their long black silk robes swishing against the dirty pavement.

The time of day wasn't helping either; it was just past one o'clock in the afternoon, and every oyster shop, coffee house, tea room, and tavern seemed to be filled to capacity with luncheon hour customers.

Jack eyed the crowd. "How are we planning to find Abelard Shirley in all of this?"

Following his gaze, my stomach dropped, because he was right. We could spend hours—if not days—trawling through this ocean of London's legal professionals before we found the one solicitor for whom we were looking.

"Did you pick up any specifics about Mr. Shirley when you spoke to his clerk?"

Jack frowned, clearly calling up the memory of Abelard Shirley's offices.

"Not young," he said. "He'd left a spare hat and overcoat on the coat tree, and they were both a good twenty years out of date."

"How do you know they weren't the clerk's?"

"Wouldn't have fit him. The clerk's short and thin."

"So." I ticked the points off on my fingers. "Probably somewhere above forty years of age, frugal, and tall."

"Frugal?"

"He's still wearing a twenty-year-old hat and coat."

"Or else the soliciting business hasn't been any too profitable for him," Jack said. "Which would explain how he got mixed up in all of this."

I nodded. "Anything else?"

"Got a sweet tooth," Jack said. "I could see into the inner office, and there was a half-empty box of Turkish delight on the desk."

"All right." I still probably should have felt overwhelmed by the task before us, but I was choosing determination instead. Failing to locate our one tenable lead in the search for Holmes wasn't an option. "That should be enough."

Jack gave me a raised eyebrow.

"It's luncheon time." I gestured at the crowds around us. "If he's fond of sweets, Abelard Shirley is more likely to visit a bakery than one of these other places. And he's most likely to visit the one that's closest to Lincoln's Inn."

That was stretching the bounds of logical deduction slightly, but a man who kept Turkish delight on his desk wasn't likely to be in the best of physical condition—which would make him unwilling to walk very far in search of his mid-day meal.

"True." Jack didn't have to add that all the *likely's* in that series of suppositions didn't add up to certainty. "What do we do when we find this bakery, though?"

"It will be all right. I have a plan."

LUCY

48. SIGHTING THE TARGET

It took us nearly three-quarters of an hour to search our way through the maze of narrow cobbled streets around Temple Bar and Westminster Hall. The nearby church bells that marked the time had my teeth on edge with every chime. But at last we came in sight of a bakery that nestled between an oyster house and a small, slightly shabby-looking hotel.

Unlike the majority of the eateries on this street, which sold good, solid English fare like plum puddings and steak and kidney pies, the bakery seemed to have a distinctly French flair. The sign over the pink and white striped awning read *Patisserie*, and the display window was filled with cream eclairs and lace biscuits and tiny frosted petit fours.

A small crowd was clumped around the doorway, waiting to go in, while more strode purposefully down the street, the bakery their clear destination: three men in barrister's robes, their wigs flopping down against their cheeks a little like a spaniel's ears; four very young men who had junior clerk stamped all over them; two whose sturdy tweed suits made me think they must be witnesses to a court case called up to London from the country.

And four heavyset men who were, at the least, solid possibilities.

I drew in a breath, raising my voice to be heard over the noise of the street and called towards the cluster of men. "Mr. Shirley! Mr. Shirley!"

Jack gave me a sidelong look. "That's your plan?"

"It worked, didn't it?"

One of the heavyset men nearest the bakery shop had stopped in mid-stride, his head lifting and turning in response to my call.

He looked to be somewhere in his middle fifties, with a heavyset build beginning to run to fat. His face was red and fleshy, with a network of broken veins across his nose and cheeks that spoke of a fondness for drink.

His gaze scanned the crowd, searching for whomever had called to him, but he hadn't yet spotted us.

"How do you want to handle him?" Jack asked.

I eyed Abelard Shirley, taking in the worn quality of his morning coat and top hat, the prominently displayed tie pin and signet ring that proclaimed him an alumnus of Baliol College, Oxford, his weak chin, and the lines of ill-temper—or possibly strain—that gathered around the corners of his eyes.

Everything about his initial letter to Jack—and everything about the man before me—spoke of a man puffed up with his own sense of self-importance, but also of a man who was fundamentally a coward.

"We need to get him on his own," I murmured back. "Confront him someplace with witnesses—someplace where he's well-known, like his offices—he'll just try to bluster and deny everything. And I think we'll stand the best chance of intimidating him into telling us the truth if he's caught off balance.

He's less likely to feel threatened if he thinks I'm on my own—at least at first." I gestured to the small hotel next to the bakery. "That looks like the sort of place that would have a private parlor or tea room, a place where litigants up from the country can consult with their attorneys. Give me ten minutes to maneuver Mr. Shirley inside and then come and join us?"

Jack nodded, already stepping back from me to blend invisibly into the rest of the street traffic. "Done."

BECKY

49. FLYNN HAS NEWS

Becky drummed her heels against the wooden chair rail and wished that she had something to read. Or better yet, something to do.

Constable Thomas, the policeman Jack had asked to look after Becky for a little while, wasn't a bad sort. But he was busy with his own work—and anyway, he thought she was too much of a little girl to talk to her about anything interesting.

Right now, Becky was sitting on a chair in the New Scotland Yard basement, just outside of the evidence room, where Constable Thomas was cataloging evidence for some case or other. She was bored. Worse than that, she was *scared* and bored—and no matter how many times she told herself to think about Lucy, who was clever and brave and never seemed to be afraid of anyone or anything, the cold, shaky feeling in the pit of her stomach wouldn't go away.

Ping!

Something clattered, the noise echoing down the dimly-lit hall.

Ping!

Becky frowned and turned her head, trying to find out where the noise was coming from. Then she jerked backwards, almost falling off her chair. She bit her tongue, too, trying to hold back a yelp of surprise.

Almost directly above her head was a window, set high in the wall and looking out at street level onto a narrow alleyway. And peering in at her through the metal bars on the window was Flynn.

Becky clambered up on the chair and scowled at him. "What are you doing here?" she hissed through the glass.

Flynn rolled his eyes. "Looking for you, o'course." His voice came through muffled, but she could still hear him all right. "I've been round and round this place four times, 'oping I might catch you. Lucky job I 'appened to spot the window."

"Do you ever just knock on the door and come inside like a normal person?"

Flynn snorted. "Me inside a police station? That'll be the day."

Becky didn't point out that if he was caught peering in through the windows of Scotland Yard, he'd probably be in a lot more trouble than if he had just come in and asked to talk to her.

"What's been happening?" she asked. She hadn't seen Flynn since she and Lucy had come back from Shellingford. "Do you know who took Mr. Holmes?"

Flynn didn't answer right away. He looked down at his feet, the corners of his mouth turned down.

"I didn't see it happen. I wasn't there."

"You weren't there?" It wasn't really fair to be mad at Flynn, but Becky couldn't stop her voice from rising. "You were supposed to always follow Mr. Holmes and Dr. Watson, whenever they went out!"

"You think I don't know that?" Flynn's eyes flashed back up to hers. His cheeks had flushed under the usual layer of grime. "I *know* I was supposed to be there! Maybe if I 'ad been, we'd 'ave some idea where to find Mr. 'Olmes! Maybe we'd even 'ave gotten 'im back by now. But I wasn't following Mr. 'Olmes when 'e got taken. I was asking questions around town about your old man. Trying to find anyone else just out of the clink who might 'a known 'im."

Becky's knees felt wobbly all of a sudden, and she had to fight not to sit back down on the chair. "So it's my fault."

Flynn's expression changed. "I wasn't saying that." His voice sounded gruff.

"But it is my fault." Becky hadn't thought she could feel any worse than she already had, but she'd been wrong. "If I hadn't asked you to see what information you could find about my father—" She swallowed, because thinking that way wouldn't do anyone any good. "Did you find out anything about him?"

Flynn shook his head. "Nothing." He was silent for a second, and then said, "I did find out about the 'ouse, though."

Becky had no idea what he was talking about. "What house?"

Flynn gave an impatient jerk of his hand. "You know. The one Mr. 'Olmes was looking at—the one 'e saw the estate agent about."

"Oh." That didn't sound particularly helpful, but Becky asked anyway. "What about it?"

"Well, I don't know which 'ouse it was exactly, but it's proba-bly somewhere in St. John's Wood."

"St. John's Wood?" A jolt of excitement went through Becky, the first she'd felt all day. It was so much better than being scared. "How do you know—" she started to ask. Then she shook her head. "Never mind, you can tell me later."

They probably didn't have long before they got interrupted, and who knew when she'd get the chance to see Flynn again? Jack and Lucy weren't letting her out of their sight, unless she was somewhere they considered absolutely safe. Which she understood, but it made things like planning out her own investigations difficult.

"Can you come to the house tonight?" she asked.

"I reckon." Flynn glanced over his shoulder. "I'd better be getting back now. I'm supposed to check in with Dr. Watson, see whether 'e needs me for anything."

Becky nodded. "Yes, all right. But then come and find me wherever you can, either at Baker Street or at the house. We have to get to St. John's Wood."

Flynn's blond eyebrows knitted together. "All right, but why?" he asked. "I already told you, I don't know which house Mr. 'Olmes was looking—"

"Yes, but I do," Becky interrupted. "It's—"

A pair of uniformed constable's legs appeared at the side of the window, and a deep voice barked, "Hey, you! What do you think you're doing there!"

She couldn't see the constable's face, just his arm and hand as he made a grab for Flynn. The policeman's fingers just brushed Flynn's coat collar, and her breath hitched up.

She could probably stop Flynn from getting arrested, but it would take a while to convince the policeman to listen to her, even if she was Jack's sister.

But Flynn wriggled away, as quick as an eel. The last Becky saw was him pelting away down the alley until he was lost to view.

LUCY
50. TEA WITH A SOLICITOR

"There, there, Miss Bates." Abelard Shirley reached across the tea table between us to pat my hand.

The hotel did in fact have a private tea room: a small, comfortable chamber on the ground floor, with pale blue velvet upholstered furniture, oriental rugs, and darker blue velvet drapes that shut out the mud and the fog outside. Gas jets over the mantle cast a warm, pleasant glow.

"The case is not so hopeless as some that I've successfully handled," Mr. Shirley went on. "I'm sure that with the right sort of pressure applied, we can make your uncle see reason."

He patted my hand again. I held myself tight in check to keep from jerking away at the press of his large, moist fingers against mine and, instead, picked up my teacup.

Since Mr. Shirley, in my estimation, liked to feel that he was stronger, more intelligent, and more capable than anyone else, I had approached him in the role of more-than-slightly-naive victim. I had spent the last seven minutes tearfully pouring out a story of a recently deceased grandmother whose entire estate had been usurped by a wicked uncle who had coerced her into signing a will on her deathbed.

"Thank you so much." I lowered the handkerchief I'd been weeping into. "I'm afraid I have a confession, though."

"Confession?" Mr. Shirley's expression changed from confident and tolerantly reassuring to slightly puzzled.

"Yes. My name isn't actually Catherine Bates. I don't actually have a grandmother—well, I do, but not one who was coerced into signing an unjust will. And my only uncle is Mycroft Holmes."

Mr. Shirley's face had been growing progressively redder with indignation, but at the mention of Mycroft, he blanched visibly. He'd clearly heard the name before—and understood what an extremely bad enemy Mycroft made.

"What—"

"My name is Lucy James." I interrupted him.

Jack and I had discussed it in advance and decided that we didn't want Mr. Shirley to know exactly who we were or what connected us to the letter he'd sent on behalf of Benjamin Davies—at least, not yet.

I glanced up at the door to the tea room, where Jack was just coming in. Precisely on time. "This is my husband, who is also a police sergeant with Scotland Yard. We'd like to ask you some questions."

Mr. Shirley's expression had been swerving between surprise, annoyance, and confusion. Now he settled on looking wrathfully affronted.

"You might have told me the truth from the beginning without all of this tarradiddle."

I set down my teacup. "For that to happen, I would have had to trust that you would exchange truthful answers for a true story. And I don't—not even slightly."

Jack pulled out a chair and sat down beside me, giving me a questioning glance. I nodded. I had succeeded in throwing Mr. Shirley off balance, but the simple fact was that he would find Jack far more intimidating than he did me, and time was short.

"What do you know about Lord Lynley, of Shellingford?" Jack asked.

"N-nothing." Mr. Shirley's cheeks went from pale to mottled red again, but he shook his head. "Never heard of him, the name means nothing to me, and I am under no obligation whatsoever to answer your questions." He shifted his weight, starting to push his chair back from the table. "I wish you good day—"

"Sit down." Jack's voice was completely calm and quiet, but something in his tone stopped Abelard Shirley in mid-word, causing him to pause somewhat comically, half in and half out of his chair. Then, looking at Jack's face, he swallowed and dropped back into his seat.

"That's better," Jack said. "Lord Lynley is dead. Shot through the head in his own warehouse."

I saw the shock of the words register in Mr. Shirley's gaze, but before he could speak, Jack went on.

"Now we can do this one of two ways. You can answer our questions here and now. Or I can bring you down to the Yard to talk. In which case word is bound to get out about how helpful you've been about assisting the police in our inquiries."

Mr. Shirley's mouth opened, but no sound emerged.

"These people you're working for," Jack said. "They've already proved they're happy to commit murder. What do you think your odds are of surviving to the end of the week if they find out you've been talking to the police?"

"I—" Mr. Shirley tugged at his shirt collar as though it were suddenly too tight. "I don't know what I can tell you."

His eyes darted nervously around the room, plainly searching for any sign that we might be spied on or overheard, and then finally came to rest on Jack.

"I was hired by Lord Lynley to draw up some legal documents. That's all."

"What legal documents?"

Mr. Shirley's bulky shoulders rose and fell. "One or two leases on the tenant properties that Lord Lynley owns. A business agreement concerning the disposition of profits earned on certain imports."

"Opium?" I asked.

Mr. Shirley's gaze swiveled to me, and I saw the brief impulse to deny it cross his expression.

"And what of it? The trade is perfectly legal—a straightforward business transaction."

"So perfectly straightforward, in fact, that at least two people are now dead, and two more are missing."

I thought of Holmes again, and pushed the thought aside. My father would be the first to tell me that emotion interfered with investigation.

"While you were in Shellingford, did you have dealings with anyone besides Lord Lynley? Did anyone else employ your services?"

"I—no." Mr. Shirley shook his head. "No one."

Beneath the edge of the table, I felt my hands curl in frustration. Mr. Shirley might be lying—but I didn't think he was. His shock at hearing the news of Lord Lynley's death had been genuine; whether His Lordship had been murdered or committed suicide, I doubted very much that Mr. Shirley had been involved.

Which meant that we only had one card left to play.

I leaned back in my chair. "Benjamin Davies."

Mr. Shirley was in the act of drawing out a handkerchief from his waistcoat pocket, but at that, he froze. His gaze traveled from Jack to me and then back again, and I saw the precise moment when sudden recognition crossed his gaze.

"Wait a moment. You're—"

"That's right," Jack said. "Which means that I've already got enough reason to dislike you. In your shoes, I wouldn't want to add one more."

His voice was still dead quiet, but Abelard Shirley's gaze fell away from his, and he swallowed visibly.

"Davies," Jack said. "Where can I find him?"

"I don't know." Mr. Shirley swallowed. "I was asked to write a letter on his behalf, and I carried out the task. That was the end of it."

"A letter demanding that a ten-year-old child be given into the custody of a known felon," I said.

Mr. Shirley straightened, pressing his fleshy lips together in an expression of self-righteousness. "I don't make the laws, I only follow and uphold them."

Then again, maybe there was a time to allow emotion to have full sway. I leaned towards him across the table, channeling all the anger I'd been suppressing since the letter from Davies arrived, sinking every bit of it into my words. "You uphold the law. That is funny, Mr. Shirley. That's really very, very funny. So if Jack were to get his superiors at Scotland Yard interested in investigating your affairs—a task that wouldn't be at all difficult, I might add—they would find everything completely open and above board? No evidence whatsoever that those legal documents you helped to draw up for Lord Lynley concerned the disposition of smuggled goods?"

Mr. Shirley didn't speak, but I saw a heavy sheen of sweat break out on his forehead.

"I want you to think very carefully, Mr. Shirley," I went on. "I'm going to ask you politely one more time and only once more: where we can find Benjamin Davies? We know he's in London. And unless you give us a straight answer now, a month, two months, maybe a year from now, you'll be sitting inside of a jail cell, and you'll be able to pinpoint this exact moment as the time when everything in your life went terribly, terribly wrong."

Mr. Shirley's Adam's apple bobbed as he again swallowed convulsively, and then mopped his forehead with his handkerchief.

"I only met Mr. Davies the one time, in Shellingford. He was introduced as someone who dealt with the distribution of … certain imported goods in the Liverpool area."

That tallied with what I already knew of Benjamin Davies's background.

"Introduced by whom?"

Mr. Shirley blinked. "By Lord Lynley. I composed a letter according to His Lordship's instructions," Mr. Shirley went on, wiping his face again. "And posted it here in London, once I returned to town. I never saw Benjamin Davies again. But—" he added the final word before I could decide whether further threats would produce more information. "I overheard him speaking to Lord Lynley about where he could be contacted. It was an address in Limehouse that he gave. The Stagg Inn, on Burdett Road. Now, may I go?"

Jack and I exchanged a look.

I nodded. "Yes, fine."

Without waiting for me to change my mind, Mr. Shirley crammed his hat back onto his head and hurried out—moving more quickly than his bulk would have led me to believe.

Jack watched the door close behind him. "He's relieved. Thinks he's gotten off easy."

"Exactly." I already knew we'd been thinking along the same lines. "And relief in most people tends to breed carelessness. Not that I honestly think he has any more that he can tell us, but someone might get into contact with him. I'll get Flynn or one of the other Irregulars to watch his offices." I frowned, replaying the course of our conversation with Mr. Shirley in my mind. "What did you think of him?"

"You mean, do I think he knows anything about your father's kidnapping?"

"Well, I could just mean, 'Do you think he's a slimy, second-rate shyster?'"

"You could, and I wouldn't argue," Jack said. "But that's not what you're thinking about."

"No." I tried without success to erase the image of Holmes, freezing and starving in an underground prison, and leaned my head briefly against Jack's shoulder. "If this is how you felt when I went missing this past fall, I'm even sorrier than I was before."

"It's all right." Jack squeezed my hand. "Comes with the territory."

That was true. Caring about Sherlock Holmes was, and always would be, tantamount to swimming in shark-infested waters.

"You didn't ask Shirley about your father," Jack said.

"I know. I thought about it, but it's not really likely he knows anything—he's just a peon, a minor cog in the wheel, not the man in charge."

"And we don't need word getting back to the higher-ups that we're asking those kinds of questions."

"Exactly." I couldn't risk giving whoever was holding my father captive any excuse for retribution. "Limehouse, though," I said. "The Stagg Inn."

Jack nodded. "It's a place to start, anyway."

"Davies isn't going to be as easy to intimidate as Mr. Shirley, though." I was trying to hold onto the anger I'd felt for the man, but it was ebbing, leaving only a chill emptiness behind. I straightened, trying to shove the cold feeling away. "Still—"

The door to the parlor burst open, revealing a skinny, blond-haired, and extremely dirty boy in a tattered coat and a cloth-checked cap.

Behind him, a uniformed hotel maid was trying ineffectually to drag him back out again.

"It's all right," I told the maid. I had to speak over the sudden pounding of my heart. "We know him." I turned to Flynn. "What is it? Is there any news about Holmes?"

Flynn was out of breath, gasping for air. "No, miss. Nothing about Mr. 'Olmes. It's Dr. Watson. 'E sent me to fetch you, on account of Inspector Plank's been found dead—murdered!"

WATSON

51. DEDUCTIONS, AND DIRE NEWS

When I awoke, it was afternoon.

My mind swirled with questions. Did Macartney know something important? He had not wished to have to explain my presence at the Chinese Legation, and I did not want Macartney telling the police how I had gone there in search of clues to the kidnapping of Sherlock Holmes, so we had left the steward to explain how he had discovered the body when attempting to open the hatch. Now I wondered if there was something I ought to have asked him, or whether I should have waited for the police to arrive.

The discovery of Plank's body had amplified my frustrations. I was convinced that learning the truth about why Plank had shot himself was critical information for the case and, following Holmes's kidnapping, even more certain that what Plank knew would help us locate those who wanted him to stay away from the hunt for the missing opium. Now that Plank was dead, we would never learn the truth from him—what Plank had been doing at the Legation. Why had he shot himself? Was he really only trying to warn Holmes away from Limehouse? And why would he do that?

I realized I needed help. First, I tried unsuccessfully to telephone Lucy and Mycroft, but to no avail. Then I went out to the snow-clogged street, hoping that one of the Irregulars was keeping watch. I was in luck. I sent messages to Lucy, Jack, and Mycroft, asking them to meet me at Baker Street. I trudged through the snow down Regent Street with the vague intention of returning to the Chinese Legation. Then the aromas of bacon and sausage wafting from a small restaurant made me realize I had not eaten since late the previous afternoon and was not much good to anyone in my current state. I stopped and, though it was hours past lunchtime, had a proper breakfast.

Upon my return to Baker Street I found Lucy on our sitting room sofa, in the company of little Becky.

"Jack was called to the Chinese Legation to investigate Inspector Plank's murder," Lucy said. "But Becky and I came to hear everything that you can tell us, Uncle John."

She spoke calmly, but the clear worry in her green eyes—and the hope in Becky's face as she fixed her gaze on me—sent an arrow of self-recrimination through my chest. I felt as though I had accomplished very little in my visit to the Chinese Legation and this would inevitably let them down.

As though reading my thoughts, Lucy said, "It will be all right, Uncle John. Just tell us everything that you observed in the Legation and what Sir Halliday had to say."

I was relieved that that was her first question. I had been expecting an inquiry into how Plank had died, and since he had suffered the same type of wound that killed Inspector Swafford—his neck cut through almost to the bone—I was reluctant to recount the details in front of Becky.

I myself was struggling against the grisly images of the crime scene that I would not soon forget.

I folded my arms across my chest and proceeded to recount the circumstances and my journey from the top of the building down the next two floors. Then I went on, "I went into the kitchen—"

But before I could continue, the sitting-room door opened to reveal Mycroft, in the company of Mrs. Hudson. Our landlady's face was pinched with worry, and it struck me that I had been remiss in failing to consider what she would be feeling at Holmes's disappearance.

Lucy must have felt this as keenly as I, for she got to her feet and held out a hand. "Mrs. Hudson, there's no real news of my father, but you're welcome to stay—"

Mrs. Hudson shook her head. "Thank you, no. I've dishes that need tending to in the kitchen." Her gaze traveled over our small assembled party, and she pressed her lips together. "You will let me know if there's any word?"

I nodded. "Certainly."

Mycroft made his way to the chair nearest to the fire and lowered his bulky frame onto the cushioned seat. Of all of us, he appeared to be the least unsettled. Though the Holmes brothers might not resemble one another in a physical sense, they shared both the same towering intellect and the same near-unshakable calm.

"Newman's death was announced today," he said. "I mention that event only on the chance that it may have some bearing on Inspector Plank's murder, which may possibly have been to avenge Newman's death; some are claiming it was not a suicide."

I shuddered inwardly. If Plank had been killed to avenge Newman, the next target for revenge could very well be Sherlock Holmes.

"You've been to the Chinese Legation?" Lucy asked Mycroft. I startled, in surprise.

Lucy added as an aside to me, "His shoes and the hems of his trousers are damp with melted snow. And there's a spot of grease on the arm of his overcoat, which makes me think he must have been questioning the kitchen staff."

Mycroft glanced at his coat sleeve and tsked under his breath at the grease stain, but then nodded. "I have been to the Chinese Legation, yes."

I felt renewed foreboding. Never had I known Mycroft to personally inspect the scene of any crime. He, too, must believe Holmes's position to be grave indeed if he had taken it upon himself to leave Whitehall.

"Your husband and the other police officers are still occupied with the cataloging of evidence and the interviewing of witnesses," Mycroft told Lucy. "But I judged it most beneficial to proceed here, so that you might hear the latest reports on the unfortunate Inspector Plank's murder without delay."

"There were no witnesses to the crime?" I asked.

"None to the crime itself, but a statement given by an itinerant knife grinder who had set up his stall on the corner has proven most informative." Mycroft drew out a small leather-bound notebook and, opening to a page, read aloud, "The police inspector walked past my stall on his way to the rear entrance of the Chinese Legation. I saw him go behind the house. He didn't come back out."

"Did he see anyone else go in or out?" asked Lucy.

"It would appear not."

"And you believe that we can take this man at his word?" I asked.

Mycroft pursed his lips judicially. "I believe we may be cautiously confident in the veracity of his statement, yes. Business was non-existent, leaving him with no other occupation than to watch the comings and goings of passers-by. And he struck me as less unobservant than the majority of his type."

"So that means that someone was waiting for Plank, either outside the Legation or inside," Lucy said.

"Since spending any length of time outside tonight was a cold and most unpleasant business, as I myself can attest, I believe we can take the hypothesis that Plank's killer or killers waited for him inside."

"You were just telling us that a part of your tour of the Legation included the kitchen, Uncle John. What did you observe there?"

The weight of responsibility settled over me once again as I tried to separate my feelings of frustration and anger from the events that I had experienced. "The shelves and workspaces had not enough space to conceal a man," I began.

"But there were servants already working there?" Lucy asked.

"A cook, a Chinese fellow, and two attendants—and a waiter, who was going out. There was a gathering of guests in the dining room. A meal was being served. And there were drinks available for the visitors attending a lecture—"

"How long were you in the kitchen?" Mycroft interrupted.

"Only a minute or two. As I said, I only wanted to ascertain the possibility that a man—"

"Yes, yes." Mycroft waved that aside. "What was being cooked?"

"Why, a stew of some sort. Fish I think."

"You could smell fish?"

"Yes, but I do not see what—"

"Tax your memory. Was the odour strong, faint, pleasant, unpleasant?"

"It was not particularly noticeable," I said. "Certainly not overpowering."

"Were there seasonings? Garlic perhaps? Peppers, soy sauce, fermented vegetables? Concentrate, and allow your mind to furnish the recollections for you."

I did so. "Yes, and now that I think of it, there was also a deep fryer going. Dumplings of some sort. The chef was taking them out of the fryer."

"How was the kitchen separated from the dining room and the other gathering rooms?"

"Why, by the ordinary swinging doors. I remember seeing through the glass panel, just before we went in. The cook had his back to the door. One of the wait staff was coming out, so I stepped back."

"And that is a most valuable piece of information," said Mycroft. "Tell me. Was there a pantry or a storage facility, connected to the kitchen work area?"

"There were shelves—wooden shelves—with canned goods—"

"Was there a door to the outside?"

I remembered. "There was."

"Open or closed?"

"Why closed, of course. The weather—"

Mycroft sat back in his chair. "Then it had recently been opened and I would expect that was the access point for the killer to go out, commit his crime, and then re-enter."

I stared at him in astonishment. "How can you be certain?"

"Because of what you have told us."

It was an answer that might have come from Holmes himself, and it made me feel his absence even more keenly. I frowned. "I still don't understand."

Becky had been silent until this moment, sitting close beside Lucy, but at that she spoke up. "You told us you could see plainly through the glass window before you went in. And you said the cooking odors were faint. If the outside door had been shut the whole time, the kitchen would have been steamy, and you would have smelled more of the fish."

Mycroft gave her an approving nod before going on: "Now, I believe you said that one of the wait staff was leaving the kitchen as you came in. Can you cast your mind back to that moment when he passed you, and tell us your impressions?"

I closed my eyes with the effort, but no recollection came. I shook my head.

"Did he brush past you, or step aside?"

I remembered. "He turned away from me."

"As you passed one another, was he on your right side or on your left?"

"On my left."

"Excellent. Now, what else can you tell us about this man?"

"He was taller than I am. Unusually tall."

"What was he wearing?"

"Why, ordinary attire. He had a towel draped over his fore-arm. A white towel. It stood out against the black jacket."

I thought harder. "His shirt was white, starched in the usual manner, and his necktie was black. Ordinary waiter's attire."

"Wearing a Chinese cap?"

"Yes. Black silk. Round top. No brim."

"White gloves?"

"Yes."

"And what was he carrying—a tray? A tureen?"

"I don't remember that he was carrying anything."

"That is highly suggestive. But let us pass on to the remainder of your inspection of the ground floor. Can you please describe what you saw?"

I gave my account as best I could recall.

"The waiter who had been leaving the kitchen. Was he there?"

"There were several waiters present, but I cannot recall seeing that one. As I said, he was unusually tall."

"They wore similar black caps?"

I nodded.

"Where did you go after the dining room?"

"There was this larger room. A lecture hall of sorts. Twenty-five people. Or perhaps a few more."

"What did you hear of the lecture?"

"The gathering was to discuss a cure—that is—"

I hesitated. An impression came to me. "The tall waiter. He had turned his face away coming out of the kitchen, but I believe I also saw him at the lecture. He was a former patient of the lecturer, and he had been cured of opium addiction."

Lucy sat forward. "What was his name?"

I remembered. "Kai-chen."

She asked, "Was there an older man with him?"

I nodded. "The lecturer was an older Chinese man, with a scarred face that I will not soon forget."

"I know them both," Lucy said. "This cannot be a coincidence."

And then the telephone rang.

I picked up the receiver and heard the voice of the Secretary of War.

"Dr. Watson? Lansdowne here."

His voice was unusually somber.

My voice caught with apprehension as I replied, "Mr. Secretary."

What I next heard through the telephone receiver caused my entire body to go numb.

"I very much regret to inform you …"

The words seemed to come from a great distance. Indeed, they might have come from another universe.

WATSON

52. DARKNESS

I gripped the receiver in shock. The room seemed to whirl around me.

Lansdowne went on. "... that on the Thames near Limehouse Basin this afternoon, Mr. Sherlock Holmes was shot while on board a small Chinese vessel. My witness says he cannot possibly have survived."

I put out my hand, involuntarily, to catch my balance, and realized that my fingers were touching Holmes's desk. The accompanying surge of emotion made me gasp.

"Are you there, Dr. Watson?"

My jaw clamped shut. I saw red. Heard an inner voice.

Whoever did this will die at my hands.

But then Lucy was at my side. I heard myself saying, "I am. Go ahead."

I held the earpiece out so that we both could hear the voice of Lord Lansdowne. "The murder was witnessed by the captain of HMS *Daring*, which is now moored at the Royal Naval College. I am on my way to Greenwich now. I have sent a carriage to Baker Street. Will you come?"

Darkness had fallen by the time we reached Greenwich. A few harbor lights glittered over the wide expanse of black river, barely illuminating the low outline of HMS *Daring* along the dock. Lansdowne was waiting for us, hatless, at the entrance to the West Building, his aquiline features readily identifiable. His tall frame was stooped and hunched against the cold. He gave a momentary glance to our group, which consisted of Mycroft, Lucy and me. We had left little Becky in the care of Mrs. Hudson. As an added precaution, Lucy had insisted on waiting for the arrival of three police constables, who would guard the Baker Street residence until our return.

To Lansdowne we were all familiar faces. All of us had been inside Lansdowne House and with him in the adjoining Devonshire House, just six months earlier, when the Jubilee Ball had nearly ended in catastrophe.

On that occasion a traitor had been unmasked, and we had shared with Lansdowne a grim triumph. Now, I could not help thinking that there was no triumph. There was catastrophe.

"I am so terribly sorry for your loss," Lansdowne said. "Lieutenant Commander Bradley is inside. I will take you to him."

The commander, clean-faced and ruddy, about forty years old, stood in his blue uniform at attention outside a tall door just off the front entrance. His blue eyes looked inquiringly at our little group, then at Lansdowne as we approached.

"Commander Bradley, I shall introduce you to each of these people in turn. They are the next of kin to Mr. Sherlock Holmes."

We shook hands with him as Lansdowne made introductions. Then he opened the door to reveal a well-lit conference room, with a large oak table surrounded by a dozen empty chairs.

On the table lay a misshapen dark pile of fabric.

"His coat," said the commander. "It's all we have, I'm afraid."

I picked up the coat to inspect it, catching the scent of damp wool and river water. It was Holmes's black tweed Inverness. I put my finger through a small hole in the front of the cape, through the coat beneath, and then through the heavy wool fabric at the back. As I did so I realized that traces of reddish liquid were coming off on my hands. There was no mistaking the coppery scent of blood, diluted though it had been by the waters of the Thames.

There was also no mistaking the inevitable conclusion. A bullet passing through Holmes's cloak in this manner would inevitably have gone through his chest. From the angle between the holes, the shot might have missed the vital organs, but there was no question that significant blood loss would have ensued.

"A miracle that he survived to take this off and attempt to swim," said Commander Bradley, looking from me to Lucy and to Mycroft.

We took chairs around the table. Bradley told us what had happened. Authorized by Lansdowne, Holmes had asked for his assistance to watch the Red Dragon Inn and monitor boat traffic in and out. "Something to do with opium smuggling," the commander said. "We hove to on the south side of the river, just opposite Limehouse Basin. We had a good view of the Red Dragon. It was a gray afternoon, but the weather was clear enough."

"What time was this?" Lucy asked.

"About three o'clock," the commander said, "We saw a motor launch pass us, heading straight for the Red Dragon, close enough so that we could see the crew was Chinese. There was no name and no flag. The boat docked briefly under the pier, unloaded a few barrels of cargo, and then maneuvered away from the dock, to head downstream. At that moment Mr. Holmes appeared on the dock, running at full tilt."

"You could identify him at that distance?" Mycroft asked sharply.

"Not at that time. I had my binoculars, but no, I could not distinguish his features as he ran. I did see that he was brandishing a revolver. He jumped onto the Chinese boat just as it was pulling away from the Red Dragon dock. In a few moments, however, I could identify Holmes. He was on the deck, and the Chinese boat was moving rapidly in our direction. Then there were shots fired. The man I now know to be Sherlock Holmes was clearly visible, and he was hit by one of the shots. He fell into the river."

"Could you see his face when he was in the water?"

"Yes. Plainly. It was Mr. Holmes."

"You had met him before?"

"Yes. This was the man who had asked me to keep the Red Dragon Inn under surveillance."

"And he had identified himself as Sherlock Holmes?"

"He did, and to confirm his identity he asked me to call Secretary Lansdowne in his presence."

"Holmes made the request to me on the phone," Lansdowne said. "I recognized his voice. Then he put Commander Bradley on the line, and I gave the authorization."

"What happened then?" Lucy asked.

"I knew the water was dangerously cold. As you know, freezing water can paralyze a man's limbs in no time. There were blocks of ice here and there, but none close enough for

Mr. Holmes to hold onto. We lowered a dinghy to rescue him. I watched throughout. He was struggling to stay afloat. He took off his coat, which was dragging him down, and tried to swim to the dinghy. It was a valiant effort, but before we could reach him, he went under. He was gone."

The commander was silent, as were we all.

After a long moment, Lucy asked, "Did you see blood in the water?"

"The sky was too dark and the sea too rough and we were too far away. But there is blood on the coat."

"What happened to the Chinese motor launch?" I asked.

"It had gone out of sight by the time we had the dinghy and the coat back on board."

"We have given a description of the launch to the police," Lansdowne added, "and to the harbor patrols."

"The body will be impossible for a diver to recover," the commander said. "The river is nearly eighty feet deep off Limehouse Basin, and this was at high tide."

"Tell me again, Commander," Lucy said. "We need to be absolutely certain. You saw the face of the man when he was in the water. How far away were you?"

"Perhaps a hundred feet."

"Yet close enough so you recognized Sherlock Holmes."

"There is no doubt in my mind."

She turned to me. "Let me see the overcoat."

I picked up the coat once again. The label read, *Made by Stanley Lampert, Draper*. I handed it over to Lucy.

"It's the coat he bought from that little shop in St. Margaret's, two years ago," Lucy said. To the commander, she added, "In fact, I selected it. We all waited while the draper's wife added a pocket."

She looked steadily into my eyes and handed the coat back to me. I turned over the wet wool fabric, finding the pocket.

I reached inside.

Felt something.

"There is a small piece of wet pasteboard in the pocket," I said. "Very wet."

"Be very careful," Lucy said.

I withdrew a small, soggy, pink-tinged rectangle from the pocket. I flattened the object out on the table.

It was a one-way railway ticket from Shellingford to London.

In my memory, suddenly I was with Holmes once again in Scotland Yard. His words seemed to echo in my mind.

Now I must pursue my own lines of inquiry.

I turned to Lucy. "We must go to Shellingford."

In Lucy's eyes I saw the same conflicting emotions that I myself felt. I saw her faint flicker of hope that Holmes might somehow yet be alive. Yet I could also see her despair at the weight of evidence stacked up against his survival.

She came closer and shook her head, her voice steady. "Not yet, Uncle John. These people are very, very dangerous. If we are to return to Shellingford, we must be fully armed with as much information as we can gather. There is something I would have you do."

She glanced over her shoulder to where Mycroft had drawn a little apart to speak to Lord Lansdowne. She lowered her voice. "But you must tell absolutely no one." A shadow crossed her features. "I don't think I can even tell Jack."

I felt my eyebrows rise. "What you plan is illegal?"

Lucy's expression remained steady, her voice firm. "Extremely."

53. OUTSIDE THE LAW

"Did you sleep at all last night?" Jack asked.

I shook my head. It was barely six o'clock in the morning, and Jack had only just come home from Scotland Yard to find me in the kitchen, staring into a cup of coffee that I had no intention of actually drinking.

"No. But I'm all right."

Outside, the weather seemed to be doing its best to match my mood. Last night's snow had turned into freezing sleet that clattered on the roof and hissed against the windowpanes. Everything felt dull. Even the usual life and bustle of London muted in submission to the winter elements.

I looked up at Jack. "Do you think there's a chance that my father is still alive?"

I knew that I could trust him to tell me the truth, and not what he thought I wanted to hear. "I keep telling myself that he's done this in the past, and that he's Sherlock Holmes, so, of course, he can't actually be dead. But as much as he seems legendary, larger than real life, he's still human—just a mortal man—and maybe everyone's luck has to run out sooner or later."

I swallowed to keep my voice from shaking. "There's one thing. One thing I thought of and that I keep holding onto, even though part of me thinks that it's crazy. That red powder that was found at the scene of Holmes's kidnapping—the chemicals that produced the smoke?"

Jack nodded, a line appearing between his brows.

"Well, it's used in fireworks, just as Mycroft said. He was looking at it as proof of the Asian connection, and maybe it is. But it's also used in the theater."

Jack nodded again. "In *The Mikado*. You said."

We were both speaking in low voices to keep from waking Becky, who was still asleep in her bed upstairs. She hadn't wanted to sleep last night any more than I had, but sheer exhaustion had finally taken over somewhere around two o'clock in the morning. I wanted her to get whatever rest she could.

"Exactly! I've seen it used at the Savoy—and Holmes would know that. He'd know I would recognize it. What if it was a message to me? Letting me know that all of this—Holmes's kidnapping, his apparent death—was something he himself had orchestrated. Another sort of theatrical production, albeit with much higher stakes than *The Mikado*."

Spoken out loud, the whole theory sounded even more tenuous and insubstantial than it had done inside my own head. But Jack didn't say so. Instead, still frowning, he dropped into the chair beside me, loosening the collar buttons on his blue wool uniform.

"What do you think? Am I crazy?" I finally asked. I was almost afraid to hear his answer, just because I knew that he wouldn't tell a comforting lie.

But Jack shook his head. "I think your father's alive until you know for absolute fact he's dead. Could he be in danger, even if he got out of the river alive last night? Obviously. Could he have drowned or died of a gunshot wound? The evidence looks that way. But until we know for certain that he's gone, I think we have to believe he survived. And if that's true, he still needs our help."

I let out a shaky breath. "Thank you." I managed a small smile. "You're useful to have around, you know that?"

"Speaking of which, what time are you meeting with Dr. Watson to get started on the plan for this morning?"

My head snapped up and I stared at him, words momentarily failing me. "How did you … did Uncle John …"

"No. I just know the way you think, that's all. Benjamin Davies is our best lead to whoever's behind all of this, but he's not going to be easy to crack. You're planning to go after him this morning."

"I'm sorry." I searched Jack's gaze for any sign of anger. "I wasn't trying to keep secrets from you, I just thought that it would be better if you didn't know I was planning to commit at least one felony today."

"It's all right." Jack lightly smoothed a stray hair away from my face. "He's your father. And we can't waste days thinking up a safer way to approach Davies. Time's important."

That was true; it was the reason I had approached Uncle John with this plan in the first place, but I still shook my head. "And your not getting thrown off the police force in disgrace is also important." I swallowed. The words were hard to force out, but I still needed to say them. "If you tell me not to do this, I won't."

"You think I'm that crazy?" Jack stood up. "I don't have to be back at the Yard until four o'clock. I'm going to go upstairs and change so I don't look like a policeman at first glance."

It took half a second before the meaning of his words jolted through me, and then I stared at him all over again. "You're planning to come with us?"

"This will all go better with three people involved."

That was also true. I'd been prepared to execute the plan with only myself and Uncle John, improvising as necessary, but Jack's presence would make it infinitely easier. My throat still closed off at the thought of what would happen if we were caught. "Jack." I reached for his hand. "You really don't have to do this for me."

"Yes, I do." He smiled briefly, squeezing my fingers. "I seem to remember standing up in front of the Archbishop of Canterbury and promising something of the kind."

"You promised to love, honor, and cherish. Unless your memory is better than mine, there's nothing in the marriage vows about taking part in whatever reckless, illegal, and possibly stupid plan your wife decides on."

Jack laughed, then shrugged. "It wouldn't make a difference, even if I could claim I didn't know what you were doing, even if I had nothing to do with it. We're married. That means I'd more or less be held responsible by the higher-ups at the Yard anyway if you were caught and found guilty by the law."

"That's meant to make me feel better?"

Jack bent and kissed me lightly. "It's meant to say, I trust you not to get caught. Now. Let's go kidnap Benjamin Davies. All else aside, I can't think of anyone who deserves it more."

LUCY

54. KIDNAPPING A SCOUNDREL

I peered out of the mouth of the alley onto the street beyond. Burdett Road was, for East London, a comparatively wide thoroughfare. It consisted largely of uninspired square brick buildings housing butcher shops, second-hand clothes stalls, several taverns, and one or two so-called "*ragged schools*," run on charity for the children of the poorest districts.

The Stagg Inn stood on the left side of the road, about five hundred feet from my place of concealment. It was still early morning, and chill fog hung heavy, partly concealing the inn's half-timbered walls and the painted sign over the door.

Beside me, Uncle John stamped his feet in an effort to keep warm. The two of us were alone, Jack having gone ahead to our ultimate destination to make sure that everything was prepared.

Uncle John blew on his gloved hands. "How do we know that Davies is actually inside?"

"We don't." The early hour made it likely that Benjamin Davies would still be asleep in the room he had engaged on the Inn's upper floor, but not certain. "If he's not, we'll just have to try again later. Or tomorrow." My skin crawled at the thought of having to wait that long. "At least we know for certain that he's staying there."

We couldn't afford to stand here indefinitely, waiting for the chance that Davies would come out of the inn. We had to draw him out. To that end, Uncle John had delivered a message to the inn's manager—an urgent message, asking that Davies come without delay to the address we already had for Abelard Shirley.

It was as certain a guarantee as we could think of that Davies would obey the missive and come outside.

Uncle John studied me. "Something's troubling you, though."

So far this morning, we had carefully avoided all mention of my father. Like me, Uncle John seemed to be operating on the plan to keep hoping until all hope was absolutely, definitively gone. But I wondered if, like me, he was also afraid to so much as bring up Holmes's name for fear that the words, *What if he really is dead?* would come out of one of our mouths.

"It's Becky," I said. "Ordinarily I would have expected her to do everything in her power to take part in this sort of scheme. But she didn't even try to argue about being left out of it all."

Flynn was even involved. At the moment, his skinny, ragged form was slouched against an empty doorway near the Stagg Inn. But Becky had gone to Baker Street to stay with Mrs. Hudson without so much as a murmur.

"Davies is her father," Uncle John pointed out. "It is only natural that she should feel distress at the thought of his involvement."

"I know. You're right." It was yet another reason I felt absolutely no compunction about what we had planned for Davies.

I straightened up, my heart quickening as the door to the inn opened and a man emerged.

I had never met Benjamin Davies before, but Jack had described him as he remembered from years ago, and we had Davies's characteristics from the police records, besides.

Height: five foot ten inches. Weight: a hundred and sixty pounds. Eyes and hair color: brown.

Even without that, there couldn't be too many men staying at the Stagg Inn with the characteristic pallor of a man who has recently been incarcerated.

Davies wore a checked suit of a pattern so loud that it would give the members of the Diogenes Club collective heart failure. He pulled on a brown overcoat and tugged the brim of a fedora hat over his brow, scowling at the fog and the mixture of mud and icy slush underfoot.

Practically no place in London is ever completely deserted, but at this hour of the morning and with a drizzle of sleet continuing to fall, Burdett Street was quiet. A milk wagon creaked slowly past, and a few dock workers hurried towards their day's employment, shoulders hunched against the chill.

Benjamin Davies came towards us. Behind him, I saw Flynn detach himself from the wall and saunter after Davies, hands in his pockets, with a deceptively casual stride.

I glanced at Uncle John. "You have everything ready?"

Watson nodded, patting his right coat pocket. "Yes indeed."

Putting on a burst of speed, Flynn darted forward, pretending to crash into Davies from behind.

"Oh, sorry, gov."

I was scarcely predisposed to like Benjamin Davies, but the enraged snarl he directed at Flynn did nothing to improve my opinion.

"Watch where you're goin', you little—" Davies broke off,

his gaze landing on something in Flynn's hand. "That's my pocketwatch!"

Flynn had protested this part of the scheme mightily, saying that it was the mark of a clod-headed amateur to pick a pocket so clumsily. But we needed Davies to have absolutely no doubt that he had been robbed.

Clutching the watch, Flynn took off running towards us at full tilt, and Davies came after him, big and clumsy, slipping on the muddy slush, but determined nonetheless. His face was red with fury.

I drew back into the shadows of the alley and looked at Uncle John, who nodded, reaching into the pocket of his coat.

Flynn burst into the alley and dove past us, taking shelter behind a stack of broken packing crates.

A moment later, Davies appeared as well, breathing hard. I stepped forward, tripped him, which sent him staggering forward … straight into Uncle John's waiting arms.

I couldn't actually remember the last time a scheme like this had gone exactly to plan. I just had to hope that we weren't slated to pay for the good luck later.

Smoothly, in a single swift motion, Watson raised the hypodermic syringe he'd brought with him and stabbed the needle into Davies's neck, depressing the plunger.

Davies gave a roar of outrage, thrashing in Uncle John's grip and struggling to break free.

"Let go o' me, y' crazy old—"

Before he could finish the insult, both his voice and his movements slowed, like a child's mechanical wind-up toy coming to a halt.

He staggered again and shook his head, obviously trying to

clear his mind. "What … what …"

"It's quite all right, Mr. Davies." Watson had maintained his tight grip on Davies's arms, and now supported most of his weight. He spoke in the reassuring manner of a doctor to his patient. "Just come along with us, we'll soon have you feeling better again."

Benjamin Davies made another feeble effort to break free, but his muscles refused to cooperate. He barely managed to flail one arm. "I don't … I'm not …"

"Now, now, Mr. Davies, none of that. Just come along with us, that's right."

Still supporting the majority of Davies's weight, Uncle John propelled him towards the opposite end of the alleyway.

I took a place on Davies's other side, ready to catch him in case he fell, while Flynn brought up the rear.

Benjamin Davies's face had gone slack, his eyes unfocused, and he shuffled along with the loose, uncoordinated stumbling of a drunkard.

"That was very quick," I murmured over the top of his head. "What was in that injection you gave him, Uncle John?"

"Horse tranquilizer. Combined with an additional ingredient of Holmes's own devising. He assured me when he developed the formula that it was perfectly safe for humans, since he'd tested it on himself."

I saw a quick twist of pain cross Watson's face as he spoke, and wished I could think of something encouraging to say. But Uncle John wouldn't be comforted by hollow reassurances any more than I would have been.

The street beyond the alleyway was busier than Burdett Road had been. Leaving Uncle John to manage Davies's increasingly dead weight, I stepped forward and hailed the first Hansom cab that rolled past.

The driver—an elderly man, muffled nearly up to his bushy white eyebrows in scarves and a tartan overcoat—looked somewhat askance as Uncle John hauled Davies forward.

"I'm a doctor," Watson told him. "And this man is seriously ill. I must get him to my surgery immediately."

One of Watson's great strengths was that he was such an honest, utterly reliable person that even complete strangers found him trustworthy.

The cab driver's expression cleared and he nodded at us to get inside. "Right you are, guv'nor. Where to?"

Watson gave the address of his own surgery in Paddington, which we had agreed on as the safest place to conduct our endeavors.

Davies flailed again, slurring something unintelligible as Uncle John propelled him up the metal steps and into the cab, depositing him with a thump onto one of the cracked leather seats.

"Yes, yes," Uncle John replied. He still spoke with hearty reassurance. "I know the pain is severe, my friend. I promise that we shall do our utmost to help you."

Davies seemed to have passed the point where he could even try to fight back. He sat sprawled on the carriage seat, his hat tilted at an angle and his jaw slack. Only his eyes continued to glare blearily at us for a moment more—but then his lids drifted closed.

I turned to Flynn, about to ask whether he wanted to accompany us, but he shook his head, hands in his pockets. "Nah, but thanks all the same. Dr. Watson already paid me, and I got things to do."

With the quickness that made him such a very effective Irregular, he turned and, in another moment, had vanished into the pedestrian traffic on the street.

I climbed up into the cab, and Uncle John gave the signal to the driver, who clicked the reins. His team of twin bay horses clip-clopped forward, and with a lurch, the wheels of the cab began to roll—on the way to break Benjamin Davies's will.

LUCY

55. Scaring a Scoundrel

"Hold still, Uncle John." Steadying myself with a hand on the back of the chair, I applied another layer of greasepaint to Watson's face.

Uncle John obediently tilted his head and remained motionless. "Quite like old times, eh?"

We had played out a variation of this interrogation technique before, during the Diogenes Club murder investigation, although in that case, Watson's role had been somewhat different, and his new face had been manufactured by Holmes.

I might not be as skilled as my father at the art of disguise, but working in the theater had taught me a great deal about the use of cosmetics. At the moment, I was engaged in giving Watson a rather spectacular black eye and a split lip that had dripped blood down his chin.

"There." I added a final yellow-purplish accent to the bruising under his mustache and stood back. "I think that's good enough to be convincing."

It might not hold up in bright light, but we were in one of the small, windowless examination rooms in Uncle John's surgery.

The only light came from a flickering oil lamp set on the floor that cast weird, unruly shadows over the blank white walls.

Uncle John nodded, gingerly touching the tiny strips of sticking plaster I'd used to make his eye appear swollen shut.

"We'd best get into position, I think," he said. "It looks as though Mr. Davies is beginning to come around."

In preparation for our activities, all the furniture had been moved out of the examination room, save for two plain wooden chairs.

Benjamin Davies was currently tied to one of those chairs. He was slumped forward with his head resting on his chest, but Uncle John was right; his closed lids were beginning to flutter and he gave the occasional twitch or snort as the effects of the tranquilizer began to wear off.

Watson sat down in the chair beside Davies, holding out his hands with the wrists joined, ready to be tied together as Davies's were.

"Are you ready for this?" I asked as I looped a length of rope around his wrists and tied a knot that was tight enough to be convincing without being too uncomfortable.

I knew from long experience that Uncle John was far more intelligent than readers of his stories might give him credit for. But at the same time, I felt a flutter of uneasiness that a large majority of our plan rested on his acting abilities.

He had many talents, but the art of dissembling wasn't typically one of his strongest.

"I believe so." I thought Watson looked slightly nervous as well, but he nodded, firmed his jaw, and settled himself so that he was slouched back in a mixture of exhaustion and defiance.

Davies let out a low groan. I took my own position opposite

the two chairs, using these few moments to study him.

Benjamin Davies was somewhere around forty-five years of age. He had wheat-blond hair, and a face that probably had been extremely handsome in youth. His features had coarsened with age, the skin loosening over his cheekbones and under his chin. But he still might attract all sorts of female attention whenever he went out.

Looking at him, I could understand why Jack and Becky's mother had been drawn to him. I might never sympathize with her decision to abandon Jack, but I could see why Benjamin Davies had caught her eye.

His eyelids fluttered again, and I drew a breath, meeting Uncle John's gaze and nodding. The curtain was about to rise.

"Is that all you have to say?" I demanded.

Watson flinched backwards. "I … I think—"

I leaned in and spoke with deadly calm. "Tell me. Has anything that has so far transpired given you the impression that I care in the slightest what you think? I want answers! Now!"

Watson cringed as I spoke the final words, giving a convincing impression of fear. And Davies simultaneously opened his eyes and thrashed out against his bonds, abruptly realizing that he was tied at the wrists and ankles.

"What in—who—" His gaze was still bleary, his voice hoarse. He turned his head and glared at me.

"Quiet," I snapped. "I will deal with you presently."

If Davies had been his usual self, I thought he might have argued back, but he was still groggy and off balance from the drug. He blinked in confusion but didn't speak again.

I leaned back over Uncle John, placing my face mere inches away from his. "Do you really need another reminder of what happens when you refuse to tell me what I want to know?"

Uncle John cringed back again, frantically shaking his head. "No ... I ... I ..."

I remembered my father once observing that most humans are, at the core, social animals, taking their emotional cues from the other humans around them. Put a man in the audience at a theater and he will likely laugh when the rest of the audience does, even if he doesn't fully appreciate the joke.

Put a man next to someone who is clearly terrified, and he'll be likely to believe that he, too, has a reason for fear.

Out of the corner of my vision, I saw Davies's throat work as he swallowed, and he tugged again at the ties around his wrists.

I ignored him, crossing to the door of the examination room and knocking twice. The door opened instantly, and Jack strode in. His expression was grimly set, which I doubted was requiring any particular acting ability on his part.

"Our friend here needs another course of motivation to help us," I said.

Without a word, without even glancing at Davies, Jack hauled Watson out of his chair and dragged him out of the room.

"No!" Watson struggled ineffectually, the flickering lamp light showing up to full effect the bruised and battered appearance of his face. "No, please ..."

The door slammed behind them, and a moment later I heard Uncle John's voice break on an agonized scream. If this had been an actual theater production and I was giving notes on his performance, I would have cautioned him not to overdo it.

But Davies was looking visibly shaken. Another constant of human nature is that we tend to fear what we cannot see.

At the moment, the screams and occasional thumps coming

from the outer room were creating far more terrifying images in Benjamin Davies's imagination than anything he could have witnessed with his own eyes.

With, of course, the added benefit that Uncle John wasn't actually being hurt. Another crash echoed from the other room, and then silence fell. Davies's throat contracted as he swallowed again, and I could almost see him silently rifling through his options, trying to decide on what approach to take with me: angry, defiant, conciliatory ...

I obviously didn't know Davies, but my own money would be on—

"Look 'ere." Davies's mouth stretched in an attempt at a smile. "I think there's been some kind o' mistake."

His smile and his tone of voice were so thick with ingratiating charm you could have spread them on toast.

At least I'd guessed rightly on his reaction. I was female; therefore, Benjamin Davies's habitual response would be an attempt to charm me.

I kept my face completely blank of expression. "I assure you, Mr. Davies, the only mistakes here are the ones that you have made."

Davies startled just a little, and I nodded. "Yes, I know your name—and quite a bit more about you, besides."

Behind me, the door opened and Jack stepped back into the room. He didn't speak, just came to stand against the wall beside the door, his arms folded across his chest.

A week ago, when Abelard Shirley's letter had first arrived, I'd been afraid of what Jack might do. Now he exuded angry menace, but also still-muscled control. No matter what happened, he wouldn't let his temper snap and endanger the success of the plan.

Davies still flinched, instinctively trying to retreat although the fact that his ankles were tied to the chair legs ensured he had nowhere to go. His gaze flicked from me to Jack, and he licked his lips.

"Who are you people?"

I needed his focus on me; that was what we had agreed on: that I would do most of the talking. "I am someone who wants to talk to you." Without turning, I nodded towards Jack. "Whereas he is someone who wants to break both your legs. I suggest you answer my questions."

Davies's expression verged on panicked, but his face still twisted in an ugly sneer. "You think you can scare me? I'm—"

Without giving him a chance to finish, I stepped forward and kicked Davies's leg just below the kneecap, calculating the blow to be hard enough for pain but not quite so hard as to do lasting damage.

Davies yelped, smacking the back of his skull against the chair rail as his head snapped back.

I kept my voice level. "I said that breaking both your legs wasn't my highest priority, Mr. Davies, not that I couldn't accomplish it if I so chose."

56. SQUEEZING A SCOUNDREL

Benjamin Davies blinked and stared up at me, seemingly at a loss for words.

"What do you want?" he finally asked.

"The name of the individual who controls the opium smuggling in the town of Shellingford."

Davies's expression tightened fractionally in surprise. Then a calculating gleam came into his eyes. "What's in it for me if I tell you?"

"What's in it for you is your continued ability to walk and use the fingers on both your hands," I snapped. I nodded towards the outer room. "Do you really want to find out what will happen if you continue to make this as difficult as our other guest chose to do?"

Davies's throat bobbed, and he changed tack, trying again for a conciliatory tone. "Look 'ere, there's no need for that. No reason we can't all be friends 'ere."

It would take all the pages of the phone directory to list the number of reasons why we couldn't. But I kept silent, and Davies went on.

"I don't even know who the man on top is. I only ever dealt with the toff."

"Lord Lynley?"

"Yeah, that's right." Davies gave a disgusted snort. "Bloody gentry."

"You didn't like him?" I asked.

"Like him?" Davies eyes narrowed as though remembering an insult. "Thought 'e was too good for the likes of me, didn't 'e? Until he gets a fit of the morbs just because that mutton shunter's brother came sniffing around. Then 'is 'igh and mighty-ness starts up talking like I'm 'is brickiest chum."

This was where it might have been smarter to have Jack doing the questioning, because I'd understood only about half of what Davies had just said.

"Lord Lynley was worried about Inspector Swafford's brother coming to Shellingford?" I was reasonably sure I could infer that much.

"Yeah, that's right." Davies jerked his head in a nod. "Pigeon-livered meater. Didn't 'ave the stomach to do what 'ad to be done. 'Ad to leave it to me, didn't 'e?"

My heart sped up, but I kept all trace of expression from showing on my face. "By which you mean, taking care of Tom Swafford?"

"Yeah, that's right." Davies shrugged indifferently. "Wanted me to bring 'im in to the estate for a little chat. Wanted to find out who he'd talked to."

"You mean, find out else knew about the opium."

"Yeah, but he weren't in a mood for conversation. Nearly did for me instead. So I snuffed 'im out on the fens and dumped the body in an irrigation ditch. Old Lynley had a fit when I told 'im.

Wait a tick—"

A light seemed to go on in Davies's eyes as a sudden disturbing thought occurred—more disturbing, apparently, than the memory of having committed cold-blooded murder. He sat up straighter, looking from me to Jack. "Is this some kind o' setup?"

"We're nothing to do with the police, if that's what you mean," I said. It was becoming progressively more of a challenge to keep the revulsion out of my voice, but I pitched my voice to sound calm, even pleasant. "And we don't care about Tom Swafford's murder. All we want to know about is the opium smuggling. You never found out who Lord Lynley was working for?"

I had my own theories, but it would be nice to get confirmation.

"Nah." Davies settled back in his chair, shaking his head.

"That's not particularly helpful." I still kept my voice level, but I sank just a bit of menace into the words. "And your being unhelpful gives me significantly less motivation to allow you to walk out of here alive."

Davies's breathing hitched and he muttered, "The Red Lantern Room!"

"What is that?"

"That's where the dope goes out." Davies spoke quickly, the words almost tumbling over one another. "I never been there, but it's in some hotel along the beach."

I let out a slow breath. I'd been right. It might not make Holmes's odds of survival any greater, but at least we wouldn't be returning to Shellingford completely blind.

"Is there anything else you can tell us?"

Davies's gaze shifted, his expression turning cagey. "What

else do you want t' know?"

I stepped forward, took hold of Davies's right index finger, and bent it backwards, just hard enough to let him know that I could dislocate the joint if I wanted to.

The thought of the man in front of me taking Becky away gave me all the motivation and needed to speak with icy menace.

"You seem to think that you're in a position to negotiate, Mr. Davies. Let me assure you again that you are not. Tell me everything you know. Now."

Standing this close, I could smell the sharp, cold-sweat odor of Davies's fear.

"Fine! Fine!" He drew a ragged gulp of air. "It weren't much, anyway. Just something I overheard Lynley say once, when 'e was on the telephone. 'The Duchess.'"

"'The Duchess?' What does that mean?"

"I don't know!" Davies's eyes were wide with the effort to make me believe him. "I swear, it was just something I 'eard. Maybe it's the name of the ship the stuff comes in on?"

I supposed that was possible. We would have to consult shipping manifests to be sure.

The silence dragged on long enough for Davies to shift in his chair and ask, with a thread of anxiety in the words, "What happens now?"

I recollected myself and glanced at Jack, who gave a barely perceptible nod. "Now, Mr. Davies, you will remain right here until we can send a telegram to the Lincolnshire police. Then I expect you'll be arrested for the murder of Tom Swafford."

Davies stared at me, a disbelieving expression on his face, as though he were expecting at any moment to hear me say that I was only joking.

When that didn't come, he stammered, "But … you said …"

"I lied." I turned to the door. "Good day, Mr. Davies. You'll forgive me for saying I hope we never meet again."

LUCY

57. A PLAN, AND A SHOCK

"Did you hear all of that, Uncle John?" We were in the larger outer room of the surgery, where patients could sit and wait for their appointments. "And I appreciate the sacrifice of your furniture, by the way."

A small chair with a cane seat lay broken on the ground—the source of the crashes that Davies and I had heard.

Watson waved that aside. "It was nothing. And yes, I believe I caught all of Mr. Davies's confession perfectly," he said.

"He killed Tom Swafford." I glanced at Jack but he didn't say anything. "That gives us much more reason for him to be sent back to jail than I'd even hoped for."

"As long as we can make the charges stick," Uncle John said. "And to that end—" He took out a handkerchief and began to scrub the greasepaint from his face. "I had best be in touch with Lestrade, so that he can telegraph the police in Shellingford."

I thought of Chief Constable Slade's careworn face and hollow, worried eyes. Maybe this nightmare would soon be over for him, too.

"He'll need backup before he can investigate," I said. "Chief Constable Slade, I mean. He's almost certainly being watched."

Watson nodded. "All the more reason for us to move quickly. We now have a place to begin to look in Shellingford, as well. The Red Lantern Room."

"We may have more than that," I told him. "But I'll wait to tell you until we're actually on the train."

Uncle John stood up. "Indeed. I will contact Lestrade at once, but that means that the two of you had best depart." He nodded to Jack and me. "Shall we reconvene at the train station in, say, an hour and a half?"

"That will be fine." I turned to the examination room, where Benjamin Davies was still captive. "Will you be all right, Uncle John? Kidnapping is still a crime, and Lestrade is still an officer of the law."

"Kidnapping?" Uncle John's smile was grimmer than any I had ever seen from him. "I have yet to hear any mention of kidnapping. Benjamin Davies accompanied me here for a friendly chat, during which he happened to let slip that he had been responsible for a man's death. When he became violent, I naturally sought to restrain him in self-defense so that he might be handed over to the law."

I raised an eyebrow. "And you think Lestrade will believe that?"

"The stakes are higher than we thought before. The charge brought against Davies will be murder, rather than simply smuggling. I do not think Lestrade will work particularly hard *not* to believe it," Watson said. "Especially in light of—"

His mouth twisted, a quick spasm of pain crossing his face.

Holmes's death, he had been about to say. I was as certain of it as though he'd actually spoken the words out loud—and equally certain that neither of us wanted to acknowledge it.

"We'll go, then," I said. "I'll meet you at King's Cross Station."

* * *

The temperature had dropped since the early morning, and a biting January wind buffeted us as soon as we stepped from Uncle John's surgery back out into the street. It was just past noon, but the dark skies overhead and the shadows clinging to the doorways felt more like early evening. Carriages rattled across the cobblestones, the drivers wrapped in scarves that were white and stiff with their frozen breath. Pedestrians hurried past, every single one of them probably wishing that they were at home in front of a roaring fire.

The only figure who seemed content to remain in place was a bearded street doctor who had set up camp on the pavement two doors down. He might have been hoping to appeal to those who either couldn't afford to visit one of the doctors' offices on this street—or to whom modern medicine offered no hope of a cure. He had a suitcase open on a stand beside him stocked with bottles that promised themselves as a cough preventative.

I wondered fleetingly whether the mixture in the bottles contained opium. More than likely, it did.

I hailed a cab, giving the driver the Baker Street address, and Jack and I climbed in.

As the cab started to roll, I studied Jack's expression. It was rare that I didn't know what he was thinking, but at the moment I could only guess.

"He didn't recognize you," I finally said.

For safety's sake, we had agreed in advance to make no mention of Becky. I had every hope that Davies's next abode would be inside a jail cell. But even if we failed to get him sent back to prison, we did not want to give Benjamin Davies cause to use Becky for an instrument of revenge.

Jack had been looking out the cab window and at that seemed to come back from a long way off. Then he shrugged. "I was seven the last time he saw me."

I put a hand on his arm. "I'm sorry. I wanted to murder him in there, practically every time he opened his mouth. I can't imagine how it must have been for you. He's the whole reason you grew up alone."

Jack raised one shoulder again. "And I'd have been better off if I'd had to live with him? I don't see that I have any grounds to complain."

I shook my head. "You're a much better person than I would be."

"Sometime I'll remind you that you said that." He smiled briefly but then sobered. "I wouldn't change anything that's happened to me—because then maybe I wouldn't have ended up where I am now."

"A police sergeant with Scotland Yard?"

"That part's nice, but I meant that maybe I wouldn't have ended up here, married to you." He threaded his fingers with mine. "That's all I really care about."

I started to smile up at him, then froze, ice running down my spine. The cab had drawn up in front of 221 Baker Street, and Mrs. Hudson's familiar figure was standing on the front steps. She was wringing her apron.

"Oh, Miss Lucy! Sergeant Kelly!" Mrs. Hudson didn't even wait for us to climb down from the carriage, but hurried to meet us at the curb, her usually plump, motherly face a mask of frightened agitation. "Thank the good Lord that you're back,

I didn't know what to do!"

"What is it, Mrs. Hudson?" I caught hold of her hands, trying to speak with more calm assurance than I felt. "Everything will be all right, just tell us what's happened."

Mrs. Hudson took a shuddering breath. Tears stood in her eyes and on her cheeks. "It's young Becky, Miss Lucy. She's gone!"

PART FOUR

BATTLE STATIONS

BECKY
58. CAUGHT

The lockpicks slipped in Becky's fingers, almost falling onto the muddy ground. Lucy would have had the door open five minutes ago. But then, Lucy could do practically anything.

Beside her, Flynn shifted his weight uncomfortably. "Are you trying to make this take for-bleeding-ever?"

Becky ignored him. "Here, hold this."

She slipped Prince's leash off her wrist and held it out to Flynn. Prince was usually good about waiting patiently, but maybe Flynn's twitchiness was getting to him, too, because he kept whining and tugging on the leash. Which wasn't helping her pick the lock.

Flynn gave her a disbelieving look. "You want me to get near that thing?"

"No, I want you to learn how to walk through doors the way they do in magic shows," Becky snapped. "But I'll settle for you holding onto his leash. And he is *not* a thing!"

Flynn scowled at her, but took hold of Prince's leash gingerly. "Sooner or later one of the rozzers is going to come by on patrol, and then we'll be for it."

Flynn had the annoying habit of being right—maybe not always but a lot of the time—and now he had a point. Beat constables patrolled this neighborhood regularly, and if one of them spotted the pair of them trying to pick a lock on a door, he'd be blowing his whistle and calling for them to stop in the name of the law before Becky could blink twice.

Or else someone else would call the police on them. Becky had dressed herself up in boys' clothes that matched Flynn's: boots, tattered trousers, oversize coat and a hat pulled down to shade her face and hide her braids.

Becky had learned a long time ago that boys had a lot more freedom to roam around the city, which wasn't fair but it was just how the world worked. Even Lucy dressed up like a boy sometimes, just to be safe and so that none of the street toughs would give her trouble for being so pretty.

This wasn't that kind of a neighborhood, though. St. John's Wood was near Regent's Park, the kind of a place where gentry lived: the houses weren't called houses, they were Something-Something Villa or This-and-That Lodge.

In other words, she and Flynn stuck out like a couple of sore thumbs.

"If the police come by, we'll just have to make a run for it," Becky said. She stuck the picks into the lock again and started wiggling them around, hoping to feel something she could catch hold of.

Flynn tipped his head back, looking up at the plate over the door, which read, *Bryony Lodge*.

"Why'd Mr. 'Olmes want to go and rent this place?"

Becky shrugged. "Mr. Holmes is funny."

That was actually one of her favorite things about Sherlock

Holmes: he never thought about things the same way ordinary people did, which was exciting because it meant that you never knew what he might do or say next.

She glanced up at Flynn. "You don't think he's really dead, do you?"

Flynn shook his head. "Nah, not 'im. Got nine lives like a cat, Mr. 'Olmes does."

Becky thought he spoke the words a little too forcefully, as if he was trying to convince himself as well as her. Flynn was worried, even if he wouldn't say so.

The lockpick scraped uselessly inside the lock, and a drop of sweat trickled down the side of Becky's cheek.

"Maybe we should have just come clean with your brother and Miss Lucy," Flynn said. "They could have gotten us in here by now."

Flynn was—possibly—right again, but Becky shook her head. "I don't want to get Lucy's hopes up in case I'm wrong." She'd never seen Lucy as worried as she'd been last time she saw her. "Mr. Holmes is her father. She doesn't want to think that he could really have drowned, but she's afraid that he did."

She blew out a breath and bent over the lockpicks again.

Maybe Mr. Holmes wasn't easy to predict, but she should have known he'd change the locks on the windows and doors.

Irene Adler—the famous lady from one of Dr. Watson's stories—had rented this place while she was in London. Becky had thought of it right away, as soon as Flynn had told her Mr. Holmes had been looking at a house that was most likely in St. John's Wood.

She'd read that story so many times she practically had it memorized, right up to the way Mr. Holmes had described the place to Dr. Watson: a bijou villa, with a garden at the back, but built out in front right up to the road; two stories; Chubb lock to the door; large sitting-room on the right side, well furnished, with long windows almost to the floor, and those preposterous English window fasteners, which a child could open.

That had sounded promising, but now Mr. Holmes was the one renting the place.

At least, she *thought* he was the one renting the place.

Becky ran through the evidence in her head. Flynn had struck up an acquaintance with the boy who ran errands for the estate agent that Mr. Holmes had seen, and found out that the only property the estate agent had rented in the past two weeks had been in St. John's Wood.

And while she'd been at 221B Baker Street early this morning, she had snuck into Mr. Holmes's room and examined the soles of all the shoes in his wardrobe.

One pair—a pair of very elegant suede shoes that she couldn't picture Mr. Holmes wearing unless he wanted to look like an aristocrat—had been speckled with crumbs of reddish-brown mud. Becky had compared it to the monograph Mr. Holmes had written about all of the different types of London soils, and found that the mud had probably come from St. John's Wood.

There were three or four other places in London that had similar types of dirt, but this had to be the most likely. It just had to.

Getting in to check whether they were right was turning out to be much harder than she'd thought, though. The long windows Mr. Holmes had talked about were now covered with heavy wooden shutters and fastened with locks that you'd need bolt cutters to get through.

Maybe she should go back to Baker Street and try getting some bolt cutters? Although the second she set foot inside, Mrs. Hudson would probably lock her up and never let her out of her sight ever again. Or else Mrs. Hudson would cry, which would make Becky feel even more guilty about having gotten away from her.

Well, with any luck, she and Flynn could finish here and be back at Baker Street before Lucy and Jack came to collect her. And if they found something really useful, everyone—including Mrs. Hudson—would understand.

"Do you think your brother and Lucy are done with your father yet?" Flynn asked.

Jack and Lucy had told her what they were planning, and what they'd left out, Flynn had filled in.

Becky wiped sweat out of her eyes and shrugged again. "I don't know."

She focused on the lock. Part of her wanted to ask Flynn to tell her everything he could about her father, since Flynn had actually seen him just hours ago. But the bigger part of her didn't even want to think about Benjamin Davies, much less talk about him.

Flynn seemed to hesitate for a second, then dug in the pocket of his coat. "'Ere. I wanted to give this to you."

Becky glanced up to see him holding out a pocket watch. It wasn't as nice as Mr. Holmes's or Dr. Watson's, but it still looked like it would sell for enough money to keep Flynn fed for weeks.

She frowned. "Why would you want to give it to me?"

"Because it's the one I nicked off of yer old man," Flynn said. "Dr. Watson and Miss Lucy never thought to ask me about it, so I hung onto it. But I reckon it oughta be yours."

Mr. Holmes would probably say that Flynn's logic left something to be desired. Becky jerked backwards, staring at the watch and starting to feel sick to her stomach. "I don't want it!"

Flynn shook his head. "Don't talk like that. You might need it—or the money you'd get for it. I know a bloke with a pawn shop down on Commercial Road who'd give you a couple of bob for it, easy."

Becky frowned, about to say that she didn't want the money from the watch any more than she wanted the watch itself.

But Flynn kept on going, leaning forward and shaking the shaggy blond hair out of his eyes. "You've got to have a plan. Just in case your father gets away and 'e does try to make you come and live with 'im."

"Lucy and Jack won't let that happen."

"Yeah, but what if it does? You never know." Flynn licked his chapped lips and then said, "I was thinking, you could always run away, if 'e did try to take you. You could come and stay with me. 'E'd never be able to find us."

That was probably true, but Becky was still stuck on the first part of what Flynn had said. "You'd let me come and stay with you?"

She was so shocked she almost dropped the lockpicks again.

Jack and Lucy would have tried to find Flynn a proper home and a family, if he'd wanted. Or let him come and stay with them. But Flynn always refused straight-out. And he didn't tell anyone where he lived, not ever.

Becky didn't think even Mr. Holmes knew exactly where Flynn stayed when he wasn't working on a case. It was probably somewhere in Whitechapel, because there was a pub near Mitre Square where Mr. Holmes could send messages. But apart from that, no one could find Flynn unless he wanted to be found.

He shrugged awkwardly. "Well, it'd just be for a bit, right? Just until we figure out how to get your old man locked up again?" Becky's eyes stung and she had to swallow a giant lump in her throat. Flynn would think she was a baby if she cried. *She* would think she was a baby.

"Thank you," she said. "I'll think about it." She made herself take the watch and slide it into her coat pocket, too. You never knew what might happen, just as Flynn had said.

The deepest, most buried fear she had—the fear she'd been trying to ignore for days—tried to rear its head again.

"What was your father like?" she asked Flynn. "I mean, are you anything like him?"

"'Ow'd I know? I told you, 'e died before I was born." Flynn gave her a look that said he thought she was crazy.

Becky stifled a sigh. "Never mind."

She pressed again with the lockpicks … and inside the lock, something suddenly clicked.

She was so startled that for a second she just looked at it blankly.

"What's wrong?" Flynn asked.

"I think … I think I just got it open."

"Well, I got an idea. What if we don't just stand 'ere staring like a couple o' mugs and go inside?" Flynn said.

Becky's heart hammered as she put her hand on the doorknob, but it turned easily. The door swung open, and Flynn ducked in.

Becky shook herself and followed. She had to stay focused, just like Mr. Holmes would say.

She shut the door behind them and locked it.

They were in a front entrance hallway with a marble floor, and gilt-trimmed mirrors hanging from the walls. It would probably be pretty when all the lights were on, but right now the curtains in the house were drawn and the windows shuttered. It made the place feel like something out of that story about the old woman who'd shut up her whole house and stopped all the clocks because she'd been abandoned on her wedding day.

"What are we looking for?" Flynn asked.

"I don't know," Becky whispered back. There wasn't really any need to whisper since they were alone, but normal speaking voices just didn't seem to belong here. "Any sign that Mr. Holmes has been here, I suppose."

What she'd really been hoping was that Mr. Holmes would be here now—that he'd somehow escaped the river and was using this place as one of his bolt-holes, to hide and recover. But she didn't even have to search the whole house to know that he wasn't. Bryony Lodge had that empty, silent, abandoned feeling that places got when there was no one inside. She already knew there wasn't another living soul here, Mr. Holmes or anyone else.

Flynn shrugged. His hands were thrust into his pockets, trying to look casual, but she could tell from the set of his shoulders that the place was making him nervous, too.

"Where do we start?"

Becky scanned the shadowy rooms she could see branching off from the front hallway. "What about in there?" She pointed to a room that looked like a parlor, with some chairs and sofas. It had to be the very same room where Holmes had pretended to be an injured clergyman and Dr. Watson had thrown in a smoke bomb to make Irene Adler think her house was on fire. Any other time, she would have been thrilled to think about actually seeing it in person.

She pointed towards the part of the room nearest to the windows. "You take that half, I'll look over here," she told Flynn.

For a while they searched in silence. Not that there was very much to search. Except for the furniture, the room was practically bare. No books, no pictures, no papers.

Becky dragged a chair over to the mantle, the legs screeching against the polished wood floor with a noise that sounded loud as a police whistle.

"What are you doing?" Flynn asked. "Trying to wake the dead?"

"In Dr. Watson's story, Irene Adler hid the photograph of the King of Bohemia in a secret recess," Becky told him. "There's a sliding panel just above the right bell-pull near the mantle."

At least, that was the way Dr. Watson had written it.

Becky maneuvered the chair closer to the mantle and hopped up, standing on tiptoe so that she could reach the bell-pull.

"Anything?" Flynn asked.

"I don't know. There's definitely something here."

Her fingers traced the outline of what had to be a secret compartment, built into the wall. Her heart started to race a little as she pushed, sliding the panel open, then looked inside.

"No. Nothing here."

The small compartment was empty, except for dust.

"Oh, well, never mind," Flynn said. "Mr. Holmes probably wouldn't use that hiding spot anyhow, not when anyone who's read Dr. Watson's stories would know about it."

"I suppose that's true."

If Mr. Holmes had been here at all, that was—which, Becky

had to admit, was looking less and less likely.

She studied the fireplace, hoping there might be ashes in the grate or some sign that someone had lighted a fire here recently. There were some coals in the coal-scuttle next to the hearth, but the fireplace itself was bare and empty, too.

Becky stayed on the chair for a second, though. The only thing on the mantle was one of those spill vases, the kind that held rolled up strips of paper to use when you were lighting a fire.

This one held five strips of rolled up newspaper. Becky frowned, staring up at them—

Outside, something rattled at the front door. As if someone else was trying to open the lock without a key.

BECKY

59. A DISCOVERY

Becky jumped, her heart trying to leap up into her throat. More than anything, she wanted to dive under one of the sofas or find somewhere else in the house to hide. But she made herself tiptoe back to the front door and look out through the peephole.

"What is it?"

Becky jumped again; she hadn't realized that Flynn had followed her out into the hall, but he was standing right beside her.

"Is it the rozzers?"

Becky shook her head. "No." Her heart was now trying to sink all the way down into her boots. "Worse than that. It's my brother."

* * *

"Well? What do you have to say for yourself?" Jack asked.

Jack didn't get angry often, and he'd never, ever shouted at her, not once. But she could tell he was struggling to keep hold of his temper right now.

"I'm sorry!" They were back in the parlor, sitting on the sofa. Well, she and Jack were sitting; Flynn was hovering near the windows, looking as if he was ready to bolt through them at any second.

Becky bit her lip. "I just didn't want to scare Lucy. She's already got her father to be worried about."

"And you didn't think she'd be worried when we found you'd disappeared?"

Put like that, Becky had to admit that she hadn't really thought things through. "I'm sorry," she said again.

Jack raked a hand through his hair. "Now she's on a train up to Shellingford with Dr. Watson, but I had to come and find you—which I wouldn't have been able to do at all if you hadn't left Mr. Holmes's shoes and his study of London soils out, open on the floor."

That was the trouble with her family—however clever you were at putting clues together, there was a solid chance that someone else would get it figured out just as fast.

"You knew we were here just from Mr. Holmes's shoes and his monograph?"

"No. Lucy went through her father's papers and found a newspaper clipping, advertising this place as available for leasing …" Jack stopped, raising an eyebrow at her. "You wouldn't be trying to change the subject, would you?"

"No. And I'm *really* sorry, Jack." Becky spoke quickly, before he could start talking again. "Really. But I think I found something. Look."

She jumped up and went over to the fireplace, lifting the spill vase down from the mantle and carrying it back to the couch.

"These newspapers." She took one of the rolled-up strips out and handed it over to Jack. "Look at the date on the top. 13 January. That's yesterday."

Jack had been frowning at her, but now he looked at the paper in his hand, his expression shifting.

"Someone was here, in the house, just yesterday!" Becky said.

"Someone who didn't want it to look like anyone was living here, but thought they might come back and be in need of a fire," Jack said.

"Exactly." Becky didn't say anything more out loud, but the words beat in time to her own pulse. *Please, please, please let it have been Mr. Holmes.*

"All right." Jack stood up. "Let's see what else we can find." He scanned the room, frowning, until his gaze stopped on the fireplace.

"I already checked the hidden compartment from Dr. Watson's story," Becky said. "There's nothing there."

"No, it's not that." Jack shook his head and stood up, crossing to kneel on the hearth. "Look here." He pointed at a small spot where a crusty white substance had dried on the hearthstones. "Someone dripped water here, and it left the salt behind when it dried."

He frowned for another second, then ducked, reaching up inside the fireplace, up into the chimney.

Something tumbled down onto the hearthstones—a wadded-up bundle of what looked like damp clothes: trousers and a shirt, wrapped around rough workman's boots.

"Cor!" Flynn had come over to see what was happening, and now stared at the bundle, his eyes wide.

"Is that—" Becky's heart was beating so hard she could hardly get the words out. "Do you think those are the clothes that Mr. Holmes was wearing when he went into the river?"

Jack was examining the clothes, shaking out each article.

"I couldn't prove it beyond all doubt, but it looks that way."

There was something else wrapped up with the clothes, too. Jack shook the stained and dirty cotton shirt, and a waterproof oilskin packet fell onto the hearth.

"Cor!" Flynn breathed again as Jack slit the packet open. "What is it?"

"It looks like a map of Shellingford!" Becky said, trying to crane her neck to peer over Jack's shoulder. The map was hand-drawn in blue ink, and a little moisture had seeped in through the oilskin, blurring a few of the outer lines. But most of the picture was clear.

"It's more than that." Jack's finger traced a line on the map. "It looks to be a diagram showing an underground tunnel between the docks and ..." He bent his head, studying the map more closely. "And the Grand Hotel."

Flynn didn't often look impressed, but at that he gave Jack an appreciative look. "I wouldn't 'a thought to look up the chimney."

Becky had to admit that she wouldn't have, either. She hadn't seen the dried spot of saltwater on the hearthstones.

Jack refolded the map and slid it back inside the oilskin. "Good to know I can still spot something the two of you overlook."

He was still trying to look stern, but a slight smile tugged at the edges of his mouth. It was enough for Becky to risk asking, "Are you ... Does that mean you're not mad at us anymore?"

"We'll talk about that later." The furrow between Jack's brows was back, but even still, Becky felt slightly better. He straightened up. "But for right now, Lucy needs us—and the way things look, so does Mr. Holmes."

WATSON | LINCOLNSHIRE

60. NŌ ROOM AT
THE GRAND HOTEL

Lucy and I reached the railway station at Shellingford early in the evening. An open carriage brought us to the Grand Hotel after a freezing ten-minute ride, passing the now-deserted boardwalk and a clock tower, built only last year to commemorate the Queen's Jubilee. A cargo ship was approaching a nearby dock.

The hotel, a sprawling affair, had been recently constructed for the seaside summer vacationing crowd. Bright lights blazed in the lobby area, but nearly all its upper windows were dark.

A bellman stood outside the lobby entrance, a woolen muffler partly concealing his face.

The coachman put our suitcases on the ground and drove away.

The bellman did not move. I looked at him expectantly, but he might as well have been a guard outside Buckingham Palace, for all the notice he took of us.

Leaving Lucy beside the bags, I strode deliberately to him.

"It don't pay me to help you," the bellman said. "You're the fourth one this evening. You'll want me to shift your baggage for you and take it to your room. But there ain't no room for you."

I was in no mood to take no for an answer. "Explain," I said.

"The Chinese fellow's clientele takes all the rooms this time of the month. So you see, you'd be disappointed and I'd not get my tip."

"We'll see about that," I said. I went back to Lucy and told her what had happened.

"The manager's name is Mr. Torrance," she said. "Chubby little man. Middle age. See whether he will help. But don't mention my name. Say it's two rooms, for you and your niece."

I took the suitcases into the lobby, set them down at the concierge's desk, and turned to the registration desk. A rotund dark-haired man looked up at me. His thick lips grimaced in an artificial smile, revealing stained and crooked teeth.

"I'm sorry. We are fully occupied."

"I have a personal invitation from Mr. Ming," I said.

"Indeed?"

"At the Chinese Legation. He told me of the event. I am a doctor, and he assured me that the presentations would be of interest." I paused. "You are Mr. Torrance, the manager?"

A wily look came over the plump man's oily features. "Mr. Ming mentioned my name, did he?"

"He did not. I learned it from the doorman outside."

At that moment, I saw the hunched form of Ming himself on the staircase, coming down into the lobby. He was followed by the tall, young Chinese man who had been cured by his treatment.

In for a penny, in for a pound, I thought, and waved to him. "Mr. Ming!"

My efforts were rewarded. Ming saw me from the staircase, and at first did not appear to recognize me. Then he smiled and said something to his younger companion. They both joined me at the desk. After a brief explanation, I had the keys for two rooms.

"Perhaps you will introduce us to your niece," said Ming.

I looked around for Lucy, but she was gone. "Perhaps later," I said.

"Then please join us in the ballroom. Our patients will be available for interviews in fifteen minutes," he said. "We will have refreshments available. I am sure you will appreciate that after your long journey from London."

I made polite thanks, gave the bellman my room number, and went upstairs with him and my suitcase. The room was small, and on the top floor. Inside, the bellman gestured to a gabled window, framed by a triangular cut-out in the low ceiling. "You have a view of the Channel," he said brightly as I pressed a shilling into his outstretched palm.

A few minutes after he had gone, I heard a knock at the door. It was Lucy.

"I followed you."

I handed her the key to the other room.

She took it, but then showed me another key. "Whatever they said about it being full of Chinese visitors is just not true. This is the key to 304 downstairs—I kept it from when Becky and I stayed there last week. The room is empty. I saw hardly anyone in the corridor."

"Why would they say they were full when they weren't?"

"They don't want witnesses," she said.

61. THE BALLROOM

Lucy accompanied me to the hotel ballroom, where the demonstration had begun. From the entrance at the side of the room we saw thirty upright chairs arranged in two rows to face the speaker.

All of the guests appeared to be Chinese. All bore the same prosperous appearance as those I had seen at the Chinese Legation. I had the impression that they were all married couples. The women wore silk dresses of various subdued colours, and their sleeves were very large and wide, so as to make it impossible to see whether they held anything in their hands. Their sleek black hair was tightly braided and adorned with various forms of metallic jewelry, each resembling a small tiara. Occasionally one would turn and whisper to the other, but for the most part all listened with polite attention.

Ming was the speaker. He spoke in the same dry, soft voice I had heard a week before. He stood between two empty upright armchairs that faced the assembly like two small thrones, though barren of adornment. Occasionally he would shuffle sideways to rest his right hand on the back of one of the chairs. His left hand, the injured one, I recalled, he kept close to his chest.

Lucy and I took seats at the end of the second row of chairs. Ming did not appear to notice. He continued to speak, his Chinese words completely unintelligible to me. He continued for several minutes. Then he nodded, as though his introductory points had been made. He picked up a small brass handbell from the chair on his left and rang it.

The guests leaned forward in expectation. Behind Ming, a door opened. A slender, dark-haired Englishwoman took a hesitant step into the room. She turned and looked back as though seeking reassurance. Then another Englishwoman, this one taller and with flaxen hair, followed her. Both wore black dresses. They stood next to one another, not looking at each other, but waiting. Then in the doorway behind them appeared a tall Chinese man, the same man Ming had introduced to me at the Legation as a successfully cured patient.

Closing the door behind him, the tall man took a firm, confident step to stand between the two ladies and offered his arm to each. Each took it without hesitation. The three advanced into the room in a manner reminding me of actors at the end of a stage performance taking their curtain call. No one applauded, however. The guests simply observed politely as the Chinese man seated each of the ladies in turn and then stepped back to stand between them, his fingertips lightly resting on the tall back of each chair.

Lucy spoke softly into my ear. "I know all three of them. The taller woman is Lord Lynley's widow, and the other is the wife of Slade, the chief of police in Shellingford. Both are most definitely addicted to laudanum."

Ming stepped forward to face the two ladies. He bowed formally. Then he turned to his audience. "I shall speak in English, as these two good ladies have no Chinese. Perhaps one day they may wish to learn. Each is already making great progress in her struggle to break free of the drug that has enslaved so many unfortunate souls around the world. I shall ask each to simply tell her story in a brief manner, so that you can understand how she has come to be here and how she now holds hope for the future. I shall start with Lady Lynley."

Lady Lynley hesitated.

"Madam?"

"Forgive me," she said. She appeared lost in thought for another moment. Chen lightly touched her shoulder. "Oh," she said, glancing up at him. "I don't know why I am so hesitant to speak all of a sudden. Normally I can talk to anyone." She gave him what I thought was a coquettish smile. "Perhaps I might have another one of those pink pastilles? No? Well, I suppose it's not time yet.

"I will be brief. I heard about the cure from a friend in London, but I didn't pursue it. Though I ought to have. I was feeling quite vile, without energy, no drive, if you know what I mean, and the only thing I really wanted was more laudanum. I was irritable without it. It became embarrassing, because of my social obligations. People were wondering what was wrong with me. Then I came back here for my husband's funeral."

She gave a little grimace, as though the event was a distasteful interlude. She looked out at the audience. "You may all think me heartless, but I felt nothing at the ceremony. We had stopped loving each other years ago—if we ever did. But that is irrelevant now. To get on with life is what I want. I will find someone else. I am a titled lady, and quite wealthy enough to attract someone. And with my laudanum—what shall I call it, my laudanum compulsion?—with that behind me, and with my new medicine working so well, I do have hope."

A low murmur came from the audience as she concluded, along with some impolite stares, the guests no doubt appalled, or at the least astonished, by the degree of candor they had witnessed from a member of the British aristocracy. But Lady Lynley took no notice. She folded her hands in her lap and lowered her gaze, withdrawing within herself once again.

Ming spoke. "Thank you Lady Lynley. Now, Mrs. Slade?"

"I'm not a good speaker," the dark-haired woman said, her hand going momentarily to her mouth. "I am very different from Lady Lynley, of course. I have a husband. A good husband. A good man. A policeman …"

Her voice trailed off. Chen tapped her shoulder and whispered something into her ear. "Oh," she said. "My daughter. Yes, I had a daughter. I lost her. For a while, my nerves were quite bad. Then for a time, laudanum helped. But it becomes expensive. My husband is a good man, as I said, but we could not afford to pay Mr. Seewald. Then Mr. Chen here told me there might be a better way, a way to free myself. I have been free of laudanum for nearly a week now. All I need is a little pastille, which is no more expensive than—" she broke off, then giggled "—than penny candy! It is too good to be true, but it is, quite true. My hunger for laudanum has gone. Mr. Seewald will not get any more of my money!"

Ming stepped forward. "Thank you, ladies," he said, giving a slight bow. "And thank you, also, honored guests, for your attentive patience. This will conclude our demonstration."

At this, Chen stepped between the two ladies and helped them to their feet. He offered an arm to each, and then turned with them in tow.

Lucy and I also got to our feet to make way for the other guests who had been seated in our row. She took me aside. "Something was not right about that," she said. "I want to talk to Mrs. Slade and Lady Lynley. Can you ask Ming about the cost of those pastilles of his? And how long the treatment will last and where the pastilles come from? I will meet you in your room."

Just after Lucy left, Ming saw me and came over to ask for my impressions of the demonstration. He was quite forthcoming regarding the details of his cure, so much so that it seemed to me he was somehow invested in the sales of the product.

"As I explained," he said, "our cure relies wholly on a purified form of opium. It is poetic justice, as you English call it. The poppy itself, when skillfully worked upon, sufficiently creates an elixir that can undo the horrible damage wrought by its more primitive forms. The refined product conquers addiction to morphine and opium, and the patient suffers none of the dangerous symptoms that occur when these more primitive medicines are discontinued. The new product is truly a hero among drugs, and for this reason the manufacturer has named it heroin."

"The treatment consists of only those pastilles that the ladies spoke of?"

"The pastilles are all that is necessary."

"And the cost to the patient is low?"

"The manufacturing cost is not much greater than the cost to produce morphine. Heroin can be produced with only a few simple additional steps in the refining process. However, I am certain that establishments such as this will seek to expand the expenditure made by patients—and their own profits, of course—by adding diet and exercise, massage, steam baths and hot tub hydrotherapy. Already those services are available here, in the hotel spa. One has only to walk down a flight of stairs or use the lift. Perhaps you would like a tour in the morning."

I wondered if the spa was where the two women had been taken. But at that moment Ming caught sight of another guest, likely an important investor, and excused himself. "Forgive me," he said as he shuffled away, leaning on his cane. "Please stay here as long as you like and partake of the refreshments."

LUCY

62. A MESSAGE AND A DECISION

"Miss! Miss!"

I turned to find Bill, the hotel bellboy, calling to me from near the front desk.

"Telegram for you, miss! It's just come."

I glanced at the hotel's front entrance, where Lady Lynley and Mrs. Slade had just gone out. My skin was prickling with impatience to catch up with them and speak to them both about what had just occurred. I couldn't pinpoint an exact reason, but everything about the demonstration we'd just seen had felt wrong to me—not least because I hadn't seen a sign of Chief Constable Slade, only his wife.

I might not know the chief constable well, but I knew he wasn't the man to send his fragile wife out to speak in public without at the very least being by her side to offer support.

But I was also trying to avoid attracting undue attention, and I'd only arouse suspicion if I told Bill that the telegram could wait.

Besides, it might be from Jack.

I tore open the envelope. The message was brief, and it wasn't signed; Jack was being careful, as well. I read the handful of words.

Both packages recovered. Will send by first post.

I exhaled a quick breath of relief. In other words, Jack had found both Becky and Flynn, and they would all three be taking the first available train to Shellingford.

What was implied but not written, I knew, was, *Try to keep out of trouble for that long.*

I tapped the paper against my hand, quickly sorting through my options. I could find Mrs. Slade—or Lady Lynley, but of the two of them, Mrs. Slade seemed the most likely to give me honest answers—

I went still, my thought snapping off at the sight of Mr. Ming and Kai-chen, going out through the hotel doors.

I didn't have time to go upstairs and fetch my outdoor things from my room. But there was a dark blue woolen cloak draped over the back of one of the lobby chairs, the owner presumably intending to come back for it later.

In an instant, I picked it up, threw it around my shoulders, and pushed my way through the hotel door.

I could question Mrs. Slade. Or I could follow the two men who, increasingly, seemed to be at the heart of this affair.

LUCY

63. A PRISONER IN DARKNESS

Outside, night had fallen, and a few light flurries of snow were drifting down, illuminated by the chill light of a rising moon. The air was clear and so piercingly cold it almost hurt to breathe. I stayed in the shadows of the hotel and watched as Mr. Ming and Kai-chen walked slowly along the front of the Grand Hotel—then turned, circling round towards the back.

I remembered once asking my father why he very nearly always assumed the worst about people, and Holmes had replied calmly that presuming the worst saved a significant amount of time.

I had no absolute proof at that moment that there was anything sinister about Mr. Ming and Kai-chen's errand. They could just be going back to the tea shop or in search of a late supper.

But every instinct I had screamed at me to find out. I did a quick calculation, weighing my options. I wasn't unarmed. From the second we'd set foot on the train to Shellingford, I'd known I didn't want to be without a weapon. Right now I had a knife in the top of my boot and my Ladysmith in my skirt pocket. True, I was alone. But if I went back to find Uncle John, I would lose all chance of finding out where they were going.

I sent a silent apology to Jack, then quickened my pace and followed, reaching the corner of the hotel.

A narrow service alleyway ran alongside the Grand, presumably used by tradesmen for delivering coal and groceries and the like to the back entrance.

And right now, raised voices were coming from somewhere in the darkness of that alley.

Both voices were speaking Chinese, but I didn't need to understand the words to recognize Mr. Ming's dry, precise tones and Kai-chen's lower-pitched ones—or to know that both men were angry.

It sounded to me as though Mr. Ming was berating his younger assistant for something, and Kai-chen was voicing an increasingly furious defense.

I risked a quick look around the corner, but the alley was pitch dark, with mounds of trash and wooden barrels forming looming black shadows. I could scarcely see my own hand in front of my face, much less the two men—although I could still hear them.

Mr. Ming said something else, the words bitten-off and curt, the tone icily … final.

I managed to scramble back from the alley entrance just in time, taking refuge in the small alcove formed behind one of the hotel's jutting bay windows. Footsteps approached, coming out of the alleyway.

I held absolutely still, pressing my back against the brick wall behind me as the drifting snowflakes swirled and stung my cheeks. If Mr. Ming chose to turn this way, he would pass by me—and there was absolutely no chance whatsoever that he wouldn't see me.

If he saw me, I would lose all chance of finding out the purpose of Kai-chen and Mr. Ming's errand, and the cause of their argument. Not only that, but I would put them on guard—unless I could come up with a plausible reason for being out here, other than a wish to follow them.

A toothache, a lost dog …

I was trying out and discarding possibilities that sounded ridiculous, even in my own mind, when the footsteps reached the entrance to the alley … and turned the other way.

Away from me.

I let out a long, slow breath and waited until the sound of the footsteps had died away. Then I walked swiftly and silently back to the entrance of the alleyway. I still couldn't see anything, but I strained my ears, listening.

Everything felt muffled by the snow and the cold, swirling wind. But I caught what sounded like a jingle of keys, followed by a soft thud.

The opening and closing of a door?

I waited, still listening and debating with myself. Everything was silent, which suggested to me that Kai-chen had gone inside, somewhere back into the hotel. Or on the other hand, he could be standing at the other end of the alleyway, just waiting for me to walk straight into him.

As much as I hated the thought of inaction, staying in place here was safest.

Three minutes dragged past, then five. I tucked my freezing hands together, wishing I'd been able to liberate a scarf and gloves from the hotel lobby, as well as the cloak.

I had counted off seven minutes inside my head when I heard footsteps coming towards me, almost at a run. I didn't have time to retreat to my former hiding place. I barely managed to crouch down behind an upturned wooden packing crate before a man's shadowy form came barreling out of the alley.

Kai-chen.

As he reached the alley's entrance, a stray gleam of ambient light from the hotel above showed his face. He looked pale and strained, his mouth set in a tight line, his black hair streaked with droplets of water from the snow.

I held my breath, but he went past me without a sideways glance and strode off into the night.

I counted off twenty seconds to make sure he wasn't going to turn back around, then straightened up.

I now had another set of options to debate. I could try to follow Kai-chen, although given that we two seemed to be the only souls out on the streets right now, that would be next to impossible to achieve without his noticing.

Or I could find out what Kai-chen's errand had been inside the hotel. Because he *had* been inside. The snow on his hair had been melted into water droplets, which meant that he had spent those seven minutes some place where the temperature was above freezing point.

I very much wanted to find out where that *some place* had been.

The alley was even more littered with rubbish than I had realized. Kai-chen must have navigated it often to have avoided tripping over the assortment of barrel staves and rusted bed-springs and broken wagon wheels that were piled high. My eyes had at least partially adjusted to the dark, allowing me to see vague shapes, but even still it took a maddeningly long time for me to pick my way to the passage's other end.

When I emerged, I found myself in the hotel's rear yard: a small, square area paved with flagstones that contained both the tradesman's entrance and the metal hatch through which coal would be delivered to the furnace room in the hotel's basement.

The tradesman's entrance probably opened into the kitchen area. Light was filtering out around the edges of the door and through the narrow transom window, and I could hear the sounds of voices, the clatter of dishes and the metallic clank of pots and pans.

The hotel staff must be preparing food for any guests who wanted a late supper.

I very much doubted that Kai-chen's errand had taken him into the kitchen. For one thing, the light dusting of snow in front of the door was undisturbed, and for another, a trip to the kitchens wouldn't be a likely cause for the argument with Mr. Ming.

That left the coal cellar—where, I saw, the dusting of snow had been shifted off the double-sided metal hatch and onto the flagstones. Footprints marked the ground there, as well, both going in and coming back out again.

For just a second, my ears buzzed and weight compressed my ribcage. Of course. It had to be the underground coal cellar.

Just once, I would love it if an investigation led me into an open, airy apple orchard. Or a sunlit cottage garden.

A metal padlock held the coal hatch closed, and I didn't have my set of picks—but I did have a hairpin, and the lock was a simple one. A few quick twists and it snapped open in my hands. And the door's hinges had been recently oiled, too, so it opened silently when I tugged one side of the hatch open and peered inside.

A straight drop into near-pitch darkness greeted me—since two-ton deliveries of coal didn't need sets of stairs to walk down. But I could just make out the top of the coal pile, maybe six feet below me, which made it slightly risky to jump, since I had no guaranteed way of pulling myself back out again.

But not actually suicidal.

Probably. Depending on what else besides coal was down there.

My heart still hammered, though, and I had to squeeze my eyes shut against the cold flood of memories that squirmed through me.

This place wasn't an exact replica of the place where I'd been held prisoner. But it was deep, dark, and underground, and that was enough to make my stomach clench and my skin start to crawl.

I'm afraid had always been my two least favorite words in the English language. But right now, I would rather do almost anything else than go down into the Grand Hotel's cellar.

Holmes could be down there. If he was still alive.

I took a breath, eased myself backwards over the edge until I was hanging by my hands, and then dropped. Landing on a shifting, unstable pile of coal made me stagger and almost fall, but I gained my balance and picked my way downwards to the floor—forcing myself to notice details rather than think about how easy it would be for someone to slam and lock the coal hatch and trap me down here.

The cellar was dark, but from somewhere up ahead of me, I could see a faint, pale sliver of light near the floor, as though from the crack under a door.

I could also hear something from up ahead, beyond the coal

cellar—something that sounded, incongruously for a basement, like the splash of running water. As I edged my way towards both the light and the sounds, an odd scent stung my nostrils and crawled down the back of my throat—a harsh, chemical smell, like paint thinner or vinegar.

I reached the source of the light, which proved to be a heavy wooden door. Feeling around the edges, I found no lock—just a heavy metal bolt that had been drawn across, holding it closed from the outside. Putting my ear to the wooden panel, I listened.

The splash of running water was louder, closer, now, making it hard to hear. But I thought I could just make out a rustle of movement, and a soft, irregular sound, like someone breathing—or sobbing.

I slid the Ladysmith out of my pocket with one hand and flipped the safety catch off. Then I drew the bolt slowly back, wincing at the squeak of the metal, and swung the door open.

The room was small, windowless, and looked to be a store room of some kind. The light from a single oil lamp showed cans of paint, brushes, and a few workman's tools on the shelves which stood against one wall. And in the center of the room, a young woman was tied, at the wrists and ankles, to a wooden chair.

She gasped at the sight of me, her blue eyes flaring wide as she stared through disheveled strands of pale blonde hair—first at me, then at the revolver in my hand.

I slipped the Ladysmith back into my pocket and spoke above the pounding of my own heart. "It's all right. Are you Alice Gordon?"

She stared for another second, then jerked her head in a nod, still looking too shocked—or too frightened—to speak.

I let out a slow breath. Against all odds, Alice Gordon was alive. Finally, something in this investigation had gone right—or it would, if I could get both of us out of here.

"My name is Lucy," I told Alice. "You don't know me, but I've been looking for you."

WATSON

64. TAKEN

Thinking to keep watch for Lucy, I waited in the lobby. I felt uncomfortable remaining in the room where the demonstration had been held. Ming had seemed too eager in his invitation. Something about the man did not seem genuine. It was a cold night, and the wind pressed against the pair of lobby doors, pushing them open slightly, whistling and howling as the sea air struggled to get in.

I waited a few minutes.

Then I decided to investigate the facilities downstairs, testing my idea that this was where Kai-chen had taken the two ladies and thus where Lucy would have gone to follow them.

But the stairway door to the lower level was locked. The lift attendant shook his head when I asked him to open it. "All closed up until tomorrow."

I was beginning to have an intuitive sense that something was wrong. Lucy should have been back by now.

I had the lift operator take me to the third floor. The corridor was empty. I knocked on the door to her room, but there was no answer. I took the stairs up to my own room and the adjoining room I had secured for Lucy. Both were empty.

I felt the overpowering urge to get out, to do something, to take control somehow. I wrote a short note and addressed it to Jack, telling him my room number. I left the note with the receptionist. Then I put on my overcoat and went down the stairs to the lobby floor. I tested the door to the lower level, but it too was locked. I went into the lobby, hoping to find Lucy. But she was not there. I pushed through the outside doors to the front portico and the steps leading down to the pavement and the street.

The bellman was still standing in his position. He gave me a curious look.

"Not leaving us already?" he asked.

"Fresh air," I replied.

I strolled around to the back of the hotel. The sea was far from calm. Even in the harbor, waves slapped against the sides of the cargo vessel we had seen coming in on our arrival. The ship was now docked at the pier, about a hundred yards along the boardwalk past the hotel. The hum of the ship's engines mingled with the splash of the waves. I could see men working on the deck, and I wondered at the activity at this time of night. I wondered why the men were silent.

The silent men were unloading cargo from the hold of the vessel. I could see their shadowy figures pulling on a rope connected to a hammock—like cargo sling, guiding it and its contents down to the dock. The crates appeared to be heavy. I could see wispy bunches of packing hay protruding from beneath the lids. Two men stood guard.

I watched for about ten minutes before I realized that the shadowy outline of the stack of cargo on the dock had not changed. It had grown no larger, or smaller, yet the cargo sling had continued to be lowered full, raised empty, and lowered full again and again with more pallets, each laden with sacks and crates.

Perhaps ten loads of pallets. Perhaps a hundred sacks and crates.

They had to be going somewhere.

I strolled. Casually. One of the guards saw me and came forward.

"State your business."

"My business is medicine," I said. "I am a doctor."

"This is private property."

"I am a guest at the Grand Hotel."

"I suggest you go back there. It's a cold night. If you're a doctor, you should know that the cold air can be dangerous."

There was no point in arguing, but I was certainly not going to give up. I bade the fellow good night and walked back to the hotel, continuing around to the street pavement at the front. Then I continued walking along the street until I had got well past the cargo ship. It was only a dim outline, about two hundred yards away.

I could no longer see the workers on the cargo ship, or their guards, which meant they could not see me. I walked directly towards the Channel, leaning forward into the sting of the January wind. I had not brought my hat, scarf, or gloves, but I had my Webley revolver in my pocket.

A full moon was just rising, but its pale silver glow failed to brighten the dark outlines of the cargo ship and the dock. The icy sea wind tore at my coat. I had to fight to keep my balance on the wet beach sand as I made my way forward.

I did not want to look at the Channel. I could hear it surging and booming as the waves broke and hissed along the shore. Much of the sea was in shadow. Here and there wavetops caught a few reflections from the ship's lanterns, or from the town street lights, or from the moon.

I did not want to look at the Channel, because each glimpse of the dark water made me think of Sherlock Holmes.

I was close enough to the waves for my shoes to be wet. From that angle I could look back up the coast and see the ship, the dock, and, further to the left, the wooden columns that supported the dock.

From somewhere beneath the dock, three men were coming out.

They were bent over, leaning forward, pushing something.

Crouching low, I moved forward on the sand to get a better view.

The three men paused, looking upward to see another pallet swung on its rope above their heads, moving with the wind and the waves as the crane gently lowered it from the cargo ship.

I now could see that the pallet was being lowered to rest, not on the dock as I had thought, but beneath the dock, onto whatever it was the men had been pushing.

The men waited. The pallet and its cargo came to rest. The men moved around it. One of them bent forward and the others did the same. Then the rope swung clear. The ship's crane hauled the rope up to the deck of the ship.

The men came around between the pallet and the ship. They bent over and braced themselves, hands on the cargo. Then as if on cue, they pushed. The cargo and the men moved away from the ship, then beneath the dock, then out of my view. I heard the clatter of metal wheels on steel rails.

A railway, I thought. Smugglers. Bringing contraband cargo ashore under cover of darkness, then hiding it in some chamber excavated below the dock. Would they have something to do with Ming? Or the opium chest that had launched this adventure? But what I had seen were crates and sacks, not even faintly resembling the chest we had found in the room of Inspector Swafford.

The chill wind of the Channel was picking up, and I was beginning to shake from the cold—my body's involuntary reaction and attempt to keep warm. I could move forward and brave the further chill, and the chance of being discovered by the loading crew and the guards. Or I could come back in the morning. The unloading process would have concluded by then, and I could walk on the dock and find a reason to climb down and inspect the area beneath the dock. I could also tell Lucy what I had found, and perhaps she could assist.

Concluding that this was the more reasonable course, I turned to walk back up the beach to the paved road.

But two burly men had crept up to stand behind me, only a few feet away. They blocked my path. One of the men was the guard I had seen nearer the dock. Even in the shadows, I could see that other man was holding a pistol.

The gun was pointed at me.

65. NOT ALONE

Alice Gordon's eyes were still wide, frightened and uncomprehending. "I ... I don't understand." Her voice was hoarse and choked. Seen closer, her hair was dirty and tangled, and her face was streaked with grime, except where recent tears had washed clean tracks down her cheeks. "Who ... how did you ..."

"I'll explain later. Right now, we need to get away from here."

I spoke quickly, drawing the knife from the top of my boot and kneeling down to slice the ropes that kept her ankles bound to the legs of the chair.

Both those ropes and the ones around her wrists were padded with rags, to keep from chafing the skin. The remains of a food tray sat on the floor beside the chair, too, containing the crust-end of a loaf of bread, a cheese rind, and a half-empty bottle of milk.

If Kai-chen was the one who had locked her in here, he had tried to keep her from suffering.

I cut through the ropes on Alice's wrists. "How do you feel? Do you think you can walk?"

Alice drew a shuddering breath, seeming to scarcely hear the question. Instead she brought her two hands around to the front, staring down at her fingers as she clenched and unclenched them.

Sudden tears welled up in her eyes, then, and she started to cry—hoarse, gasping sobs that had her doubling over as though in pain.

I gripped her shoulder, sympathy warring with impatience. "Alice, we need to leave, do you under—"

A step sounded behind me and I cursed myself for the stupidity of not keeping a better watch.

I spun around, my knife at the ready.

Kai-chen stood in the doorway, leveling a snub-nosed revolver at me. For a split-second, he looked momentarily even more stunned to see me than I was to see him. Not so shocked, though, that he let the gun waver, and in barely a heartbeat, the shocked expression had flattened out into one of grim determination.

He kept the barrel of the revolver aimed directly at me.

"Put the knife down."

Unfortunately, I didn't have a choice. With another opponent, I might have tried throwing the knife—it might not kill, but it would certainly injure. But I already knew how quick Kai-chen's reflexes were. The second my knife-hand twitched, he could fire off a shot, and I would be dead before the blade came within a foot of him.

The same went for trying to draw my own revolver. I was kicking myself for having put it away so as not to frighten Alice—it would take far too long for me to reach for it now.

I crouched down slowly, setting the knife on the ground. I'd cut the ropes binding her, but Alice was still huddled on the chair, and still sobbing.

Obviously, I couldn't look for any help there.

"Kick the knife over towards me," Kai-chen ordered.

I did as he said and sent the knife skittering across the flag-stones. But I kept my gaze on Kai-chen's, refusing to break eye contact.

"You're not going to kill Alice. You can't."

A flicker of some expression flashed across Kai-chen's features and was gone, too quick for me to identify. "You know nothing."

My mind was spinning through possibilities, trying to identify a plan of escape, and so far failing. But one of Uncle John's sayings from the army was that a distracted soldier was a dead soldier, and the saying worked outside of the battlefield, as well.

A distracted enemy was often a dead one. And if I could keep Kai-chen talking and distracted, a way out of here might occur.

"I know that Mr. Ming ordered you to kill her tonight, and that you came here for that purpose," I said. I kept my eyes on the barrel of the revolver. "But you couldn't bring yourself to do it. You care for her."

The quick twist of pain that crossed Kai-chen's face was more pronounced this time. "But I came back." He straightened his shoulders, his expression flattening into determination once more. "I will do as Mr. Ming asks. There is no other way."

He had so far avoided looking at Alice, but now his gaze just touched her before flicking away again. "Death will be instant. She will not suffer."

His breathing had quickened, just slightly, and his eyes were dilated. He was talking himself into action.

Not good news for either Alice or me.

"Rubbish." I kept my voice calm. I thought of the bronze statuettes in the tea shop, the little game players, meant to provide friendship to their owner into the next life. "You don't think it will pain her to know that the man who killed her is the same man who was supposed to love her? She loved you enough to leave her friends and defy all social convention for you—how many girls would have done the same? Does Mr. Ming show you that kind of loyalty? Does—"

"Stop! Stop talking!" Kai-chen's hand holding the revolver shook ever so slightly.

I fell silent, but also tensed all my muscles and watched Kai-chen closely. Despite what many believed, unless you were an expert marksman the odds of shooting someone even at close range weren't strongly in your favor.

If I dodged and dove low, under Kai-chen's guard, I might be able to knock him off balance and then get the revolver.

Before I could decide on a moment to act, the sound of angry voices broke the silence—muffled by the thick basement walls and the sound of running water, but still not far off.

"Unhand me at once!"

The majority of whatever was being said was lost, but some trick of acoustics carried those words to me plainly. I froze, shock inching its way down my spine.

I knew that voice, almost as well as I did my own. It was Uncle John.

66. DOWNWARD

"They're not here."

Jack's voice was quiet and completely calm, but Becky could tell just by looking at him that he was worried. He was looking around the hotel room where Dr. Watson was supposed to be staying. They wouldn't have known where that was, but Dr. Watson had left a note for them at the hotel desk and told the receptionist to give it to them when they arrived.

Now it was after midnight, and the whole hotel was eerily dark and quiet, the only light coming from the couple of electric torchiers set into the hallway's walls. Dr. Watson's room was completely dark, too, the curtains drawn. But Becky could see it was empty—and they'd already checked Lucy's room next-door and found it just as deserted.

Wherever Lucy and Dr. Watson were, it wasn't here.

"I don't understand." Flynn had been silent up until now, his shoulders hunched and his whole pose uneasy as they made their way through the hotel. If he didn't like to be inside even on a good day, the amount of luxury and rich furnishings in the Grand was probably enough to turn his stomach. "You're a … copper, right?" he asked Jack.

Becky knew that was a more polite word that he would usually use for the police.

"So why don't you just go down to the desk and tell 'ooever's in charge that they better tell you everything they know about Miss Lucy and Dr. Watson and 'elp you find them, or else? Becky told me about that Mr. Torrance, that runs this place. 'E sounds like a shady character, to me."

Jack looked as though he were almost tempted to try that idea. But he shook his head. "That's not how it works. I'd need a warrant to search this place. And if we alert Mr. Torrance—or anyone else who might be guilty—to the fact that we're here, and looking for Lucy and Dr. Watson—"

He stopped talking, and Becky saw the line of his mouth go tight.

She didn't need Jack to fill in the rest of what he had been about to say. If Mr. Torrance had taken Lucy and Dr. Watson prisoner somewhere, then he might hurt them—or worse—if he thought that anyone was here looking for them.

Becky felt as if invisible hands were wrapped around her throat, trying to strangle her. She had lost count of the number of times she had said *I'm sorry* on the train ride up here, so she didn't say it again, but it felt like the words were stuck in her throat, like sharp-edged rocks.

If she hadn't gone off to look at the house in St. John's Wood, then Jack would have been able to come up to Shellingford with Lucy, and maybe Lucy and Dr. Watson wouldn't be missing—

"It's thanks to you that we found the map, Beck," Jack said quietly. He must have known or guessed what she was thinking. "That's important—it's the best lead we have right now, in fact. But I need you to do something for me." He kept going before

Becky could ask what it was. "I'm going to go down to the docks and take a look at this tunnel the map showed."

"No!" Now Becky felt like the invisible hands had shifted, trying to squeeze all the air out of her chest. "Not by yourself, you can't!"

Lucy and Dr. Watson were missing, Mr. Holmes might be dead, and if Jack got caught, too—

"I'll be all right. But I have to go by myself. There's a lot less chance I'll be seen that way." Jack hadn't raised his voice, but Becky knew from his tone that there was no point in arguing.

She *couldn't* really argue. Three people were more conspicuous than just one.

"I need you and Flynn to stay here," Jack said. "Right here in this room where you'll be safe, all right?"

The lump in Becky's throat swelled and the back of her eyes burned, but she nodded.

"Good." Jack smiled at her and tugged one of her braids. "I'll come back soon, Beck. Promise."

* * *

Becky stared at the clock on the mantle. Jack had said that they could light one of the gas jets over the mantle, so that they could see better, as long as they kept the curtains shut tight and a pillow stuffed under the edge of the door to keep anyone outside in the hall from noticing that a light was on.

Seventeen minutes after twelve ... Eighteen minutes after twelve ...

It felt as though the seconds were crawling by. Finally, the minute hand ticked over to read twenty minutes past midnight.

She jumped up. "All right. Let's go."

Flynn had been slouched in the easy chair by the fireplace—not asleep, maybe, but Becky suspected he'd been on his way to dozing. Now he startled, blinking at her.

"What d'you mean, let's go? Your brother said to stay 'ere, remember?"

"I know. But he didn't specify how *long* we were supposed to stay here." If Jack had been less worried about Lucy, Becky knew he wouldn't have made that mistake—but it worked out well for her purposes. They had been here a total of ten minutes, which meant that strictly speaking she hadn't lied when she'd agreed to do as Jack asked. "Besides, I have a better idea."

The edges of Flynn's mouth pulled down in a scowl. "I don't think we agree on what the word *better* means."

Becky ignored him. "We're going to search the rest of the hotel and see whether we can find any sign of where Lucy and Dr. Watson may have gone—or where they're being held, if they've been taken prisoner."

Flynn's scowl deepened. "Oh good. 'Ow'd you know I was just sitting 'ere, 'oping for a chance to get myself caught or killed?"

"You're not scared, are you?" Becky asked. That wasn't really playing fair, since she knew Flynn would rather die than admit to being afraid of anything. But she was long past caring about fair tactics versus dirty ones.

Flynn stood up, still glaring at her. "Where do we even look? The 'otel's a big place. It'd take us all night to look in all the rooms—and that's if we 'ad keys to them all, which we don't."

Becky let out her breath. It might not sound like it, but she knew she'd won. "I know. But I found that map of the tunnel that leads from the hotel to the docks—and the only sensible place for it to start is down in the basement, below ground. So that's where we'll start. Downstairs in the cellars."

LUCY

67. LIES FROM OUR CAPTORS

Kai-chen prodded me in the back with the barrel of his revolver. "Sit down."

Uncle John was already sitting, bound and gagged, on a wooden chair that had clearly been cast off from the hotel's restaurant upstairs. One of the legs was cracked, but the gilt-edged white paint and rose-colored upholstery made for a bizarre contrast to the dankness of the cellar's walls.

Alice, still weeping, was tied to a second chair next to Uncle John's, and a third one waited for me beside hers.

I stayed where I was, ignoring the press of the gun against my rib cage. "I don't think so."

I didn't know what they had planned for us, but I did know that the moment I allowed myself to be tied down, I would be helpless to stop it.

Behind me, Kai-chen gave a growl of frustration. His voice sounded even more ragged than before, his nerves more frayed.

Bad for him, good for us.

My eyes sought Uncle John's. Above the length of white linen that formed the gag, his gaze was steady and clear, and as

I looked a silent question at him, he gave me a barely perceptible nod.

I had just been given permission to try whatever means of escape I could, regardless of the risk.

Duck, spin, knock Kai-chen's gun-hand up, at the same time aiming a kick at his left knee.

I gave the maneuver about a sixty-seven percent chance of working—and I had in the past acted on worse odds than those.

I drew in a breath …

And a man's hunched figure stepped out of the shadows, clearing his throat and beaming as though this were a gala ball and he was the host, welcoming me to the evening's delights.

"Ah, Miss James. Or perhaps you would prefer Mrs. Kelly? I beg that you will not attempt whatever assault you were about to perpetrate on Chang Kai-chen. The outcome would be unfavorable to you both, I assure you."

I held very still, ordering myself not to react—although I could feel tiny crystals of ice burrowing into my skin. Ming had just called me Mrs. Kelly, which meant that he knew exactly who I was.

He seemed to pick up the thought, because his smile grew even broader. "A wise man once said, 'If you know the enemy and know yourself, you need not fear the result of a hundred battles.'"

"Sun Tsu also said, 'Convince your enemy that he will gain very little by attacking you; this will diminish his enthusiasm.' I've read *The Art of War*, too."

It was one of the very few ancient texts we had studied in history classes at school that I had really enjoyed.

Ming tipped his head back and laughed. "Remarkable. Just as

I thought, truly you are a remarkable young woman." He scrutinized my face, nodding as though I had just confirmed some long-held theory. "My only regret where you are concerned is that we could not have made one another's acquaintance under more harmonious circumstances. However—"

He was only a foot or two away from Uncle John. A quick step brought him to Watson's side, and he drew a hypodermic syringe from a fold of his robe. He set the point of the needle against Watson's throat.

"Sun Tsu also advises, 'Begin by seizing something which your opponent holds dear; then he will be amenable to your will.' Sit down in that chair, or I will inject the full measure of heroin in this syringe into your friend. I assure you, the dose will prove fatal."

My pulse was beating in short, hard bursts, but I stayed where I was. "I'm very sure that you intend for tonight's activities to prove fatal for us in any case. And I think I can safely speak for both myself and Dr. Watson when I say that I would very much prefer to be shot than to die by heroin injection."

"Fatal?" Mr. Ming's eyes widened, and his mouth rounded in surprise, like a child wrongly accused of naughty behavior. "Oh, no, no, no. Not fatal. At least, not necessarily so. I give you perhaps a seventy percent chance of surviving the night, provided that you do as I say."

It ought to have been the least of my worries, but it was still was oddly unsettling to realize that the odds Mr. Ming had just given me were nearly identical to my own earlier calculations.

"Shall I tell you how it will be?" he went on. "You will be given a dose of heroin—not a fatal dose, you understand, merely enough to induce a pleasant lethargy followed by sleep—then you will remain here, soundly asleep, for the rest of tonight, and will wake in the morning none the worse. Always provided, of course, that you suffer no adverse reactions to the heroin, which, of course, I must admit that some do. Yes, I cannot lie, there are, where opiates are concerned, certain risks involved." Mr. Ming lowered his eyes, shaking his head at the sadness of it all. "But there is, as I say, a strong chance of your waking up tomorrow morning."

"I see." The needle still rested against Watson's throat—and Kai-chen still held the barrel of the revolver pressed against the small of my back. At that moment, I had no other strategy than to keep Ming talking. "And what is to stop us from coming after you then?"

Mr. Ming clucked his tongue. "Ah, no, no, no. By morning my associates and I will be long gone. This area has proved to be a convenient base for our operations for some time. But Lord Lynley's unfortunate death has complicated matters. It is now time for us to move on. By morning, we will be on a ship, sailing for … ah, well." He shook his head like an indulgent uncle cautioning a wayward child. "You can hardly expect me to tell you that. But we will be hundreds of miles away, and you and Dr. Watson here will awaken refreshed and ready to commence a return to your ordinary lives."

I drew in a breath. "If by 'refreshed and ready' you actually mean, 'dead, drowned in the hotel's hydrotherapy baths,' then yes, I'm sure things will happen exactly as you say."

I had to credit Mr. Ming: his start of surprise was very slight and almost instantly masked.

"I've been hearing the sound of running water ever since I came down here," I said. "It's coming from the hotel's hydrotherapy rooms, isn't that right?" I had actually forgotten about the hydrotherapy until I remembered what Bill the bellboy had said about the Grand's spa weekends. "Some people believe that submersion in water stimulates blood circulation and treats the symptoms of a variety of diseases. But there's absolutely no reason for the hotel to have the machines running now, at this hour of the night."

I looked over at Alice Gordon, who was still slumped in the chair with her long blonde hair hanging into her face, scarcely seeming to hear anything that was said. I wondered whether they'd been already dosing her with opiates—in her food, maybe—to keep her quiet and compliant while they held her captive.

"Alice found out through Kai-chen about your smuggling operations—and that the cures you offered to opium addicts were actually nothing of the kind," I continued. "That's why you kidnapped her and held her prisoner here. Although at first, I'm sure Kai-chen didn't know that. Until you told him the truth, he genuinely didn't know what had happened to her.

"Your plan was to dose Alice with enough heroin to render her unconscious, then leave her in the tanks to drown. That way, you could dispose of the body ... where? My guess would be in one of the irrigation ditches in the fens, and her death might feasibly be ruled simple accident—since it would be a death by drowning, after all. But Kai-chen was worried that Alice would suffer. Drowning is a very unpleasant way to end one's life, so he left her, unbeknownst to you, and came back with a gun. But now you're planning to include Dr. Watson and me in your original plan."

Mr. Ming's eyes narrowed just fractionally. If I'd read him

rightly, behind all his smiling, eccentric mannerisms, he liked to imagine himself the cleverest person in the room—and he didn't at all appreciate my having deduced his actual intent.

Unfortunately, knowing his real plans didn't help me think of a feasible way to stop him from doing with us exactly as he chose.

Above the strip of the gag in his mouth, Uncle John's eyes were resolute, steady and clear. But the second I tried to attack Kai-chen or draw the Ladysmith, Mr. Ming would depress the plunger on the syringe, injecting the fatal dose of heroin into Uncle John's bloodstream.

I kept talking. Delay was the only tactic I had. "Also, I don't believe that you really intend to quit this place forever and start your operations somewhere else. You've got a ship docked nearby—I saw it for a moment when I went outside. The ship was unloading cargo. Maybe it still is. But if you were shutting down your operations, the ship wouldn't be bringing in supplies.

"You're planning to keep right on with your operation, and you're planning to kill Dr. Watson and me so that we can't interfere. And, by the way, what are you planning to do with Lady Lynley and Mrs. Slade? Where did you take them? What was the purpose of having them make those touching, hopeful speeches to your audience this evening?"

Ming just stared at me. But I saw something in Kai-chen's eyes. The same flicker of shame he had exhibited when he had looked at Alice.

Then I knew.

I went on, still trying to buy time, "I think I know why. Shall I tell you?"

Ming stared, still silent. Kai-chen looked down.

"Those people in your audience. They know that Lady Lynley and Mrs. Slade will be bitterly disappointed. Because whatever cure you're pretending to give, it really isn't a cure. It's just opium or laudanum or morphine, only in a more concentrated form. It's just enough to create hope, and then betray that hope. And I was watching your audience while they were listening to the two English ladies. You said they were here to find a cure for their friends and relatives who are addicts. But it wasn't hope and empathy that I saw on their faces.

"At first, I couldn't quite identify their expression, but now I think it was satisfaction. Self-centered, vindictive, satisfaction. They're going to buy those pastilles from you and take them home, but not because they want to cure anyone. They're going to sell the drugs, aren't they? They may even give the drugs away to people who are their enemies. They've come here to see how your new drugs will enslave their customers, and make their enemies suffer."

Ming said nothing.

"Both those two ladies looked very anxious for their next dose. Maybe you took them somewhere where your audience could watch them wait, and grow more and more desperate, and beg, harder and harder and harder. A demonstration."

Across the room from us, Alice was curled up in a ball, sobbing.

"Have you already done that with Alice here? Put her on display?"

Still silence.

"You are as hideous on the inside as you are on the outside, Mr. Ming," I said.

No reply. Not even defiance in Ming's eyes. Just a dry, patient glitter, like a snake.

I went on, determined to provoke a reaction if I possibly could. "Kai-chen, how can you look at your own reflection in the mirror, knowing you are working for a man like this? Is this truly who you want to be?"

Kai-chen was about to speak, but Ming silenced him with a warning glance. Then he turned to me.

BECKY

68. A DESPERATE MOVE

Becky didn't recognize the dry, raspy voice. It came from down
the hall, in some other room, but not too far away. It said, "You
need not speak, Kai-chen. Miss James, the subtlety of your mind
is quite astonishing, for a barbarian."

The voice made Becky's skin crawl, all the way from the base
of her neck to the soles of her feet.

"We have to do something!" she hissed.

She and Flynn were crouched in the shadows of the service
staircase they'd used to get down into the cellar.

The Grand Hotel's basement covered the footprint of the
entire sprawling structure and was laid out like a maze: dark
narrow hallways and windowless rooms.

They'd blundered around a bit in the dark and found a room
that looked like a bigger version of the chemistry laboratory
Mr. Holmes had in his Baker Street rooms—beakers and burners and test tubes, all laid out on tables. The air smelled like
a chemistry experiment, too, harsh and sour. It was beginning
to give Becky a headache.

But all she cared about now was that she'd also heard Lucy's voice, coming from behind the closed door she could see off to their left and at the end of another narrow hallway.

Panic was pulling tight under Becky's ribcage. "Whoever's in there is going to kill Lucy and Dr. Watson, too, unless we can stop them!"

Flynn frowned. Then he picked up a stray half of a broken brick that lay on the floor, weighed it in his hand, and threw it down the hall.

It landed with a crash.

Becky stared at him, opened mouthed. "Are you out of your mind?"

Flynn shrugged. "They can't kill Miss Lucy if they're trying to find out where the noise came from. We can stand 'ere arguing about it, or we can run, so that we're not 'ere when they do come."

69. A NEW ARRIVAL

When the crash came, I was tied in a chair, by hand and foot, with a gag stuffed into my mouth.

Not pleasant. Not pleasant at all, not to mention having my neck pricked by the tip of a hypodermic needle.

But not hopeless, either. I had given hundreds of injections to hundreds of patients, using a syringe just like the one Ming held. I knew I was not helpless. Far from it.

To begin with, there was Ming himself. He was holding the syringe with his good hand. The other was tight against his chest, as always, as if it were held in some sort of sling. That meant he could feel the syringe, but he could not feel my body movements, the subtle tensions I would be going through, as my muscles prepared to make some kind of movement.

If I were preparing to move.

Which I was.

The second point in my favor was that to inflict real damage the syringe would require two moves on Ming's part. First, he would have to penetrate the skin of my neck, and second, he would have to depress the plunger, delivering the contents of the syringe into my system. Without the second movement, the first would be no more than a scratch, or an inconvenient insect bite. A small prick of pain, but not any permanent damage. Nothing to incapacitate me.

The third point in my favor was Lucy James. I knew what she could do.

The problem was Kai-chen, of course. The big strong Chinaman had his revolver jammed into the small of Lucy's back. If I moved, Lucy would be fully occupied with him—possibly fatally—before I could have any effect on Ming.

But then the crash had come from outside the room, and my spirits soared.

Ming pressed the syringe into my neck all the tighter. But he said, "Kai-chen. See to that. Take the revolver. Miss James, stay where you are. Or the syringe in my hand will do its work."

I waited until Kai-chen had gone. Then I prepared myself for my move, rehearsing it in my mind. I would crunch my knees up to meet my chest, leaning forward, jerking my body, curling up, which would pull my neck away from Ming. My plan was to hit the floor, then roll into Ming's legs, chair and all, knocking him off balance. With no Kai-chen to contend with, Lucy could do the rest. I was completely sure of that.

I made my move. It caught Ming unawares, and my neck came free of the syringe. Knees up, I rocked forward and toppled sideways, still bound to the chair. But my forehead struck the stone floor.

I saw blackness.

But I heard scuffling.

It took me a moment to realize that the blackness had come from the lights in the room going out, and not from the blow to my head. I struggled to get myself upright. I heard Ming call out in anger, and then came the sound of another impact, like a slap.

Then, in my ear, a familiar voice. A voice that made me gasp.

"Just a moment, old friend."

That voice was that of Sherlock Holmes.

70. TOUCH AND GO

A profound feeling of relief surged through me. Holmes was alive! And while we had been searching for him, he had found us!

I felt relief, but I also felt outrage. How could Holmes have let us believe that he was dead? How *could* he?

I felt a tugging at the ropes that bound my wrists, and a moment later my arms were free. In the next moment the lights in the room came on.

I saw Jack, at the light switch, and Lucy, kneeling, one knee digging into the back of the prostrate Ming. The tip of her Ladysmith revolver was pressed firmly into his ear. Lucy's flashing green eyes shone with a cold fury.

My hands freed, I pulled away the gag. Holmes knelt beside me, cutting away the ropes that bound my ankles. He slid the ropes across the floor to Lucy, along with those that had bound my wrists.

I started to speak, but Holmes put a finger to his lips.

I very nearly disobeyed his clear instruction and spoke anyway.

So many questions surged to my angry mind. Why had he allowed us to think he was dead? Had he staged the incident on the Thames? He must have done! Had the commander been in on a charade? If Holmes could trust the commander, why could he not trust us? And it had been four days since that awful event. During that time, why had he not gotten word to us that he was safe? Why had he not somehow explained to us what had occurred? He may have needed the public to believe he was dead. I understood that. But why could *we* not be trusted?

As I got unsteadily to my fee, I saw Jack, pocketing a revolver. Holmes was whispering something into Jack's ear.

I patted my coat pocket and realized that the revolver Jack had taken was my Webley.

Jack nodded at Lucy, who nodded back. Then Jack left the room.

Lucy was still silent. I realized that there must be a reason that she was not talking. She had been just as shaken by Holmes's disappearance and presumed death as I. She would have had the same questions and pent-up feelings as I.

Yet she was still silent.

Looking at her once more, I saw she was binding Ming's arms behind his back, using the ropes that had bound me. Her eyes still blazed, but she was looking at Ming, and not at Holmes.

So she was not furious with Holmes.

She must have understood something I had yet to fathom.

Holmes tapped me on the shoulder. He whispered, "Can you assist Jack?"

Then I realized.

Kai-chen.

Kai-chen had left the room to see what the disturbance had

been. He would return soon—or he had already become aware of Holmes's presence and was biding his time, waiting to return when our guard was down. Or he was going for reinforcements, possibly to bring back the men who were unloading the ship. We needed to find him and overpower him.

I nodded, stepping out into the dark hallway. Looking back for a moment I saw Holmes crouched at Lucy's side, wrapping a length of rope around Ming's ankles.

I took a few paces down the hall. Ahead of me I heard a metallic clatter. Then breathing. Intense, short sharp breaths, indicating exertion. I took a few paces more and saw the room to my right. Through the doorway I could see Jack and Kai-chen, circling one another like two tigers. Kai-chen held a knife, outthrust. Jack's hands were empty. Kai-chen must have kicked the revolver out of Jack's grasp. Jack was brave and honorable, but I feared for his chances in a hand-to-hand struggle against Kai-chen's oriental fighting skills. And now Kai-chen had a knife, and he held the knife as though he knew precisely how to use it.

I waited. The two were circling one another. Kai-chen's eyes were on his opponent. He did not see me. A few more paces and his back would be to me.

I waited.

Three more paces. Two. One.

I charged, putting all my strength into my run, lowering my head, using my body weight behind my shoulder for maximum impact, hitting the Chinaman with a powerful bull rush, carrying him forward. My fighting instinct had taken over. I would not stop until we both had crashed into the stone wall. I tried to turn Kai-chen so that his head would strike the hard surface with all the force of my body weight behind it. He realized his danger and twisted around to take the force of the impact on his side and shoulder. We crashed into the wall together, falling to the ground.

Then Jack was behind us, his boot stamping hard on Kai-chen's knife hand. I heard the bones crack. Heard Kai-chen's hiss of pain. I got both hands under his chin and gouged my thumbs and fingertips into his throat. He thrashed and kicked, flailing his arms, driving a knee into my midsection so that I nearly lost my grip on him.

Then I heard the crunch of metal on bone. Kai-chen's hands went involuntarily to his cheek, where Jack had hit him with the handle of my revolver. His neck was now exposed. His knife was on the floor at my side. I could have picked it up and cut his throat.

Instead I shoved it away and slammed my forearm down on his windpipe and his chin, driving the back of his head into the stone wall.

Kai-chen went limp, although he was still breathing.

Jack pressed the muzzle of the Webley into Kai-chen's ear. "I have my handcuffs on my belt. Dr. Watson, would you do the honors?"

I was about to reply, but then I heard Becky's voice. "He needs to hold that man's legs. I'll do it."

And Flynn's voice. "I've got the knife."

WATSON

71. THE STOLEN HOARD

We cuffed Kai-chen's wrists behind his back. Then we marched him to the passageway, where Holmes waited with Lucy. I saw Ming on his knees. His hands and ankles were tied.

"Now, Holmes," I began. I intended to say that now that Ming and Kai-chen were both secure, Holmes could tell us how he had come to be here and where we would go next with our prisoners.

But Lucy was looking at me. With a finger to her lips.

So there was something else that she knew that I did not.

What was it?

"Jack, would you please take Ming and Kai-chen to the dock," Holmes said. "Becky, Flynn, please run ahead of him. You will find Mr. Lansdowne there with the Royal Marines. Tell him that Jack is on his way with two prisoners and that he should order the preparation of two cells in the ship's brig."

"On what charge am I to be jailed?" Ming hissed the question.

"There is no shortage of charges, and there is an abundance of evidence."

We waited as the others left the room.

"I'm coming with you," Lucy said to Holmes.

"You cannot."

I could contain myself no longer. "What are you talking about?"

"There was a reason we could not know the truth," Lucy said, stepping forward to face Holmes. "I know why you are here, where you are going, and what you are planning to do. You think you have foreseen everything, and that your plan is the only way. But I do not agree. And you cannot stop me from coming with you."

"Then I am coming as well," I said.

"Neither of you can be part of this," Holmes said, and started to walk. "It is essential—"

Lucy cut him off. "On my wedding day, you said that we would do things together."

She now was walking ahead of Holmes, down a corridor. Ahead of us was a metal door. It appeared to be watertight, the sort one would find on a naval vessel. It was open. From within I caught the odor of chemicals. The sharp smell of ammonia mingled with the sour scent of vinegar. There were tables with glass containers and Bunsen burners. The room was unoccupied.

I asked, "What is this place?"

"This is where Mr. Seewald gets his laudanum, and where Ming's heroin pastilles come from," Lucy said.

Pride and annoyance appeared to war with one another on Holmes's sharp features as he looked at his daughter. "Quite correct. This is the laboratory where raw opium is converted to morphine." He gestured to a wall of shelves. "There is the lime and concentrated ammonia used in the process."

"I can smell the ammonia quite plainly," I said.

Holmes continued, "Then soda ash, acetic anhydride, and chloroform are used to convert the morphine into heroin. The acetic anhydride has a characteristic smell of vinegar. When it combines with water vapor in the air, in fact, it *is* vinegar."

Lucy was at a shelf that contained a number of small bottles and a stack of paper. "These are the bottles and labels for Mr. Seewald's laudanum. Probably there is a supply of alcohol around here as well." She turned to Holmes. "That may be useful."

"I had something else in mind," said Holmes.

He was at the far side of the room, opening another metal door. I heard the sound of the ocean and caught the scent of sea air.

"A tunnel," Holmes said. "Products are carried out, and supplies are carried in. They are brought here from the hotel dock—" standing in the tunnel, Holmes flung open another metal door "—and stored in this room."

"Along with the opium," Lucy said.

"The cargoes of three ships, and possibly more," Holmes said.

"Which is why you didn't want us here," Lucy said.

"I still want you to stay out," Holmes said. "You should be able to say that you never saw the missing chests of opium. You should be able to testify to that in a court of law. You should be able to swear to it with a clear conscience."

"My conscience doesn't work that way," Lucy said.

She stepped around Holmes and threw a light switch. Electric lamps blazed. "Now we can see what a million pounds' worth of opium looks like," she said.

I gazed into the room. A cavern had been dug out, an extension of the basement and hydrotherapy rooms, but one that went on as far as or perhaps even farther than the foundation of the hotel.

I saw wooden chests, coated with pitch, identical to the chest we had first seen in Swafford's room and later in Mrs. Newman's home. Chests by the thousands, stacked along the wall on shelves about a foot above the concrete floor, to guard against damp. There were perhaps fifty electric bulbs shining throughout the room, hung from the ceiling. They would provide abundant illumination for the loading and unloading process, making it difficult for a thief to conceal and get away with anything of value.

On the shelves were also hundreds of glass bottles of varying sizes. "Supplies," Holmes said. "Alcohol, lime, acetic anhydride, ammonia, Activated charcoal. Now you have seen it. For the first and last time."

Lucy stepped into the room. "We are all three in this," she said.

Holmes pulled something tubular from inside his coat pocket. It had a string. I realized it was a tube of dynamite. Perhaps a foot long, perhaps two inches thick.

"Powerful enough for its purpose," said Holmes.

He led us out of the storage room, partially closing the metal door. As we waited in the tunnel, he struck a match, lighting a wax candle that stood in a wall sconce next to the door. "I will shut the door after I light the fuse," Holmes said. "We need not go all the way down the tunnel."

Then from behind us in the laboratory room, came a familiar, raspy voice.

Ming's voice.

"Drop it, Mr. Holmes."

72. BATTLE

The shadowy light cast by the wall candle played over Ming's scarred face, making it even more hideous.

With Ming was little Becky.

Ming's good hand clutched Becky by her hair, pulling her head back to reveal the sharp point of a steel hook that gleamed in the electric light. I realized the hook came from the end of what we had thought was Ming's immobile arm. The back of the hook was pressed into the soft white skin of Becky's exposed neck.

"Drop it, Mr. Holmes," repeated Ming, "or this little girl will suffer the same fate as Inspector Swafford. And you will watch it happen."

"We thought his hand was just crippled," Becky said. "We didn't know the hook was inside."

"In weakness there is strength," Ming said, with an evil leer.

"He cut the ropes with it," Becky went on. "We ought to have been watching, but we didn't know."

"Where is Jack?" Lucy asked. "Where is Flynn?"

"Kai-chen is guarding them," Becky said. "He has the revolver."

"You are wrong," said Ming. He tightened his grip on Becky's hair and pressed the back of the hook more tightly against Becky's neck. Then he turned slightly. "Isn't that correct, Kai-chen?"

In answer, Kai-chen stepped forward, into the light. His face was scraped and misshapen from our earlier struggle, and his broken knife hand dangled at his side. In his other hand he held my Webley. His grip on the revolver was firm.

The gun was aimed directly at Lucy.

"Your friends are locked into the therapy room," Kai-chen said, "along with Alice and the two other British ladies."

"Not so clever now, are you Mr. Holmes?" Ming smiled his hideous smile. "I presume the tube you are holding is some kind of explosive. You will drop it immediately. Or I will order Kai-chen to shoot your daughter. Her death will not be a quick or painless one."

"Kai-chen admires you, doesn't he, Ming?" Holmes said.

The two were momentarily silent.

Holmes went on, "I wonder if he knows the truth about how you were injured. Does he know how you really got your face burned and your hand crippled?"

"In a battle with the British," Kai-chen said.

"No," said Holmes. "This man, Ming Donghai, was burned, but not in a battle with the British during the Opium Wars. That conflict ended more than thirty years ago. Ming's injury came only four years ago, in Hong Kong, when he became a bit careless with the chemicals and the heating flame while working in a morphine factory. His investors, who owned the factory, were not pleased, as the fire caused them considerable financial loss. To atone for the loss, he came up with the idea of turning pirate, only in a more efficient manner. He would bribe captains and officers of three vessels sailing from India. His audacious plan earned him the respect of the emperor, and the funds to pay for the bribes—and the murders that followed to hide the piracy."

"Sheer fabrication," said Ming. "You have made this up out of whole cloth."

"Associates of Sun Yat Sen are my source. They were only too happy to describe what they knew of you."

"They are notorious liars," said Ming.

"Others knew the truth—in particular, those who were involved building this facility, which you needed to store your stolen cargo. Swafford's brother saw the cargo being unloaded two years ago. He went to sea, but his greed drove him to return. He recovered one of the opium chests from this hoard and took it to London, where his brother thought it would serve admirably as bait in a police investigation. You killed Inspector Swafford personally, with the hook that I ought to have realized you kept with you at all times. You were seen committing the murder."

"By whom?"

"Hasson, that very robust owner of the Red Dragon, saw you. Now that Newman is dead and his gang is in disarray, Hasson has thrown in his lot with the police."

"Hasson is unwise," said Ming.

"You had the help of Newman's gang to alert you to Swafford's activity. You hired them to make certain that Swafford's fiancée would not reveal what Swafford and his brother knew. Your money paid for the murders of two innocent women."

Ming said nothing.

"You hired Newman's gang to continue their watch on the

police investigation, and they alerted you to the activities of the unfortunate Inspector Plank, who wrongly suspected Swafford of being in league with opium smugglers. He was so anxious to keep me from discovering what he thought was a shameful secret that he wounded himself, in a clumsy ruse intended to frighten me away. He came to the Chinese Legation hoping to learn the identity of Swafford's opium source. You lured him there, Ming."

Ming said nothing.

Holmes turned to Kai-chen. "You were there at the Legation that night, young man. Did you distract Inspector Plank so that Ming could attack from behind? Would you have done so, if you had known the truth about Ming—that for his own profit he creates addicts, both in England and in China, and perpetuates all the human misery that goes with addiction?"

"Lies," said Ming. "Kai-chen, these are lies."

"I have proof to the contrary," said Holmes. "Sun Yat-Sen's associates were very helpful. I have photographs of you with the Chinese Legation, taken five years ago. Your face is undamaged, and both your arms are intact."

"It seems you have been very active for a man who supposedly died four days ago," said Ming.

"Lansdowne and the British Navy have been active as well. As I said earlier, Royal Marines will soon be inside this tunnel."

"You are bluffing," said Ming. "And I have had enough of your falsehoods. Kai-chen, I order you to change your target."

Kai-chen hesitated for a moment. Then he trained the revolver on Holmes.

Ming's raspy voice purred with pleasure. "Now you must die again, Mr. Holmes."

As if contemplating a reply, Holmes gave a long look at the tube of dynamite in his right hand.

Then in one swift move, he turned to the burning wall candle and lighted the fuse. The glowing tip of the cord crackled and sparked.

Brandishing the dynamite, Holmes stepped towards the partially opened door to the storage room. He held the lit dynamite stick at arm's length. His hand and the dynamite were inside the doorway. "It is a thirty-second fuse, Ming."

For a moment, we all stared, fascinated by the thin smoke and tiny sparks that emanated from the fuse, only a few inches from the dynamite.

Ming screamed to Kai-chen. "Shoot him!"

Then Holmes flung the dynamite into the storage room.

LUCY

73. ACTION

Time seemed to skitter and slow down as I watched the lit stick of dynamite arc through the air, land with a thump, and then roll across towards the far side of the storage room floor.

Ming screamed another order at Kai-chen—probably repeating his order to shoot Holmes, but the words were drowned out by the thunder of my own heart in my ears.

Holmes had a plan. He had a plan and was trusting me to know that and to carry out my part.

Jack and the others could be dead. My throat felt clogged with the thought of how easily Kai-chen could have lied about that.

But right now, Holmes must have a plan—and my part was to block out absolutely everything else and take advantage of the split second my father had just given me to act.

Ming had been caught equally off guard by Holmes's lighting the fuse, and for just this brief moment his attention wavered, his muscles going momentarily slack with shock.

I dove forward, wrenched his arm away from Becky's throat, and in the same movement hooked my ankle around his, throwing him off balance.

Kai-chen could shoot me at any second, but I had to trust that Holmes had a plan for that, too.

Becky was ready, and the moment I touched Ming, she wrenched herself free and slid, eel-like, out of his grasp.

I struck his face with the heel of my hand, then turned and elbowed him in the throat.

Wheezing, he bent over but then brought his arm up. The knife-sharp edge of Ming's hook slashed barely an inch from my eyes. I ducked aside, readying myself for my next move.

But I never got the chance.

Ming threw himself forward, weakened and gasping, but still scrambling towards the stick of dynamite Holmes had thrown. It had rolled towards the far wall, maybe twenty feet away. And it had ... how long? Maybe twenty seconds left on the fuse?

Kai-chen's gun still hadn't gone off, and I had no idea why—until Kai-chen himself flew backwards past me, staggering into the storage room, crashing into one of the shelves that lined the walls.

I spun, and saw Jack, breathing hard.

The breath I'd been holding rushed back all at once, a sharp stab in my lungs.

Jack had a darkening bruise over one cheekbone and a cut over one eye. But he was alive.

"Thank you."

Jack's expression was grim as he watched Kai-chen. He had taken possession of the gun, but still was braced for the other man to come at him again.

"I owed him one."

"Holmes!" That was Uncle John, who was shouting from near the doorway.

Glancing over my shoulder, I saw that the chemicals from the shelves had spilled onto the floor, forming a widening pool of liquid between us and the dynamite—and that Holmes was poised over the spreading river with another lit match.

He tossed the match, and instantly flames sprang up, separating us from the dynamite by a leaping wall of fire.

"Don't be a fool, Ming," Holmes said. His voice was deadly calm.

With a snarl, Ming ignored him and lunged again—not for Holmes but for the dynamite. The fire licked the hem of his silk robes, and he sprang back with a furious cry.

Holmes caught hold of my arm. He turned to Kai-chen. "You have a choice, young man."

Kai-chen's expression was still dazed from his impact with the wall. But he blinked, shook his head to clear it—and then ran towards Ming and the burning fuse and the spreading flames.

Outside in the tunnel, Uncle John led the way, while Jack carried Becky. I held tight to his other hand.

The tunnel sloped downwards and was slippery underfoot, making it treacherous and impossible to run—as much as I could almost feel the fuse on the dynamite growing shorter by the second.

"How did you get free of the hydrotherapy rooms?"

"Becky managed to slip Flynn her lockpicks. Well done, Beck," he added. "Almost makes up for your not actually staying where I asked you to."

"Alice and the others?"

"Flynn is leading them out. Should be upstairs in the hotel by now."

"Hurry!" Holmes was following close behind us all. "Watson, open that door!"

We were already in sight of a heavy metal door that I assumed must lead to the harbor. Uncle John wrenched it open, and we burst through—nearly running into the tall, aristocratic figure of Lord Lansdowne.

The cold light of the full moon illuminated the scene. Lansdowne was standing over a group of trussed-up men lying on the ground, who were also being guarded by a group of sailors in Royal Navy uniforms.

Lord Lansdowne raised his eyebrows at the sight of us. "Ah, Mr. Holmes. I trust you were successful?"

Holmes, together with Watson, slammed the heavy metal door behind us—just as the great, thundering boom of an explosion rent the air and made the ground shudder under our feet.

Only when the last lingering echoes had died away did Holmes turn back to Lord Lansdowne.

"Indeed, my lord. I believe I may say that this part of the affair has been brought to an entirely satisfactory conclusion."

LUCY

74. A NEW SUSPICION

"How are you feeling?" Becky asked.

On the surface, very little inside the Slades' cottage had changed. The sitting room was still dusty, the piles of laundry and newspapers and half-drunk cups of tea still exactly where they had been the last time Becky and I had been here.

There was something indefinably different in Mrs. Slade's expression, though, as she lay on the sofa and smiled wistfully up at Becky.

The three of us were alone in the cottage. Chief Constable Slade was still down at the Grand Hotel, cataloging the evidence and supervising the builders who had come to determine whether the explosion in the cellar had caused lasting structural damage.

Mr. Torrance himself was, at the moment, residing in the holding cell of the police station next door. The last I had heard, he had been stridently maintaining his innocence and claiming that he had no idea of the morphine being manufactured in the cellars of his hotel. But I very much doubted that the judge and jury at his eventual trial would believe him.

Holmes, Jack, and Uncle John were already back in London. They had left on the first morning train and were even now no doubt meeting with the plethora of officials who would want answers as to what exactly had happened to the huge quantity of opium they had hoped to recover.

Becky, though, had wanted to say goodbye to Mrs. Slade. I still hadn't entirely recovered from seeing her pinned with Mr. Ming's hook at her throat the night before. Probably, I never would grow used to Becky's being in danger—just as my father would probably never grow fully comfortable with my taking part in his investigations. But I *had* come to accept that Becky was no ordinary ten-year-old girl, and that I had to trust her to know her own mind. She had slept without any nightmares for what remained of last night, and now seemed a little quiet, but almost her usual self.

So I had agreed to her pleas that we go to see Mrs. Slade, and we had stayed behind to take a later train.

Now Mrs. Slade was looking pale, her face drawn with exhaustion. And yet there was a look of clarity, almost peace in her dark eyes that I hadn't seen there before.

"I feel terrible," she said. The wry smile deepened. "Positively, absolutely dreadful."

I didn't doubt that. The after-effects of the drugs Mr. Ming had given her would still be lingering in her system, and would, according to Uncle John, take some days to fully subside.

"But—" Mrs. Slade bit her lip, looking down at her joined hands, and seemed to hesitate before going on in a stronger tone. "But I *wish* to be better. That was why I went to see Mr. Ming. I wanted those pills he gave me to work. I did want to get better."

"Then you will get better," Becky said.

Mrs. Slade's expression softened as she looked at Becky. "I hope so. I have been thinking … no." She stopped, suddenly squaring her shoulders. "I have decided. I am going to London, to stay at a clinic there. A real clinic, that is. Dr. Watson told me of it when he came to see me this morning, on his way to the London train. He thought the doctors there could help me."

Becky beamed. "If Dr. Watson said that, then it's true. And if you're going to be in London for a while, then we can come and visit you, can't we Lucy?"

I smiled. "Of course we can."

* * *

Outside the cottage, Becky slipped her hand into mine. "Do you think she really will be all right?"

"I hope so." I glanced over my shoulder at the small cottage, framed by the backdrop of the fenlands. The flat, spreading pools of water glittered silver in the pale winter sun. "She has a difficult journey ahead of her, but she seems determined to help herself, and that is half the battle."

Becky was silent for a few steps. Then she said, "If Mrs. Slade does start to get better at Dr. Watson's clinic, I'm going to introduce her to Flynn."

Flynn had chosen to accompany the others back to London on the earliest train. There was, he said, too much fresh air up here, so far outside of the city.

"To Flynn? You do realize that there's a significant chance of him murdering you if you try to get him adopted to a family where he has to do things like bathe regularly and sleep under a roof?"

Becky looked unperturbed. "It would be good for him to have a family—people he can trust, people to care about him."

"Maybe." I squeezed her hand. "At the very least, he has us—and he has you for a friend. He's lucky there."

"What about Alice?" Becky asked. "And Lady Lynley? Have you heard what's going to happen to them?"

"I saw Alice last night—or rather early this morning." After Becky had—to her only mild indignation by then—been bundled off to bed. "Remember Connor Faraday, from the Lynley's stables? Apparently his mother lives in a cottage not far from here, and she's going to let Alice stay with her for a while, until she's recovered from the shock of everything that's happened."

"Do you think Alice will marry him?" Becky asked. "I hope she does, he's nice."

"You sound like a village matchmaker." I glanced at her. "You're awfully anxious to see everyone settled into domestic arrangements today."

"Well, families are nice to have." Becky's grip on my hand tightened a little, and I knew without asking that she was thinking of her father—the father who would never be able to take her away from our home. She was safe with us.

"I certainly won't argue with you there."

Becky walked in silence for a few steps, then looked up at me. "Lucy?" She seemed oddly braced, as though she'd been nerving herself up to say something, and when she spoke the words came all in a rush. "Do you think there's any chance that I'll turn out, like, you know … like *him*?"

"Like your father? Is *that* what's been worrying you these past days?" For the sake of her feelings, Jack and I had spared Becky the ugliest details of our interview with Benjamin Davies.

Maybe she would be ready to hear them someday, when she was older, but not today. I shook my head. "Becky, I don't think you could turn out anything like your father even if you tried."

Becky blinked quickly, brushing impatiently at a loose strand of hair. "We're related. No matter how much I want to, I can't get away from that. You don't understand, your father is Mr. Holmes—"

I put my hands on her shoulders. "Did I ever tell you that there was a time when I thought that I was Professor Moriarty's daughter?"

Becky's eyes widened, and her jaw dropped a little. "You thought—"

"So did Professor Moriarty's brother. That's why I grew up with the last name James—for James Moriarty. It was the name Professor Moriarty's brother gave me to honor the man he thought was my father. I didn't find any of this out, though, until I came to London and met Mr. Holmes for the first time."

Becky was still staring at me, wide-eyed. "But you must have thought … you must have felt …"

"Yes." I smiled a little. "I don't think anyone really wants to discover that they're the last living descendant of one of the most villainous criminal masterminds of all time. Or at least, I certainly didn't. But then I decided that whatever my father had been or done, it was nothing to do with what I was now. Professor Moriarty once told my father that they were very much alike in their intellect, in their talents—and it's true. The difference lay in what they chose to do with those talents. Just as I had a choice what to do with mine. There's a poem called 'Invictus' that I read while I was at school. It has a line: 'I am the master of my fate: I am the captain of my soul.' It's true. Everyone gets to choose the direction of their lives: Holmes. Professor Moriarty. Your father. And do you know what else I found out about my name when I first met Holmes?"

Becky shook her head.

"I met my mother for the first time—and I learned that she was the one who had named me Lucy, after Saint Lucy, who was so brave and so strong that she couldn't even be moved by the wicked governor's whole team of oxen when they tried to drag her away." I squeezed Becky's shoulders lightly. "You're not just your father's daughter—you are your mother's daughter, too, and she loved you and tried to do the very best she could for you. You're Jack's sister, and mine, and Sherlock Holmes's honorary niece—and above all, you are yourself, your own person, the captain of your own soul. Do you believe me?"

Becky's eyes searched mine for a long moment, and then she let out a shaky breath and nodded. "Yes."

I hugged her. "Good. Now let's go home."

We kept walking. Becky was quiet, but her steps had a bouncing skip to them that had been missing these past days.

Maybe both I and Invictus made matters sound a bit more simple than they were, in the cold, hard truth of real life. But I did believe it to be true: everyone had the power of choice in this world.

It was the reason I hadn't spoken to Becky of Lady Lynley's future, or Mrs. Torrance's. Mrs. Slade might have the strength and determination to overcome her addiction, but I doubted that Lady Lynley—

I stopped, frozen.

LUCY

75. A NEW SUSPECT

"Lucy?" Becky stopped walking, too, and looked up at me. "Lucy, what's wrong?"

I shook my head. Seemingly-random jigsaw pieces were swirling together in my mind, but for the first time they were—just possibly—beginning to form a coherent pattern.

We were still in sight of both the Slades' cottage and the police station.

"Becky, I need you to run back to Mrs. Slade's and stay there with her, all right? I have to go into the police station for just a minute and look in on Mr. Torrance."

Becky's brows knitted themselves together. "All right, but—"

She was about to ask why, I knew, but seeing my expression changed her mind, and ran back up the Slades' front walk.

I took a breath and sped to pound on the police station's front door.

Constable Meadows—who I'd met only briefly and in passing the night before—opened the door. He was a tall young man with sandy-colored hair and an amiable, square-jawed face that registered surprise at the sight of me.

"Why, hello there, miss. Can I help—"

I interrupted him. "Has anyone been here to see Mr. Torrance this morning?"

The constable looked still more startled by my tone. "Only his wife, poor lady. Most upset, she was, crying and carrying on—"

I ignored the rest of what Constable Meadows said and plunged towards the door at the back of the room, which I assumed led to the holding cells.

The constable's voice followed me. "Miss? Miss, I'm not sure you should go back there—"

He broke off, sucking in a sharp breath and stopping short—just as I had done a moment before—as he saw what lay inside the jail cell.

Mr. Torrance's body lay crumpled on the floor, his arms outstretched and his head lolling awkwardly to the side against the steel bars. His eyes were open, staring sightlessly up at the ceiling.

Constable Meadows started forward, but I shook my head. I had already reached inside the bars to feel for a pulse and found his skin lifeless and cold.

"He's dead." I jumped up. "Your telephone—where is it?"

"In the other room." The constable gestured. "But—"

I was already halfway across the room, towards the telephone cabinet.

I lifted the speaking piece, tapping my fingers against the receiver until I heard the exchange operator's voice. "The Grand Hotel, please." I barely managed to avoid adding, *hurry*.

The wait as I was connected to the hotel's front desk felt interminable, as did the wait after I had asked to speak with

Chief Constable Slade.

But at last the Chief Constable's voice came on the line. "Yes? Is something wrong—"

I didn't let him finish. I didn't even have time to explain to him what had happened. "I need you to find Mrs. Torrance! Is she there?"

I could picture Chief Constable Slade's eyebrows drawing together into a heavy frown, but apparently he had developed enough trust in me not to ask further questions—yet.

"Just a moment. I'll have a look round."

There was a light thump of him setting the telephone receiver down, and then another interminable stretch of waiting, during which I could hear the background noise and voices from the hotel lobby.

It felt like hours, but the clock on the wall told me that only five minutes had passed by the time that Chief Constable Slade's voice came back on the line.

"Hello? Still there? Yes, there's no sign of Mrs. Torrance anywhere. We've searched the hotel, but she can't be found. Now." The Chief Constable's voice turned stern. "Would you mind telling me what this is all about?"

"Yes. But you'd better come back to the police station." I would tell him, of course. About the vague feeling of un-easy *wrongness* I'd had about Mr. Ming's false demonstration of his supposed cure—and about how today, it had suddenly struck me: Mr. Ming had trotted out Mrs. Slade and Lady Lynley and even Kai-chen like obedient little show ponies. Why not Mrs. Torrance, as well?

It might have been that she simply hadn't sought him out for a cure.

Just as it might be that the *Duchess* that Benjamin Davies had spoken of was actually the name of a ship.

But right now, I very much doubted that it was.

76. A REPORT

Two days had elapsed since Holmes had incinerated the great hoard of stolen opium. He had barely rested since our return to London from Shellingford, spending much of his time away from our Baker Street rooms and not telling me what he was doing.

We were now at the Royal Exchange, for a meeting at the Lloyd's Underwriting Room. Holmes had insisted on making a personal report to the Chancellor of the Exchequer, and to the Society of Lloyd's. I was puzzled, for I saw no apparent reason for him to do so. After all, he had flatly refused to accept the chancellor and the society as his clients.

What would Holmes tell them?

In the cavernous expanse of the huge Lloyd's office area, it seemed as though we were participants in a ceremonial procession. I felt the gravity of the occasion.

Lansdowne and Holmes walked behind Avery Jacoby, who, despite the serious import of the subject at hand, led with his usual jauntiness. Lestrade and I brought up the rear. Mycroft was just ahead of us, his broad round back partially obscuring our view. Of our group, only Holmes and I knew all that had happened in the underground storage room at Shelling-ford. Lansdowne, who walked alongside Holmes, knew that the opium chests and their contents had been destroyed, but, as I understood it from Holmes, Lansdowne had agreed not to disclose the result until this meeting, when Holmes would be present to provide answers and explanations.

Our procession continued. We approached the majestic columns that supported and surrounded the Lutine Bell. The gilded surface of the bell shone brightly against the polished dark wood, capturing the pale winter sunlight that streamed through the tall glass windows.

Jacoby gestured upward, towards the gleaming brass relic. "So, Mr. Holmes, will we ring the bell once for bad news, or twice for good?" He added: "People here are making bets on the outcome."

"Soon you will have your answers," Holmes replied.

Lansdowne said nothing.

I felt a pang of dread. Seeing the matter with the eyes of the Society and the chancellor's office, I was certain that they would view Holmes's report as an utter and complete disaster. Sir Michael Hicks Beach, Chancellor of the Exchequer, and his assistant, Lord Ernshaw, badly wanted the return of the six thousand opium chests. As did Jacoby. And Ernshaw had officiously warned that anyone interfering with those chests would be committing a treasonable offense.

So if Holmes gave a complete report of what had happened in the underground storage area of the Grand Hotel, he would be confessing to the destruction of government property on a massive scale, and thereby exposing himself and all who had been with him to a trial for treason and then to the hangman's rope.

I could not imagine him doing that, but neither could I anticipate what he would say. And, of course, he had given me no indication of his plans.

"Never been here before," said Lestrade, walking at my side, his beady eyes darting nervously around the enormous room. The tall ceiling dwarfed us all, and the stares from what must have been a hundred pairs of eyes seated at a hundred polished wooden desks made both of us uncomfortable. "Don't know why I should be here now," Lestrade continued.

"Holmes did not enlighten you?"

Lestrade looked me expectantly.

"Nor did he enlighten me," I said.

Lestrade shook his head in resignation.

A few paces more, and we reached the entrance to the directors' room. Jacoby pushed open the heavy oak door. At the end of the long conference table, two men sat across from one another, waiting for us.

Lord Ernshaw, tight-lipped, sat with his bony hands clasped on the tabletop before him, his posture reminding me of a huge praying mantis.

Sir Michael Hicks Beach sat with his arms folded, his dark, wolfish features only a little softened by his heavy black mustache and close-trimmed black beard.

Sir Michael leaned forward, nodded, and spoke in a sympathetic tone. "Gentlemen, please do come in. Mr. Holmes, we are happy to see you in our midst. We had heard most distressing rumors of your demise."

"The experience was most distressing to me as well, I assure you," replied Holmes. "But most necessary. I had the help of Secretary Lansdowne, here, and his men, who did an admirable impersonation of a Chinese crew on a small vessel, an impersonation good enough to convince the captain of HMS *Daring*. To complete the illusion, they also used a prototype of the latest undersea gear."

"Based on the Bruce Partington plans," said Lansdowne. "For the recovery of which we had you to thank, Mr. Holmes. So, we are even on that score."

Ernshaw looked impatient. "All very well about that, I'm sure," he said. "But now, Mr. Holmes, we are anxious to hear what has occurred concerning the recovery of the opium."

Holmes turned to Lansdowne. "Mr. Secretary," he said, "would you like to say anything before I make my report?"

Lansdowne inclined his high-domed brow just a fraction of an inch. Then he shook his head. "I shall save my comments for later. You should proceed now."

Holmes steepled his fingertips beneath his chin in his characteristic expository pose. "The case has been a complex and difficult one," he said. "However, I know the financial implications of this endeavor are the most prominent in your minds. I shall immediately come to the point you are waiting for. I located the missing opium. It had been hidden away in an underground storage facility, beneath the Grand Hotel in Shellingford—"

"Wonderful!" Jacoby interrupted.

"—but the opium has been destroyed."

The faces of Sir Michael, Ernshaw, and Jacoby registered first shock, and then disbelief.

Finally, Jacoby spoke. "Is that all? Just—destroyed? Gone, poof, nothing to be done?"

"I am happy to provide further detail," Holmes replied. "I merely desired not to keep you in suspense as to your principal concern."

"But all the same, you are telling us it's all gone," said Ernshaw. "You are admitting that you failed in your assignment."

Holmes held up an admonishing finger. "I took no assignment from you," he said.

"Then why are you here?" Ernshaw's lip curled in a resentful challenge. "Why have you wasted our time to tell us of this—this, debacle?"

"I have come here to report the facts. This group is free to draw its own conclusions."

"Go on," said Sir Michael.

"Very well. Dr. Watson can bear witness that he and I saw a huge quantity of sea chests, in numbers sufficient to account for three ships' worth of cargo."

I nodded.

"As I mentioned," Holmes went on, "the chests were all stored in an underground facility. We did not have time to open the chests or even to count them."

"So what happened?" asked Sir Michael.

"Shortly after Dr. Watson and I saw the chests, they were destroyed in an explosion that resulted from an altercation with two men. One of those men, named Ming Donghai, was principally responsible for the theft, by fraud, or piracy, that brought the opium to England. Both men perished in the blast. Dr. Watson and I were fortunate to escape with our lives. No others were killed or injured."

"There is no doubt that this Ming and his accomplice were killed?" asked Lestrade.

"Inspection of the storage cavern yielded enough of their remains to confirm their identities. Both men had been working with others, using the opium to produce various narcotic products for sale in England, and, internationally, to enemies of the Crown."

"But the opium is gone. You failed," said Ernshaw.

"I never agreed to recover it," said Holmes.

"Can any of the opium be salvaged?" Sir Michael asked.

Holmes shook his head. "The inspection of the storage cavern included a detailed evaluation of that possibility by the local constabulary and a party of Lord Lansdowne's Royal Marines. The chests were sturdy and built for seagoing voyages, so I, too, thought it possible that some of the opium—itself quite sturdy and compressed in the spherical form in which it had been stored—might still be usable.

"However, the cavern where the chests had been stored also contained supplies of chemicals used in the conversion of the raw opium to the other forms of narcotic. Alcohol, in particular, and acetic anhydride were present in substantial amounts. The containers containing these substances were shattered in the explosion, and the chemicals reacted with the raw opium, and the pitch covering the chests, causing fire and a cascade of further chemical reactions. There is no possibility of ever using any of that opium for its intended purpose. It has no value. It is mainly foul-smelling ashes."

"I am sure we all appreciate your clarification and the accompanying detail," Ernshaw said. "Yet you are describing failure, nonetheless."

"No need to dwell on it, Ernshaw," said Sir Michael.

"Indeed," said Holmes. "I may also add that other persons were involved in the narcotics operation at the hotel in which the opium was stored and manufactured. One, the local pharmacist, was employed in the conversion of the raw opium in a laboratory located on the premises. He was apprehended by the local police. Another, one Mr. Torrance, the manager of the hotel, was arrested and jailed. Mr. Torrance has been since found murdered. The principal suspect is his wife. Mrs. Torrance visited him in his cell and left just before his body was found. She has gone missing. The local constabulary is tracking her."

Lansdowne added, "As is the navy, in the event the woman tries to leave England."

"Well, I suppose that is rough justice," said Sir Michael, "One apprehended, one dead. And we have the possibility for a third to be brought to the Crown's justice. That is something, at least."

"Still a failure as far as the economics of the affair are concerned," said Ernshaw.

Jacoby looked over at Holmes. "You did everything you could, I'm sure."

"Quite correct," said Holmes.

"Do you have any idea," Sir Michael asked, "why this Ming and his associate would have destroyed the opium?"

"They did not confide in me," Holmes said. "But I doubt that they wished to undergo the disgrace of a trial in a British court."

"Perhaps they had booby-trapped the storage room," offered Mycroft. "And the trap went wrong."

"They must have known the game was up," said Lansdowne. "My men arrested their sailors—the crew that was bringing in a fresh load of supplies."

"It may have been a spiteful act," said Jacoby. "An 'If we can't have it, no one can have it' kind of thing."

"Pity you weren't able to bring them to justice," said Ernshaw, getting to his feet. He turned to Sir Michael. "Well, Mr. Chancellor, I know you have a very busy schedule. It seems there is nothing else to be done to help the situation and therefore nothing further to keep us here."

Holmes held up a cautionary finger. "There is just one thing."

77. A TRAP IS SPRUNG

Holmes's voice had taken on that silken tone I have heard many times before, and a thrill went through my entire frame. I did not know what was about to occur, but I recognized very clearly the signs that Holmes's web had been spun and that his prey was soon to be trapped.

Ernshaw and Sir Michael settled back into their seats.

"Yes, just one thing," Holmes went on, "if you could be so kind as to spare us a moment or two more. And perhaps your assistance. I think it may prove most valuable in the interests of justice."

"*My* assistance?" asked Sir Michael.

Holmes shook his head. "Forgive me for not making myself plain. It is Lord Ernshaw's help that might assist us."

"Only too pleased to do what I can," said Ernshaw. He smiled politely, placing his elbows on the table and clasping his hands once more.

"Then, Lord Ernshaw, would you tell us what you know of the whereabouts of your sister."

The polite smile remained fixed on Ernshaw's face, but I now thought it had turned lifeless, a forced grimace, rictus-like and devoid of genuine feeling. He said, "I don't see why you would ask that."

"I shall explain," Holmes said. "But first, Inspector Lestrade, would you kindly step over to stand behind Mr. Ernshaw."

Lestrade gave me a look of grim satisfaction as he got to his feet. He whispered, "*Now* I know why I'm here."

"Once again I shall be brief," Holmes said, after Lestrade had taken his position. "Gentlemen, Mr. Ernshaw's sister, Clarissa Ernshaw, has the married name of Torrance. Do not trouble to deny the connection, Mr. Ernshaw. The records at Somerset House are quite explicit. I have examined her marriage certificate and both your birth certificates."

Ernshaw stared haughtily at Holmes. "And?"

Holmes went on, "I wondered if she might have been in touch during the last two days, considering that she is your business partner and fellow owner of the Grand Hotel in Shellingford."

"I know nothing—"

Holmes held up his hand. "Do not trouble to deny that, either, Lord Ernshaw."

Mycroft spoke for the first time. "The Grand Hotel is listed as an asset of Empire Holdings, a corporation which was floated for public subscription several years ago. Not all of the shares were publicly subscribed, however. The majority is held in your name, Lord Ernshaw, and that of your sister. I presume that you floated only the amount you needed at the time.

"The two of you were most clever and most enterprising. Three years ago, as part of the government and railway program to bolster the tourist economy in Shellingford, you arranged for a substantial quantity of public funds to be set aside for the renovation of the Grand Hotel, as a destination that would attract the vacationing public. You failed to disclose, of course, that you were profiting by the transaction, since it added value to the hotel and thus to your own personal fortune, at the expense of the British taxpayer."

"I categorically deny any wrongdoing."

Mycroft shrugged. "There is more. Sherlock?"

"Indeed, there is," Holmes said. "When the hotel was constructing its hydrotherapy rooms and equipment, you arranged for additional expansion, to include excavation of a large underground storage room and a tunnel leading to the hotel dock. The dock itself was also expanded. The new structure enabled the unloading and loading of cargo vessels—not the size of the freighters that ply the London docks, but large enough for your purposes. Do not bother to deny that you authorized the funding for the construction, Ernshaw. Your signature is on the approval documents, which the excavation and construction companies insisted upon seeing as proof of funds before commencing the work. I was able to view those documents for myself at the hotel office, after the explosion and before I returned to London. I also saw records of rental payments to the hotel that were so generous as to be excessive. Upon my return, I found that those exorbitant payments came from Ming Donghai, the man responsible for the theft of the opium. I also found that you and your sister both were seen in the company of Ming, in London, on the day after my death had been reported."

"Seen by whom?"

"One of my Irregulars followed you, at my instruction."

"A packet of lies," said Ernshaw, staring fixedly ahead. "The testimony of a street urchin. Laughable."

"There will be proof enough when you are tried in a court of law," said Holmes. "Or in the House of Lords, if you insist on being judged and humiliated by your peers. Since your actions provided a place of concealment for the stolen opium, you will be charged with abetting the theft of British Government property. Given the high value of the property involved, as you pointed out less than a week ago, your actions constitute a treasonable offense. I am sure you are aware of the penalty for treason."

Ernshaw's hand went involuntarily to his neck, which appeared even thinner and more frail than I recalled from our first meeting.

Holmes continued, and his voice took on a graver, more solemn tone. "In Kensington, there was a young woman who loved a London Police detective. The two intended to marry. The detective went missing and the young woman came to me for help. She became my client. But within the week, both the detective and the young woman were murdered. The mother of the young woman, and another police detective, were also murdered; that second detective leaves behind a widow and three children. All four murders were committed to conceal the stolen opium hoard from which you profited, Lord Ernshaw."

"You cannot prove—" Ernshaw began.

But Holmes cut him off, his tone inexorable. "I repeat. Four innocent lives taken, and four more irrevocably harmed. Eight lives for which you, Lord Ernshaw, will one day be called to account, if not in this world, then in the next."

Holmes gestured to Lestrade. "Now, Inspector Lestrade, will you please arrest this man."

The inspector placed a hand on Ernshaw's bony shoulder. "You are under arrest," Lestrade said, "and anything you say may be written down in evidence and used against you."

"I admit nothing," Ernshaw said. "Sir Michael, none of this can be proven. I have done nothing wrong."

Sir Michael looked at Ernshaw with disgust. "Inspector, please take this person out of my sight."

A moment later, Ernshaw was handcuffed. We waited in silence as Lestrade led his prisoner from the room.

78. THE BELL TOLLS

After a few more moments of silence, Sir Michael gave an involuntary shudder. "What a serpent I have harbored," he said. "I worked with him every day and I never had the slightest notion. I hope you'll catch his sister, Lansdowne," he added.

"We'll find her," said Lansdowne.

Sir Michael turned to Holmes. "What made you suspect Ernshaw?"

"At first, it was only a trifle," said Holmes. "If you recall, Mr. Chancellor, you were to meet with us here, on the morning after the first chest of opium was discovered. But you did not attend, which was most unlike you, given the enormous financial implications, and the possible link to the diamond case we had concluded last November. I asked Mycroft to look into the matter. He learned that you had gone to Buckingham Palace due to a last-minute summons, which later turned out to have been a clerical mistake. Yet no one on the Royal staff would say why the summons had been sent."

"You think Ernshaw arranged for the mistake?" asked Sir Michael.

"I do now. At the time, I thought it odd that you would have sent a substitute, when you might simply have asked for the meeting to be rescheduled. I wondered if there was any connection with the location of the meeting having been at Lloyd's. I have since learned that Lloyd's insures the Grand Hotel. I expect Ernshaw wanted to be on hand to steer the conversation away from what might have become a sensitive topic."

"Or simply to learn how you proposed to locate the opium," Mycroft said, "so that he could take precautions if necessary. That became moot, of course, when you refused to take the case."

"Indeed," said Holmes. "I noted his attempt at studied indifference when I declined. He is not a talented actor. His facial expressions betrayed his glad relief that I would not be meddling in his affairs, and then his suspicion that I would investigate on my own. On that point he was correct, of course."

Jacoby looked puzzled. "If he didn't want you to investigate, why did he lay such emphasis on the treasonous nature of any crime connected with the stolen opium? He said it would give you such great powers."

"He made the argument for appearance's sake, hoping we would believe he truly wished me to take the case. On reflection, I think he also feared exposure for his treasonous involvement with the opium hoard. This genuine fear provided a foundation for his otherwise hypocritical emotion."

"But you kept searching for the opium," Sir Michael said. "Why?"

"Swafford's murder was an affront that I could not allow to stand unpunished. Then the following day, I learned that two innocent women had been killed in London," Holmes said.

"And one of the women was your client. She had to be

avenged as well."

I saw the familiar tight little smile on Holmes's face. He gave a brief nod of acknowledgement.

"Then you learned that Lord Lynley had been killed in Shellingford. And Lucy was in Shellingford," said Mycroft.

"She was," Holmes said.

"Is that why you had to die?" asked Sir Michael.

Again, the little smile. "I had to create the illusion that my investigations had been conclusively ended."

"Glad it was only an illusion," said Sir Michael.

"I only wish we could get our money back," said Jacoby.

"I have two suggestions that may help you," said Holmes.

Jacoby brightened. "You do?"

"First, I believe there is legislation allowing the Crown to recoup losses for property stolen from Her Majesty's Government."

"By seizure of assets owned by the thieves," Mycroft said. "Good idea. I would think the Grand Hotel would fall into that category."

"Also, Lord Ernshaw's estate is considerable," said Holmes.

"Then we might sell it," Sir Michael mused. "And the hotel, if we can find a buyer—"

"—and then you might share the proceeds with the Society," Jacoby added.

Holmes interrupted. "You can work those arrangements out among yourselves. As to my second point, Lord Lansdowne, I would further suggest that the Department of War has realized considerable financial savings from the recent events at the hotel, since the opium will no longer be available for sale to those who would attack the Crown. I would suggest that some of this savings might also be applied to the purpose of compensating the Crown, and, of course, the Society, for its previous financial injury."

"Hear, hear!" said Jacoby, brightening considerably.

"I might add that Ming had the support of the Chinese Emperor," Mycroft said. "We may be able to use that point to our advantage as we negotiate our new Hong Kong treaty."

"We will take it under advisement," said Lansdowne.

"I hasten to add," said Holmes, "that I want no monetary compensation for myself."

"Won't argue with that," said Jacoby.

"I do, however, have one request," said Holmes.

Holmes stood, walked over to Jacoby, and spoke for a brief interval, so quietly that the rest of us were unable to hear.

Jacoby nodded.

A short while later we left the Underwriters' Room. Holmes was a few steps ahead of us. I walked with Jacoby, Mycroft and Lansdowne, reflecting inwardly on how much had changed since our little procession had first entered this vast space only a short time earlier this afternoon. At that initial moment I had feared we might be marching to a stern confrontation and a grim outcome. Now, thanks to Holmes, the villainous Lord Ernshaw had been led off to face punishment, and we were leaving in triumph.

Then I heard a single, sharp, clear ring emanate from the Lutine Bell.

It had been struck once: the signal for a loss.

A shocked hush fell over the Underwriters' Room. I stopped and looked back.

Within the rotunda and beneath the bell stood a Lloyd's attendant, an old fellow wearing a red robe. He was holding a thick white rope attached to the bell.

Then he reached up and pulled down hard on the rope, puffing out his cheeks with the effort, ringing the bell again, and again, and yet again. After the eighth ring he stopped, let go of the rope, and stood motionless.

Eight rings, I thought.

Eight lives.

The echoes of the eighth ring died away.

Beside me, Jacoby was speaking, his tone hushed. "We're starting a fund for police widows," he said. Then he added, "Mr. Holmes thought you'd want to help."

My emotions surged. I turned to where Holmes had been.

He was no longer in the room.

THE END

HISTORICAL NOTE

This is a work of fiction, and the authors make no claim that any of the historical locations or historical figures appearing in this story had even the remotest connection with the adventures recounted herein. However …

1. In 1897 Sun Yat Sen published *Kidnapped in London,* the account of his kidnapping and incarceration in the Chinese Legation the previous year. The government of China continues to occupy the building described in that book as being located on the corner of Portland Place and Weymouth Street. The building is now the Embassy of the People's Republic of China.

2. The Grand Hotel in the fictional seacoast town of Shellingford was inspired by the Royal Hotel, a grand old Victorian structure still operating in the very real seacoast resort town of Skegness, in Lincolnshire, where recently were found the ruins of an underground hydrotherapy center. No smugglers' tunnel has been discovered at the Royal, although that portion of the Lincolnshire coast was notorious for smuggling and for underground storage bunkers built into the sand dunes.

3. Another hotel tunnel on the other side of the Atlantic, however, is known to have been used for smuggling purposes.

At the Congress Hall Hotel in Cape May, New Jersey during the 1920s, American bootleggers smuggled cargoes of alcoholic beverages from an oceanside dock directly into the hotel basement. Today that basement is enjoyed by visitors as an underground sports bar and pizza restaurant.

4. The HMS *Lutine* disaster was the most famous maritime loss in the 330-year history of the Lloyd's Company. The ship, a former French frigate converted for Royal Navy transport use, sank in a gale while carrying gold and silver in sufficient quantity to prevent a stock market crash in Germany. Divers still search for the sunken treasure, which is rumored to include the crown jewels of Holland. The ship's great bell was salvaged in 1858. The bell continues to hang in the atrium of the Lloyd's underwriting room, where formerly it was rung once for bad news and twice for good, for the very practical purpose of ensuring that all underwriters heard bad news or good news simultaneously. The bell is now rung to commemorate special occasions.

5. The theft of three opium cargo ships insured by Lloyd's underwriters is, as far as the authors are aware, entirely fictional.

6. The authors make no claim that the events described herein were in any way connected with those occurring in June 1898, when the Government of China signed a 99-year lease with Britain granting possession of the New Territories and increasing the Hong Kong area under British control by more than twelve times.

Lucy James and Sherlock Holmes will return.

A NOTE OF THANKS TO OUR READERS

Thank you for reading this latest book in the *Sherlock Holmes and Lucy James Mystery Series*.

If you've enjoyed the story, we would very much appreciate you going to the page where you bought the book and uploading a quick review. As you probably know, reviews make a big difference!

The other seven adventures in the series are currently available in e-book, paperback and audiobook formats.

To keep up with our latest escapades, please visit our website: www.SherlockandLucy.com

About the Authors

Anna Elliott is the author of the *Twilight of Avalon* trilogy, and *The Pride and Prejudice Chronicles*. She was delighted to lend a hand in giving the character of Lucy James her own voice, firstly because she loves Sherlock Holmes as much as her father, Charles Veley, and second because it almost never happens that someone with a dilemma shouts, "Quick, we need an author of historical fiction!" She lives in Maryland with her husband and three children.

Charles Veley is the author of the first two books in this series of fresh Sherlock Holmes adventures. He is thrilled to be contributing Dr. Watson's chapters for the series, and delighted beyond words to be collaborating with Anna Elliott.

CONTENTS

PART TWO
HEADWINDS

PART THREE
CUT ADRIFT

PART FOUR
BATTLE STATIONS

CPSIA information can be obtained
at www.ICGtesting.com
Printed in the USA
BVHW082038250219
541124BV00007B/30/P